Nowhere to Hide
An Erie Canal Adventure

iUniverse, Inc.
New York   Bloomington

Nowhere to Hide
An Erie Canal Adventure

iUniverse books may be ordered through booksellers or by contacting:

iUniverse
1663 Liberty Drive
Bloomington, IN 47403
www.iuniverse.com
1-800-Authors (1-800-288-4677)

ISBN: 978-1-4401-1830-2 (pbk)
ISBN: 978-1-4401-1831-9 (ebk)

Printed in the United States of America

iUniverse rev. date: 02/25/2009

Nowhere to Hide
An Erie Canal Adventure

Charles T. Harrell
Rhonda S. Harrell

Also by these authors:

History's Moments Revealed, American Historical Tableaus: Teacher's Edition, 2006.

Tears of Sadness, Tears of Joy, 2006.

Introduction

Nowhere to Hide reveals the timeless conundrum between guilt for one's past and hope for one's future. Set during the beginnings of America's great migration westward (1825), the story tests the theory of whether the frontier acts like a steam boiler's pressure valve, allowing frustrated Americans to escape a tumultuous past. In poor Jeduthan Higby's case, no matter how far he travels, his decisions continuously haunt him.

What embodies his nightmares is reminiscent of his own shortcomings. Fearing betrayal, he has difficulty developing sincere relationships. He doubts the compatibility of mankind's engineering achievements with nature's everlasting perseverance. He observes hypocritical religious leaders, impeding his faithfulness. Though he tries to rationalize his feelings and dreams, he must face the guilty pangs that result from his poor choices. Nevertheless, he continues onward, hoping to flee from his evil deeds. He sadly finds that he cannot long escape, but must live each day with a dread that his doom awaits only a few steps behind.

We set about publication with a desire to put in writing a simple story describing the reasons for Jeduthan Higby's removal from his New York home to the Virginia frontier about the mid 1820s. We hoped to place him at important historical sites, observing great events that have shaped America's character. However, while developing his personality, we found ourselves seeking answers as to why a person would leave his family and set off on an adventure from which there could be no return. We are not satisfied with a *no-fault* excuse and find it hard to understand the detachment that this unfortunate man must feel as he abandons his family and community. Therefore, we searched our souls, attempting to justify Jeduthan's actions.

Both of us agree that Jeduthan Higby retains a sense of wanderlust and enjoys its accompanying liberty. However, after intense discussion, we realized that his past does not allow him the total freedom he seeks.

His dreams are constantly blocking his path and he is only able to forge ahead with the help of an outside force, seemingly detached from guilt. He finds this savior in his companion William Bartlett, a traveling artist, charming and witty, who seemingly leaves life to chance. Jeduthan obediently follows his friend on exciting escapades, relieved of responsibility and haunting memories. When Bartlett departs and Jeduthan again faces responsibilities of his own making, his worries return and therefore he flees again, attempting to hide from a past that will not release him.

Charles T. Harrell
Rhonda S. Harrell

Table of Contents

List of illustrations

Escape

Jeduthan slowed his horse to a walk, sweat streaming from the beast's neck after his turbulent ride southward. The aging man's legs ached from the early morning hours spent in the saddle, riding through the dark night, all the stars hidden by foreboding clouds overhead. However, as the morning sun shown upon the eastern horizon, its warming rays peeked from under the weather, reflecting the splendid colors of a countryside full of life, free and triumphant as any spring morning. Soon, the ominous clouds receded and the sun warmed nature's sweet wonder.

With the sun's position in the sky and the gnawing hunger in his belly, he guessed the time at midmorning, possibly ten o'clock. He extracted a small silver watch from under his coat. The spring-loaded cover opened with a snap, confirming his estimation. Funny, he always had a unique gift of accurately estimating time.

The early morning hours had put seven miles between himself and home. Home. The woman's image concealed on the watch's interior reminded him of home. Her soothing blue eyes beckoned him to return, urged him to reconsider, and cried from an earthly grave for him to restore to Turin and to its principal family, its preacher and father. However, the blue-eyed womanly figure was gone, dead these many, many years. Another replaced her; a woman who never filled his heart with comforts that only his beloved mother could. Home. He would have to stop thinking of it as home; rather, it was only an empty house, devoid of warmth, lacking sentiment, destitute of faith. Home. He had left, and no one could force him to return, not even his mother's ghostly apparition. He must stop reflecting on what he left behind and imagine only the future possibilities of freedom. He must think about starting a new life. However, he could not right now, possibly later when his tormented emotions were not so fresh.

He closed the silver watch, turning it over revealing its smooth polished metal back. There, etched in delicate script, was his family genealogy, the founding patriarch prominently evident.

Zaccheus Candee
Sarah Candee Higby
Jeduthan Higby, Sr.
Jeduthan Higby, Jr.

All were gone now, save himself, the last of a proud and stubborn lot. History ought to have freed him, yet his father's legacy still burned his mind and haunted his memories.

He glanced over his shoulder, wondering how long before a mounted search party would come looking for him. Fleetingly, he dwelled upon that thought, eager to distract his mind from images of his wooden store and family's house. However, it was not to be. Visions of father, supervising the framing of the homestead, judging his work with a critical eye, and all the while Jeduthan perched among the rafters, soaking with sweat, a beam precariously balanced both overhead and between his feet. This homestead was where he had fathered children and raised his younger sister, Adah. This house was where he read his endeared collection of classic novels, studied Latin and Greek, and played music on his beloved scheitholt.

Nevertheless, it was also the house where he and his wife, Florinda, sat each evening, wordlessly glaring at each other across a barren table. Neither shared the other's interests. Unlike himself, she was not a Godly person. He only saw in his wife a woman, distorting faith and substituting drama for worship. In that house, in that community, he felt penned in, like some hog waiting for slaughter. He ached for freedom, and during the dark hours of last night, had stolen himself away like a runaway slave in quest of liberty. With these thoughts, he drifted southward, no particular destination in mind except to flee and hide, away from home.

As he crested a hill, Jeduthan estimated that he was far enough away now to be safe from his pursuers. Halting his horse but for a moment, he lifted his canteen to his lips and drank thirstily of its cool, refreshing water. A trickle of liquid leaked from the edge of his mouth and dripped across his chin. A brief rest would refresh him. Yet, paranoia also gripped his mind. He must not let his guard down, even for a moment, so he gave Nimrod rein.

Old Nimrod, his steadfast horse, served him well over the years. Throughout the week, Jeduthan relied on the steed for visiting members of his congregation. When required, Nimrod could also haul merchandise from market to his general store. Moreover, each Sunday morning, he dutifully hitched Nimrod to the wagon, and the beast loyally hauled the family to church. Today, though, old Nimrod provided him a means of escape. Yes, this valiant steed, though not swift, was sure and dependable, knowing always to keep on the road unless otherwise commanded. He was a good, faithful horse.

Faithful! A pang of guilt swept over Jeduthan as he contemplated the word. He had not been faithful. He longed to be! As a member of the community, a husband, a father, and an elder in the church, he so desired to be faithful! However, for many years bitter seeds grew within him. He tried to recall the first moment of his discontentment. He could not place the specific date or time, but he had memorized the conversation. He re-played it in his mind once more.

His father commented on the benefits and qualities of a good merchant and his own reply, "But I don't think I'm cut out to be a merchant, Father. I don't seem to be naturally inclined to buy, sell, and deal with people all day long!"

However, his father's immortal words haunted him. "Be faithful to what you are, boy! You can learn our trade, son. Granted, I'm not questioning the Good Lord's provision and His limitations for you, but I don't want you to work as hard as I have. So buck up, boy! Do as you are told!"

Jeduthan acquiesced, although he found the four walls of the store stifling. He felt he had sincerely tried over the years to become a merchant. However, his father's meddling hands had intruded too often for him to feel any sense of accomplishment at the work. Father had set up the business. Father chose the location. Father selected the stock. Father set the prices. Jeduthan imagined his life as a pawn in his father's horrendous chess game for profit, parental control, and dominance. This unseen parental fist was oblivious to his inclinations and desires. Moreover, that parental grip controlled all his decisions. For that, he loathed his father. His death, these five years past, should have freed him from the heavy hand that felt nigh unto slavery. However, it did not. The ghost of his father faithfully tormented his dreams both day and night.

Particularly annoying was his father's instruction for a store keeps' mindless banter with the public. Along with the continuous book-keeping, recording profits, calculating margins, and managing costs, Father insisted that when townspeople entered the storefront, a successful merchant must encourage customers to gossip about their neighbors, the church, the harvest, and a myriad of other topics including the weather. Weather! He hated even the sound of the word! Nobody could alter its course. The entire topic seemed irrelevant. Often, while confronting an offending individual, he found himself fantasying about a gruesome event that might overtake the hated gossiper. He prayed the offender would get what they came for and just leave his presence. Why did they have to stand around, wasting his precious time? He would rather be reading a book, preparing a sermon, or playing checkers or chess with one of his children.

He dropped his head and sighed. No one felt pity for him, no one tried to comfort him, and only Nimrod accompanied him through the woods today. He was utterly alone and faithless.

Journeying southward, the land began to open, revealing small fields separating the vast wooded frontier. High on a significant prominence and opposite Sugar Creek from Jeduthan's path emerged Constable Hall, home to Widow Mary McVicker Constable. Poor woman!

Jeduthan had been present the day the accident happened which ultimately took her dear husband's life. William Constable, esquire, invited him to the final phase of constructing the grand manor house. He arrived by carriage from the north side of the residence as workmen and Mr. Constable carefully manipulated cables suspending a gigantic stone above the front portico. The Constable children eagerly watched as the great stone inched its way toward its perch atop the foundation. Mr. Constable called for Jeduthan to tend the children during the critical placement of this ten-ton stone slab for the grand hall's front entrance.

Jeduthan gladly consented and led the youngsters a respectable distance away to the shade of a giant oak tree on the front lawn.

There, he began amusing the children with nursery rhymes including *Humpty Dumpty* and other ancient fables. He loved the children and often teased them following church on Sunday afternoons. Chuckles and giggles were heard all around as Jeduthan playfully teetered on one leg and then the other, much like a drunkard who left sobriety far behind. All was happy and gay. However, on this day while he was busily occupying the children under the enormous oak tree, a catastrophe occurred. An iron pike that Mr. Constable was using as a lever snapped under the load of the great stone. The colossal weight immediately fell upon the doomed father's leg, crushing and pulverizing the bones.

Jeduthan bounded to the rescue. All afternoon, he, along with the construction laborers, carefully worked to unpin the master of Constable Hall. By nightfall, it was plain to all that the land-baron was done for. Days passed as Mary Constable tended her invalid husband. Jeduthan dutifully reported weekly on Mr. Constable's condition in prayer requests, but knew the man's condition was critical and likely mortal. However, as his convalescence continued and the weeks turned into months, William Constable refused to submit to his wounds. By year's end, he again engaged his energies in completing his mansion. His restless toil cost him dearly, though. His leg, useless and limp, continued to pain the man. A putrid stink hovered about him for two years before his body, poisoned by the shattered leg, succumbed to his wounds and was laid to rest in the cemetery. All that remained was thrust upon the cheerless widow. How she must suffer!

She suffered in silence, though. Before the next spring, Widow Constable sought tenant farmers to work her land. This morning, to the east of the road, Jeduthan spied one of her many resident farmers plowing the estate's bottomland. He was intently focusing on the haunches of a mule hitched to a worn plow. With each successive step, the metal blade overturned the soft fertile soil making straight lines burrowing their way across God's productive earth.

The farmer's rows reminded him of his brother and the eventful day when Solomon announced his desire to become a soldier. That was over a decade ago in the year 1812. The local militia stood waiting for the order to march off to war. Just like the farmer's straight furrows, the soldiers stood in orderly ranks. Their backs rigidly straight, their guns held straight. Everything about them was straight. Narrow. Proper! Such was the life Jeduthan's father desired for all his children. Orderly and proper!

Accordingly, Solomon joined the militia, becoming the family hero. Returning home safely from the war, his brother's service distinctly lacked heroics but Father heralded the young citizen soldier, showering him with accolades. Solomon soon married a charming maid before becoming, with the aid of Father, the local Justice of the Peace. Over the next decade, Solomon fathered four sprite children living happily and comfortably in Turin, his life all planned and proper, just as Father demanded. As Nimrod trotted past the farmer's field, Jeduthan gazed at the isolated farmer. The man, no doubt, took pride in his straight lines, just as Solomon took pride in his straight, narrow, confined, and proper life. He resented Solomon from an early age. His younger brother succeeded easily at everything he tried. Everything Solomon was, Jeduthan was not.

"Well, they can have it!" Jeduthan almost shouted in frustration and anger. "I can't plow a straight line and I can't live such a confining life!" Only two people knew the competitiveness between the siblings; himself and mother.

His mother, her image delicately sketched inside his silver watch; oh how bittersweet was her memory. He knew that the only way to survive in the family was by conforming to Father's wishes; and that she did. When necessary, she could be as precise as father. However, her compassion tempered her Puritanical nature. She repeatedly made up for Father's severity and lack of understanding with warmth and sympathy.

Mother died only two months after Solomon marched off to war. Jeduthan speculated that grief and worry for his younger brother's safety contributed to his mother's early demise, leaving only himself as the target of Father's wrath. He resented Solomon for that, as well. Without Mother to comfort and praise him, Jeduthan allowed seeds of bitterness to take root in his soul until Father died.

Seeking an escape shortly after Father's death, Jeduthan suggested to Florinda that they sell the store and try some other venture. Her reply stung him as a wasp might attack an intruder.

"Why would you want to give up this comfortable life? I have everything I've ever wanted!"

Hounded, he conceded defeat. No one else in the small village of Turin wanted to change their occupation. No one wanted to take over his lot in life. A year later, in desperation, he tried once again.

"Florinda, I feel the need for a change! We could go to the frontier. I could set up a shop there, homestead the frontier, or even spread the gospel. Think of what an adventure it would be!" he explained.

Her reply felt like nails driving a lid into his coffin.

"Why would I want to do that? My family is here. My friends are here. This is all I've ever known!" retorted his wife.

"My point exactly!" he tried to reason. "Wouldn't you like to go see what else is out there in this great nation of ours?"

"So now Turin isn't good enough for you! Isn't my family good enough for you? My friends? Moreover, what about me? All of a sudden, am I not good enough for you either?" Florinda accused him.

He remained silent, routed, engulfed, defeat washing over him like the waves swamping the sides of a sinking ship. He knew another word would only lead to another argument. Florinda refused to see his side, his needs. Therefore, he let himself drown in sorrow, self-pity, and pessimism.

In reflection, Jeduthan spent his life trying to please others. He squandered his childhood trying desperately to win his father's acceptance. He wasted his adulthood attempting and failing to please his wife. Well, no more! Now it was his turn. He was emotionally prepared to please no one but himself.

However, what did please him? What did he truly enjoy? He pondered long and hard. Introspection did not come easily to a man accustomed to doing the bidding of others.

The huge mansion upon the hill glistened in the morning light. He remembered the many pleasurable hours he had spent among the walls of Constable Hall, tutoring the young Constable children. Their attentiveness to religious themes and playful banter warmed his heart. He soon concluded that what he really wanted was to delight in reading, savor the pleasures of classical study, and revel in sharing knowledge with others. He visualized the pleasant faces of youngsters with inquiring minds looking to him for knowledge and intellectual growth. He smiled in his fantasy. No doubt, he should seek a position as a teacher or tutor to fulfill this future. Perhaps a rich family, much like the Constables, with a house full of inquisitive and well-mannered children will hire him as a classical educator. Yes, that is a possibility that would bring him great pleasure. Books, Latin, Greek, music, adoring faces looking to him with eyes yearning for more knowledge would be a perfect situation.

Nimrod's step changed and, for an instant, Jeduthan was nudged back into reality. Clouds began filling the sky, dulling the sun's bright rays of the early morning. A sweet spring rain might dampen his enthusiasm, but he continued contemplating his dream, his plan only momentarily niggled.

Where, then, should he seek employment? New York, and particularly this part of it, is much too close to home. He might be discovered and hauled back to Turin. Pennsylvania? He had not heard of many wealthy landowners there who could afford private tutors for their children unless he was to live in a large city. He wondered what life might be like in a metropolis. Would he be supplied a genteel room flooded with warm sunlight overlooking a placid park? No, more likely only a dank closet with a lone porthole providing dim light in the shadow of smoky soot belching from factory chimneys. He dreaded the life of a decrepit indentured servant. No, the city would not suit his longing for open spaces and nature.

He must go farther, possibly into the southern states and the grand countryside in America's rural society. There, his knowledge would be appreciated and valued. Yes, he would aim far south into Virginia's hill country. There he would seek a wonderful position as a tutor for the offspring of a rich, luxuriant plantation owner where he would be housed in a quaint summer cottage, birds chirping in a trestle garden and students eagerly awaiting to be inspired. Moreover, he reasoned, Virginia is far to the south. No more harsh winters! No more fighting the cold, snow, and wind that bite at a man's bare face or turn hands and feet into useless appendages, as is so often the case in New York's northern frontier.

As he dreamed, a slight smile crossed his face, the first in many, many months. Although barely aware, he gently nodded his head with this first glimmer of hope for a new and better life.

His stomach growling, he extracted a hefty slice of bread from his haversack secreted from home before his hasty departure. Biting off a generous morsel, he noticed how stale and crumbly it had become. His mouth instantly dried. Lifting his woolen covered canteen to his lips, he metaphorically compared the dry, crusty bread to the home he was leaving behind, a faithless home devoid of happiness. He was finally free.

Cresting a ridge, Jeduthan inspected the countryside that lay before him. All morning he had intently focused on his problems while failing to notice the natural world all about him. With a new alertness, he realized that absent mindedness was not to his benefit. One of any number of nosey townsfolk traveling this same route might see him and report his whereabouts to the authorities in Turin. No doubt, the constable, at the behest of the church deacons, proceeded assembling a posse in search of him on this very morn. Additionally, other travelers might want to talk or, worse yet, ask questions; questions which he hoped desperately to avoid. Fear swept over him like an ice-cold wind from an autumn squall rushing off Lake Ontario, chilling him to the bone, even though the sun's warmth should have penetrated everything its rays touched. Paranoia caused him to look around sharply with heightened senses.

The extended wood lining this portion of his trek had only recently begun budding leaves, enabling him a rather unobstructed view for some distance between the light tints of green spotting the countryside. Occasionally, the white flowers of dogwood contrasted sharply to the sycamore's red hue. Unlike the Tug Hill plateau's barren wintry landscape, this region seemed vividly fresh and clean. Cardinals sang their melodious tunes loudly, staking claim to territory. Robins pulled worms from the earth, intent on a delicious meal from nature's bounty. It was a pretty season, a time of year ripe with aromas and colors of new hope.

He reasoned that God meant for humanity to enjoy and relish nature's beauty rather than be caged inside a dark, dank building, as was his life in the village of Turin. He imagined that the freshness of spring held a scent of promise. He envisioned new beginnings and a new life ahead. Yes, he had chosen the right time to leave!

Traveling along the road for about an additional hour, placing a few more miles between his past life and his future, he noticed the beautiful New York countryside. He had traveled this road many times before, but only today did he discern the vibrant life lining its route; a life not unlike the warmth and hope that he experienced in a small country church just last autumn.

While visiting Joanna S. Floyd, wife of the late General William Floyd[1] in the quaint village of Westernville only a short journey from his own congregation, he learned of a young pastor named Charles Finney[2]. The elderly woman told of this youthful minister in glowing terms. During the late general's funeral, the traveling preacher inspired the congregation with vivid and emotionally filled stories of faith, sacrifice,

---

[1] William Floyd was a Revolutionary War Veteran and signer of the Declaration of Independence. He married (1784) second Joanna Strong and by 1804 moved his residence to Westernville, Oneida County, New York. (http://colonialhall.com/floyd/floyd.php).

[2] Called to the ministry in October 1821, Charles Finney spent his early years in western upstate New York. One of his revivals included the Township of Western. By 1824, many Presbyterian ministers adopted his new methods and he was evangelizing in many eastern cities. More may be found on Finney's life in his autobiography at (http://www.gospeltruth.net/1868Memoirs/mem16.htm).

repentance, and hope. She added that Finney was to preach again the following Sunday and Jeduthan decided to call to hear for himself the moving words.

When the day arrived, Jeduthan dutifully traveled the many miles and witnessed Finney's methods just as Mrs. Floyd described. One by one, Reverend Finney called for the gathered brethren to repent, asking Jesus into their hearts. The listeners responded openly. Inspired by the pastor's fervent and emotional beckoning, Jeduthan experienced a similar spiritual awakening in his soul. The preacher saturated the multitude so that Jeduthan hoped he too might move his own flock in a similar manner. However, on that day in Western, he hesitated committing to Finney's call for repentance. He did not step forward and kneel at the altar. Religious impotence shamed him. Nevertheless, scores of parishioners rededicated their lives that fateful Sunday. Later, after the sermon, Jeduthan vividly remembered grasping the young reverend's hand while departing the sanctuary. Its warmth and softness contrasted sharply with Finney's fiery eyes.

The following Sabbath, he returned to his own pulpit and used Finney's methods to call his flock to immediate repentance. Emotionally charged and spiritually engaged, the words flowed from his mouth with the authority of the Holy Spirit. Tears dripped from his cheeks while his voice echoed through the sanctuary. However, no one, not a single soul, came forth. Not a single wretched heart from Turin's Presbyterian Church responded to the message, a message as emotionally compelling as he had experienced in Western. Only stern expressions from faithless eyes accosted him. Later that evening, Florinda condemned him for "... such devilish methods." Adding insult to injury, the deacons rebuked him with a letter of reprimand.

"Do not be tricked by the radical message of Reverend Finney," stated the letter. "You are to follow the prescribed format during worship. Do not distress the parishioners!" Devastated, he retreated and did not divert from the accepted ways of his Presbyterian congregation again, though his heart ached for the sincere faith that he witnessed the previous Sunday while away from Turin.

He paralleled Black Creek's western flank, traveling southward through the wilds of Lewis and Oneida Counties. He hoped to avoid the thriving town of Rome, a pleasant growing settlement where he often traveled when trading with several local merchants. Therefore, when the roads forked, he chose to remain with the farm road following the creek. He planned to descend deep within the hollows and gullies of the Adirondack Mountains where few dared to venture. There, he could breathe the fresh air and regain a sense of emotional balance.

Hours passed as he traveled the forested road and yet not a person did he encounter. All afternoon the eastern edge of the road skirted only forest, the sweet sounds of nature occasionally creeping from within its depths. Birds chirped, squirrels scampered about, and a few rabbits peeked inquisitively at him. Once, a deer darted across the path after feasting in the meadow under the late afternoon sun.

As his horse crested a knoll, he was able to peer ahead down the road for nearly a mile, for the woods thinned, forming more of a sparse glade instead of the impenetrable forest for which the indomitable Adirondacks are known. However, in the distance, he soon spied an approaching rider. He panicked! Glancing into the deep, penetrating wood toward his left and rear, he searched for an escape route. However, there was none.

He rationalized that he should veer into the underbrush and out of sight of the road or risk discovery! Once hidden by undergrowth, he could stop and act as if he were relieving himself, waiting until the rider passed before returning to the road to continue his trek. It was his only prudent choice! He started to pull slightly on the reins, but abruptly changed his mind. No! That was the old Jeduthan Higby. Cowardly. Sniveling. Acquiescent. If he were ever to alter his course in life, the time must be now! He must confront the on-comer face to face! If asked questions, he would boldly answer them! He would not run! He would not hide!

He straightened his body in his saddle, riding forward with determination set in his jaw. The distance narrowed and he noticed that the stranger's large, brimmed hat had slid over his eyes as if the rider was asleep. He imagined the approaching rider might well already be aware of his identity and the ploy of slumbering meant to gain an advantage. Nevertheless, his nerve remained firm until, when only a few yards separated them, he heaved on the reins, darting into the ravines east of the path. Nimrod obeyed immediately, scurrying through the dense pinewoods along the sloping hillside.

The evergreens seemed to swallow the pair, closing in behind them as the old steed maneuvered between the tightly packed trees for twenty yards before halting. His heart raced! He did not want to draw any additional attention with sudden movements, not that he could have moved anyhow, for horror froze his bones. He breathed deeply, trying to stabilize his racing heartbeat. The blood pounded through his veins, echoing loudly in his ears. He feared the sound would resonate throughout the far hills and valleys, alerting everyone.

For an eternity, he watched and listened for his pursuer. His eyes scanned the thicket, searching for escape routes, if he might need one. The sleeping rider though, passed by, oblivious to the drama played out in the pine copse only a rod's length from the road. Soon, his logic regained control, chiding him for succumbing to fearful emotions.

The constant battle within his mind was nothing new. Irrationality and guilt overcame him and instilled a deep-seated fear embedded in his heart. Shortly, anger boiled within his breast, causing him physically to lash out in frustration in payment for his mental weakness. He beat his chest, tore at his ears, and cascading tears erupted from his desolate eyes. Minutes seemed like hours as he slowly regained some tranquility with its accompanying rationality. Emotionally exhausted, he desperately needed rest.

Nudging Nimrod forward through the evergreen thicket, dodging trees for a quarter mile, he approached Black Creek at the bottom of a deep gully. He had yet to view the stream before the faint sound of a trickling brook weaving its fresh water among rocks and downed timber reached his ears. Thirst instinctively led his beast toward the refreshing water and soon both horse and owner slurped the cool liquid.

He relaxed on a large rock, wetting his handkerchief. Grime crusted his face. Instinctively, he wiped the dust from his brow and cleansed his hands. He remembered a little verse his mother used to sing to console him as a child. "...Always tidy will make you mighty." Here he rested for an hour, calming his nerves and regaining his composure. The trees cast shadows upon the water and he perceived his reflection within the still pool at his feet.

The motionless water transported his mind back to Turin's Presbyterian Church of forty-eight hours previous. Sitting on a rough wooden chair, he slowly counted the donations deposited by the parishioners. For many weeks, this agonizing chore rested on his burdened shoulders. He was charged with opening, examining, and recording each pitiful tithe from the day's religious service into the treasury journal and noting which families faithfully shared their earthly success with heaven's church. Often, his investigations revealed that the village's poorest inhabitants far exceeded the generosity than those who flaunted their privileged positions.

However, he reached a breaking point on this day. Once again, the deacons postponed their promised meeting to settle accounts. Lingering expenses financially hobbled him. Moreover, each time he presented his accounts to the church elders, they demurred. "We have not the time this week, Reverend Higby! We shall convene again after planting," they had promised. However, he knew their hearts. They had strayed far from God's purposes! Each sermon had become only a choreographed script, no heart-felt repentance, no seeking God's mercy, only just a game played out each Sabbath.

He counted the last of the funds and briefly scrutinized the assorted coins in his hands. Just like each week, a small safe stood open, ready to receive the tithes. The dark hole reminded him of a snake's lair nestled in the side of an exposed rock cliff. He imagined the darkness contained a poisonous viper laying silently for its victim. Only then, in the darkness that engulfed the church storage room, he paused before slowly gathering the coins into a small leather bag and slipping it into his vest pocket rather than the safe. Today, he would not feed Satan's treasury. The Devil's fangs will be disappointed!

However, deep in the safe's dark chamber, he perceived a faint, perturbed hiss soon followed by an acidy spit. He shivered from its cold, chill sound. Suddenly, a serpent's head emerged from the safe's cavernous innards and lunged for his throat!

He fell backward, his hind parts landing in a cool pool of creek water. A small, slithering snake disturbed the calm, black liquid at his feet, awakening him from his trance. Nimrod stood firmly on the creek bed and tugged upon some green moss anchored snugly onto a nearby exposed tree's roots. He picked himself up, grasped Nimrod's bridle, and slowly advanced along the creek bed.

The lengthening shadows and darkening wood revealed that few hours remained before sundown and he soon located a suitable clearing for establishing a camp for the night. Tethering his horse and placing oats in a muzzle bag for Nimrod, he laid his blankets upon a mattress of pine needles. Sitting upon his saddle, he extracted his meager rations of two hard-boiled eggs, a slab of cheese, and four hefty slices of bread from his haversack. He carefully peeled the eggshells and swallowed the egg whites whole. As for the yokes, he vigilantly flattened them into his palm, making a sort of flat paste that he positioned onto his slices of bread. Breaking the cheese into squares, he carefully placed them onto the remaining bread slices. Lifting the bread to his lips, he devoured the sandwiches by munching the dry crust first and then the softer centers. He chased the entire meal with a liberal amount of water from his canteen. Nourishment strengthened his muscles.

He laid in the twilight, relaxed, nature's sounds surrounding him. The previous chill from the creek bed seemed to dissipate as stars began appearing in the heavens. He leaned backward upon his saddle and felt the bulge of his beloved musical instrument protrude into his ribs. Sitting upright, he extracted the scheitholt from its blanket wrap, placing it upon his lap. He remembered pleasant times with his musical instrument as he might an old friend, plucking its strings and performing musical notes of joy for his children. They laughed and sang old folk tunes by the dim fire light of the hearth.

He plucked a few chords and they echoed through the darkening wood with an unex-pected vibrancy. Then he stopped and realized the night sounds, too, had ceased. He held his breath for an eternity before the peeping and calls of nature's nightlife once again resounded throughout the wood.

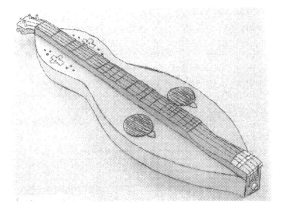

He decided that tonight he would fall asleep with nature's tunes resonating through his mind instead of man's noise. He hoped that the hoots, peeps, and chirps of the night would relieve him of the frightening nightmares that seemed to haunt him since he first envisioned his escape from Turin. He was sadly disappointed, though, as there would be no escape.

Imagined spirits from his past haunted his dreams in the deep woods that night, causing him fitful uneasiness and little sleep. There was the apparition of his father, hands resting authoritatively upon stout hips, shaking his head slowly while clucking his tongue, expressing disappointment in his son. His aged mother kept her head down, resting her gray hairs in her hands, weeping silently at his broken trust and lack of commitment. Finally, he imagined his abandoned wife and children gazing hopelessly into the distance, through cold frosted windows, their hands shading tear-filled eyes from the brightly shining early morning sunlight, ever looking for their father and husband. These visions burned into his mind as a hot iron might sear a brand into livestock. The specters haunted him throughout the long night, peaceful sleep eluding him once again.

Pursued

As the sun's first rays lightened the dark sky with the brilliant colors of dawn, Jeduthan arose, stretched, and saddled Nimrod. Although his bones and joints protested, he well understood that today was the defining moment of his new life. He could never return, or even look back toward his unfortunate past. Instead, he must look forward, toward a hopeful future and a better life.

Mounting Nimrod, he turned to face the rising sun, feeling its warming rays touch his clammy skin. He attempted prayer, much as he did each morning. Yet this morning his words came only haltingly. He felt empty. His prayer seemed like meaningless ritual. He began to wonder if Florinda's faithlessness had permeated his own spirituality over the years. Cold and icy, he felt a wet tear descend his exposed cheek. Was this the life of the faithless?

Ascending the steep embankment, he made his way back to the roadway leading southward toward Rome. Slowly, Nimrod stepped off a deliberate, rhythmic gait along the lengthy path of his new life. However, his destination must not include Rome or Utica, both bustling cities planted firmly in his path. Too many people might recognize his presence in both locales.

In his past life, he had often traveled to Rome in pursuit of business. Many months had passed since his last trip there. On that day, he purchased blankets, ironware, glass, and pottery for his floundering store in Turin. The danger that the town posed to Jeduthan included the town's various mills, attracting farmers and merchants from throughout northwestern New York, some of whom might include his former neighbors and parishioners. Utica offered only slight advantage, but its several breweries attracted the less desirable characters that might expose his past in exchange for the Devil's drink. As the two towns were about 20 miles apart, he decided to divert his course, using farm lanes through the countryside, placing both cities on his flanks.

He soon left the main road and turned eastward along a little used farm lane. The large mud holes and deeply rutted roadbed caused him considerable delay, but as the sun reached its zenith, he spied a small community in the distance. Doubt grabbed his conscience. Should he avoid this village? Yesterday's moment of weakness and cowardice still burned in him like the after effects of swallowing the broth from a bitter root disguised as sweet soup. No! Rather than dodging this village by skirting its flanks, he must boldly ride through its middle, holding his head high and bravely entering its environs. He vowed never to cower again. Therefore, he approached the village with neither increasing nor decreasing his horse's pace.

The rutted roadway improved into soft gravel the closer to the village he approached. Within one hundred yards, he viewed a small village commons and a few scattered buildings strewn along both sides of the lane. A few children played in its roadbed while numerous women, obviously mothers of the playful children, stood by a rail fence discussing community news. He could hear their chatter, much like chickens clucking near a hen house before feeding. Thoughts of his parishioners' gossiping voices echoed in his mind. So much time wasted by idle hands; a true Devil's playhouse. These women ought to engage their children rather than gossiping. Expose their adolescents to nature's beauty, enliven their children with lovely poetry, or inspire their hearts with God's words expressed through His holy scriptures. Alas, no! The old hags allow their brood to wallow in the mud while they seek temporal pleasures in light conversation with their peers! Jeduthan silently fumed.

As Nimrod glided gently by, his anger went unnoticed except for one small set of eyes. Not over seven years old, she sat naked in a muddy garden, neglected by her parent. Her eyes followed each step that Nimrod paced down the path. They were intensely blue, much like his daughter's eyes. They pierced his soul as a savage's arrow might skewer its victim during an Indian raid on the frontier. Had a Divine spirit entered into her mind and through her eyes beckoned him to return to his past life? If only she were to command him, *Retrace your steps, old man!* he would obediently comply. Yet her lips never parted. He cast his eyes downward in shame, breaking the possessed child's grip. When he again saw her, she was playfully patting large, round mud pies with her palms as if he was of no importance.

He often felt of no significance. For forty-two years, few people expressed interest in Jeduthan Higby. He obediently conformed to expectations and was never encouraged to question authority. He supposed that these suppressed feelings might have caused his recent rebellion. Insecurities fueled his drive to throw off a contented lifestyle that so many other rational individuals seek and embrace. Thus, he desired an uncertain life outside his tiny borough. He was sure a great adventure awaited him only a few score miles ahead. However, here he was nobody, insignificant and ignored, even by a possessed child.

At the southern edge of the village, he discovered a small cemetery adjacent to a clapboard-meeting house, reminding him of his parents' burial plot at Constableville. Solomon's family tended their parents' grave a few short miles south of Turin. Each year, the younger sibling inquired what flowers Jeduthan thought should adorn the gravesite. Each year, he responded with a deep sigh, head slumped upon his shoulders.

The last time he visited the burial site was the 15th day of October 1820, shortly following his father's demise to nature's fury.[3] The intense moment still burned in his memory. Father and son had traveled to Pulteney, in Steuben County, to investigate importing a herd of sheep. There they had met with four local farmers, George Copper, Jonathan Wales, Nobel Sweet, and Chauncey Phelps. These men regularly conversed by post with the elder Higby and offered an enticing trade of twenty-five fine sheep and fourteen barrels of pork for six bolts of calico. Jeduthan had just deposited the cloth with Mr. Copper and harnessed the team to the wagon when Father burst forth from the barn.

"Boy, we need to hurry! Bad weather is coming."

Jeduthan scanned the peaceful sky, only a few clouds dotting the heavens. He began to protest but shut his mouth realizing its pointlessness. Father never heeded his advice. Soon all six men were bound for Sodom, the town's major village where the awaiting herd of sheep and casks of ham were located.

---

[3] *Daily National Intelligencer*, November 13, 1820.

The air was warm and humid, but there were few signs of the frightening temptress that was soon to engulf the party. A sweet smell lingered in the air from the last of the flowering blooms from the year's Indian summer. By afternoon, though, storm clouds appeared in the western sky. Ever expanding, the dark gray clouds were reminiscent of smoke from hell's inferno. Jeduthan gazed upon the dark phenomena, wondering if locusts would soon appear from within its bowels and devour the Earth as described in *Revelation*. Yet, he held his tongue, for debating with his father was useless.

Soon, the tremendous thunderstorm let loose its deadly wind, terrific lightning, and torrential watery downpour. Mr. Sweet called for a temporary halt in their journey. However, Father stiffly refused. The group continued onward. Nevertheless, when the wind began to howl through the treetops, Sweet and Phelps both abandoned the wagon for the cover of a nearby woodshed. Jeduthan was about to join them when Father ordered him to dismount from the buckboard and take hold the horses' reins, leading the frightened beasts onward through a walnut grove rather than wisely seeking protective shelter. Jeduthan began to object, but he had long since learned that a commandment from Father was as firm as a legal statute. Dismounting and grasping the reins, he proceeded only a few hundred yards through the deluge before a great gust of wind swayed the enormous trees with the power only Satan might employ.

From the treetops came violent cracking sounds followed by a tremendous snap. The horses reared up and broke the son's hold upon their halters. A broken limb resembling a great ship's mast crashed down, crushing the forward wheels and, combining with the animals' strength, broke the harnesses, freeing the maddening creatures. Jeduthan landed upon his rear, stunned by the tumultuous wind, the frantic horses' cry, and the sound of the wagon shattering in thousands of splinters. By the time he righted himself, the wind had ceased its violent assault and a gentle spring shower engulfed the glade. Peace reigned about his being. He imagined angels' protective arms embracing his body as might a protective mother's arms embrace a newborn.

The minutes seemed as hours before reality gripped his mind. A giant limb lay where, only a few moments before, Father, Mr. Wales, and Mr. Copper had sat. Its massive weight, detached from the uttermost extremities of a colossal walnut, had crashed down upon the wagon and smothered the three men. Jeduthan tried in vain to lift the massive bough from off his father's collapsed chest, but to no avail. Falling backward onto the muddy ground again, he wept. The image of his father's arms burned into his memory, twisted and contorted as they were between the branches. In a split moment, the man who dominated his life was no more. Sweet and Phelps soon arrived, but they could do little more than console the lone survivor. Jeduthan felt that day an invisible hand lift from his heart an enormous weight in the oppressive spirit of his father. Nevertheless, it was short lived. Somehow, his father's spirit continued to haunt him like the solid salt pillar of Lot's wife standing vigil over the doomed city of ancient days. To this very day, five years after the incident, as he passed a simple graveyard far from his former home and cheerless life, his father's memory continued to oppress his spirit.

Gliding past each tombstone, he examined the carved names carefully. *Carter* appeared four different times in separate plots. Two large marble markers displayed *Petersen*, identically carved with intricate scrolling on their upper portion with the same date recorded as deceased. No doubt the Petersens paid dearly that dreadful day.

Reaching the last marker nearest the path, his body became rigid as he viewed the inscription, *Higbie* in bold letters. He never thought that relatives, besides his immediate family, might reside nearby. He reached deep into his memory, attempting to recall and sort his family history. However, he only knew of his father and two uncles, Zaccheus and John, moving from Connecticut to Lewis County, New York. Their move occurred an entire decade before his own travels to the frontier. Nevertheless, the brothers had all kept in close contact before the war with Britain. Who might this rogue *Higbie* be?

When first called to Leyden's Presbyterian Church only a few miles from his father's frontier homestead, the church deacons were impressed by the Higby name, repeatedly voicing praise of his father's character during the required interview. "A thrifty, pioneer farmer!" the men exclaimed, and no doubt his father's reputation cemented Jeduthan's appointment, instantaneously gaining him the elders' confidence. However, within a year, friction began.

Father interfered with church matters for which Jeduthan, as pastor, ought to have conducted. Many times the deacons deferred to the elder Higby on financial matters, leaving the son unsure of his position. Finally, his father's meddling reached a climax when he interrupted Jeduthan's Sunday sermon by quoting a scripture passage from memory that had little relevance to the message. Jeduthan exploded from the pulpit in a fit of anger. By the sermon's conclusion, he felt embarrassed, not only from his father's behavior, but also his own.

Conditions worsened when numerous parishioners ridiculed him for his outburst. He secretly wished to disown his father. Therefore, Jeduthan sought appointment to a neighboring church in Turin, miles away from his embarrassing father. Many months passed before father and son conversed again. Moreover, never again did the father attend church where the son preached.

A bell sounded from behind. Jeduthan peered about and realized that he had left the small village far in his wake. Only the chapel bell echoed through the immense pastures that surrounded him. Ascending a tall rise along his path, he faintly spied the village on the far northern horizon, now the buildings appeared as only small dots in the distance.

Before him lay a lush valley, studded with patches of wooded glens and open fields like to a grand quilt in northwestern New York's terrain. The wonderful panoramic vista bathed his eyes, made even more spectacular by the crystal-clear air. Halting Nimrod, he breathed in deeply, swelling his barrel chest and smelling a wondrous sweetness of a virgin countryside, unspoiled by wickedness. A fresh spring breeze rustled the trees and the tall meadow grass teemed with life.

As he descended into the valley, birds chirped and sang. One song resounded from a cardinal. He knew that cardinals endured harsh weather, unlike robins that migrated south for the winter. He smiled as the sun bore down upon his right cheek.

"So then, I am more like a robin than a cardinal. But I've got autumn and spring reversed!" he found himself exclaiming aloud while Nimrod leisurely tread his path southward. His words rang true. Each spring he yearned to fly away as did the robins. Walls seemed stifling and confining; the out-of-doors, harmonizing with the birds and breathing fresh air, soothed his soul.

He did not hope to mimic the legendary explorers Daniel Boone or Meriwether Lewis, but rather he just enjoyed the outdoors. Jeduthan recalled his many acquaintances who were farmer's sons complaining bitterly of daily chores, tending livestock, and attempting to outguess the whims of nature each year. The never-ending work with little time for relaxing fouled his taste for farming, so he desired to escape into the wilderness, not to tame its wilds but to enjoy nature's freedom.

Nimrod's evenly paced steps and gently rocking momentum acted like a sleeping potion. Jeduthan's eyes became heavy and his head bobbed upon his shoulders. A warm sensation crept around his ears and thoughts of traveling the wilderness permeated his mind. Recalling lines within his copy of the *History of the Expedition under the Command of Captains Lewis and Clark* that he secreted amongst his beloved books, he visualized his participation in their great trek into America's Louisiana wilderness. Marveling in wonderment, he imagined the majestic open plains, the mysterious *Hill of Evil Spirits*, and the enormous falls of the mighty Missouri. Indescribable flora and fauna decorated the open domain in his imaginary world. Surrounded by an unknown land abounding with dangerous animals and savage natives, he delighted his senses in their endless variety. Oh, how wonderful that life must be! These New York forests, glens, and glades must pale in comparison.

Jeduthan was jolted back to reality by Nimrod's sudden halt. A large snake stretched full length across the path, obstructing his journey. His old steed stood fast while Jeduthan studied the serpent for a full minute, noticing its shiny scales as it sunned its body in the afternoon light. He doubted that many traveled this roadway and expected that the snake often found its way here to warm itself. How strange that this creature exhibited no fear from his presence. Perturbed, he recollected passages in *Genesis* describing the devious serpent and its participation in man's downfall. What sign might this docile creature foretell of his future? Is the snake a precursor to dreadful events lurking along his path? Might its venom symbolize poison that might befall him? Was this Satan come to collect his soul for the great sin he held within his heart?

Jeduthan patted Nimrod's neck and whispered gently, "Back, now, old fellar. Back." The steed tenderly backed away from the snake. The horse's movement startled the creature, and like a flash, the reptile raised its head a full foot from the rocky path. Jeduthan watched as the snake's head abruptly changed shape and hissed, its tongue slithering from between deadly jaws. He held tight to the saddle as Nimrod hastened a quick retreat. Within a moment, the roadway was clear and no sign of the monster remained.

Jeduthan's stomach gurgled and a deep pang indicated that he must soon stop to eat. Fearing that the cheese in his haversack might spoil and knowing his last morsel of bread must be hard and stale, he passed quickly along the roadway and proceeded several hundred more yards before stopping to consume his lunch in the shade of a large oak tree.

Dismounting, he examined the contents of his haversack. His speculation concerning the bread proved correct. Crumbled into nearly a handful of powdered starch, it would prove uneatable as bread for much longer. Therefore, in a calculated decision exemplifying the mood of his new, adventurous lifestyle, he consumed every morsel of food remaining. He thrust off his old frugal nature, insisting on confronting his fears of future survival.

However, the countryside soothed his trepidation as much as it abounded in nature's bounty. Nimrod gently grazed on the lush grass that provided a soft cushion beneath his feet, much better forage than the northern wilderness afforded during cold winter months. There, on the rocky precipices of Tug Hill plateau, only meager and monotonous forage exists. However, here tasty clover, wild onion, and luscious meadows bless the countryside. Such a bountiful region must surely contain an abundance that could support the likes of one more inhabitant within its bounds. Jeduthan pledged to find Nimrod a fine stable and plentiful oats before the sun set in the western sky. Mounting his steed once again, he set a route southward, confident and optimistic of his course.

Late in the afternoon, he sighted a town along his path. Having gained confidence from successfully piloting though the village earlier in the day, he rode Nimrod directly toward the hamlet, almost daring anyone to speak to him. Looking eastward, he noticed a small gathering of parishioners in front of what looked to be a church near the far end of the dirt street. They gathered around a notification board that many small villages rely upon to convey important information. As he approached, he noticed a substantial placard with the word **Wanted** in bold, prominent letters.

Could it be that news of his crime had already spread here from Turin? He suspected that his crime, so dastardly to Presbyterians would undoubtedly travel quickly, but he doubted the news would trek as rapidly as he could upon Nimrod. It is true that notification boards post official announcements! They must have found him out! How did they expose him so soon? He did not recall any riders overtaking him. Word must have traveled by some other path! Panic gripped him again. His mind raced. "Yes, that's it. I've just been taking my time, leisurely traveling when I should have been sprinting like the wind. Oh, I am such a fool!"

As he had not commanded Nimrod to change path or gait, the trusty mount steadily approached the Presbyterian Church as a condemned man might to the hangman's noose. The distance narrowed and he plainly saw many characteristics of the people gathered at the vestibule. A rather large woman wore a flowered bonnet. A skinny man was dressed in a dark, homespun suit. A hunched-backed man, whose bent posture allowed only small steps, hopped about the crowd's periphery. Others, too, gazed upon the notices. All the people appeared disturbingly familiar. Could they all hail from this tiny hamlet...or possibly Turin?

"That's an incredible amount of money!" the large woman said in a manly, booming voice that echoed from the church's clapboard siding. Her voice and words made his blood run cold.

"Can you ever imagine doing such a thing?" the thin man asked a younger gentleman standing nearby.

The younger man replied, "Money drives desperate men to desperate acts, even to selling their bodies and souls into everlasting damnation."

Panic tightened its grip upon Jeduthan's chest. His fingers froze about the reins. He could not loosen his hold upon the leather. Fear of detection forced him to lower his head, hiding his eyes and face in shame with the brim of his hat.

An unseen bystander whistled and said, "I never heard of such, not in all my born days, unbelievable! So much money!"

"It's a hideous crime!" shouted another old man in the crowd who looked amazingly similar to Jeduthan's father.

Within moments, Jeduthan must ride past these same people who surely would know the actual reason why he had left Turin in a frantic hurry. They would turn, recognize him, yank him from his horse, and condemn him. His brief breath of freedom had ended. Whether they returned him for trial in Turin or simply lynched him here, in this isolated village and under the church's eaves, did not matter. Either way, he was doomed. He could not escape!

"I admit it!" he yelled, his deep voice rumbling through the village. "I took the money! But, I deserved it! It was rightfully mine!"

The townspeople stood motionless, shocked by his words. Wordlessly and with one accord, they grabbed at him. The large woman's fingernails sank deep into the skin of his forearm, causing blood to trickle forth. The skinny man grabbed at his waist, jerking him roughly down from his horse. Thrown to the ground, the bent man, using his strong legs and feet repeatedly kicked at him, bruising his torso. Others, nameless and faceless, chanted hysterically, "Lynch him! Kill him! Throw him in jail!"

Jeduthan attempted a meek defense. "The church never paid me! I was faithful for three long years! I have a wife and family to feed, clothe, and provide for! I have expenses! I did my best! Please spare me!"

A young boy ran in front of old Nimrod, startling the beast into an abrupt halt only a few yards short and slightly behind the crowd peering at the notice board. The nightmare of the few minutes before had not occurred. His words, along with the crowd's insults, were only imagined fears. Most citizens remained focused on the announcement board, some continuing a low unintelligible mumble between themselves. A few young boys played fetch with an excited dog. He glanced toward both flanks, perceiving that in the world's reality, no one had moved, no one had accosted him. No one noticed him as he approached. No one knew his name or his crime. No one recognized his face or discerned the distinctively nervous sweat on his body. No one cared.

Hiding on the Canal

Jeduthan dismounted his horse and approached the gathered town folk. From ground level, the crowd did not look nearly as hostile as he had imagined only a few moments before. The large woman donning the flowered bonnet radiated a pleasant child-like smile, while the stooped man flashed a genuinely pleasant toothy grin. The nervous sweat that had streamed from his brow

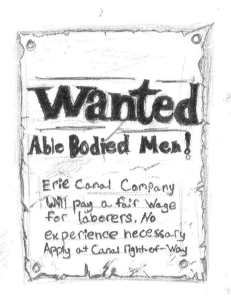

quickly abated as his anxiety eased and he regained a sense of calm.

Approaching the bulletin posted on the village notice board, he investigated the announcement more closely. Below the bold and prominent *WANTED* were inscribed the words, *Able Bodied Men...* These three words resonated through his mind. *Able Bodied Men!* This notice was not about some fugitive criminal or desperate rogue, but rather an advertisement for laborers! He nudged his way forward, weaving through the assembled onlookers in order to read the details written in smaller letters upon the posted sheet. *Erie Canal Company will pay a fair wage for laborers. No experience necessary. Apply at canal right-of-way.*

An elaborate plan instantaneously developed deep within his mind. A lone rider passing through villages, hamlets, and towns might arouse suspicions. However, the constant stream of canal workers might provide him opportunity to disappear into the masses, as one of many unfamiliar faces. Therefore, he could gain the anonymity he so much desired. Later, he could plan his escape southward.

He only needed to find the canal right-of-way in order to sign on for work. Therefore, gathering courage, he glanced about, searching for one friendly face to ask for directions to the right-of-way. He spied a few youngsters gathering flowers near the church's white picket fence a few rods from the announcement board. Approaching ever so cautiously and humbly, he inquired of the oldest, a young girl of about fourteen, where he might find the canal.

"Easy, mister. Just foller this here road 'til ya reach de red barn on de right. Take de path to de left not more than five hunerd yerds and there it be."

"Thank you very much, young lady," said Jeduthan. Parting, he glanced back over his shoulder to the young lass and thought what a pitiful sight she presented. Uneducated to a point of near imbecility! He was sure that within only a short time he could tutor the ragamuffin, changing her deportment so that she could grow into a gracious young lady, refined and gentlewomanly.

He had proven his tutoring skills many years before by schooling his youngest sister, Adah. Left motherless at age nine and, figuratively speaking, fatherless pretty much since birth, she craved attention. For nine long years, Jeduthan groomed young Adah, compelling her to improve her speech, to refine her manners, and to organize her possessions. In time, he induced her to marry Mr. Fallus E. Taylor, Esquire, who arrived from Connecticut but only a few months ago. Adah and Fallus had been a fine match and would sprout excellent children in time.

This memory overwhelmed his mind with grief and a sense of mortification. *Compel, organize, refine, induce!* All were words used by his father to direct his own life. He trembled with an aching heart. Had his actions toward his baby sister sown the same seeds in her heart as harkened in his own? A tear formed from the corner of his eye as he gazed sorrowfully at the adolescent, while she and her young compatriots scurried around the low fence and into the churchyard, happily and innocently gathering wild flowers alongside the clapboard building.

He soon remounted Nimrod who stood patiently nearby, the only creature witnessing the internal conflict rattling its owner. Following the young girl's directions, he obediently proceeded along the road to the red barn and then left down the path to the canal right-of-way. What the girl lacked in culture, class, and etiquette, she made up in common sense, for at the end of the path lay his destination. The hiring tent was a dirty gray shelter with a large canvas fly shading an old man from the warm sun. A few paces away lay a recently dug ditch. Its muddy slick sides were no more than six feet deep and a little water trickled along its bottom.

He dismounted and tethered Nimrod to a low branch of a nearby willow tree. He stood on a soft mat of green clover, which would satisfy his trusty steed with fresh forage and tasty grass to munch on while he inquired about employment. "How content you are," he said, as he stroked the animal's muzzle. "Good boy."

After tracing a dozen steps toward the hiring tent, he glanced back to Nimrod confirming that his belongings were intact and safe. As nobody disturbed his mount, Jeduthan took a long, deep breath and moved to the end of a line of four men standing in front of the fly. He stood sideways with one eye on Nimrod, slightly inhibited and uncomfortable, until another man came up from behind. He then turned forward, avoiding eye contact with the other men.

Agitated by Nimrod's distance from his person and the man between him and his horse, his palms began to sweat nervously. Tied loosely on the animal's saddle hung his scheitholt and secreted in the instrument's recesses, his sizable amount of money, money stolen from the church funds. Minutes nervously passed. Paranoia threatened to sweep over him again as he imagined the horse, as calm and obediently as Nimrod might be, bolting and throwing his musical instrument loose from the tack and falling onto the ground, crushed under the animal's hooves, thus exposing his crime. Moreover, the hiring line moved extraordinarily slowly. Minutes seemed like hours of torment.

"Hey, you looking for work too?" a man directly in front of Jeduthan asked.

Surprised by the man's words, he nearly instinctively snarled, "Would I be standing in this line if I didn't?" However, he stopped himself, keeping his mouth closed and his annoyed sarcasm to himself. He only nodded and released a deep grunt.

The fellow briefly turned his head around, glancing at him as if he had taken offense. Ignoring the man, Jeduthan held his reply. He readily assumed by the fellow's yellow crooked teeth, unkempt oily hair, pocked face, and dull watery eyes, that he was not the sort of man for socializing and discussing any civilized topic. What could such a commoner have to convey? His interest piqued, he wondered if everyone awaiting employment was of the same caliber. He studied the back of the man two ahead of him in line. His hair was thinning and gray. His shoulders were broad and his clothes patched.

"Another common, ignorant laborer," Jeduthan huffed to himself.

At the front of the line, bent over a table shaded by the tent fly, he saw a man drudgingly signing papers. He thought that if he can sign a paper, perhaps he can read and write, a far cry from *Mr. Crooked Teeth*! Jeduthan smirked and the man in front turned to expose his disgusting teeth, as if reading his thoughts. The man ejaculated a great wad of yellowish spittle from between his greasy lips, the huge gob landing near Jeduthan's shoes. Using his filthy hand, the man wiped a long trail of saliva from his chin before regaining his stance in the hiring line. Attempting to avoid conflict, Jeduthan glanced to his rear, confirming Nimrod's position a few yards off.

Concluding that the local workers were an uninteresting and dreary lot, he surveyed his physical vicinity. It was flat here, unlike the rolling hills that he had traveled through earlier in the day. The tent fly stretched above a rough wooden table behind which a distinguished looking older man sat in a straight-backed wooden chair. Ink stained the table from bleeding though cheap paper or dripped from quills of clumsy men unused to writing. Behind him, four crates stood piled two by two. Jeduthan could only speculate at their contents. A lantern hung from a cord draped over the ridgepole. After a long wait, he finally arrived at the line's front.

"Next!" bellowed the old man, gruff as an old miser driving a stubborn mule team in an unplowed field. Jeduthan stepped forward and nervously announced, "I am." Only then did the old man raise his head, revealing a pleasant smile, much like a politician when requesting a vote.

"Good afternoon! Looking for employment?" the man smiled.

Again, Jeduthan thought about being sarcastic, but held his tongue as there was no need to make enemies here.

"Can you tell me more about the opportunities available?" Jeduthan queried.

"Well now! I can see that you are not a common laborer as are these miserable souls, but that's all I have available at present. Are you willing to dig ditches?"

Jeduthan almost panicked! If this stranger could determine so easily and quickly that he was not similar to the other common laborers, his chances of finding employment narrowed while his chances of being exposed widened. He contemplated fleeing, but a voice within urged him to make light of the man's comments.

"Does it matter who or what I am if I am willing to work?" he responded while trying to give his most convincing grin.

"You have a point, sir. My job is not to question the motives of our laborers. My job is to sign on workers. Again I ask, are you willing to work?"

"Yes. Can you tell me the specifics of the work?"

"Right now, we need men to work at removing stumps and smoothing the tow path. Can you do that?"

"I believe that with the help of my trusty horse, I can do justice to that job." He pointed toward Nimrod tethered next to the ditch, taking the opportunity to confirm that his horse and his belongings were still unmolested.

"Good, then. Sign here."

"A few more details first please," Jeduthan solicited. "How much does it pay and when am I to be paid? What provisions are there for lodging and food? What about my horse?"

The man stared caustically at Jeduthan for a long moment, much as if being admonished by some young, insolent boy. His face tensed as he mechanically stated, "The pay is fifty cents per day. The workers who wish to sleep in company tents pay back five cents daily. Those who have horses pay back another five cents a day for a boy to feed and groom the animals each evening. Plus, if you wish to join the company food mess instead of preparing your own rations, that's another ten cents a day."

"So what you're really saying is that I would make thirty cents per day, after expenses," Jeduthan analyzed.

"Yes, if that is what you are willing to do!" retorted the older man.

"That is what I am willing to do! I's work for ya mister," Jeduthan responded less refined, hoping better to blend in with the host of laborers gathering about. By this time, the line had significantly lengthened to include over twenty individuals.

"Then sign here," grunted the old man, poking at the stained paper on the wooden table. "Today is April 20, 1825. I will start your wage tomorrow."

Jeduthan glanced down the list of names, noticing that only a few made their marks on the paper. Surprisingly, most workers had signed their names in the designated spaces, a development which he had not expected only a few moments before. He questioned silently if many of the Erie Canal workers were educated. He did not dwell long as he obediently signed in the vacant space at the bottom of the lengthening list of newly hired laborers. He contemplated using an alias, but decided against one.

The old man pointed Jeduthan toward the laborers' camp situated alongside the muddy ditch a few hundred yards farther along the pathway. There he found his assigned tent and arranged his scant baggage on one of the two empty cots inside the cramped shelter. Soon, an aroma of spicy beef stew drifted from a large pot at the cook's open fire, enticing his nostrils. After securing Nimrod at the camp's corral, Jeduthan set off toward the lengthening meal line, awaiting his turn at rations served by the Erie Canal Company.

While he stood patiently in the dinner line, an assemblage of tourists in a large wagon rolled past, stopping a few rods beyond the cook's tent. He examined each member disembarking the wagon onto the muddy path. The first was a man about Jeduthan's own age, who wore a fine tunic of green with large lapels. How out-of-place the fellow appeared at a dirty construction site. His hair was powdered white, much as the rich merchants he remembered in Connecticut as a young child. Two women were next, both wearing dresses with great hoops, which he expected a frontier woman might wear only to a wedding. The older of the two women expressed disgust when first stepping into the mud, most likely due to difficulty balancing upon her narrow shoes that seemed to slip somewhat in the muck. The younger woman smiled broadly when she exited the wagon, grasping a gentleman's hand from within the coach to steady her descent.

When the gentleman emerged from the carriage, he stood with his back toward Jeduthan, only his handsome hair visible from under an elegant hat. He carried a distinctive cane with a silver knob at its end that he used to steady himself upon the slippery path. The man stood erect with authority, a sense of majestic resilience pervading his appearance, steadily peering westward toward the setting sun as if enthralled with its beautiful hue. The statue-like figure remained motionless as a flock of children descended from the conveyance and moved about like two-legged insects just discovering a discarded pastry. Jeduthan thought it quite strange that a man would stare for such a length of time toward the setting sun while pandemonium reigned about his feet. However, the gentleman stood frozen in time, much like a magnificent dramatic tableau.

The children moved so quickly that Jeduthan did not try counting them. They were like a sea of frenzied fish surrounding the four adults, each child trying their best to attain the attention of the green-jacketed man, hurling question upon question at him. The younger woman tried desperately to settle the children, but soon surrendered to their excitement and instead grasped the young gentleman's arm affectionately. All the while, the younger gentleman's gaze never left the horizon.

The minutes of commotion finally abated and the children hushed when the white haired man spoke. "Children, listen attentively to our lesson today. You are living at an extraordinary time in history; a time which no other generation since the days of old Egypt can compare. Behold, many call this feat of engineering, *The Eighth Wonder of the World*! For eight years past, thousands of men, young and old, educated and not, rich and poor, have endeavored to bring to life mankind's dream; a dream to connect the great interior of our fine continent to the enormous port cities of the Atlantic Coast!" The older man grandly gestured with his arms toward Jeduthan and his compatriots awaiting in the stew line.

"Whose dream is it?" inquired one small girl with golden curls.

"Why, my dear lass, it is all mankind's dream. However, our own enlightened governor, his Excellency Mr. Henry Clinton and the investors of the Erie Canal Company will succeed where others have only imagined." The man affectionately patted the youngster's head. "The canal's four foot depth and forty foot breadth will provide a communication and transportation link which will make our great state the richest of the entire known world."

"And how might that be accomplished?" piped the younger of the two women who turned her head toward the children yet remained beside the young gentleman whose vision was fixed on the western horizon. She flashed a bright, broadening smile from her pink lips as if she already knew the answer.

"My dear, since the opening of the western lands and taming of its frontier wilds, many thousands of tons of raw material reaped from the mighty prairie could only flow along the rivers southward toward New Orleans in far western Louisiana and the mighty Gulf of Mexico beyond. That city is grand indeed, but it is far distant from the growing markets of our eastern metropolises. This canal will shorten the travel distance between goods and markets from four thousand miles to a mere 363-mile trek. Its course from the shores of Lake Erie to the swiftly flowing Hudson River and then to the port of New York City beyond will strengthen our economy tremendously. There, within our large factories and warehouses, those same raw materials will be processed and returned, via the same canal waterway, to the frontier farmers as finished goods, enhancing our wealth and ensuring our future security. I assure you, Madam, once the Erie Canal opens, travel time westward and freight eastward will be cut by six times. A mere ten day's junket will replace the three month expedition that our forefathers experienced."

The older woman interjected, "I agree with you, sir, but for eight years men have toiled, animals have struggled, and we have endowed the company as investors and yet have seen little return. This route from Albany west to Buffalo might be jinxed for all I know, awaiting destruction by some unforeseen calamity. I say," she smirked, "that *Clinton's Ditch* most likely will be a failure! How much longer do we wait, I ask you?"

The white haired man waved her off. "Fear not, dear Mrs. Beman, before the weather turns cold, our own governor will celebrate the canal's completion by pouring water from the Atlantic Sea into the western waves of the great Erie Lake. Moreover, what a grand commemoration it shall be! Children, your eyes have beheld the great aqueducts over swift flowing streams and cavernous gullies. Even the mighty Mohawk River, a scant one day's travel from your front steps, could not stop the impressive hands of our engineers. Have you not picnicked next to huge manmade ship locks within sight of the boundaries of our own quaint city of Troy? I ask you! Does not the engineering that amazes your wondering eyes excite your emotions? I expect this marvel to inspire artists, poets, and essayists to produce their craft stimulating the world to American ingenuity and genius. Humanity's conquering spirit has cut its swath across nature's wonders in an unprecedented flight across the countryside."

The younger gentleman, still set like stone silhouetted against the reddening sky, spoke. "My dear Mr. Howard, I expect your predictions are accurate. Humanity has indeed struck a gash upon nature's brow. Its scars surely must be everlasting."

"Hush now, cousin. Father only wishes to captivate the children's minds. Come, let us return to our accommodations before the long ride home on the morrow," interjected the young woman. She turned her head toward the young gentleman and Jeduthan took special notice of her profile as the sky ebbed purple. Her plump lips pouted a silent plea.

"Of course, dear cousin Betsy, I cannot deny any of your desires," the young gentleman offered as the party re-embarked into the wagon. As the vehicle slowly pulled away, Jeduthan thought about the young gentleman's words and their meaning. By working upon the Erie Canal, was his employment a sin against nature? Was he part of Satan's tools to wreak ruin upon God's gracious world? If so, how many more evils must pervade his soul before answering heaven's God?

He felt a poking stick in his back and heard a gruff, "Move on, you stupid mic! Take up your plate and be gone!" He had reached the head of the stew line; back in the realm of reality, grim and unforgiving as it is.

Jeduthan awoke to a crisp spring morning. The weather turned cold during the night and some areas of the muddy towpath froze. Exiting his tent, he walked toward the corral to check upon Nimrod's condition. Often he heard a distinct crunch under foot as the mire beneath his feet gave way to his weight.

A grimy-faced character greeted him in the corral. Startled by this unkempt fellow, Jeduthan inquired of his position. A harsh voice replied, "I am your foreman, you lousy 'scuse of a man. You be working for me today. An I don't take no back talken' from me workers!"

Jeduthan patted Nimrod upon the muzzle, holding his chin high. However, the foreman closed upon him, exhibiting such an intimidating growl that Jeduthan cowered. "Yes, sir. I will do as you ask."

"Wise choice, ol man! Today we work on de path. Ya horse and ya, folla me crew. Weed be takin' de stumps outa de path today an' I spect ya lose some of ya flab before too long," snapped the foreman. Jeduthan complied, following the supervisor out of the camp and along the path with Nimrod in tow.

The laboring was difficult the first day. Back pain and sore muscles caused Jeduthan hours of restless sleep during the night. Early the next day, the same foreman met him at the corral and the insulting hiring ritual repeated. Again, Jeduthan trailed the supervisor to the worksite and labored intensely. For three long weeks, he obediently pursued a similar itinerary of arriving at the corral, enduring the foreman's insults, laboring in a massed gang, and then recovering during the night hours. One wet morning, the grimy, disgusting foreman failed to appear at the accustomed corral meeting. Jeduthan busied himself by grooming Nimrod, patiently waiting for over a half an hour and still the supervisor failed to materialize. Just about to retire to his tent, he saw an approaching man, robust and smartly dressed, calling for him.

"Pardon, sir," puffed the large man nearly out of breath. "I regret to inform you that the canal company has reorganized its contractual arrangements with your former supervisor. Unsatisfied with his gang labor scheme, we have terminated his employment. We do, though, wish to offer you an opportunity to continue on with the company as a sort of independent contractor, you might say."

"What are the terms?" asked Jeduthan, avoiding eye contact with this new canal company representative.

"Same as before, but you shall be working alone. We feel that your new duties will best serve the company if you can use some individual initiative to work more effectively to complete the canal. We expect you to clear brush, trees, rocks, and stumps from the towpath, smoothing the surface sufficiently for horses, mules, and oxen to trod as they move barges along the canal. As you can see, the work is much the same as before, except no pushy foreman with which to contend." The man grinned.

Jeduthan cracked a broad smile as the gentleman announced the demise of the hated foreman. "Yes, I agree to your terms, sir."

"Good," replied the man. "I have drawn you a map with the region of your responsibilities. Can you read a map, sir?"

Jeduthan nodded as he took hold the parchment. "I have no difficulty with my letters and words."

"Fine!" Wagging an accusing finger toward Jeduthan, the man lectured him further. "Now I expect you to keep me informed of your progress, as we must endeavor to meet our construction schedule. I am sure our new arrangement will be much more to your liking. I am Mr. Albright." He held his hand out in a friendly gesture that Jeduthan refused, eyes cast down toward the muddy ground. Albright retracted his hand at the affront and turning, snidely huffed, "Good day to you, sir."

Jeduthan studied the map, his finger tracing the canal's path westward from Rome. Circled in ink was his assigned section, a fair distance from the present camp, probably over five miles away. After obtaining an ax, shovel, spade, and a long length of rope, he mounted his steed and proceeded westward.

He passed by many workers, some laboring in gangs as he had these past weeks, others working independently much like his current assignment. Along a portion of the canal path, he paused for Nimrod to drink from a trough near four stonemasons pursuing their trade. They must have been shaping stones for one of the many locks or possibly a nearby culvert on this day. Such skilled work did not appeal to him for he hoped to remain oblivious to the outside world, a seemingly non-entity amongst the masses. Even his recent independent status frightened him somewhat. Within the gang laborers, he blended in as only one in a crowd of many. Now he could be pinpointed, identified, and acknowledged, which caused him considerable worry.

Yet, as the days passed into weeks with no prodding eyes and little interference, Jeduthan came to enjoy the tough work. His body, unaccustomed to strenuous physical labor, rebounded after the first week. Even the aches in his strained muscles subsided. Within two months, he found that he could lift loads undreamed of before. His new strength amazed him. Forty-two years of age, he was bronzed and muscular like never before in his life. He took pride in his physical prowess, liking the comments that younger fellows mentioned such as, *Look at that old man go!* and *Don't challenge him to any kind of contest because you won't win!*

Clearing the ten-foot wide towpath of brush, trees, and rocks so that horses, mules, and oxen could trod their life-long mission of moving canal boats was a hard, tedious job, but it gave Jeduthan a sense of accomplishment which had evaded him so long in his previous vocation as minister to a dying flock of non-believers. He surveyed his assigned path each morning, taking pride in its smooth, even course. Felling trees with his axe and using heavy ropes and Nimrod's strength, he uprooted stumps by the score. On rare occasions, the team cleared away rocks the size of large furniture with only a shovel, an improvised lever, and brute force. Finally, with the towpath cleared of all debris and obstacles, he would hitch Nimrod to a rolling log, flattening and smoothing the pathway so as to appear similar to a brick lined street in a fine city.

His days were uneventful, lost in hard work and quiet reflection; however, his nights were tumultuous. Uninvited nightmares plagued him. Sometimes he dreamed of his son Jimmy threatening to injure the younger children, Philander and Lysander, with a bloody axe. In his dream, the nine year old Jimmy would lean back and laugh at his two younger brothers' bodies hacked to pieces, exclaiming "That'll show you to get in my way! I run this house!" In another haunting, Jeduthan dreamed of his sister, Adah, standing on the far side of a river, crying, her eyes red with tears and her face, arms, and legs bloodied and bruised. Jeduthan attempted to cross the rushing stream to her aid, however, each time the current would sweep him away. Twice he dreamed of men from his former congregation coming after him with wooden clubs, pitchforks, and shovels, intent upon his capture. Their evil cries echoed within his mind. They called for his life, carrying a dangling noose meant to stretch his cursed neck. These specters caused him to lash out with his arms, flailing in the darkness and pummeling his unsuspecting tent mates into sudden consciousness.

"What is your problem, old man?" cried one tent mate after a violent nightmare. "Take hold of yourself! I need sleep!" Jeduthan regained his composure and lay awake in the darkness the remainder of that night, cursing his foolish dreams. The following night, the dark vision returned. He awakened to find his tent mate struggling to restrain his arms.

"Look here, old man! I will not allow this foolishness to continue! Restrain yourself or I will!"

The next morning, Jeduthan asked for his own tent, willingly paying the extra five cents daily for the benefit. Mr. Albright refused. "We simply do not have extra accommodations!" By morning, several men in the camp thought he was completely insane. Others were simply wary of him. As rumors spread of his strange nighttime behavior, men avoided Jeduthan and only newcomers were assigned to share his tent. He feared these nighttime fracases drew unwanted attention his way and he spent more time in prayer, hoping for a savior who would free his mind from his torments.

Only when rain poured from the skies and a few select Sundays would he take a day of rest. It was during these interludes that Jeduthan remembered the long ago time when he used to read his books and play his music which so calmed him during his previous life as a merchant. He imagined the lovely tunes that resounded from his scheitholt's strings, but he dared not play his beloved instrument now. Prying ears might inquire who could bring to life the wondrous tunes, jeopardizing his anonymity. The greatest risk that he ventured upon during those rare days in camp was retrieving his Bible and reading quietly in his corner of the shelter, alone and unobserved. He purposely avoided conversation with his tent mates. Several occupants shared his tent, but few stayed more than a single week, which suited him well, as he wished to circumvent any prolonged and intimate discussions with anyone.

Most canal workers were local men who preferred to venture only a short distance from their homes earning a little extra money. Few remained as long as Jeduthan. For him, tent mates were only acquaintances, forming no lasting friendships. Each man avoided eye contact as he awakened each morning, staying to himself, with only an occasional grunt for a greeting. After a hurried breakfast, the men lumbered off for another grueling workday along the canal. Returning to camp late in the day and then standing in the supper line awaiting the same beef stew each night, most workers spent their few moments of relaxation in silence before the retreating sunlight darkened the camp. A few workers poked in the campfires in the dark, but the majority retired to their bunks for much needed rest. The next day, each began the regimented work again. This life suited Jeduthan, for it was simple and solitary. No one imposed on him and he imposed on no one in return. He needed time; time to hide.

William H. Bartlett

One rainy Sunday afternoon, Jeduthan spied a smartly dressed stranger lumbering into camp, attracted, no doubt, by the sheltering canvas stretching over the camp kitchen and the smell of food cooking over the fire. His large, green frock coat studded with brightly polished brass buttons reminded him of visiting ministers who once adorned his country church, too rich and pompous for honest work and believing that their mere presence benefited the frontier. Mr. Albright conversed briefly with the newcomer and Jeduthan overheard the stranger boast theatrically, "...filling my belly with the best beans and bacon I ever tasted!" Mr. Albright nodded affirmingly and pointed toward Jeduthan's tent. The man bowed slightly before darting across the muddy ground toward the shelter. Jeduthan averted his eyes.

"Hello, let me introduce myself, old fellow," the man roared, stretching forth his hand in greeting. "I am William H. Bartlett, artist and engraver." He waited for Jeduthan's cordial response, which was not forthcoming, before continuing. "I am here to capture the grand images of this awesome behemoth being built across your great Empire State. Wise politicians and benevolent businessmen will revel at my sketches and artistry depicting your beautiful countryside and the marks of mankind upon its skin!" A broad smile breached the newcomer's lips.

While Bartlett announced his quest, Jeduthan could sense by the man's smug smile and twinkling eyes that the intruder did not take others, or even himself, too seriously. Yet there was something vaguely familiar about the newcomer that Jeduthan could not place.

"What are you really here for?" Jeduthan asked, curtly. His new guest's appearance was anything but of a laborer. Definitely much too clean and smooth to work on a dirty canal. The man reminded him of one of the posse members whose rope awaited his neck in his nightmarish dreams.

"Exactly what I have said, dear boy! I am commissioned, by *The New York Review and Athenaeum* to draw sketches of this serpentine waterway through nature's spectacular wilderness. Its very existence has captured the imagination of readers nationwide." Bartlett paused, awaiting some emotional reaction to his pronouncement. Jeduthan severely disappointed him.

Bartlett continued. "Your grand and enlightened investors, including our dear governor, his Excellency the Honorable Governor Dewitt Clinton, are hoping that fantastic illustrations will generate immense interest by the wealthy propertied class who, consequently, will desire traveling by canal on fanciful excursions across this fair land." He paused again. Realizing that his grandiose proclamations were getting him nowhere with Jeduthan, he matter-of-factly stated, "Alright, I have been assigned this tent by your foreman, Mr. Albright."

Jeduthan began to protest when Bartlett raised a defiant hand and continued, seemingly without a breath. "Stop! Before you raise a calamitous complaint, he instructed me to inform you that there is no other option. I must bunk with you! You see, old man, it's all about money, I tell you. I have more than you, and your employer said my fifteen cents a night tent rental far out paces your mere ten cent rental."

Jeduthan began to speak, "But…"

Bartlett interrupted again, "Now, now, my dear fellow, no buts about it! I am the artist your employers, who are far richer and much more powerful than you, have seen fit to employ sketching the scenic beauty found all along this miserable, wretched, four foot deep sink and I get first choice of tent mates. So, I choose you! And, by the way, you cannot leave either, for I just might need your assistance with my equipment. Now, isn't that a nice arrangement? I get to do what I enjoy most; draw. You get what you enjoy most, a break in the tent rental. So, old man, no complaints!"

Taken as if by storm, Jeduthan found himself dumbfounded and speechless at this recently arrived hurricane of a man. Contemplating a rebuttal of sorts, Jeduthan decided against any hasty comments. He would continue his masquerade as an ignorant laborer for the time being. Quite possibly, Mr. William H. Bartlett might determine that, by Jeduthan's silence, he was actually a foreign immigrant unaccustomed to English speech. Besides, there seemed a strange, charming quality within this high-strung newcomer's personality, which intrigued his intellect.

Bartlett continued in monologue, "If I can make money drawing, which is my lifelong ambition and God given talent, and in turn, my employers achieve their monetary ambitions by my talents, then that is a satisfactory arrangement for all parties involved, don't you think?" Without allowing his tent mate a chance for comment, Bartlett reached outside the tent, grabbed two substantial trunks and a large rucksack, throwing them carelessly into the front two-thirds of the tent. He then quickly remarked, "I am so glad we have reached an understanding. I must go now but fear not, for I shall return before the sun once again shines on the eastern horizon. I go to investigate an interesting rock formation that might make an ever so delightful backdrop for a portrait I am considering on the morrow. Goodbye, old fellow, and don't mind the luggage." Not waiting a response, Bartlett departed as quickly as he arrived.

Jeduthan sat stunned. Was Bartlett truly who he claimed to be? Had his haunting dreams aroused suspicions that he was ever so carefully hiding during working hours? Had he failed to remain anonymous in the crowd of canal workers? Concerned and puzzled, he decided to keep his ears and eyes open while keeping his mouth shut until he could determine how to deal with William H. Bartlett, artist and engraver.

Poor weather always had a dismal effect on Jeduthan's mood, and he had realized its effects even as a youngster. Sleep was his only cure. "Sleep the weather gone," he repeatedly told himself. Therefore, he longed for the sweet release of sleep as the rain pounded the campground, turning the right of way into a mire of red clay muck. However, restful sleep continued to elude him.

In his dream he imagine following his eldest son, Milton, into a large red barn on his father's farm. The boy's assigned chores included regular milking of Father's cows. Approaching the stall, he diligently found the boy engaged at the task. Milton's hands squeezed the teats and fresh milk slowly filled the waiting pail. Jeduthan smiled at this simple chore, proud of raising his child in a manner not to shun honest work.

However, as the boy industriously toiled, a rat darted between the animal's legs startling the beast. The sharp movement of the prancing cow upset the milk bucket, angering the youngster. In retribution, Milton slapped the cow's udder with the back of his hand, resulting in a kicking outburst by the cow. The lad received a swift hind hoof to his scalp, leaving a terrible gash freely flowing with red, sticky blood.

As the boy lie on the ground in a growing puddle of red ooze, Jeduthan heard his father shouting, "Serves you right, you clod! Treat animals with respect!" Turning to rebuke his father for insulting the child, terror engulfed him. There, in the midst of the straw scattered about the barn's floor, his father stood not. The offender was none other than himself! Where had this anger and bitterness come from? Where was his parental sympathy and compassion for his own mortally wounded child? He awoke in a dripping sweat.

"Do you need my assistance?" a voice uttered from the darkness across the tent. "I am somewhat of an amateur phrenologist. Come now, let me examine your skull..."

Jeduthan muttered "No!" Pausing, he added, "Thank you, no. I am fine."

The stranger struck a lucifer, revealing on the opposite bunk, erect and attentive, his newly assigned bunkmate. Jeduthan's disgruntled response had not escaped the attentive ears of the artist. Had he been observing Jeduthan throughout his entire nightmarish dream?

"Look, old man, you must relax to obtain a restful night's sleep! This thrashing and mumbling about late into the evening must stop. I was warned about your nightly haunts, but I am much too busy to lose a night's sleep caused by your imagined anxieties. Now settle down! We have an eventful day tomorrow and I must gain a good repast. Good night, old fellow."

Jeduthan lay restless and confused. He was too frightened to close his eyes once again, fearing that Bartlett might hear a nightmarish tirade and possibly find out his terrible crime. The rain ceased. The tent flap gently swayed in a light breeze allowing him a view of the night sky. He could see a single lone star in the heavens. How he wished his body could become like that star, shining brightly and illuminating nature's beauty with its dim light.

As morning cast an orange shade upon the sky's horizon, Jeduthan stirred in his bunk. His body yearned for additional moments of sleep as his difficult, restless night had left him exhausted. However, true to his character, he mechanically arose, adjusted his suspenders, affixed his hat on his head, and exited the tent, ignoring the sack-like appearance of Bartlett's body and the haphazardly scattered paraphernalia about the small shelter. He stretched in the early morning sunlight, gaining strength from its warmth before glancing over his shoulder once more at the artist's pile of blankets, pillows, and clothing.

"Rich dandy!" he thought. "No sense of real work for some people." He peered across the laborers' camp and saw the morning ritual beginning. First, stand in line for breakfast, a second line for lunch provisions, and then to the corral to get old Nimrod before finally heading to the work site along the Erie Canal's towpath.

Jeduthan had laboriously tugged, chopped, and dug on one particularly stubborn oak stump without success during the previous Saturday. He dutifully reported to the stump again this morning, finding that yesterday's rainstorm had filled his work hole to the brim with chilly rainwater. He pondered the work ahead of him. How much we seem to work at a chore only to find it all for naught upon our return.

Bracing his body upon the slippery stump, he reached among the roots with rope in hand. The water enveloped his arms as he slipped the lashings around the stump. With the last knot secure, Jeduthan began to extradite his upper half from what had now become a mud hole when a melodious voice interrupted his labors.

"Say, hello there, Mr. Higby."

Jeduthan, startled, lost his footing upon the side of the slippery slope, and fell face first into the muck. Extraditing himself, he heard a bellowing laugh echo across the canal as he glared upward, finding Bartlett grinning from ear to ear.

"Mighty crisp out this fine morning! My God, man, don't you know that bathing in a mud hole is counterproductive?" Bartlett smirked. "Now get out of that trench and come over here. I want your opinion as to the natural beauty of this portion of the canal."

Stunned, Jeduthan soon began clawing forward, just as a turtle might inch his way up a riverbank, repeatedly losing his grip upon the slippery slope.

"Hurry up, my good man. I do not have time to waste," Bartlett commanded. Jeduthan emerged and stood before the artist, the young gentleman paying little attention to his mud caked companion's physical or emotional condition.

"Do you see that eagle's nest over there past the curve of the canal?" The artist stretched his arm toward a large bluff about fifty yards further along the canal. "The nest atop that tree slightly askew from that large rock outcropping?" asked Bartlett.

Jeduthan mechanically raised a pointing muddied finger in the general direction.

"No, no, no! Not that tree, the other one. The one with little bark remaining on its lower trunk!" retorted the artist. "That scene is perfect for my first drawing along this portion of *Clinton's Ditch*. It contrasts sharply with the mess you fellows have done to nature's beautiful landscape with this atrocious project. Now, I need time to adjust to my surroundings before I begin my drawings, so please, sit with me. Come on now, sit!"

Jeduthan, still pointing, sat upon the ground as instructed while the strange young man gently parked himself on a small outcropping of rock near the edge of the towpath. Jeduthan stared at the gentleman as the artist raised his arm in the direction of the said tree, eagle's nest, and substantial bluff, closed his eyes, and began taking deep breaths as if he had just climbed a steep embankment. He looked ridiculous and Jeduthan was about to state as much when Bartlett shushed him, as if he knew Jeduthan's own mind. They both sat silently, on the edge of the canal for a full five minutes before Bartlett commanded, "Now, old man, go back to our tent and fetch the large brown trunk marked W.H.B."

Jeduthan began to protest that he was not in his employ when Bartlett interjected, "Hurry now, before I lose the inspiration. Quick!"

Obediently, with his head drooping in defeat, Jeduthan stood, gathered his horse's reigns, and mounted Nimrod. Distancing himself from the odd artist, he glanced back to find the man motionless, perched on the isolated rock, arm still outstretched like a bloodhound that had sniffed out its prey. How strange this new character seemed that had disrupted his simple life's plan. However much perturbed, Jeduthan was nevertheless intrigued by Bartlett's unique charming demeanor.

Soon, he returned with the requested parcel, finding Bartlett still seated, eyes shut, either asleep or immersed in his natural scene. Jeduthan speculated the artist might be in some sort of trance. Without disturbing his companion, he carefully placed the requested trunk at the artist's feet and, without pausing, retired to his awaiting tree stump obstacle and persisted with its removal. Occasionally he would pause from his work to glance toward the artist who remained unmoved, much like a statue from ancient history, until nearly lunchtime.

Tethering Nimrod to the stump that he had finally extradited from the ground, he sat apart from Bartlett, eating his afternoon provisions. He tried not to make eye contact with the artist, though the two were only a mere score paces apart. As he unwrapped his portion of cheese, he noticed a strange sound that the sketch artist was making with his nose. It resonated loud enough that Jeduthan recognized it as a sniff.

"Higby, what do I smell? Is that you or your old nag?" retorted Bartlett.

Jeduthan replied, "Probably this cheese."

"Why, Higby, you speak! I was wondering if you were some crazy, deaf mute or something. By George, I am amazed! Well, what do you think?"

"About what?" Jeduthan guardedly responded.

"About my scene!"

"I don't see any sketch."

"Why, of course you don't, silly. I haven't made a sketch. I asked you about my scene, nature's scene? It is right there," the artist gestured grandly.

Jeduthan paused, quite puzzled as to Bartlett's meaning. It was then that he realized what Bartlett was so ineffectually trying to verbalize. Nature's scene was all around him. The eagle's nest, the topography, the gentle trickle of water in the ditch, even the recently pulled oak stump, all were part of God's marvelous world. A world that Jeduthan claimed he sought solace within, but by contrast was now disfiguring with his canal labors. He replied with a sigh, "Glorious!"

"Ah, ha! I have found you out, Higby! You are not some ignorant, poor bastard of an uneducated laborer. You fiend! Cast off your disguise, old man! You are refined!" Bartlett's eyes narrowed.

Jeduthan shook nervously and scrambled to his feet, ready to escape.

"But wait, before I begin my sketch, I will eat. Higby, can you share a morsel of that cheese?" asked Bartlett.

Jeduthan peered cautiously at the thin, young man. "I suppose I can share some as you are paying my lodging fee," he cautiously replied. Dividing the remaining cheese with his knife and reaching into his haversack to retrieve two biscuits that remained from his lunch, Jeduthan handed the provisions to the artist.

"Thank you, my good man. I shall not bother you anymore this afternoon. I will be much too involved in my sketching. Please return by this spot before heading back to camp and assist me with my supplies. Thank you for now," Bartlett announced.

Jeduthan left the young artist and proceeded about thirty yards farther along the towpath to his next project, another hefty oak stump. Throughout the afternoon, he struggled, pulled, lashed, and shoveled, until at last he freed the stump from its tight grip upon the earth's soil, leaving a gaping hole in the towpath. He stepped back to inspect the scar upon the earth, from which his five hours' struggle with the stump had resulted and contemplated the work he anticipated on the morrow. Jeduthan had so concentrated during the afternoon on the stump removal task that he had not noticed the artist's actions only a few short paces away. Turning, he was pleasantly relieved to see that Bartlett was no longer in sight. He suspected the dandy gentleman had tired of the afternoon sun and returned to camp unnoticed.

He spied the previously selected rock that his artist bunkmate had used as a bench to soak in nature's scene. He then glanced abruptly back to his hole from which the oaken stump had once tightened its grip upon mother earth. Turning his head back and forth several times, Jeduthan seized upon an opportunity. His hole approximated the same size as the artist's rock. Jeduthan decided to fill his recently dug trench with a stone base and then cover it with dirt.

Using a pickaxe, he began to chip at the stone, tediously breaking off the rock flush and level with the towpath. His logical and rational solution to two jobs, filling the hole and removing the obtrusive rock, tickled his intellect; two jobs at one time! For the next hour, he toiled at the task, easily taking advantage of weak fractures to shear the stone flat and then using Nimrod's strength, dragging the rock into the vacant hole. Completed, Jeduthan hurriedly smoothed the towpath before gathering his tools and heading back to the laborer's camp.

Returning to his tent, Jeduthan was again pleasantly surprised to find that Bartlett was nowhere in sight. On his bunk, though, spread flat was the sketch that the artist must have completed during the afternoon. To Jeduthan's eyes, the eagle's nest, the gently curving canal, and the far distant tree whose trunk was bare were distinctively visible. The way the sharp shading cast by the rock outcroppings blended with the soft shading from the wild flora was intriguing. He could feel emotional warmth boiling within his heart as he examined and imagined nature's majesty displayed upon the parchment. Nature's beauty was truly captured by this aggressive and vain stranger during that brief time he stayed at the secluded spot along the canal. "Bartlett's artistic talents are extraordinary," exclaimed Jeduthan, surprised. Maybe he really is whom he says.

Careful not to disturb the placement of Bartlett's sketch, Jeduthan went forth for evening rations, expecting, and to his own surprise, hoping to stumble upon the talented artist. However, he was disappointed. His artist companion from the afternoon was nowhere to be found. He re-entered his canvas home finding all as he had left it earlier.

He arranged the blankets upon his bunk before climbing into his sleeping quarters for a night's rest as the sun's purplish hue slowly relinquished its hold upon the late evening sky. The visually pleasing hills in the distance gradually faded into the darkness, while Jeduthan's starry companion began twinkling its nightly vigil. He lay viewing the star as its soft light shone through the tent flap. His mind wandered this night from an image of his arduous work on the towpath to the eagle's flight from its nest atop the scarred tree, to the eccentric artist who had so accurately captured nature's majesty on parchment. Soon he fell fast asleep, free from his haunting dreams, and secure in wondrous, sweet images of nature's wilds.

Jeduthan awoke refreshed. For many months, horrible dreams racked his mind most nights, however today his body felt rejuvenated from his deep rest. He turned his body over on his cot and viewed Bartlett's sketch carelessly discarded onto the damp ground. On the opposite bunk lay the artist, covered in blankets and pillows, only his stout nose visible and his leather boots, still upon his feet, protruding through the disheveled pile.

Sitting upright, Jeduthan faintly smelled the acrid scent of alcohol, its distinctively sweet aroma floating in the air. He studied the discarded sketch again and imagined himself within the picture, leisurely strolling the towpath along the canal's curving course as if in a heavenly park. The eagle had emerged from its hiding place, circling high above searching for prey to feed its chicks. The baby eaglets, partially hidden from view in their protective nest atop the lone tree, extended their necks in anticipation of their juicy morning meal from their devoted mother circling high above. A faint screech resounded across the placid valley.

Flatulence from Bartlett's bunk shook Jeduthan from his pleasant natural vision. He crinkled his nose as the odoriferous cloud met his nostrils. How could such an uncouth fellow sketch such a wonderful, pristine depiction of nature but also permeate his own living compartment with such a foul smell from his bowels?

Jeduthan prepared to depart for breakfast by pulling on his boots and raising his suspenders upon his shoulders. Glancing once more from the discarded sketch to the bunk and back again to the artist's work, he paused briefly before journeying forth in search of his meal. With hesitation, he slowly reached down and gently retrieved the discarded parchment, carefully placing it upon Bartlett's trunk. He then departed the tent to begin another routine day's work on the Erie Canal.

Tramping westward along the towpath, Jeduthan soon reached his familiar worksite. All was as he left it the previous day. Leading Nimrod past the site of Bartlett's sketch, he glanced toward where the rock outcropping had once obstructed the path. A few yards further was the once vacated mud hole from whence he wrestled the great oaken stump from the earth. He smiled at his victory as he glided over the stained earth covering the trench that he had cleverly filled with a rock base only a few short hours ago. The smoothed dirt securely hid

Bartlett's stone seat, while the two ragged tree stumps nearby contrasted sharply with his superbly sculptured and groomed towpath.

Using Nimrod's strength and two substantial ropes, he dragged the stumps from the towpath and deposited them into a nearby wood. Returning, he used his feet to smooth the gouges on the path that each stump caused and then surveyed his fine work once again. He was pleased with himself and a grin creased his lips.

A few rods further, he approached his next substantial impediment, a large pine tree that had fallen squarely across the canal's route. Its trunk, fully two feet in diameter, blocked the path and its limbs reached into the muddy canal water. He surveyed the obstacle before reaching into his rucksack on the old horse's back and retrieved a sturdy ax. Moving toward the towpath's edge nearest the canal ditch, he secured his footing and firmly gripped the tool's wooden handle. Swinging the ax over his head and into the awaiting tree trunk, large chunks of bark chipped off the fallen tree, some nearly the size of a man's face. The first impacts of the ax made quick work of the bark covering, but as the tough wood beneath resisted his exertions, the task became more difficult, requiring more energy and precision to shear off the top portion of his wooden obstacle. Within a half hour, though, the first cut was complete and the top limbs crashed into the canal, leaving only the pine trunk blocking the pathway. He rested briefly before gathering the limbs from the ditch, a task far more laborious than chopping as he had to repeatedly scramble into the muddy canal and drag the limbs, a few at a time, from the muck over the towpath to its far side.

By lunchtime, he had completed the job of removing the limbs and sat regaining his strength with his meager provisions. Again, cheese and biscuits provided his fare. As he sliced the cheese into substantial squares, he noticed a figure walking along the towpath from the direction of camp. He recognized the newcomer as his tent mate, strolling leisurely with parchment in hand. The artist stopped short of Jeduthan's position and glanced about as if he had lost some article that had fallen from his grasp. Jeduthan patiently cut another morsel of cheese as he watched the artist stretch out his arm in the direction of the eagle's nest, before continuing his scramble in search of the lost article.

Perplexed, Jeduthan continued observing this odd spectacle until Bartlett cried out, "Higby! Do you recollect the location where I began my artistry of yesterday? I believe it was nearby, but I seem unable to locate my spot."

Jeduthan stood and paced off the short distance to where Bartlett awaited in a state of great agitation. Pointing to the smoothed path where the substantial rock seat once protruded, he replied, "Right there."

Bartlett's face morphed from inquisitive, to horror, and finally into an intense rage. "What has happened to my scene? Where is the stone upon which I sat and was inspired? Some criminal has stolen…no, vandalized nature's beauty and left me empty before my sketch was complete! Tell me, Higby, what has become of my beautiful, inspirational, stone seat!"

Slightly annoyed by Bartlett's exaggerated, melodramatic scene, Jeduthan replied, "I leveled the towpath by removing it and placing the sheered off portion into the hole over which I toiled yesterday."

Bartlett exploded into a series of oaths that only the devil might allow to slip from his lips. "How dare you! How insensitive! Are you not satisfied with puncturing God's golden creation by removing stumps and slicing through nature's delicate skin just to build this monstrosity? No! Now you must gorge out an icon from its skeletal frame! An icon that exposed itself to the fury of countless seasons upon Earth's fragile skin! And then, you bury its fractured body in a grave that will become a route for worthless beasts of burden! Their cloven hooves will tread upon God's glorious works for the convenience of the destructor, mankind! I am through!" Holding his sketch high in the air as a Greek warrior might hold a sacrificial child, Bartlett cried out, "It is useless! This work of art has been defiled!" Sobbing, he plunged the parchment to the ground and stormed away.

Jeduthan, in silence, watched the artist's determined retreat down the towpath and out of sight. With his head bent, Jeduthan viewed the crumpled sketch at his feet, slightly covered with loose dirt. He had not considered the impact of the stone's removal as controversial, but Bartlett's diatribe probed at his spirituality. Had his labors these past months been a crime against nature's beauty? Certainly, tree stumps would fade as quickly as any living creature upon the landscape, but what of the rock? The stone upon which this eccentric artist perched capturing a wonderfully mastered natural scene, so emotionally inspiring, was no more. He had defaced it with his own hands in the name of progress! He bowed his head in remorse and melancholy.

Slowly stooping to retrieve the picture, he became unnerved. He felt like a criminal against nature. He studied the sketch and then raised his eyes toward the still visible eagle's nest in the distance. Tears formed as he glanced backward toward the fallen tree that he had laboriously mangled earlier in the morning. He viewed the large bark chips at his feet, fallen victim to his deadly ax blows. The branches sheared off and heaped in the pit on the towpath's far side seemed like amputated arms on some long forgotten battlefield. Finally, the tree trunk, still defiantly blocking the towpath, lay like a decapitated body on the guillotine, awaiting the executioner's last insulting task. "What have I done?" he audibly sobbed.

Alone and in silence, sketch dangling from his fingers tips, he contemplated how a few short moments ago he had only been guilty of crimes against his fellow man. Now, he stood convicted of a far more heinous sin, a crime against nature. Indicted by Bartlett's sketch and convicted by his own soul, Jeduthan prepared for condemnation. Leaving the fallen tree to its fate, he took Nimrod's reins in his free hand and still grasping the glorious sketch in his other, walked soberly toward the nearby river.

The river here was more like a large creek. No more than fifty feet wide and possibly three feet deep, its rushing water splashing upon rocks as it meandered in its valley until it emptied into a larger pool near the canal construction site. There, its waters were harnessed by the man made ditch, filling the canal so boats could trace their course eastward and westward. He stopped in a small glade where Nimrod gingerly stepped into the water's shallows, leisurely drinking its cool liquid. Jeduthan then sat on a soft pallet of leaves near the water's edge, the fresh aroma of moist air penetrating his nostrils and cooling his skin. He placed the sketch upon nature's mattress and slowly reclined, continuing his study of the picture's intricate details as he laid his head on a pillow of leaves.

Centermost in the sketch was the eagle's nest, but as Jeduthan investigated closer, many fine artistic details revealed themselves. Within the canal itself were four fowl, which he identified as ducks. One of these birds was slightly larger than the other three, so he surmised the flock was a mother and her recently hatched ducklings. Additionally, to one side of the towpath he could see the faint outline of an object seemingly tossed aside. Yes, it must be his tree stump! The same stump he had removed just before the artist's arrival. How clever to include the evidence of nature's demise within the sketch!

He closed his eyes briefly, noticing various sounds in harmony with the creek. A splash from a falling nut, the chirp of a lonely songbird in the nearby meadow, and the gentle wind blowing through the swaying trees seemed to draw him into a wondrous dream. He sensed the wind flowing through his unbuttoned vest, dried leaves beneath his feet that crunched under footsteps from approaching pedestrians. He envisioned two ghostly figures, one slightly larger than the other, strolling along the sketched towpath, hand in hand. As they approached the foreground, their faces became recognizable. The smaller was a young girl about eleven, speaking gently to her father.

"Why do eagles fly and we do not?" asked the young lass to her companion.

"It is nature's way, my darling. Birds are free and bound to no one. We are duty bound by God to tend, tame, and garden Earth's pastures, as the grandfather toad is bound to the waters of the pond ridding its murky swamp of the ever-present mosquitoes. Only the birds are truly free!"

"Higby! Wake up there, Higby."

Jeduthan awakened from his trance finding Bartlett towering above him casting an unexpected shadow upon his face, just as the Cyclops Polythemus hovered above the Greek hero, Odysseus.

"Higby! Wake up, man. I wish to converse with you about this morning's incident. Now old man, sit up and pay attention!"

Struggling to regain a sitting posture, Jeduthan peered at the sketch still lying beside him on its bed of leaves. Obviously, Bartlett had not yet observed that he had saved the work. Ignoring the sketch, he responded to Bartlett's demand, "I know of no incident this morning, Mr. Bartlett."

"Nonsense, old man! I overreacted and I accept full responsibility for your error. I had previously mentioned for you to return to assist me with my sketching supplies before the afternoon ended, and I abruptly left without giving additional instruction as to my whereabouts. You, no doubt by my hasty departure, believed my duty at that particular station was complete and continued your labors of clearing the towpath, which I now realize included defacing my natural seat. My tirade of this morning was below my accustomed stature and accordingly, I wish to express my sincere regrets for my poor behavior, no matter how your actions might have provoked such a common response."

Jeduthan sat spell bound, awed by Bartlett's incapacity to admit guilt.

"Well, with my apology offered, let us go forward in our relationship and speak no more of this episode." Glancing about, Bartlett continued. "Higby, why have I found you here, next to this lovely bubbling brook among nature's wilds instead of sweating out a miserable existence clearing the canal's towpath? I am quite sure the foreman disallows such respites from his employees. If knowledge of your hiatus were to find its way to his ears, I quite assure you that there would be hell to pay. So, sit up and speak, man! What do you have to say for yourself? Come on! Respond!"

Jeduthan intentionally hesitated with his reply while peering into Bartlett's eyes until his unannounced guest averted his stare.

"I picked up your sketch, and it being near lunchtime, I decided to come to the creek and rest under the trees' pleasant shade."

"You picked up my..."

"Yes, I picked up your sketch and have wiled away the past hours fantasizing about the scene. It comes to life with truly amazing shading and vivid imagery."

Stunned, Bartlett stood erect, as if viewing an extinct beast deep within the wilderness. His jaw seemed to drop, exposing the dark chasm between his pale lips. For the first time during their association, Bartlett seemed lost for words.

"I am duly impressed with your aptitude for the visual. A haunting contrast between the wilds of nature and man's manipulation of it is evident within your drawing," Jeduthan concluded.

Bartlett's eye caught a glimpse of the parchment still lying on the ground. Reaching down, he grasped the sketch and examined it. After an excruciating moment of silence, he announced, "Higby, I believe you're right! I am shocked that you, a commoner from the laboring classes, have such an aptitude for critiquing my drawing. However, you have gauged my intentions correctly. I desired to subtly convince my patrons of the horrific injustice which this outrageous engineering project has wrought upon nature's body." Pausing, Bartlett expected his companion to respond in kind, but Jeduthan only stood and began removing his shirt, exposing his barrel chest. His frame, muscular and ruddy, contrasted greatly from his aging forty-year-old face, somewhat surprising the young artist. "Well man, do you have a response to my proclamation?"

Jeduthan paid no attention to the artist's demand as he waded into the cool waters of the flowing stream.

"Higby, I am speaking to you! Do me the honor to respond to my declaration!"

"No. I think not."

Bartlett fumed. "I cannot believe your insolence, Higby! You spend the previous two days uttering little more than a grunt and then, from your lips burst forth a commentary upon the significance of nature's demise, and you choose to avoid its meaningful discussion?"

"Can't you see I am enjoying a relaxing swim?" retorted Jeduthan.

With that, the artist began removing his own clothes and within moments, submerged himself in the creek alongside the older man. Both men remained silent, enjoying the refreshingly cool, flowing water over their bare skin. Bartlett interrupted the silence.

"Higby, I think we have wrongly embarked upon our acquaintance. You have not been completely honest as to your station and I, too, have led you astray concerning mine. I propose we should begin anew."

Jeduthan tensed.

Standing bare-chested within the creek bed, Bartlett stated, "Good afternoon, my dear sir. I would prefer an appropriate introduction, but as nature is our only witness, I will breach proper etiquette and initiate formalities. I am William H. Bartlett. My close associates refer to me simply as Will."

Jeduthan, recognizing the artist's embarrassment, decided that his newly humbled companion might provide entertaining and stimulating discussions that he had so long hungered for. Guardedly, he responded, "I am Jeduthan Higby of Turin." As the words left his mouth, he worried that he might have jeopardized his anonymity by claiming his residence. Hoping the young man did not notice, Jeduthan tensed.

His anxiety eased a bit for his companion's personality seemed rather flighty, shallow, and somewhat strangely charming.

Bartlett, though, paid little heed to Jeduthan's words. "I, too, am an immigrant to this fair land..."

Slightly confused, Jeduthan wondered if this young newcomer had mistaken from where he hailed. Remaining silent, he allowed Bartlett to continue, unbroken in thought and word.

"...born and raised in the sulfuric laced smog of London's metropolis, I was bred from a young age, to become like my father, and his father before him, successful merchants with an ever-growing ocean fleet. Trading in silk, leather, lumber, fine porcelain, and exquisite teas, my life was foretold through my father's expectations. I attended Oxford and traveled the European continent. Twice I visited the Near East, including the exotic pyramids of Egypt and the holy shrines of Palestine. I lived a fanciful, relaxing life, never in want and always pampered. Nevertheless, as I approached my twenty-first year upon God's unholy Earth, my strong willed father insisted I learn the family business. Thus, I was thrust into the counting houses which my father operated, keeping ledgers from his many trading ventures..."

Jeduthan remembered the hours he too had spent bent over ledgers for his local mercantile business, wasting hours upon hours of his life interpreting credits, debits, balances, and the countless reports that his father, and then his bride, demanded. Bartlett's story seemed remarkably similar to his own.

"...My heart could not find fulfillment in the accountant's ledgers, though, and I rebelled, seeking achievement through art. I had dabbled with sketching and artistry at Oxford College, all the time readily and repeatedly rebuked by my professors, no doubt under the scrutinizing eyes of my father. Therefore, after three months slaving in the dank, poorly lit, and smog infested counting house in central London, I fled. I staggered from the oppression of the great city onto a sailing adventure across the ocean sea before disembarking at the great seaport of New York harbor, a free, yet destitute man. I quickly applied my artistic talents upon the streets of that fair city, sketching the wealthy sorts, sometimes individuals, but more often entire families for portraits to hang on the walls of their lavish homes. I spent many an evening socializing with the young ladies of fanciful households as my artistic rewards were often paid for with spare rooms and lodgings while completing a portrait. I am ashamed to admit that my overindulgences with numerous faint-hearted ladies sometimes required hasty departures. My work and skill as an artist became widely desired, to say so myself, and my reputation reached the printing houses of the *New York Review*. Soon, publisher William Cullen Bryant of that venture called on me to seek wondrous natural scenes upon the newly constructed Erie Canal so that engravers might reproduce my sketches for his magazine. Frightful that my many nightly courtships with the daughters of my portrait customers might seek redress, I accepted Mr. Bryant's proposal, and I departed America's greatest city for the wilderness. That is how I landed upon your tent step."

Bartlett finished his life's adventures, crossed his arms in satisfaction, and inquired, "How about you, Higby? What, pray tell, brings your aging frame into this wilderness?"

Jeduthan remained seated, the cool stream flowing past his torso. Bartlett's account seemed plausible, and though he recognized the similarity between his own reasons at flight and that of the artist's, he positively understood that his crime among Turin's parishioners far outreached the nightly rendezvous that his young companion described. Jeduthan cautiously responded, intentionally avoiding any mention of his dastardly feat in his home church.

"My life is not so different from your struggle. I, too, had expectations thrust upon me at an early age, though much before your time. Although not with international shipping, my father demanded that I live the life of a small town merchant, as he had. He consistently pushed me to follow his dreams and expectations, but without the pitfalls that shape one's character. He repeatedly anticipated success and required perfection. I could not fulfill his desires, and he continually reminded me of my failure. Only my mother seemed to console me while my father ridiculed and debased me. As I grew older, mother passed on to God's heaven, leaving me to the clutches of a tyrannical father. As an adult, his oppressive will continued to hound me. Even during his last moments of life during a summer's thunderstorm, as he lay crushed by an old walnut tree torn asunder in the violent wind and onto our small wagon, I could not fulfill his expectations. Try as I might, I heaved, pulled, tugged, and attempted to lift the tree's gigantic mass from my father's torso, while his burning eyes continued their ever present gaze of disappointment upon my ineffectual efforts and futile life."

Jeduthan paused as his chest heaved in solemn remembrance of that fateful June day five years past. It was then he had secretly begun planning his escape. He continued, "You might have misunderstood the location of Turin from which I recently claimed to hail. There are two Turin's to my recollection. Turin, Italy, is that ancient mercantile city whose fame stretches across centuries, continents, and the ocean seas. And then there is Turin, New York, a small hamlet settled by my father and his brothers only twenty-five years ago. It lies upon the New York frontier, nestled in foothills where mighty beasts and fierce Indians have roamed, even within my own lifetime. It is from this frontier village that I have made my home in the shadow of my father for these last twenty years. Here, I was trapped by Father's ever-present demands, much as your own father's expectations trapped you in London's counting houses. However, you broke free much sooner that I. You, as a young man, vital, full of life and energy, have sought your dreams of which I can only hope to experience for a few more brief years. I am happy for you."

"Buck up, my man! Do not become so despondent. Your life is not finished. You have now found a new meaning and, if I may say so, a new companion to share your future adventures. We both might have disappointing pasts. Nevertheless, I assure you our futures are bright," Bartlett remarked. "We rest among nature, enjoying the birds' freedom in wilderness as the…"

"What are you two doing lying in this creek!" boomed a voice from the wood. Emerging through the brush with pounding foot-steps appeared George Pierceson, canal foreman and Jeduthan's former immediate supervisor. Pierceson was well named, for when workers were found idle, his piercing voice launched into a tirade of oaths and insults that caused even the brashest to cower beneath his wrathful domination. As an axe man, Jeduthan was spared this creature's tyrannical rule since being offered independent status by Mr. Albright. Now, though, Jeduthan feared that his hiatus from the work site might jeopardize his special position and he might be reassigned to the work gang, coming under direct supervision of Pierceson, his measure of freedom lost.

"Higby! How dare you wile away time bathing when your portion of the canal path is still obstructed. I noticed a substantial tree trunk fully blocking the towpath. Get out now and back to work!" demanded the despotic supervisor. Not recognizing Bartlett, who was half submerged in the stream, Pierceson demanded the stranger's identity from his employee.

Bartlett announced, "Why, Mr. Pierceson, how do you do? W. H. Bartlett, artist and engraver, assigned to capture the natural beauty of the canal by your employer. I am glad once again to see your smiling and helpful countenance. Please forgive Higby. I was wandering along his towpath section, admiring the flying birds, gently soothing breeze, and lazily swaying wildflowers when I lost my footing and slid into the canal ditch. Higby, nearby, rescued me from my predicament. Covered with mud, he graciously led me to this wondrously secluded stream where I insisted we take our lunch following a short swim to rid my body of New York's infamous clay muck. He wanted to return to his infernal tree trunk blocking your precious towpath, but I insisted he remain with me in case I needed further assistance."

"Oh, Mr. Bartlett, I am sorry that I did not recognize you," snorted Pierceson. "I must insist, though, that canal employees have not been hired to assist in your pursuits."

Bartlett's face puckered, his lower lip extending as a young child might when his feelings were insulted. "My dear Mr. Pierceson, I truly regret diverting your worker from his assigned task, and I will remind myself to avoid such diversions in the future. Please report my actions to your supervisor along with the slight diversion we had over that bottle of cognac and card game you so evidently enjoyed last evening," Bartlett remarked with a sly smile.

Pierceson's countenance significantly changed as he replied to the artist. "Mr. Bartlett, I see your point. We don't need to cause any problems now. Higby, you help Mr. Bartlett out of that creek bed and return to your duties as quickly as Mr. Bartlett can release you. You've got about two hours until dusk, which should be plenty of time for you to clear that tree from the path. Please excuse my abrupt words, Mr. Bartlett, for any dilemma that I might have caused. Can I expect that we continue our association later this evening?"

Pointing his finger directly at the tamed foreman, Bartlett replied, "I will take you up on that engagement my good man, but tonight, I will bring the deck of cards and you bring the liquor along with hoards of money you wish to lose."

Pierceson returned the way he came.

Jeduthan waded to the creek's edge and extradited himself from the waters as Bartlett declared, "The power of influential connections! What a man will sacrifice to save his own skin!"

Glancing over his shoulder at the artist, Jeduthan stated, "You rescued me from a rebuking that I could scarcely endure. Pierceson is a cruel man to individuals he considers subordinates." Pulling his shirt over his body and grappling Nimrod's bridle, Jeduthan smiled at the young artist and for the first time in months uttered, "Thank you, friend." He returned to the towpath to finish his task, believing he had finally found a companion with whom he could share the glorious scent of nature.

As weeks passed, Jeduthan and his new friend, William H. Bartlett, spent much time together. He continued his labors as an axe man, clearing the canal's towpath of rocks, trees, and stumps. Moreover, for much of the time, Bartlett followed Jeduthan and found his natural scenes waiting along the same portion of right-of-way. Often the pair conversed about natural phenomena during their brief moments at lunch. Jeduthan felt impassioned by their discussions and though he reconciled his mind with his work on the canal, he dreamed of the wondrous scenery that mankind would enjoy from their comfortable seats on the touring packet boats.

Except for the ever-plentiful soaring birds, rarely did the pair sight an abundance of fauna. However, as twilights approached, animals appeared by the still waters of the canal. Small raccoons, groundhogs, and squirls disturbed the peaceful canal waters in search of a cool drink. On one occasion, as the setting sun lengthened the shadows of the hills and trees across the towpath, Bartlett caught glimpse of a strange, large, wild animal. It was an enormous buck. The deer's appearance next to the canal ditch startled the men as they leisurely strolled toward camp. They stopped and gawked at the fourteen points of its magnificent rack as it cautiously stepped its way down the embankment and slowly lowered its regal head to the life giving waters. Its ears remained constantly perched upward, ever listening for approaching danger. Bartlett's face flushed with admiration for God's handiwork. The artist stood agog at its size and magnitude. "Never have I seen such a majestic creature!" he later remarked. He explained that he had only encountered such a large, wild animal within the confines of a traveling menagerie.

Jeduthan found it hard to fathom a grown man never witnessing the grandeur of wild animals, for he had lived twenty long years on the edge of the North American wilderness. He remembered when, as young men, Solomon and he hunted the adjacent wood. On one July evening, a fearsome mountain lion ventured into Turin's darkened streets. Panic overtook women and men alike as its dangerous claws snared two young children before sunrise. At father's behest, both brothers ventured forth to secure the village from the cat's deadly vigil.

It had been Solomon, with his militia musket, who slew the beast. The following morning, he dragged its carcass into the village green for all to see. Jeduthan had gazed in amazement at the animal's glossy eyes, its ruffled fur, and fearsome claws, marveling at the predator's sleek body and shiny white fangs. Father praised the young hero and the town honored its savior with a grand thanksgiving feast.

However, for Jeduthan, the creature's demise did not bring forth celebration; only regret. The fine specimen's ruin saddened him. Mankind's triumph over God's glorious handiwork; smitten by man's ever expanding influence into its world.

The buck raised its head abruptly as if alerted to some danger. Moments later, it leaped out of the canal ditch, crossing the towpath, and disappeared into the underbrush before the two onlookers' viewing eyes.

"How marvelous," exclaimed Bartlett, a broad, amazed grin parting his lips. "I must sketch this scene immediately." He sat upon the ground cross-legged in the twilight, fumbling within his haversack for pad and lead.

"Will, there is no possible chance that you can see to sketch in this darkness. Let us go to the camp and sit within the tent where you may sketch by candle light."

"No, I must sketch now! Besides, Higby, I do not need light to sketch. The splendid animal is within my mind and must only come out through my hand," Bartlett proclaimed, stubbornly waving his extremity as if it had its own mind.

"Have your fun, my good friend, but as for me, I'm heading back toward camp to get a good night's rest. Tomorrow is pay day and I am to receive my meager wage."

As the artist would not budge, Jeduthan left him sitting on the towpath in the all-encompassing darkness. An hour later, Bartlett threw back the tent flap and called to Jeduthan, "Well, old fellow, how do you like my sketch of that fine animal we stumbled across before darkness fell upon us?"

Jeduthan grasped the parchment from Bartlett's extended hand. Holding it to reveal the image with light from the lone candle hanging in the tent, he sarcastically responded, "Yes, sir, real imagery here! I can definitely see that your skills at night portraiture are extraordinary. The problem is, though, that I cannot see your precious fauna among the scribbling!"

A large grin appeared on Jeduthan's face as he handed the sketch back to Bartlett. The artist's lower lip extended briefly before he broke into laughter. "Higby, I am glad you are my friend. I can always count on you for a candid appraisal of my work." Crushing the parchment into a tight-fisted ball, Bartlett tossed the sketch out the tent's flap into the dirt street before reclining on his bunk. "Higby, what will you do with your wages tomorrow?"

"I expect I will go to Lockport to scout for a newspaper, magazine, or possibly a bound book. I used to read far more than I do these days."

"Then, I will escort you, my friend. I believe I can also find suitable entertainment."

Holding that thought in his mind, Jeduthan leaned toward the tent's lone light and leisurely puffed the flame out with a single breath. The faint smell of tallow lingered in the darkness as Jeduthan closed his eyes and remembered how before this young, eccentric lad joined his company, he faced nighttime with trepidation, a darkness haunted by dreadful memories. However, for these past few weeks, accompanied by his friend, those terrible nightmares troubled him no longer.

Lockport

Jeduthan awoke to the usual scene of blankets and pillows heaped upon his bunkmate. Only the sight of a familiar nose and booted feet extended from the disheveled mound that Bartlett simply referred to as *his quarters*.

Exiting the tent and after obtaining his morning ration, Jeduthan hoped to beat the anticipated crowd gathering at the paymaster tent. This morning, though, he was disappointed, for as he crossed the camp to the paymaster's shelter, an extensive line of workers already congregated there in hopes of accomplishing the same early start. Disheartened, he stood in his proper place at the end of the lengthening line and waited his turn for nearly an hour before finally approaching the rather hefty paymaster.

"State your name and assigned work," the paymaster blurted out, mechanically.

"Jeduthan Higby, axe man."

The paymaster abruptly looked up from his ledgers into Jeduthan's eyes, before he stood upon his short, stocky legs and called in a bellowing bawl, "Pierceson! Pierceson!"

A few seconds later, stumbling out of the paymaster's tent, came the arrogant bully.

The paymaster asked, "Pierceson, is this the man you reported a few weeks ago taking an extended lunch break swimming in a creek, only returning to work when apprehended?"

"Yes sir, it is," responded the supervisor with a sly smirk.

"Well, man, if you remain slothful I will need to dismiss you and expel you from the canal's property. As this is your first, and I trust, only offense, I will only fine you fifteen cents for your indiscretion. But mind you, if further reports surface of extended breaks, inferior job quality, or other misdeeds on your part, you will be roughly handled before I eject you from this job site," stated the paymaster gruffly.

Jeduthan despondently looked on as the paymaster laid out his monthly wage of $7.20 on the camp table and then, methodically remove fifteen cents and place it into his own vest pocket. The paymaster grinned as he glanced toward Pierceson, confirming that the two were in cahoots. Jeduthan lowered his head solemnly, accepting the money and slinking away, as a whipped dog might cower after his master's tongue-lashing.

Arriving at his tent, he found Bartlett awake. "Good morning, Higby! What a fine morning to a wonderful day." Bartlett paused. "Why the gloomy face, my friend?"

"Pierceson!"

"What has that devious bastard gone and done now?" asked the artist.

"He reported our brief hiatus of several weeks ago to the paymaster. As punishment, I was fined fifteen cents."

"I am appalled, Higby! After giving me his gentlemanly word to overlook that slight indiscretion, Pierceson broke his pledge and reported you anyway? What a fiend! No, a brute! I tell you he is contriving with the wrong fellow, I guarantee you..." stated Bartlett, his nostrils flaring in anger.

Jeduthan interrupted his friend's pronouncement. "Let us not pursue retribution, Will. I understand Pierceson's sort. No doubt, the paymaster and he are in league together, cheating most workers of their fair wages every month. Any complaints will surely result in tighter restrictions, which is exactly what I desire not. I enjoy working alone as an axe man and I imagine my work could be completed as easily and efficiently by anyone. So, just drop it."

Bartlett continued. "I am truly blessed that my duties are not under constant critique by a ruthless supervisor. My trade gives me a rare sort of independence. If you find that I can intervene in some manner, I..." Jeduthan raised a wagging finger in protest. Bartlett, head bowed as if offended by a terrible injustice, simply finished with, "As you wish, my friend."

Jeduthan examined the seven dollars held in his rough, calloused hands. Bartlett's demeanor soon drastically altered and he stated, "Higby! Let us mount old Nimrod, mighty steed as he is, and travel together, westward, toward the impressive metropolis of Lockport, five miles hither and scout about for adventure! There, I am sure, we can find multitudes of eager youthful entrepreneurs impatient to part you and your meager wage in return for an evening's entertainment."

Peeking outside the tent flap and down the muddy street toward the paymaster's tent, Jeduthan hesitated before responding to Bartlett's request with a nod of his head. Both men exited the tent and immediately stepped off a direct path to his awaiting horse at the corral. Mounting, Bartlett in the rear and Jeduthan at the reins, the two men braced themselves, as the old horse began a steady gait past the paymaster's tent and toward the towpath beyond, Bartlett's eyes deliberately glaring at Supervisor Pierceson.

Riding on the towpath toward Lockport, Jeduthan spotted many stumps along the way. In one location, the towpath ceased to exist entirely, confirming his guess that the canal was far from complete. Soon the broad valley and gentle, rolling landscape abruptly altered. Closing within a mile of the young village of Lockport, the canal's course entered a steep canyon, bluffs towering on each side. Nimrod slowed his pace, the reins held tightly in Jeduthan's calloused hands.

As the hills closed in around the pair, vertical cliffs soared above them. Here canal crews still labored vigorously, chiseling the rock precipices with heavy hammers and drills. Constant sounds vibrated through the chasm as metal resounded off metal with a continuous clang, clink, and crash. A large tower hovered high in the sky, many ropes, chains, cables, and a huge bucket attached to its skeletal frame. High upon the hillside, Jeduthan watched the workers, ever toiling with their heavy iron bars, breaking and prying one stone at a time from its hold upon the Earth.

"Will, I am glad that I am not working as these poor men, in a canyon of solid stone. The sound is deafening and the close quarters stifling!"

"I was told about this site when I first saw the locks near Schenectady," responded Bartlett. "I inquired as to the stone required for building locks and the head mason there told me that most of his stone was requisitioned from quarries down the Hudson, but as for the construction here at Lockport, much of the stone is appropriated nearby from the limestone and granite found in the Onondaga Ridge. I suppose he meant this gorge."

Precisely then, a large boulder broke from its moorings and crashed down the bluff a hundred yards behind the pair, where only a few moments before, faithful and steady Nimrod had trodden. Both men stretched their necks backward, viewing the spectacle. Workers seemed to scurry around the boulder, ignoring the danger and the hazy dust, which spewed into the air as the stone followed gravity's course down the hillside and onto the canal's towpath.

"Hazardous duty," remarked Bartlett casually. "Much more dramatic than your moving my stone seat a few weeks ago."

"No doubt," responded Jeduthan, as he repositioned his body facing forward on Nimrod's back. Soon, he reined in the horse, coming to a dead stop in the middle of the towpath.

"What is the matter, my dear friend?" asked Bartlett, slightly annoyed at their abrupt halt.

"My goodness!" exclaimed Jeduthan. Peering forward, both men sat aghast with awe. A strange silence seemed to engulf them as they were overwhelmed by the sight. Ahead, only a few hundred yards distant and standing like an Egyptian temple, appeared five conjoined stone locks, freshly completed and rising at least sixty feet like a gigantic stairway toward heaven. The two men were spellbound by its majesty. A full minute passed before Bartlett shifted in his seat in agitation.

"Higby, I need down. Now!" Bartlett glanced into the sky. "I suppose you do not know the time, my dear esteemed traveling friend."

Jeduthan reached into his haversack and extracted his silver pocket timepiece. "One o'clock, at present. Why do you ask?"

Lost in calculations and still gazing into the sky with one hand extending into the western horizon, Bartlett ignored Jeduthan's question. "One o'clock gives me..."

"Six and one-half hours until twilight," finished Jeduthan, realizing that his friend was attempting to estimate the amount of daylight remaining. "You should begin now to complete your sketch before sundown. Pick your location carefully, though, because the gorge workers still seem hard at their task."

Bartlett began walking forward with outstretched hands framing his scene. Jeduthan, still mounted, followed a few steps behind. Soon, the artist stopped, a mere fifty yards from the lower gatehouse, and announced a solemn proclamation, "I am here! Higby, hand me my haversack, please." Doing as he was asked, Jeduthan began to comment, but was abruptly cut short. "Higby, come back at twilight. I shall be immersed in my scene until then."

Jeduthan obediently turned Nimrod toward a path leading up the steep bluff, departing from his artist friend, leaving Bartlett to his sketching without further disturbance. Peering back before the valley's rim hid his friend from view, he observed the artist's familiar stance that he assumed with each artistically inspired moment; arm stretched forth toward the majestic object that would dominate his sketch.

Reaching the hill's brow, he observed hundred of workers toiling deep within a chasm, pounding deep drills into a man made slot. For sixty feet wide and disappearing into the distance, this man-made gouge scarred the Earth. The locks, as impressive a sight that they revealed, paled in comparison. Mighty are the works of man!

Alongside this massive cut he spied a small village. Lockport serviced the magnificent locks that descended into the gorge and a construction village it was. The town contained a substantial number of frame buildings, all recently constructed. Piles of discarded lumber littered the ground. Many of the business establishments posted fanciful signs,

including *Spaulding's General Store, Johnson's Bakery, Joseph Pickard's Barber*, and three impressive taverns. It was the latter that Jeduthan sought, suspecting they were the best places to obtain a meal to purge the hunger gnawing in his stomach.

Crossing from the canal locks, he made his way through a labyrinth of muddy lanes bordered by a large tent city, no doubt erected to house a large labor force completing the locks and its approaches. He found that few workers occupied the tents at this hour, but he did come across one young lad with short britches and a green and white checkered shirt covering his thin frame.

"Good day, boy. May I inquire as to the best place to obtain a decent meal in this fair city?"

The boy eyed Jeduthan from head to foot before retorting, "Do ye take me for a young dandy, old man? To describe dis filthy, rat-infested pigsty of a place as a city is a far stretch from any trufe'. Iffin Saint Patrick hisself, along with de holy mudder Mary, come upon dis wretched place and remove its blot from mudder Earth, I'd rejoice and drink to dar' health!"

Shocked by the thick Gaelic brogue that spilled forth out of the mouth of this innocent looking lad, Jeduthan straightened his body attempting an intimidating and commanding posture. "Look boy, I wish…"

The boy interrupted, "De name tis Patrick Donnelly O'Neil and I don't take no lip from no dandy!"

Jeduthan slumped before continuing, "My apologies, young O'Neil. Where do you bunk?"

The boy's face lightened. "Now dat tis a better way to speak to an Irish Catholic canal worker. I bunk over yonder in dat tent with de two chimneys protruding from its canvas. What about you?"

"Only passing through, looking for a brief meal. Can you suggest an honest tavern?"

"Can't promise any will be honest, but the *Eagle Hotel* tis where I would stay, iffin I had de money. They tis the only establishment which will serve our kind our grog. De rest of 'em full of quackers," young O'Neil responded.

"Quackers?"

"Yea, dis here town tis full of dem. And none of dem will touch a lick of whiskey and you cain't pick a fight with dem, either. But de owner of de *Eagle*, he's a good Catholic man who takes care of his kin, and us redheaded Irish."

Jeduthan realized that O'Neil and most likely many of the laborers who slept in the tent city were Irish immigrants. He had heard talk about the large numbers of immigrant workers in the eastern port cities being of foreign birth, but this was his first encounter with an Irishman or Irish boy.

"Well, young O'Neil, as you are seemingly a man who can hold his own, will you join me, as my paid guide, to partake of said *Eagle Hotel's* fare?" Jeduthan asked, reaching into his coat pocket, retrieving a coin and tossing it to the boy.

Admiring the coin, O'Neil replied, "Well, stranger, let me show you about town."

At a brisk pace, the boy started forward toward the nearest building outside the tent city, Jeduthan nudging Nimrod along in order to keep pace with the young lad. Pointing at a small brick structure, O'Neil stated, "Dat tis de ol' blacksmith shop owned by Deacon Crocker. He, too, is a Catholic artisan from dey ol' country. And ober dar is ol' man Gardner's place. He used be a lawyer but now tis a biznessman of sorts. He owns the *Exchange Coffee House*. Is sissy, if ya ask me. And over two alleys was Mr. Jennings place, till he was murdered. Dey blamed us workers for dat, but none was found guilty by de sheriff. And talkin 'bout de sheriff, he libs right yonder in dat green shuttered fancy dwellin'. He'd be a hard man, Sheriff Bruce."

Jeduthan spied upon the sheriff's porch a notice board with three wanted posters pinned upon its wooden pallet. He wondered if he might be one of the wanted men. He hurried O'Neil passed the sheriff's home and toward the village center.

"And right ober dar is de barber. He's a colored man, suspos' to be run away from deep down south. A few years ago, men came and bound his han's and feet before they was goin' to haul him away. The whole town rose up and stood firm 'till they released de barber and they left town. I never seen such a crowd of ol' stuffed shirts stan' up for another man's freedom before, but dey did. And finally, we is here."

Jeduthan glanced around. On the far corner stood a fine establishment with large white lettering above its painted façade, publicizing *Washington House*. On the corner where Jeduthan and O'Neil stood was an unpainted two-story shack, a balcony porch extending from the second story rooms. Pointing toward its doors, O'Neil exclaimed, "I present ye, *The Eagle Hotel. Let us enter and partake* as ye dandies might say."

Entering the establishment, Jeduthan noticed a pianoforte in the far corner with a crucifix upon its wooden back. In the close corner was a man, face down upon a crude table, a tin cup on its side with a small portion of its contents spilled. Down the center were three vacant tables, one of which proved nailed to the far wall, acting as a makeshift bar. O'Neil led the way directly to the bar, where he seated himself upon a stool. Jeduthan, not finding another stool, made do with a short-legged chair from one of the vacant tables. Their portrait presented a strange sight indeed; a young lad, fully six inches higher than an old man sitting upon the chair at an improvised crude wooden bar.

A tavern keeper emerged from the back door and asked in a heavily laden Irish accent, "Young O'Neil, what have ye brought me today?"

"Mr. Holmes, this man seemed lost in yonder tent city and inquired as to victuals. Informing him, says I, *The Eagle Hotel* be the only honest establishment in this whole town. Where will that be, says he. Follow me yonder, says I. And I has brought ye a paying customer. What says ye pours a drink for ye favorite canal worker, Mr. Holmes?"

"Why sure, my lad, iffin de stranger is doing the payin'," responded the barkeep.

"Sure, give the lad something to drink," replied Jeduthan, pulling a copper coin from his pocket. "But sir, I desire some food for myself, if you please. Do you serve flap jacks here?"

"We can make anythin' happen for ye here, sir, for de right price," grinned the barkeep, gesturing toward the stairway leading upward.

"Just food for now, thank you," responded Jeduthan.

Holmes grunted as he left the shack's interior, leaving by the same path in which he had entered. Jeduthan followed the barkeep with his eyes and then turned to face O'Neil who sat smugly next to him on his stool with a grin extending across his entire face as if he had won some great award.

The two remained silent, O'Neil sipping noisily his grog, hoping to spark some type of response from his companion. Jeduthan, however, did not fall for the trick. He remained silent until Holmes re-entered the room with a large plate of steaming flapjacks. Placing them in front of Jeduthan, Holmes said, "Dat will be fifteen cents."

Jeduthan nonchalantly reached once again into his pocket and extracted the required payment. Looking at his young friend, he removed two hefty flapjacks and handed them to O'Neil. Mr. Holmes reacted swiftly. "Hey mister, dose flap jacks are for you, not him!"

Jeduthan responded haughtily, imitating to some degree his friend Bartlett. "Of what concern is it of yours to whom I give my property? Do not play me the fool, man, just because I am a stranger to these parts. Now, be gone and allow me to enjoy my meal in peace!"

Holmes seemed shaken and made a hasty retreat.

"Thanks, old man," exclaimed O'Neil.

"No thanks needed. I consider this an advance for services in the future. I might need a friend sometime and you seem ready to comply."

Stepping down from his stool, flapjacks in hand, O'Neil proclaimed, "I'd be thar iny time you call, mister." He strolled toward the hotel's door and turned before exiting. "Hey mister, what do I call ye?"

Jeduthan hesitated, slightly concerned that revealing his identity might jeopardize his position. "The name is Higby."

"Thanks, Higby!" exclaimed O'Neil before he left, scurrying toward the bustling and noisy tent city of Irish canal workers.

Jeduthan enjoyed his remaining flapjacks, savoring the soft warm sweet bread that he had regularly relished at home in Turin. However, there at home it was he who mixed the ingredients, he who stoked the fire, and he who labored over the hot skillet making the fluffy treat. His wife did not assert any talents within the kitchen, leaving the cooking to him, the children, or hired help. He imagined how life might have evolved if he had enjoyed the benefits of a domestically gifted wife.

"Is that all you want, mister! Stop daydreaming and answer me question!" bellowed Holmes.

"Pardon me. Yes, I am done. Do you rent rooms here, Mr. Holmes?"

"Yes, daily and weekly."

"I might request lodging later. Good day, sir." Jeduthan stood, turned, and departed the hotel. Entering the street and grasping

Nimrod's bridle, he walked toward the locks, retracing the path that young O'Neil had guided him through earlier, but more slowly now, noting additional signs, advertisements, and individual people going hither and thither on their daily errands or laboring with tasks that seemed perpetual and inevitable in small towns. He passed a Methodist Church, followed shortly afterwards by a Quaker Meeting House. He stopped at *Tucker's General Store*, hoping that among its collections of blankets, textiles, boots, harness, and other sundry items would possibly be some reading material. However, he was disappointed. Inquiring about any bookstore from Mr. Tucker, the gentleman replied, "Not this side of Utica!"

Obviously despondent, Jeduthan began to depart when Tucker remarked, "Closest item to a book in these parts is *The Lockport Observatory*."

"What, pray tell, is *The Lockport Observatory?*" asked Jeduthan.

"It is our local newspaper. It built this town, along with the canal locks, of course," replied Tucker.

"Where is the newspaper's office, Mr. Tucker?"

"Down the street next to *The Washington House*," replied the storekeeper.

Jeduthan left through the store's entrance and mounted Nimrod. Slowly returning to the corner where *The Eagle Hotel* stood opposite the much grander *Washington House*, he spied no sign indicating the newspaper's office. He rode past twice but with no evident placard, Jeduthan came to a complete stop in front of *Washington House*. Somewhat frustrated, he dismounted his horse and prepared to enter the hotel when he noticed, in a secluded recess of the building, a disappearing staircase with a small notice on a wooden shingle. It read, *The Observatory*, with a small white arrow pointing downward into the hotel's basement. He shivered with excitement, for finally he could read written words other than those found in his Bible, possibly locating an advertisement for a tutor far away from his previous life.

Entering the office, a cowbell attached to the door jingled obtrusively. Standing at the far brick wall was a short man, hands blackened by constantly handling ink while operating his large bulky printing press. He abruptly stopped his task and turned, facing Jeduthan. "Hello, sir. Orsamus Turner here. How may I help you?"

Jeduthan approached the intervening counter and asked, "May I purchase one copy of your most recent periodical?"

"Why yes, sir." Turner reached under a nearby stool and grabbed the topmost newspaper. "You will be quite entertained with our small paper. Most immediate news includes a projected visit by the Revolutionary War Hero, General Marquis de Lafayette. We also have narratives from survivors of the earthquake two years ago, the ceremonial opening activity of the Lockport Mason Lodge, canal progress of course, and the Thayer Brothers' execution scheduled for June 17th. We also have the schedule of events for the new Presbyterian Church opening..."

Jeduthan's heart raced. A Presbyterian Church? Who were its founders? Could they know of his dreadful deed from Turin? He quickly determined not to tempt fate, but to avoid these people at all costs. Taking the newspaper, he thanked the editor and left. Jeduthan glanced over *The Lockport Observatory's* news columns as he climbed the steps into the street.

All was as Turner had said. Yet, a small column in the lower left corner piqued his attention the most. *Sheriff apprehends fugitives among canal workers. More arrests eminent.* How many fugitives were apprehended? Was he a suspect? He remembered the wanted posters displayed at the sheriff's home. Should he risk arrest by perusing the notices? No! Better to flee the canal construction crew before any sheriff should capture him.

Folding and stashing the periodical into his saddlebag, Jeduthan mounted and proceeded directly and determinedly toward the locks. He planned to quit the region and make his escape as soon as he rejoined his companion, Descending the path to the bottom of the gorge, he found his artist companion diligently completing his masterpiece.

"Higby," cried Bartlett. "Come! Look over my shoulder at a new genre that I believe God and His will has thrust upon my being!"

Peering briefly at Bartlett's sketch, what he saw startled him. The sketch contained five dual interconnected canal locks carved from the bedrock in the midst of the wilderness. Jeduthan looked from the drawing to the locks. The locks, surrounded by large lifting cranes, men perched upon massive stones, the edge of a sinful tent city stirring to life in the evening shadows, and a multitude of buildings towering above distinctly silhouetted by the setting sun's rays, all which contrasted sharply with Bartlett's drawing.

Glancing once more at the sketch, Jeduthan commented, "Will, your depiction is not accurate! The bustling crowd, the towering buildings, all are absent from your scene. Instead, the gigantic locks are surrounded by garden-like shrubs, manicured lawns, and towering, gracious trees as might be viewed in some great European park."

"Precisely, my dear friend! My patrons will pay handsomely for this dreamy wonder. For you and I, Higby, we view reality. A lock is a construction site, filled with the grime, smoke, rubbish, and laborious activity that factually occur as man scars nature with his enterprise. My benefactors might be appalled to know that their investment has caused a travesty to God's nature. Therefore, they desire imagery and fantasy to justify their investment as a positive good. To them, man tames nature but never abuses it. So that is what I must give them; nature's wilderness improved by the almighty hand of mankind."

"Hogwash, Will. When your so called patrons come and see the realities of Lockport..."

Bartlett interrupted, "...I will be far away with my commission, handsomely endorsed to sketch the husbandry of mankind upon another of nature's wonderment." Bartlett smiled as if a victor in a game of deceit.

Slightly annoyed with Bartlett's motives, Jeduthan abruptly announced to his friend his intention of leaving the canal company. He lied, "My recent monetary arrangements with the canal company has altered my plans somewhat, my friend. I hope you are not disappointed, but I am leaving its employ, with little thanks to my supervisor, Mr. Pierceson, and his corrupt paymaster. I have found suitable lodgings in Lockport, and after returning for my personal effects, plan to stay in the village until I find other opportunities. You are welcome to accompany me if you so desire."

"Why, Higby, I am shocked by your initiative. Nevertheless, I am honored by your request and I accept. I will accompany you on your future excursions, for I have also become accustomed to your persona. We will ride back together, you, me, and old Nimrod, to the laborer's camp and retrieve our belongings." Rolling his sketch and stowing it within his haversack's confines, Bartlett lifted his hand toward Jeduthan, awaiting a response. Jeduthan hesitated only an instant before reaching down from the saddle and grasping Bartlett's outstretched arm in friendship.

Hours later, as twilight crept over Lockport, the two friends again approached the huge, imposing locks that appeared from a distance like a giant's staircase ascending the steep slope into town. The fingers of darkness stretched into the waterway, enveloping each successive lock in its firm grasp until all was swallowed up in its dark grip. As the two climbed the pathway leading to the village, the stars cast their faint light upon the works of man and subdued their grandeur until, like wild beasts in a darkened wood, they faded from sight in the all-encompassing darkness. The tent city, full of Irish workers and their families, stood out in great contrast to the shadowy canal only a few paces away. Full of life, alive with song, and speckled with pinpoints of candlelight, the hundreds of tents hummed with varying sounds.

Jeduthan, wary of the tent city's dark alleys, followed a straight path to the *Eagle Hotel,* where he assured Bartlett of available lodging. The town's streets were lonely and grim compared to the bustle among the tents nearby. At one point, Jeduthan feared he had lost his direction toward the town center. However, a pianoforte musical tone reassured him that the establishment could not be far. Using the sound as a guide, the pair found the hotel's entrance. At the tavern's portal stood a rough-hewn man of great stature eyeing the pair as they approached. By this time, both men had dismounted and close in tow was Nimrod acting as pack animal for Bartlett's two hefty trunks.

"State ye business," exclaimed the man, blocking the hotel's entrance with a broad, muscular arm.

Jeduthan began to respond when Bartlett piped up in a Gaelic brogue, "Good evening, me good Irish friend. Me business tis to procure lodging within these walls. I's have it from a good source dat dis *Eagle Hotel* be de friendliest pub in all of Lockport, 'specially for good Catholic boys. Be it so?"

"It be," the giant smiled and stepped aside, gesturing the two through the doors.

Entering, Jeduthan was surprised to find that the establishment abounded with people, the air acrid with tobacco smoke and the strong smell of intoxicating liquor. Scantily clad women and young girls dotted the barroom, their bosoms revealing their curving breasts for the perusing eyes of a large number of drunken men. In the room's center, three drunken men wagered coins in some card game. Next to the table, acting as the improvised bar stood Holmes, busily filling small tin cups from a large barrel that had been uprighted upon the bar and tapped with a rubber hose. Two shabbily dressed men sat upon the pianoforte's stool, occasionally striking a key in random order, while one young lass, not exceeding fourteen years of age, seductively sprawled on its wooden top, teasing the older men attempting to play the instrument.

"This cannot be the same place where I lunched at noontime! Then, it was bare with no customers and seemed a reputable establishment," informed Jeduthan to his friend.

"Nonsense, Higby! I see here distinct possibilities for the evening," Bartlett excitedly beamed as the noise intensified. Jeduthan noticed that Bartlett particularly enjoyed the feminine sights displayed by the young maiden upon the piano.

Visibly agitated, Jeduthan tugged at his artist friend's shirtsleeve, causing Bartlett to turn and face his partner squarely. "Will, I do not drink intoxicating liquors. Never has the devil's elixir passed through my innocent lips!"

"And no need that it start tonight," replied Bartlett. "I will do all necessary intoxicating for the both of us. Do not worry yourself, I will protect your virtue, good friend." A large grin appeared upon Bartlett's face as he turned toward Holmes who was dispensing brown liquid from the upturned barrel. "Hello, friend! Be so kind to fill a mug from ye barrel for me thirsty lips." Holmes nodded and did as asked. Bartlett deposited a coin upon the bar. "Me name tis Shamus Bartlett from County Cork in the ol' country, only recently arrived an' fresh off de boat. Me and me friend desire lodging. Can ye accommodate?"

"I can for ye, but ye friend might be too refined for me regular customers," replied Holmes.

"Oh, never mind old Higby here. He tis only a gentle giant, a heart of gold, I tell ye. When I first arrived off de boat, I found him working on de dock, lifting, hauling, and moving freight. By the end of de afternoon, I had charmed him into becoming me manservant. Though a simpleton he be, no man is more trustworthy. Me sent him, only this day to scout for suitable lodgings an' he reported that thy *Eagle Hotel* served up such a fine stack of flapjacks dat even he couldn't down all in one sittin'. An' all for an honest price! Now dat I meself, have viewed ye establishment, I too, have spied a ripe opportunity within thy walls."

Holmes eyed Jeduthan before replying to Bartlett's request, "I s'pose room three will be vacant in a moment. Me rate is ten cents per night and twenty-five cents weekly, payable in advance."

Bartlett reached once again into his pocket and extracted one coin, slapping it upon the table. "Here be fifty cents and I hope ye might provide introductions to a few lassies. I particularly believe that young lass upon de piano is tempting to me eyes."

Holmes took the coin and deposited it within his vest pocket before making his way through the crowd to the piano. There he leaned over and whispered into the girl's ear a message. The girl's eyes briefly shifted toward Bartlett and then a broad grin spread across her young face.

"Will!" Jeduthan called upon his friend. "I feel quite uncomfortable with this atmosphere."

"Fine, Higby! You go into the street and secure our luggage. Then report to room three up yonder staircase. I will join you later after I consummate our dealings with Holmes." Bartlett's attention returned to the young woman across the room.

Jeduthan obediently worked his way through the crowd to the exit. Returning carrying the pair's baggage, he ascended the staircase, glancing only briefly toward the bar, viewing his friend intimately speaking to the girl who so recently flirted with the intoxicated men at the piano.

As he climbed the rickety flight of stairs and turned left into a short hallway, he scouted for room number three. Locating the room with little difficulty, as there could be no more than ten rooms in total, he set Bartlett's trunks onto the hall floor before reaching for the iron door latch. Grasping the cold metal, he was startled, as the handle was frigid in his hand. He imagined its coldness foreshadowing the terrible evils contained therein.

He turned the handle and slowly pushed the door open, revealing a small, dark room with an undersized crate upon which stood a lone, unlit candle. The crate's rough surface substituted for a bedside table. That, along with two small beds, one on either side of the room, was the only furniture. The bed on the left side contained a disheveled woolen blanket. These items, however, were not what held Jeduthan's attention. The bed on the right side mesmerized him, for upon it lay a bare-chested woman.

He halted, eyes affixed unwillingly upon her round bosoms, slightly visible by the faint moonlight penetrating through the loose board siding. He could hear her shallow breath in the darkness and his own heart pounding within his torso, rumbling, as savage drums echo through the hills and valleys on the frontier. He remembered a weekly struggle he faced from what seemed like many years ago. While greeting parishioners at the church doors, his eyes involuntarily perused the young maidens in their fineries, breasts pushing upward, exposing their round, soft flesh to him and other gentlemen who were brazen enough to view their milky white skin. He often wrestled with sinful thoughts as the temptresses gently bowed in respect, allowing him an uncompromising view of their half-exposed breasts.

"What may I do for ye, sir?" came a high-pitched voice from the darkness. Awakened from his visions, Jeduthan averted his eyes and blandly stated, "Mr. Holmes said this room was vacant."

"It can be, iffin that's what ye desire," resounded the female's alluring voice.

"It is," responded Jeduthan, perfunctorily. "My companion and I have rightly rented these quarters. If there has been a mistake, I will retrace my path to Mr. Holmes and ask for different accommodations."

He began to turn when the woman moved from her position on the bed. "There has been no mistake." She stretched her petite frame before rising, still fully bare-chested in front of him. "Do ye like what ye eyes see?"

Jeduthan, still attempting to avert his gaze, responded, "I am a married man!"

"Now don't ye worry about dat. Many of me associations tis married men. They only desires what their cold-hearted wives will not provide. Now then..." She approached him and pushed up against his side, her bare breasts rubbing gently against the exposed skin along his upper arm, her nipple distinctly poking him as a honeybee might as it flew onto the soft petal of a wild flower bloom. He remembered many years ago, when he and Florinda, recently married, first exposed their young bodies to each other's investigating eyes and sense of touch. Her breasts were not unlike this girl's, but as the years passed, their youthfulness waned and recently had turned cold and disinterested.

He stepped backward, regaining his composure, as he demanded, "Cover yourself, child! I am an old man, the same age as your father."

The girl obediently reacted by pulling up her bodice from around her waist, covering her round breasts. He watched as her supple curves disappeared, wondering why young girls, such as the object that stood before him this evening, sacrificed their virtue for a mere pittance. He hoped his young daughter, Laura Ann, could avoid the Devil's charms and live a virtuous life. Alas, so many daughters of Eve turn away from righteous paths out of desperation. He prayed that dear Laura, fifteen years old, be strong and avoid a life of sin.

"Excuse me, old man! I need to attend to willing customers waiting for me down below," remarked the girl as she passed by Jeduthan and proceeded out of sight down the stairs.

He raised the two trunks, along with his own blanket roll, and entered the room. He placed the artist's belongings at the foot of the right side bed and then reclined upon the left. The long day had taken its toll on him, for twice he rode from the laborer's camp to Lockport, but sleep seemed to elude him. The noisy commotion of the pub below nearly shook the building's foundation. Often he could hear his artist friend leading a chorus of drunken fools in song as a choir director might lead his chorus in praising God.

He had faced the evening twice tempted by sin, and twice had overcome its devilish hold. Although his soul still heaved in turmoil, he believed that he had found a hiding place, among the rabble of the crowd where all have sinned and admittedly have come short of the glory of God. He soon fell asleep.

Jeduthan awoke with a ray of sunlight peeking through a crack in the shack's wall and striking his right eye. For many months, his only bed had been a hard cot provided by the Erie Canal Company. However, this morning he felt relaxed and warm with a restful night's sleep in a stuffed mattress. All seemed right with the world.

However, when he turned his head to view his artist friend lying amongst the familiar pile of blankets and pillow, he became rigid with fear. Stretched out beside him, providing the warmth he had thought was from the soft mattress, was the young girl of last night, her hand gently resting upon his heaving chest and her bare leg thrown carelessly about his hips. Her soft flesh touched his own, bringing forth memories of long ago. His loins burned with passion yet his mind urged him to resist temptation. Slowly reaching to the underside of the girl's thigh, he heaved it into the air, rolling her upon the floor with a thud.

"What do ye mean, manhandling me as such?" she hollered.

"Wicked woman! You tempted me with your womanly wiles, and now I am defiled," he loudly cried, tears watering his eyes.

Upon the opposite bunk, Bartlett awoke from his drunken escapade, announcing, "Dear Higby! Pardon me for not introducing you. This is young Eileen," pointing to his own still sleeping companion. "And that young darling is her sister, Kathleen," gesturing toward the naked girl upon the floor. "Now will you please regain your composure and lie upon your back and enjoy the company which I have generously procured for your pleasure?"

Jeduthan flushed with anger. "Will, I don't understand! Did I not send this young girl out from these quarters last night before I retired?"

"Of course you did, my old friend. She came down the steps a virtuous lass and complained to Holmes. Confronted with your debauchery, my only recourse to remedy the episode was by employing the sisters for the evening," grinned his companion, as he gently kissed his young cohort on the forehead. "Now, little Kathleen, you dress yourself, go to your master, and retrieve us men folk some breakfast. I will send your sister straightway."

Kathleen picked herself off the wooden floorboards and, with a huff, exited the room, pitching an annoyed scowl at Jeduthan sitting upright and rigid upon the bed. The other young girl only snuggled herself deeper within the blankets which Bartlett and she shared, ignoring the commotion of the preceding moments. Jeduthan began to fidget uncontrollably.

"Dear friend, I cannot express my guilt to you. I am sinfully ashamed of my behavior," Jeduthan stated awkwardly. His head slumped in defeat.

"Do not worry yourself, Higby. You might have slept with that beautiful young lass, but you had no carnal knowledge of her. You were fast asleep when I arrived only a few brief hours ago from my adventurous romp through the Irish community below. I tried to awaken you, but my efforts were in vain. You lay as still as that tree trunk lay across your precious towpath some weeks ago. As both sisters are assigned to this room, I had to relinquish one precious specimen to share your bed, as both could not repose in mine. So poor Kathleen, attracted no doubt by your fatherly charm, chose to lay with you while Eileen received the prize of my company. Nevertheless, do not worry yourself as you did not copulate with said young lady. I doubt, though, she would have objected, even after she informed me of your previous encounter and your reasons in rejecting her advances."

"I am sorry that I did not warn you earlier of my treacherous crime of abandonment of wife and family," stated Jeduthan.

"Dastardly, I admit, but we must all seek our fortunes. Only a sign from God himself would alter my path. That sign a few weeks ago was a vision of the setting sun casting its azure rays upon Governor Clinton's Erie Canal and your half-empty tent at the construction site. Again, the soaring eagle provided a visible enticement to sit near your workspace and intimately become familiar with your unique persona. Finally, our encounter with the majestic series of locks here in this town altered my course once again to break away from the laborer's camp and find recreation among the immigrant masses. Moreover, I will await another sign from heaven above before altering my course on more adventures. That is just my nature."

"Dear Will, I suspect that God might frown upon you as long as your travels are intertwined with my sinful ways." Looking upward, Jeduthan prayed, "Dear God, strike me down for my many sins and send a sign for my youthful companion in order for him to seek your guidance and comfort."

Precisely at that moment, a distant rumble, sounding as mighty as thunder preceding a great storm, rolled from the chasm beneath the locks. The earth swayed beneath the building, much as an earthquake might shake a hut. Moments later, a large chunk of rock crashed through the cedar shingles, splintering the roof before landing squarely between the two bedsteads where Jeduthan and Bartlett sat, and the young Eileen still slumbered. The two men's eyes widened and shocked expressions stretched across their faces. Eileen barely moved.

"Higby, I think God has sent me that sign."

Peering at Eileen, Bartlett gently nudged her awake. "Dear lassie, we need to vacate, for the sky is falling!"

Eileen's eyelids opened narrowly as she stretched her naked frame and remarked, "Do not take worry, my handsome Paddy, it be only de canalers once agin blowing de rocks from de chasm. But, as ye are not of dis place, I will arise and fetch ye such victuals ye might require to continue ye journey. Iffin ye pass by agin, I hope and pray upon the Holy mother, ye will seek me out." The young girl sat upward, exposing her nakedness fully to Jeduthan's sight as she stretched her pale white arms laterally. A moment later, she picked up the coverlet at the bed's foot and exited the room, blowing a lusty kiss at the men as the door closed behind her.

Bartlett stood. Gathering his woolen breeches, he proclaimed, "After breakfasting, I believe we should seek more suitable lodgings for tonight. Will you accompany me on my next adventure, old man?" Jeduthan, overcome and awestruck by his companion's nonchalant attitude, could only muster a head nod to the request. "Great, my dear adulterer, restless wanderer, laboring axe man, naturalist, art critic, and God only knows what other titles that I am sure to find lurking within your devious past. Yes sir, Higby, you are a far more colorful man than you present."

Bartlett opened the door, stepped into the hall, and beckoned for his traveling companion. Jeduthan obediently followed his artist friend, much like a canal boat linked by rope and chain to its mule team, and proceeded down the staircase and into the lower room.

Washington House

As the two travelers exited the *Eagle Hotel* into the bright sunlight of the morning, each shielded their eyes with their hands. The dank, poorly lit interior of their recent abode contrasted dramatically with the crisp morning sunshine. To the east, near the locks and into its descending chasm, a large dust cloud hovered, most likely caused from the morning's explosion that resulted in the large rock's descent into the two men's quarters moments before.

"Well, Higby," Bartlett stated, stretching full length in the sun's warm rays, "Your first choice of lodgings suited my tastes much more than it seems to have suited yours. However, alas, I also tire of such rambunctious escapades and very much relish the company of more refined residents. Where else do you know that would accept us wanderers as boarders?"

Jeduthan responded by raising his hand and pointed eastward, across the intersection at an imposing brick structure that he visited the previous afternoon to purchase his periodical, *The Lockport Observatory*. "In that yonder villa, we shall find our next residence. *Washington House* is famous for its high-minded consortium of learned fellows. Let us retire therein, to feast our minds and rest our bones!" mused Jeduthan.

Bartlett abruptly turned his eyes toward his companion and retorted, "Higby, I am glad to see you have not lost your eloquent diction and have awakened as the companion whom I so much enjoy. So be it, my elderly friend, let us embark upon crossing this avenue, and acquire lodging in yonder abode named so expressively for the most famous of all our founding fathers." While entering *Washington House*, Bartlett smirked, "This residence lacks its bruiser guarding the front door."

Greeting them was an imposing foyer, a thick carpet covering the majority of its finely polished wooden floor. The floor covering's construction was of various large animal hides, primarily bear, but with some deer, wolf, and, strangely enough, a single white pelt in its center, which Jeduthan could not identify.

A woman, adorned by a long polished black cotton dress sat quietly in the far corner reading a publication. She arose and stepped to the room's center greeting the men, arms stretched into the air as if announcing a royal entourage, "Welcome to *Washington House,* my dear gentlemen. I hope we can accommodate your needs?"

"Our needs will be simple, my dear madam," replied Bartlett. "We only need a single room, with an accessible window providing light for my dear friend's proclivity for reading. We will also desire meals, which I hope you provide in this friendly establishment."

"Yes sir, I can assure you that those demands will be satisfied and much more. Gentlemen of your refinement will no doubt enjoy the company we retain on regular occasions. For instance, tomorrow we will be receiving General Marquis de Lafayette during the afternoon dinner party before he inspects the locks and then departs for his next tour destination. I hope you may partake in greeting the beloved general. As for meals, we serve twice daily, breakfast, of which you have already missed, and supper served promptly at seven chimes. Our weekly charge is…"

"No matter, my dear. We need not discuss monetary concerns this early in the morn. I am sure whatever your rate, it is a fair one and I readily agree to it," interjected Bartlett.

"As you wish, gentlemen. Please allow me to show you our accommodations." The woman gestured toward a grand staircase at the far end of the foyer and the three ascended two flights of stairs to a substantial hallway. There, the group entered a room three times the size of their previous night's quarters. A chest of drawers lined the far wall, along with an elegantly cushioned chair. Two feather stuffed mattresses on two opposing beds lined each wall with a large, glass paned window providing ample lighting.

"These arrangements are quite sufficient. I am William H. Bartlett, artist, and this is my traveling companion, Higby. We are of one mind, he and I, so any messages intended for me may be entrusted to him. Thank you, Madam…?"

"Widow," interjected their hostess. "Widow Colburn. I will leave you to settle into your surroundings, gentlemen. I beg you to remember, supper at seven. I do not serve late comers." Mrs. Colburn backed out of the room and closed the door.

"Now this is a pleasant change from the bawdy house of sin across the way," stated the artist as he peered through the window. Do not worry yourself concerning the lodging fee, for my expense account is nearly inexhaustible, thanks to my friends at the *New York Review and Athenaeum*." Jeduthan silently expressed a sigh of relief, for he had worried how to explain to his young companion his monetary circumstances, ever hoping to retain his hideous crime as a secret. "Now, if you don't mind, my fellow companion, can you please see fit to obtain our luggage from the *Eagle Hotel* while I rest these weary bones? Last night's frolic among cupid's garden has caught up with me."

Jeduthan nodded as he retreated from the elegant room on his errand to retrieve the trunks and baggage. Leaving the front entrance of *Washington House*, he spied a black man passing in front of the *Eagle Hotel*. His pace was quick and determined. He had never before set eyes upon a man of African heritage and the man's strange looks intrigued him. He temporarily abandoned his errand at *The Eagle Hotel* and lengthened his stride, following the Negro two hundred yards before the African disappeared into a small shack. Approaching the building, he gazed upon the shingle hung from the rafters. He remembered his young Irish guide mentioning that the only black man in town was a Mr. Pickard, the town's barber.

To better observe the Negro's habits, Jeduthan chose to enter Mr. Pickard's Barber Shop. There were no customers and the African stood erect in front of a large glass mirror, handling a pair of cutting shears. Pickard turned and grinned a large, toothy smile.

"Good mornin' suh. I'se glad ta sees ya this fin

day. I's Uncle Joe. Can I'se be so kind as to trim ya hair? T'would take only a few minutes and I'd be through and for only two cents."

Jeduthan responded with a smile and gentle nod as he sat upon the elevated chair to which the barber motioned. "Well Uncle Joe, I have heard that you can cut hair as well as any man, so I will ask you to groom my head to be presentable to the honorable General Lafayette on the morrow."

"Yes, suh! Being dat dis dey furst time you'em has paid me a call, I'd give you a shave on de house. Yes, suh, dat Gen'ral Lafayette, he'd be here all aftanoon t'marrow and I'd bet my soul, dis town will be full of onlookers. Now suh, ya jus lay back an let'em old Uncle Joe take care of ya!" The African arranged a large linen sheet over Jeduthan in the manner typical of barbers and began his craft using a large wooden comb.

"Uncle Joe, how long have you been in business here?" asked Jeduthan, once the barber's procedure was well underway.

"Well, suh, I'd be cuttin' hair in dis town cum nay unto five years. Deys nice folks in dees parts. Some of dey nices' peoples is dey lowest, dem Irish canal workers. Only las year some slave patrol come from ol' Kentuck, lookin' for runaways and dey thought I be one. I twas bound and gagged and on me ways into slavery hadn' been for dem Irish. Dey surrounded dem two slave catchers and with tools in han' refused to move lessen dey slave catchers release me. And dey did too, and skeedaddled out of town like a bobcat that had lost his bob!" With the end of his story, Pickard grinned broadly and shook his head as if he had told a wildly hilarious joke. "Yes suh, *Skeeeee daddled*!"

Jeduthan smiled as the barber lathered up shaving soap and prepared his customer for the free shave. "I am glad for your success. So, Uncle Joe, are you a runaway?"

The barber's grin disappeared instantly as he paused, holding the razor in his hand close to Jeduthan's neck. "Why is ya asken', suh?"

"Don't you worry, Uncle Joe. You are the first Negro I have laid eyes upon and my religious background has taught me the intrinsic worth of all people, no matter what color God has endowed them. I am only curious."

"God don' always answer our prayr's, suh. But fo' me, he listens." Pickard continued with the shave. "Dem slave catchers. Dey be from ol' Kentuck so dey could not be afta' me. I'd be from Merryland. My massah, a kind man uba name ub Stuart freed me and tol' me *skeedaddle* one morn after de oberseer hab gottn' mighty drunk. He said, *Joe, you get b'fore he find out why I'd be firing him.* An I don' need da be told twice. I up an lef', headen north, ta freedom. I traveled durin' dak nights, many dak nights til I 'rived here. Dis town is friendly to my peoples. Dem Quackers, who own dis town, don' b'lieve in de slavery. So, dey let me stay. I b'come de barber and we'd all be happy t'gether ever since, save when de slavers come."

"What did the overseer do to have your master fire him?"

"I don' rightly know, suh, 'ceptn' he be a hard man on us slaves. I once told da Massuh Stuart dat he been drunk in de fiel's and dat he had stashed away some corn from de fiels and was goin' to sell it on his own. I rightly think dat is why Massah Stuart done fired him, but I still don' know fo' sure. At first I couldn't find nowhere to hide. But nows I's found me a home here."

Pickard pulled the razor one last time before wiping Jeduthan's chin and stated, "Thank ya, suh. I hope'n my wanderin' stories did not bore ya."

"No, not in the least. It was very interesting and I have better grasped your people's struggle in the process. Thank you Uncle Joe, and I hope God continues listening to your prayers." Reaching into his vest pocket, Jeduthan retrieved two cents, deposited them into Pickard's awaiting hand, and departed the shop with a friendly wave goodbye.

Standing in the street, noticeably refreshed, Jeduthan recounted Uncle Joe's story. Corrupt overseers, merciful masters, long desperate escapes, wretched slave catchers, loyal Irish friends, honor bound citizens, faithful believer in God. He wondered how similar his own situation was to that of Lockport's Negro barber, as he made his way to the *Eagle Hotel*, retrieved the luggage, and re-entered *Washington House*.

Entering the large foyer, he noticed that Mrs. Colburn was absent from her perch upon the corner chair. He hesitated only briefly before lugging the trunks up the staircase. Upon opening the rented room's door, he spied Mrs. Colburn sitting calmly in the cushioned chair opposite the window. "My dear Mrs. Colburn, please accept my apologies for intruding. I thought this was my accommodation."

"Higby, old boy! Come on in and sit down on yonder bedstead." Seated on a small stool behind the door was Bartlett, sketchpad in hand. "I am in the process of sketching our dear hostess, and your rattling might disrupt my concentration. Now Mrs. Colburn, where were we? Oh, yes, your husband. Pray tell, how did he succumb to rest in his earthly grave?"

"He contracted cholera from the hoards of Irish rabble in their tent city next to the canal locks. He was constantly ministering to those Catholic heretics, attempting to eradicate their drunkenness and debauchery. It was he, though, that succumbed to their disease-ridden cesspool. Poor man..." Her voice uttered a slight quiver. "Ezekiel, God rest his soul, brought the first printing press to our fair town. Accordingly, we became the county seat for this region. After he passed on to a better place, I was left with this house and the printing press in the basement. Therefore, I employed Mr. Turner as editor for *The Lockport Observatory* and for three years now, have operated this boarding house for gentlemen passing westward toward Tonawonda. I will not, though, cater to those devilish Catholics and have turned away all who associate with them."

Bartlett stole a hidden glance toward Jeduthan, slyly winking at him in acknowledgement, before he queried Mrs. Colburn again. "How many guests are you entertaining tonight, my dear lady?"

"You two gentlemen have completed my complement for tonight, along with Mr. Turner, my own two younger sons, George and Hiram, Mr. Dibble, Mr. Thomas Love, esquire, and Sheriff Bruce, who often enjoys his feast at my table. The late Mr. Colburn and Sheriff Bruce were close associates, and he always keeps a watchful eye upon my safety and well being."

"How charming," commented Bartlett as he finished the sketch. Jeduthan leaned over, and viewed the drawing of Mrs. Colburn sitting upon a rock seat along a gently curving section of the canal's towpath. "Mrs. Colburn, as requested, I believe your handsome figure in the midst of nature will add a touch of the wondrous outdoors to your parlor," announced the artist as he presented the likeness for her approval.

She gasped in excitement. "Dear Mr. Bartlett, I am very impressed! Your talent for inserting my portrait into your wonderful memories along the scenic portions of the canal is extraordinary. Thank you very much." Taking the portrait, she departed the room, reminding the gentlemen, "Now remember, seven chimes sharp for supper."

After she departed, Jeduthan remarked, "My dear Will, you seem to be able to charm all who hear your seductive voice."

"It's a gift, my dear old friend. A gift, I tell you." Bartlett opened his trunk, placed his haversack within, and extracted a fine dinner jacket. "Higby, do you have any suitable clothes for dinner?"

Jeduthan looked over his clothes, as if wondering how inappropriate his attire was for dinner at *Washington House*. Bartlett's accusative eyes revealed distress and signaled Jeduthan to empty his belongings upon the feather mattress. During the next few minutes, the older man displayed every possession he owned to his critical friend's eye, holding each up in turn for Bartlett's inspection. With Jeduthan's scant wardrobe quickly exhausted, the artist declared all the choices inappropriate.

"My dear fellow, you cannot attend such an occasion with those rags. Do you have anything else?"

"Nothing but this scheitholt," Jeduthan answered, despondently.

"So that constitutes the bulk of your belongings? I've wondered these many days what you kept under your bunk in the tent, but I never would have guessed a musical instrument! Do you play?"

"Of course!" huffed Jeduthan. "Do you think I would carry this thing all over the countryside if I did not?" Bartlett gazed back, blank faced, awaiting a direct answer to his query. "Yes, I play," Jeduthan blandly responded.

Bartlett returned to their original dilemma of evening attire and resolved the situation by reaching into one of his own trunks. "Please try this dinner jacket upon your boney frame," demanded the artist. Jeduthan tried on a light blue jacket and found it too tight. "No, no, no. That is much too small for your fragile bones, old man. Try this double-breasted frock. It has always been much too loose for me these past months since my labors in the wilderness," stated Bartlett almost condescendingly. "Yes, dear man, that is much better. I would not be ashamed strolling along the piazza in Rome with a gentleman dressed as you are now." Pausing briefly and examining Jeduthan's head, Bartlett asked, "Did you have your hair trimmed while I was laboring with Mrs. Colburn? If so, you must tell me who was your barber, for he did a fine job if I may say so myself." Before Jeduthan could reply, his artist friend interjected, "Hurry now, I am sure we have only a few minutes before the supper bell. Moreover, bring the schiet..., schiet..., your musical instrument. We might have opportunity to provide a little entertainment for the guests tonight."

Arriving in the foyer, the two companions met Mrs. Colburn. She was in the process of hanging some overcoats upon hooks in a small wardrobe behind the front door. "Good evening, gentlemen. I am glad you could join us for evening supper. Please enter the library, as not all my guests have arrived yet. We have a few minutes before seven."

"Thank you," replied Bartlett, as both men crossed to the far doorway. They passed into a large room lined with scores of books. Jeduthan's eyes widened as he peered through the glass cases at volumes upon volumes of classic novels, investigative theses, and descriptive poetry. He spied complete works by Greek authors including Homer, Aristotle, and Plato. Other authors included Seneca, Sir Walter Scott, and even a Danish novelist, Hans Christian Anderson. Elizabethan plays written by Shakespeare occupied an entire shelf. How Jeduthan's heart ached to view these volumes, only inches from his eager eyes, yet behind a glass barrier far beyond his physical reach.

In the room, seated upon a plush settee was a young man, about twenty. His calloused hands proved him a man who was no stranger to difficult labor. Bartlett approached him, extending his hand, "Good evening, friend."

"Good evening to you, sir," replied the stranger. "I am Orange Dibble."

"W. H. Bartlett here, sir. Artist. My older companion investigating the immense volumes of printed materials over yonder is Higby. We are travelers. What is your purpose here in Lockport, sir? I can tell by your rough hands that you must be in some kind of mechanical work."

Dibble responded, "You are quite observant, sir. I work a specialized crane at present in Pendleton's cut, lifting excavated material as workers loosen its hold upon the earth."

"I think I know of one piece of earth that has come flying out of the cut without any help from your crane, sir. A boulder in excess of ten pounds crashed through my previous lodgings' roof only this morning," replied Bartlett.

"Yes, I know of the dangers. The workers use explosive powder to loosen the more stubborn rock, and as few have blasting experience, it often results in regrettably showering our poor village with the occasional flying rock. Usually, only small pebbles rain down upon the town, but this morning more substantial debris found it way hurling its path across the sky," humorously exclaimed Dibble.

Bartlett did not smile. "Your substantial pebble nearly caused the death of two women, along with the disfigurement of my dear old friend here." Jeduthan peered over his shoulder toward the two men and raised his eyebrows slightly.

Dibble's face tensed as he uttered a low apologetic, "I'm sorry."

"Good evening, all," a smooth baritone voice interrupted the intense moment, as an older gentleman entered the room. "Thomas Love from Boston, New York at your service," the man announced with a slight bow.

Bartlett abandoned Dibble by turning and piping in, "W. H. Bartlett, London England, along with my elderly companion Higby. Moreover, sitting across the room is Mr. Orange Dribble."

"That's Dibble, sir!" corrected the young crane operator.

"Ah, yes. I beg your pardon. Dibble," repeated Bartlett.

"Yes, I've heard of you, Mr. Dibble. I am quite impressed with your new crane invention and its improved method of removing the excess dirt in Pendleton's cut. Good work, young man. I have also read about you, Mr. Bartlett in the *Review and Athenaeum*. My friend, Mr. William

Cullen Bryant, has already published some fine sketches by your hand in his periodical, enhancing the value of our nearly completed waterway. Very impressive indeed, sir. You, Higby, I do not know."

"I...I work..." stuttered Jeduthan, before being rescued by Bartlett.

"Higby works as my companion in my craft of sketching, Sir. He carries my trunks, entertains me in the field upon his musical instrument, and generally provides ears to listen to my many diatribes upon nature, politics, economics, and social injustices."

"Well, Higby, you travel in good company," stated Mr. Love, as he turned toward the entering Mr. Turner. "Oh, how nice to see you again, Orsamus. What has been keeping you these past weeks? I have only seen you about the streets of our fair town twice and then only momentary glimpses as you scurry by, no doubt on some critical errand."

"I have iron gall ink all through my hair as the temperature in this basement seems to fluctuate from one extreme to the other. Good day, Mr. Love. And good day to you, sir," stated Turner, nodding toward Jeduthan. "Have you enjoyed reading our local tabloid of news and advertisements?"

Surprised, Jeduthan stuttered before asking, "Are you Mr. Turner of *The Lockport Observatory?*"

"One and the same," responded the frail editor. "I present quite a different look away from that infernal contraption in the cellar."

Jeduthan responded, "I regret that I have been so active since my previous visit that I have not been able to spread its pages to read its broadcasts. I assure you, though, I will rectify this omission before this night descends upon us."

"Well, Higby, your momentary lapse for words seems to have passed. You exhibit quite the talent for eloquent speaking," stated Mr. Love.

"Is your name Higby?" inquired Turner.

"Yes, sir."

"I vaguely remember that name coming across my desk recently," stated the editor. "Are you from Turin, New York?"

Jeduthan instantly tensed and became suspicious. "No, I am from Middletown, Connecticut, recently traveling westward with my dear friend, Mr. Bartlett. My name is Solomon Higby," Jeduthan lied.

Bartlett turned his head toward Jeduthan with a questioning look upon his brow.

"Mr. Bartlett correctly informed you of my musical talents, and I would graciously present a musical treatise for your entertainment as we await our evening's repast," Jeduthan stated, hoping to divert the editor's thoughts from any advertisement that might reveal him as a felon.

Bartlett spoke, "Why yes, Solomon, I would very much like to hear a musical tune from your schiet…, your schiet…, whatever you call it."

"My scheitholt, dear friend, Mr. Bartlett," stated Jeduthan with a compelling look upon his brow, encouraging his friend to play along with the ruse.

Jeduthan sat in the plush settee next to Mr. Dibble, placing the dulcimer style instrument upon his lap. Taking one string at a time, he tuned the instrument before plucking *Believe Me, If All Those Endearing Young Charms.* The gentlemen politely listened to the vibrating strings as they echoed through the corridors of *Washington House,* sending a heart felt tear to Mrs. Colburn, who quietly entered the room as the song slowly concluded.

"Dear Mr. Higby, such a beautiful tune to soothe a poor widow's heart! I hope we may be graced once again by your musical talents before the night is out?" inquired the widow.

"I would gladly indulge you, madam."

At that moment, a large mantle clock chimed. "Gentlemen, supper awaits us. Please follow me, as my two sons have just arrived and have already found their places at my humble table," informed Mrs. Colburn to the gentlemen gathered within her library.

Proceeding through a short passageway, the party emerged into a dining room, a large finely finished oaken table dominating its center. At the table sat two young men not exceeding twenty years of age. They arose as the visitors entered.

"Good evening, mama," greeted one. "The servants have completed preparations and to spare us their annoyance, will only intrude upon our call. Please come, sit."

The men found appropriate seats, Jeduthan intentionally taking position on the opposite side from Mr. Turner but also next to his artist friend. Several large, covered dishes adorned the table, along with assorted breads plainly in view.

Mrs. Colburn spoke first. "Gentlemen, may we bow our heads in reverence to the Almighty that provides us with all our needs?" All the guests lowered their eyes as Mrs. Colburn continued. "Lord, bless this food to our bodies and watch for our safety and well being. It is in your precious Son's name we pray, amen."

The men raised their eyes as Mrs. Colburn uncovered the first dish, revealing meat well smothered in brown gravy. An audible stomach growl erupted from an anonymous member of the group as she revealed yet another dish. Mr. Dibble visibly smiled as he apologized for his eager appetite.

"Pray tell, Mr. Love, of the fate awaiting the Thayer scoundrels," inquired Editor Turner.

"Alas, unfortunate Israel Thayer was indicted in my poor son-in-law's murder last autumn, as no doubt you all are aware. The judge of the county appointed me the Thayers' attorney, but my skills in a court of law could not thwart their guilt. It weighs heavy on my mind. I believe Israel guiltless of the heinous crime; his three sons must be the evil perpetrators. They were found riding the deceased's horse, toting a forged legal document, and attempting to collect money owed to my unfortunate son-in-law. When the corpse was found on Israel's farm, the sheriff arrested father and sons alike. Soon afterwards, the sons confessed to the heinous crime and of attempting to conceal the body upon Israel's property. However, no substantial evidence emerged at the trial of a conspiracy that would indict Israel along with his sons. However, the jury about ruled otherwise before my appeals and arguments persuaded them to reverse the prosecution's accusations. Israel will be spared but all three dastardly sons will swing from the executioner's gallows in Buffalo on June 17th next. I expect a fair crowd will attend the ceremony."[4]

"I also anticipate a great multitude attending the execution Thomas. John was well esteemed in this community," interjected a newcomer

---

[4] Long forgotten is the epic of the Thayer Brothers' execution. A historical marker in Buffalo marks the spot but the most extensive information about the incident comes from the Boston Historical Society of Boston, NY. More may be found at their website http://www.townofboston.com/historical_info.html , 2008.

entering the parlor. All the men rose from their seats as the latecomer casually sat opposite Jeduthan.

"Gentlemen," announced Mrs. Colburn. "May I introduce my late husband's affectionate consort and ally, Sheriff Eli Bruce. You remember my sons, George and Hiram?"

"I do, indeed. You boys have matured handsomely."

"I would also like to introduce," continued Mrs. Colburn, "my house guests this evening. Besides Mr. Love, you know Mr. Turner, editor of my late husband's newspaper *The Observatory*. Also joining us is an ingenious engineer from the canal, Mr. Orange Dibble. Finally, W. H. Bartlett, and his traveling companion, Solomon Higby."

"Mr. Bartlett, how do you find our quaint city here among the fringes of the wild frontier?" inquired the sheriff.

Bartlett, never at a loss for words, responded, "Far from the wilderness, I assure you, fine Sheriff Bruce. We are only a two-week's travel, by express packet boat along the canal, from the bustling metropolis of New York City, and soon I expect your residences to explode with new travelers both passing through and settling among your precious populous. My friend Higby and I are only two examples of eager travelers who will demand services, as you provide here at *Washington House* Mrs. Colburn, as we travel yet farther westward toward the setting sun and the ever awaiting frontier."

"Well, Mr. Bartlett, you are quite fanciful with your selection of wording. What, may I ask, is your vocation?" queried the sheriff.

"He is an artist," eagerly interjected Mrs. Colburn as she lowered her head, slightly embarrassed.

"Yes, I am an artist. Only today, yonder fair mistress sat for a likeness which I hope she will soon use to adorn her fine household." stated Bartlett. "Please, madam, would you do me the great honor to show the good sheriff your sketched likeness?"

Mrs. Colburn blushed. "As you desire, Mr. Bartlett." She rose and left the room in search of her portrait.

"Mr. Higby," stated Sheriff Bruce. "I served in the militia with a soldier by the name Higby during our most recent disturbance with the British several years ago. He was one member in our brigade that attempted to repel the red-coated imperialists before we retired, leaving the poor town of Lewiston to the devastating torch of the invading marauders. Might you be related to such a soldier?"

"Very possibly," Jeduthan hesitatingly replied. "Many Higby's joined the Connecticut militia sent westward to free the Canadians from their oppressive rulers. As for myself, I remained behind, husband and father to a growing brood."

"Where is your family now?" inquired Mr. Love.

"A terrible scourge devastated our community last winter. My entire family fell victim and all have perished. I soon assumed the demeanor of a seemingly broken man and was such until I met Mr. Bartlett upon the wharfs on New York's waterfront. His company this past half year has kept my poor body and mind focused on the everlasting task of seeking out new adventures that he may record upon his many and varied parchments." Jeduthan winked an eyelid toward his artist friend.

"...And there I found him, destitute and without purpose," Bartlett finished, as Mrs. Colburn re-entered the room, portrait in hand. "Dear Mrs. Colburn, how delightful you are for your willingness to display my handiwork for your guests tonight."

Unveiling the sketch so all could view, Mrs. Colburn flushed with a slight bit of embarrassment.

"I do like how the natural aspect of your picture contrasts sharply with the refined features of Mrs. Colburn. Your work is exceptional, Mr. Bartlett," stated the editor of *The Lockport Observatory*. "Possibly might you relinquish printing rights to one of your sketches to *The Observatory*?"

"I have a wondrous sketch of your magnificent canal locks which I would part with under the proper arrangements. I will visit your office on the morrow," stated Bartlett.

As the party finished their eating, Mr. Love inquired of Jeduthan, "Would you once again indulge us with a musical note or two from your beloved scheitholt, Mr. Higby?"

Jeduthan looked for Bartlett's approval before responding, "I would gladly indulge your request with the approval of our respected hostess." Mrs. Colburn nodded her approval, and Jeduthan carefully extracted his scheitholt from its canvas casing. He gently plucked the chords of

Home Sweet Home. As he repeated the refrain, the guests around the table joined in with,

> *'Mid pleasures and palaces though we may roam,*
> *Be it ever so humble, there's no place like home.*

The room resounded in applause. "Thank you, Mrs. Colburn," piped in Bartlett. "It is now time for Higby and me to retire, as I plan an active sketching schedule tomorrow. May I take my leave?"

Mrs. Colburn assented with a nod as the two men rose to their feet.

"Mr. Bartlett, will you be available to gather with us here at *Washington House* to meet and greet the town's honored guest, General de Lafayette tomorrow afternoon?" inquired Editor Turner.

"We are delighted to accept the invitation, Mr. Turner. Au revois!" articulated Bartlett as both he and Jeduthan exited the room and retired up the two flights of stairs to their suite.

Closing the door behind them, Bartlett turned and faced Jeduthan accusingly. "Why, Solomon, what an elaborate tale you weave. What are you hiding?"

"I needed a new identity, Will. Mr. Turner has limited knowledge of my past."

"I assure you, Higby," stated Bartlett, "Men frequently abandon their wives, especially nagging and unappealing ones! I, myself, have left more than one ravenous female upon love's altar because of her domestic demands."

"My crimes far exceed abandonment, my friend." Jeduthan sat upon the bed, his head slumped in shame. "Only a few months ago, I was the heralded symbol of righteousness in my community. I was a successful merchant, eloquent speaker, elected deacon, and trusted minister to a growing parish on our far northern frontier. However, my years of toiling, drudgery, and mental anguish all were a financial burden, for which my miserly flock failed to compensate me. Though repeatedly promised, year after year, no meager salary was forthcoming. My congregation continually feasted upon my spiritual flesh, never, for four long years, reimbursing me a fair wage. I did not receive even a mere pittance, leaving my purse empty and indebted. My wife only added to my worries, as she demanded the lifestyle which an esteemed minister ought to live, but of which I could not provide."

A tear crept down Jeduthan's cheek as he prepared to admit his crime to his artist friend. "After a Sunday sermon last April, I abducted the tithes and offerings from the collection plates and bolted from town, leaving my wife, family, and friends behind for good. I absconded with over four hundred dollars from God's plate and hid among the crowds hoping to conceal my identity. Only tonight, I must be found out."

Reaching into his haversack, Jeduthan retrieved the newspaper he had so recently purchased. "Look within, my friend, and you will no doubt find my identity sketched upon its pages."

Bartlett took the paper and opened it, glancing from one article to the next. On the third page, he halted and studied the words more carefully. "Higby, you are correct! Your name does appear among these folds. However, do not worry your weighted heart, my sinister companion. Your likeness does not appear as any sketch. In a small advertisement only, buried among the various announcements and notices, does your name appear. Moreover, wrongly at that. I will read the notice to you."

"Award for the apprehension of a devilish scoundrel by the name Jed Higbed by the authorities of Turin, New York. Medium build, ruddy complexion, puncture wound upon right buttocks. May be impersonating a clergyman. Report sighting to Sheriff of Lewis County."

Jeduthan's teary face turned toward his friend reading the announcement. "See, old man, they did not even spell your name correctly and have misidentified you as a clergyman. Your escapades of recent would definitely disqualify you as a member of the church, excepting, of course, last night's ordeal with the young ladies," Bartlett remarked with a broad smile. He continued, wildly gesturing as if speaking to a great-assembled crowd, "Come, let us not worry ourselves on this matter anymore. We must live out our time on this wondrous earth seeking adventure and living life to its fullest!"

Bartlett paused once again and peeked at Jeduthan with a corner of his eye before matter-of-factly stating, "Besides, old man, when you become so morbid, I begin to tire of your company. Stay as my faithful companion and embellish me with your expressive diatribes tickling my intellectual fancies! Now, off to bed with you. We have an exciting agenda on the morrow."

Bartlett pulled off his dinner jacket, unbuttoned his vest, and then reclined on his stuffed feather mattress. "Good night, Higby," was his last words as he gently extinguished the lit candle with a delicate puff of his breath, darkness descending throughout the room.

Jeduthan remained standing. He could not judge the extent of time he stood motionless in the room's center, but as he too reclined upon his bed, he could hear the gentle breathing of his sleeping companion, motionless and at ease in his life's security. However, for Jeduthan, horrific memories that had so recently abated returned that night to haunt him.

Awakening to the sun's glare through the window, Jeduthan judged the time of day as past ten o'clock. He arose, expecting to see the familiar heap of his late rising companion on the opposite bunk. However, he was surprised to find the blankets neatly arranged and properly tucked, as if no one had lain upon them at all. Nervousness overpowered him. Has Will Bartlett betrayed him by leaving early and fetching Mr. Turner, who could then identify him as the advertised scoundrel to Sheriff Bruce?

Quickly gathering his scheitholt and other belongings, Jeduthan exited the room and descended the staircase. In the lower foyer sat Mrs. Colburn, rigid as a statue upon an altar. She held a newspaper in her grip. As he approached, the masthead clearly identified the paper as *The Lockport Observatory*.

Mrs. Colburn spoke, "Oh, Mr. Higby, I am glad you have awakened. I had my servant quietly enter your suite while you still reclined to prepare Mr. Bartlett's linens. However, as you were fast asleep, I instructed her to avoid waking you or attending to your portion of the room. Did she succeed in her task? Well, of course she has, otherwise you would have awakened long ago. I will dispatch her again immediately if you..."

Jeduthan interrupted, "There is no pressing need at present, Mrs. Colburn. Please instruct your servant girl to devote her time and energy in another arena before focusing on my bed linens." Without pause, he proceeded directly toward the awaiting boarding house door.

"As you request, sir," Mrs. Colburn responded as he whisked by. She resumed reading her periodical, paying little heed to his swift departure. However, just as he reached the exit, Mrs. Colburn added stoically without lowering the newspaper, "Mr. Bartlett asked that I inform you that he would be out all this morning on business, but would attend the General's reception at noon. I was to convey his desire of your attendance, if you were to suddenly depart." She remained motionless as a guarding sphinx, her eyes transfixed upon her reading material.

"Thank you, Mrs. Colburn. I will remember," Jeduthan sweated. He exited into the street and glancing down the intersecting boulevards for approaching agitators, he headed eastward, paralleling the canal. His pace quickened as he imagined William Bartlett leading an angry crowd brandishing weapons in frenzied search of the rascal that *The Lockport Observatory* described him as. He visualized that upon his recent companion's heels came the feared Sheriff Bruce, his hangman's noose draped upon his saddle. Included amongst the vigilante mob was the frail frame of the newspaper editor, Mr. Turner, defiantly waving his tabloid above his head and exclaiming, "There he is! Trap him, do not let him escape, the fiendish scoundrel!"

Jeduthan quickened his pace until he found himself running at full tilt toward the steep bluff overlooking Pendleton's cut. He stopped upon its brow and peered into its gaping chasm. Only the day before he cheerfully strolled along the towpath, gay and light hearted with a kindred spirit. But now, his fiendish companion had betrayed him! He felt trapped! Pendleton's Cut, steep and foreboding, lie to his front and a rushing, livid mob behind. There was nowhere to hide! He cried out, "God, forgive me!" as Bartlett swung a gigantic pole at his head and he heard the splintering noise of fracturing bone as his enemy made contact with his skull.

"Are you alright, sir?" a quiet, feminine voice heralded him as his eyes opened. "I was fixing your companion's linens when you fell from your mattress. Can I assist you in any way?" the young servant girl asked.

His head ached as he pried his body from the hard wooden floor, his sweat leaving a distinct wet spot upon the hardened planks. "No! No. My scheitholt, where is my scheitholt? My musical instrument?"

"On the cushioned chair, sir. I can retrieve it for you, if you wish."

"No. I can," grumbled Jeduthan, as he pulled his body upward and onto the bed. "Please leave me. That is all."

"Yes, sir, of course," replied the servant girl, withdrawing.

He peered across the room at where Bartlett had lain the previous evening. His linens were neat and orderly. He looked at his precious scheitholt for a long moment before gathering his belongings, determined to leave town as quickly as possible. He exited the room and descended the flights of stairs. There, seated upon her stool was Mrs. Colburn, as was her custom. In her hands was a recent copy of *The Lockport Observatory*. Jeduthan's mind raced. Had he experienced a dream? Was Bartlett playing a cruel joke on him?

"Oh, Mr. Higby. I am glad you have at last awakened. My servant informed me of your recent fall from your bed. I hope you have not bruised yourself. I will send my girl into your room to fix your linens, as she has already accomplished for Mr. Bartlett. I will dispatch her immediately if you..."

"There is no need at present, Mrs. Colburn," Jeduthan felt himself stating as if not in control of his own thoughts. "Please have your servant girl devote her time and energy in another arena before focusing on my bed linens." He headed straight forward toward the awaiting boarding house door.

"As you request, sir," Mrs. Colburn nightmarishly responded before lifting the paper to her face, continuing her reading. "By the way, Mr. Higby, your traveling companion, Mr. Bartlett, asked that I inform you that he would be out all this morning on business, but would attend the General's reception at noon. I was to convey his desire of your attendance, if you were to suddenly depart."

Hoping to break the menacing embrace that the nightmare seemed to have hold of him, Jeduthan only nodded as he stepped outside into the bright sunshine. He shaded his eyes from its brilliant rays as he struck out westward along the road that paralleled Pendleton's Cut. Every one-hundred yards or so, he glanced backward toward the village, expecting its rushing civilian population to flood out upon its streets in frantic search of him, but none did. After about one mile, Jeduthan slowed his pace, but his mind still raced. He seemed delirious, weaving from side to side as a drunkard might, hands tightly grasping his only remaining true love, his scheitholt. The sun bore down upon his brow and sweat fogged his eyesight. Sticky ooze streamed down his right cheek. Lifting his hand to swipe some imaginary insect from his forehead, Jeduthan noticed red blood upon his fingers. His body convulsed, heaved, circled around, and finally lay upon the road, his eyes gazing upward into dazzling sunlight.

Had he been wounded during his escape? Were these the last thoughts of a condemned man as he hung limp from the hangman's noose? He could faintly envision shade from a darkening storm cloud descending upon him. The bright sunlight subdued as he took his last breaths and expired.

"Higby, old man! Awaken; it is your friend, Will Bartlett! Open your eyes! There, I told you so. He is not dead, only unconscious. Right, Higby? Now sit up and drink this." Jeduthan felt cool, refreshing liquid pouring across his face, soaking into his shirt, revitalizing him.

Bartlett righted his body. "Higby, you were saved by the quick actions of our beloved General who, fifty years ago, came to the aide of a beckoning young nation. May I introduce his Excellency the Marquis de Lafayette, our honored guest," grandly announced the artist.

Where was the pursuing agitated mob? How could he have escaped the lynching multitudes? He felt a stinging upon his cheek as Bartlett slapped him out of his stupor.

"Higby, I say, welcome your savior!" Jeduthan's eyes widened and recognized Bartlett. In addition, standing over him was a smartly dressed old man, exceeding seventy years, who had a substantial cockade pinned upon his chest. "Welcome Marquis de Lafayette!" repeated Bartlett.

Jeduthan muttered a feeble "Welcome, sir" as he regained his senses. He found himself seated upon a low wooden chest in the foyer of *Washington House*. The room was fast filling with visitors, Mrs. Colburn, Sheriff Bruce, Mr. Love, among them. Most prominent, though, was the old man who Bartlett introduced as Lafayette. Could this elderly gentleman be the Revolutionary hero? His face displayed many hard days of campaigning but youthfulness still seemed apparent in his shining eyes. Were these the eyes that excited true American pride and patriotism?

"Excusez moi, my mischievous fellow citizen. You were fortunate that I appeared in my carriage before you became completely scorched. Shading you, I had my chauffer lift your nearly lifeless body into my coach. We delivered you here, where Madame Colburn sought out your companion Monsieur Bartlett. It is he who successfully revived you." The General then turned to Mrs. Colburn. "Merci beaucoup for inviting me to your humble establishment for tea as I continue my journey, Madam."

Mrs. Colburn replied, "You are quite welcome. Come, I wish to introduce you to our local sheriff, Mr. Eli Bruce and Thomas Love, esquire, also traveling eastward along the canal to Rochester." The party entered the adjacent room, leaving Bartlett tending Jeduthan.

"Will, I am sorry! I feared you betrayed me and I ran, seeking sanctuary from this place. However, now I see that I was wrong. You are a trusted friend." Jeduthan muffled a cough. "I hope you can forgive my evil thoughts and assumptions."

"Higby, you read too much into words. Often rhetoric is just talk, much of which should be discarded. You, though, are in the presence of a great man, and I am not speaking of myself today. Your chance encounter with General Lafayette should be exploited to its maximum potential, so do not dally. Stand, old friend, and let us mingle with our hostess' party."

Entering the adjacent room, Jeduthan smelled a variety of specialty delights placed upon the oaken table. As hunger gnawed upon his stomach, he loosened his grip upon his companion's arm, made straightway to the table, and chose a few hearty samplings from the variety of small breads and fruits. The juicy fruit seemed to revitalize him best and with a second helping in hand, he stood erect and glanced about the room filled with more than twenty strangers.

From across the room he heard the General speak, "Ah, Monsieur Bartlett, I am informed that you practice the fine craft of sketch artistry. How wonderful! I wish I could wield the artists' quill as well as the soldiers' sword, but that is not my calling. I must though purchase some token sample from your collection of drawings. Before I proceed on my journey, please seek out my chauffer, present him with your best work, and he will handsomely reward you. And what of your injured traveling companion?"

"He has regained his footing, General. He was delirious this morning, no doubt due to the excitement your visit has stirred within our small community," declared Bartlett with his usual flare.

"General, may I suggest Mr. Bartlett's friend play a short song to entertain us?" asked Mrs. Colburn.

"Splendid idea, Mrs. Colburn," confirmed Attorney Love. "We listened to his skillful tunes only last night, and we were left breathless. Mr. Higby, would you do the General the honor?"

Jeduthan searched for his scheitholt upon his person before throwing up his hands in disappointment.

"Your scheitholt is still in the foyer," exclaimed Mrs. Colburn, as she darted out of the parlor and returned, moments later, instrument in hand.

Slowly extracting the instrument from its casing, Jeduthan thought of an appropriate tune he should play for the Revolutionary War hero. Soon a smile crept over his face and he carefully sat in the General's corner. He laid the instrument upon his lap, and deliberately plucked the tune *Yankee Doodle.* Few in the room altered their expressionless faces until the General broke into a broad, grandfatherly grin and proclaimed, "Ah, the song of our victorious army." He then chimed in with his broken English,

"Yankee Doodle went to town, riding on a pony,
Stuck a feather in his hat, and called it macaroni!"

The entire room exploded in laughter and gaiety, nearly all joining in with the chorus,

*"Yankee Doodle keep it up, Yankee Doodle dandy,
Mind the music in your cap, and with the girls be handy!"*

Jeduthan continued strumming the tune four times before concluding. A clamorous round of applause resounded throughout the halls of *Washington House*.

"Now, Madame, I regret that I must leave you and your enchanting company, for my schedule demands prompt departure below Pendleton's Cut. I bid you a fair adieu." Ever so slightly, the General bent at the waist and he gently kissed Mrs. Colburn's hand before departing through the front doors where an immense crowd cheered wildly.

The General paused briefly at the threshold while a tall, slender man with a smooth beaver fur hat hushed the assembled mob. "Ladies and gentlemen, please let us all toast America's favorite living hero, General Lafayette!"

More applause and cheering rumbled through the thoroughfare before Lafayette stood upon the top step of *Washington House's* portico. Raising his goblet in toast, the General responded, "I give you the county of Niagara; first in the wonders of Nature and first in the wonders of Art!" An eerie hush stilled the air as the old gentleman sipped from his glass and then lifted both hands high into the air and proclaimed, *"Viva la France, Viva la United States!"*

Wild approval resounded throughout. As the General waved, a large red carpet was summoned and laid at his feet. Two small boys awkwardly unrolled the textile from the foot of the portico to the street beyond while a fancifully decorated carriage waited at street's edge. The General and the tall man descended onto the carpet and stepped gingerly toward their conveyance when a tremendous explosion reverberated from below the locks. A grave look stretched across the General's face.

"Fear not, General," announced the fancifully attired tall man, "We honor you with a salute. We, being deficient of proper artillery, have laboriously drilled over one hundred holes on the canal's bank, filled them with explosive powder, and ignited them in mass to celebrate your visit to our community!" Cheering continued as Lafayette and company boarded their carriage bound for the lower reaches of the canal and points east.

Jeduthan viewed this spectacle through the shimmering panes of his third story suite window. Dragging his weary frame up the long staircase to his room, he had left his artist friend when Lafayette departed *Washington House's* parlor. Jeduthan only gathered enough strength to gaze at the old general addressing his admirers before his body, weakened by his earlier escapades, forced him to lie upon his mattress, exhausted.[5]

He did not know how long sleep maintained its grip on his weakened body but his recent nightmares did not return; however, neither did any pleasant dreams. He felt as if he had lain down and within moments was once again awake. Light streamed through the window, striking his artist friend's linens, which once again were folded and tucked as if not slept upon. His mind remembered when the empty bed had panicked him. Had he only dreamed about two scenarios that could play out in the coming day? Was his meeting of General Lafayette only an addendum to his continuing nightmare?

Jeduthan closed his eyes again and prayed, "My Lord God, please direct my thoughts toward your goal. Rest my mind in peace. Protect your sinful servant and throw off the turmoil that torments me. Yet, Lord, if these trials that beset me further your glory, I pray, let Thy will be done! In the name of Jesus, I pray, amen." A calming aura seemed to descend upon his soul. Would he fall into a nightmarish trick again today? No! Rather, he would allow God to direct his path. No, he welcomed the Lord's direction.

Contemplating his attachment with William Bartlett, Jeduthan accepted the artist's intervention in his new life as an act of a merciful God. He did not know how his newly found friend was to affect his life, but deep within the confines of his heart, he had no doubt of Will Bartlett's devotion as a friend, confidant, compatriot, and companion.

---

[5] Lafayette's visit to Lockport, New York in June 1825 was but only one stop of many the Revolutionary hero graced upon the young United States. His romp across the heartland lasted for nearly two years. For a detailed account of this travels, see http://www.lafayetteinamerica.com/ for a copy of Alan R. Hoffman's translation of Auguste Levasseur's, *Lafayette in America in 1824 and 1825*. My information concerning Lafayette and the locality of Lockport's taverns comes from a splendid assemblage of articles and clippings housed in the Niagara County Historical Society, Lockport, NY, Ann Marine Linnabery, Assistant Director.

Jeduthan sealed his eyes and sat upright on his feather mattress hoping equilibrium would return to stabilize his body. To his delight, he was not dizzy or light headed. Standing, he pulled suspenders over his shoulders and beheld a loose sketch upon Bartlett's trunk at the foot of the bed. It displayed a magnificent soldier in blue tunic and bi-corn hat eagerly listening to the tunes of a scheitholt played by a faceless man. The sketch confirmed the reality of his wondrous memories. Silently, he thanked William H. Bartlett, artist, for recording the historic moment and confirming his own sanity.

Dressed, he soon joyfully bounded down the stairs in search of his confidant. Entering the foyer, Mrs. Colburn, as was her habit, sat perched upon her seat with book in hand.

She remarked, "Mr. Higby! Glad to see you are finally joining us after your extended rest. Mr. Bartlett requests your attention in the library."

"Good morning," beamed Jeduthan. "And thank you, Mrs. Colburn! You are such a joy to this phenomenal planet!" The woman peered over her reading with a slightly annoyed look upon her brow but her air did not disturb him as he proceeded straightway toward the widow's library.

Entering, he saw his friend examining the shelves of books. Bartlett's finger touched the glass case as if he were searching for a specific volume. "Good morning, Will!" piped Jeduthan.

"Morning? It is nigh unto three o'clock in the afternoon, old man. You have slumbered for an entire afternoon, evening, night, morning, and nearly another afternoon. I am slightly annoyed that you have delayed our progress for so long with your napping. Nevertheless, dear friend, you have awakened, and now we may proceed. We are off to Buffalo today. I fear your identity might be in jeopardy."

"By whom? Mr. Turner?" inquired Jeduthan.

"No, a client of his. He was at the reception yesterday and heard you play upon the schiet..., schiet..., the instrument. By the way, your resplendent selection of *Yankee Doodle* tickled the general and was a stroke of genius. A variety of townsfolk whispered that the tune was an insult to our heroic soldiers. However, when their ears heard the General's voice echo its immortal words, many altered their opinions. Brilliant, I say Higby. Just brilliant," beamed Bartlett.

Jeduthan's mood remained grave. "Who is the conspirator, Will?"

"What conspirator, Higby?"

"The man of whom you believe might identify me!" insisted the older man.

"Oh, that conspirator! The man of whom I speak is prominent in the Presbyterian denomination. He stood next to the refreshment table in *Washington House's* parlor as the General sang your inspirational melody of yesterday. I believe his name is Mr. Finney, clergyman about these parts. Rumor is that he leads a congregation that will soon open a new church building within the boundaries of this quaint village. During your hiatus in the upper room of late, I used the time and inquired into arrangements for publishing one of my sketches in *The Lockport Observatory* when Mr. Finney overtook Editor Turner. The preacher seemed very agitated, so I excused myself briefly on pretext of relieving myself in the nearby necessary. Upon my return, while still outside *The Observatory's* office, I overheard the dastardly Mr. Finney intimately speaking to the editor about a *Higby scoundrel*. Observing the two in heated discussion through the newspaper office's window, I saw Mr. Turner decidedly waving off the entreaties expressed by the visitor. I suspect Mr. Finney might be on your trail, my good old cohort."

Jeduthan, much to his own surprise, did not tense his body in fear or trepidation, as was his recent habit. "If I am to be caught, I willingly await my fate."

Bartlett, unwilling to risk loss of his friend to the fiendish clutches of the religious persecutors inserted, "Sorry, my friend! We are leaving today. Gather your belongings, bring my trunks, and fetch old Nimrod. I will await you here, in the library."

Perplexed by the demanding commands emanating from the young artist, Jeduthan tried a resolute stance with his friend. He puckered his lips, creased his brow, and narrowed his eyes. Bartlett though, responded with a simple smile and wave of his hand, shooing Jeduthan on his errands as an aristocrat might a troublesome servant. Rage should have gripped the older man, but Bartlett's sparkling eyes were irresistibly comforting. Obediently, Jeduthan complied, not as a scolded dog but as a child might run on some chore for a caring mother.

When he returned within an hour, errands complete, trunks in tow, he found Bartlett, seated and relaxed upon a settee. "Ah, are you done, my old friend?" queried the artist.

"Yes, all is packed and ready to depart. Nimrod is tied to the hitching post just outside."

"Excellent!" Standing, Bartlett stepped toward the stacks of books that he had previously been studying. "Jeduthan?"

Slightly astonished, as this moment was the first time Bartlett called him by his given name, he replied, "Yes?"

"Do you enjoy reading?"

"I relish any chance as much as you enjoy your artistry, but as of late, our adventures have denied me the blessed opportunity to indulge in its pursuit," replied the older man.

"Today, old friend, as part of settling our accounts with Mrs. Colburn, she has granted us the privilege of selecting one volume among the many decorating her library's walls. Call it a gift or possibly payment for your splendid musical entertainment for the General yesterday, she insisted I require you to select one volume of your choice." Bartlett's white teeth gleamed in a broad smile as he motioned toward the cabinets as a sales clerk might entice a patron with sparkling souvenirs.

A puzzled look stretched across Jeduthan's brow as he peered at the books within the cases. The selection was enormous. He imagined the immortal lines of the Odyssey, anticipated the lovely verse of Cicero, and envisioned the haunting tragedy filling the volumes of Shakespeare. His voice shuddered. "Oh, the selection is marvelous! I have read so many of these volumes in my past life. The choices are…"

"Overwhelming? I know, old boy. That is precisely why I allow you to choose. Come now, we do not have time to dilly-dally. Pick one which you have not already read, and plan to read it aloud to me so that we both can enjoy new, marvelous reflections while journeying this wondrous summer season," insisted Bartlett.

"You are so correct, Will. A work that is fresh." Jeduthan rested his fingers on his pointy chin, much as a confounded schoolboy might in deep contemplation.

Bartlett stood, arms folded, as if annoyed by his companion's delay as Jeduthan carefully raised his hand, index finger gingerly pointing toward *Works by Geoffrey Chaucer.* "I will take that one."

The artist's eyes rose slightly. "It seems so short! Are you not sure that a large volume would be more fitting?" inquired the young artist.

"It is not the size of a book that matters, my young artist companion, it is the words within its pages and the images they convey that bring joy to a reader's heart. For example, do you judge the quality of your sketches by their physical size?"

"No! Many of my most moving scenes are miniscule versus the monstrous portraits that I am commissioned to complete."

"The same is true with the written word," explained Jeduthan in a fatherly tone. "Your recent comment concerning rhetoric as mere words, so often spoken not to be heard by others but by oneself, describes the waste that humanity prescribes to language. There is no need continuing to speak when there is nothing to say. Blessed is silence! Believe me, my young adventurer, the most descriptive of verses contain the fewest of words."

Bartlett's lower lip extended, as was his custom when another had upstaged him. However, he quickly retracted it with a large grin. "I expect you are correct, dear Higby. Choose and I shall retrieve your blessed novel."

"My choice remains firm. It is Chaucer."

"Then you will have it, my good friend," stated Bartlett opening the case, retrieving the bound volume, and then stepping into the foyer to finish his transaction with Mrs. Colburn. Jeduthan studied the other works until Bartlett returned, beckoning with his waving hand, directing Jeduthan to the door and the sunny street beyond. A few minutes later, the pair reached the edge of town. "Goodbye, quaint city of Lockport!" proclaimed Bartlett, much like a minstrel exiting an actor's stage.

The pair made their way westward, alongside the still incomplete Pendleton's Cut for several miles before they ended their trek at a neatly manicured canal basin where many barges unloaded their precious cargo. There, great multitudes of crates, sacks, pallets, and barrels which lay stacked one upon another, awaiting portage around the unfinished excavation. Numerous construction crews continued at their work of breaking loose the tough rock in Pendleton's Cut, delaying completion of the canal to Buffalo for what would be many more months. However, at the canal basin, a multitude of wagons rolled from the nearby town's boulevards, keeping up a brisk trade while laboring backs hauled freight around the unfinished cut. Many an Irishman could find employment at this task long after the stone locks at Lockport were completed.

However, canal work was no longer Jeduthan's objective. The pair sought transportation westward. Here, among the bobbing barges and sleek packets, Bartlett searched for a boat to Buffalo. He soon found one. A neatly painted shingle upon its cabin boasted, *Bound for Buffalo, Passengers Welcome.*

A Wondrous Summer

"Perfect!" proclaimed Bartlett. "Higby, old man, I believe I have found our conveyance." The artist rubbed his hands together as a shyster might when formulating a fraudulent transaction. The pair approached the barge and Bartlett let fly, "Ahoy, ye owner of this fine vessel!"

From within the cabin a man's voice sounded, "No one man owns the *Seneca Chief*, young feller. She's a company boat." An old man with dark hair emerged from the boat's aft compartment. He was bent and crooked, evidence of a harsh life in severe weather and hard circumstances. Leaning over the boat's railing, he ejaculated a wad of tobacco juice from between his lips. "What do you want?"

"We seek passage westward, toward the frontier settlement known as Buffalo. May I and my elderly friend, along with a swayback horse book fare?"

The old man replied, "We rarely take horses as passengers..."

Bartlett extracted a gold coin from his pocket and tossed it to the man.

"...but I suppose that if you will pay for its berth, we will allow all three of you on board," replied the old man as he dragged a tremendous plank from the barge's hold to act as a bridge to shore. With extraordinarily long strides, the barge captain crossed the plank to the shore and inspected Nimrod. "He seems sturdy enough. Ever pulled a barge before?"

"No," responded Jeduthan.

"Well, there is nothing to it. If you ever want to part with this animal, seek me out. He would make a fine worker."

"We are not interested in selling our horse," interjected Bartlett. "We wish to book passage to Buffalo!"

"So be it, mister. Come, let's load the beast. Hardest part is getting the horse flesh aboard. Young feller, take hold of its tail while I lead it aboard."

Bartlett's expression altered substantially. "Sorry, old timer. I will leave the business end of this monster to my aged companion."

With raised eyebrows, Jeduthan eyed his artist companion before submitting.

"Suit yourself, mister, but we got to *tail* this animal before we leave." The captain gestured toward the animal's rear and instructed Jeduthan to grasp tightly its tail. "Now, what ever you do, don't let go or into the drink the horse will go!"

Slowly, Nimrod stepped onto the creaking plank while the old canaler pulled the horse's reigns and Jeduthan held back its tail.

Bartlett snickered. "If you two gents were built more like the legendary *Atlas*, I could imagine the poor creature torn asunder!"

"'Tis the only way horse or mule flesh will board a canal barge," replied the old captain as Nimrod stepped its last strides aboard the barge. "We call it *tailing*. Most times, I can do it myself, but this beast ain't broke to the ways of the canal. Therefore, to guarantee its good behavior, I always have the owner take hold of its tail the first time. Now boys, we leave soon. You get comfortable anywhere you like."

Soon the two men, along with old Nimrod tucked away in the packet's floating stalls, were westward bound.

As the evening shadows from the nearby trees extended across their path, Jeduthan and Bartlett reclined on a large pallet of grain sacks at the barge's bow. A long rope attached the slowly floating boat to four mules slowly stepping along the towpath. An occasional flap by the rope upon the still water and the slow stomp of mule hooves were the only sounds that greeted the pair as they stared into the brilliant hues of the setting sun.

Jeduthan, arms stretched back holding his neck, thought about how he recently toiled upon this engineering feat with only a dull future awaiting him. Now he was embarked upon a grand adventure in the company of a remarkable individual whom he had come to trust. A half moon rose slowly in the darkening night, casting a faint glow upon the still waters. "Friend, will we reach Buffalo on the morrow?" inquired Jeduthan.

"We will reach our objective before the moon rises its full course, my good comrade, as these packet boats average more than four miles per hour. I expect to find lodgings within the city and arise refreshed by noontime. Then, I will ready myself to seek wondrous scenes for my eager pen. In the meantime, you shall tantalize my ears with words nestled among the pages of your newly acquired volume."

"That I shall, Will."

A few hours later, the pair viewed the approaching Buffalo docks as they emerged from darkness' grip. The brevity of their journey surprised Jeduthan somewhat. He had never traveled so leisurely before. How wonderful this canal will be to multitudes of future emigrants to the American continent as they make their journey westward. Soon Bartlett stepped onto the pier from the *Seneca Chief's* rail and led the way into the night streets of Buffalo. After securing a livery for old Nimrod, they settled in at a small tavern bordering the canal, snug and comfortable on soft mattresses for the remaining hours of darkness.

Over the next week, the two adventurers investigated the confines of Buffalo, often spending time sketching scenic views and hearing a few inspiring words from *Chaucer*. Only on one occasion did Jeduthan accidentally cross paths with a familiar acquaintance. It was the attorney, Mr. Love from Lockport. He was on hand for the expected execution of the Thayer criminals, his recent unfortunate clients. The two exchanged polite comments, including a brief reference to Jeduthan's musical talents, recounting the pleasant party they had shared at *Washington House* before they departed on their separate ways.

All seemed right in Jeduthan's world until the fate-filled day of June 17th. As the sun rose, the town hummed with excitement. While the Thayer brothers awaited their execution scheduled for noon, thousands crowded into the city, some traveling dozens of miles to see the hangman's noose tighten around the doomed brothers' necks. Bartlett was determined to sketch the event, even over Jeduthan's protests.

"Will, the loss of any man's life should be a time of reflection, not celebration."

"Dear Higby, your words might have impact upon the lives of the innocent, but these men were found guilty of a heinous crime, the murder of their neighbor. Does not the Bible teach, *Love thy neighbor as thyself*? Besides, this historic moment should be preserved for future generations, and I hope my pen and sketch board might provide the medium for just that!"

"Yes, but did not Mr. Love mention the injustice committed upon Israel Thayer at the trial? The old man averted doom only by the attorney's talented arguments. When the boys finally threw themselves upon the mercies of the court, the judge refused leniency. I suspect the public demands blood," Jeduthan reminded his companion.

"Possibly! However, Mr. Love might be prejudiced in favor of the defendants as he was their appointed attorney. Be that as it may, the execution can not be prevented by our feeble efforts, so better to capture the likeness of the scene rather than let it fade into the past as only a mention in the local journal," retorted the artist.

Jeduthan surrendered to Bartlett's logic. When the artist set his mind to accomplish a task, little debate swayed him to the contrary. During the morning hours, the two companions made their way toward the waterfront, viewing the magnificent lake spreading to the horizon from atop Commerce Bridge. Smells of the fish houses permeated the air. Large nets tied to heavy cranes lifted barrels by the hundreds from the bowels of the canal barges and into awaiting lake schooners. The wharves teamed with business.

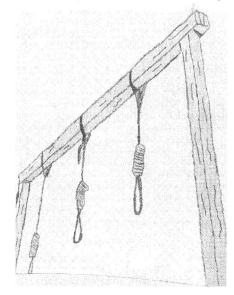

As the noon hour approached, the pair weaved their way through the ever-expanding crowd toward the courthouse and the nearby gallows. As Jeduthan spied the wooden platform with its stout beam looming above and its three ropes dangling, he worried that some day he too might hang from a similar gallows in payment for his crimes.

"Why, Mr. Turner, fancy meeting you here in this thriving metropolis," Bartlett announced as the travelers pushed their way into the shadows cast by the executioner's platform.

"Good day, Mr. Bartlett, Mr. Higby. What brings you to this momentous occasion?" responded the editor of *The Lockport Observatory*.

"Most likely the same purpose I suspect you have for traveling the many hours from your quaint village; to record this historic moment for posterity," replied Bartlett.

"You are absolutely correct, my fine sir. *The Lockport Observatory* will become the primary published account of these men's last moments. Are you going to sketch?"

"Yes, I am. Is your periodical interested in purchasing said sketch for an engraving?" queried the artist.

"I suspect the newspaper might pay a handsome price for an accurate rendering."

"So be it, my fine editor. My lead is at your service." Opening his sketchbook, Bartlett began drawing the gallows, empty of the condemned.

Jeduthan glanced about, concerned that others from Lockport might have traveled to town in order to view the same execution. "Mr. Turner, have many other citizens of your fine city journeyed from their peaceful homes to view this hideous spectacle?"

"I suspect many have, Mr. Higby. The town virtually emptied onto many waiting canal boats bound for Buffalo early this morning. I suspect many a citizen has made the journey into a day's outing by packet boat to see the festivities. I fear, though, the odds of meeting any one of them are slim in this crowd of thousands. Our chance meeting, I assure you, is an oddity," replied the editor.

Jeduthan continued his visual scan, hoping that the inquiring Reverend Finney was not among the growing multitude.

Soon, a low grave drumbeat sounded from across the plaza, beating a rhythmic, morbid thump as the condemned men slowly exited their confinement in the nearby county jail. Jeduthan watched as the three convicts slowly paced their final steps along the path toward their demise. A large man walked alongside the condemned, a brightly polished constable's badge prominently displayed upon his chest. The crowd hushed. The clinking sound of the men's shackled feet shuffling along the gravel reverberated in Jeduthan's ears before each in turn ascended a short flight of steps onto death's platform. He closed his eyes tightly, reciting a short prayer. Only God's mercy could forgive humanity for the crime it was about to perform.

Never before had Jeduthan witnessed a man's demise by the justice of law. He opened his eyes to see the nooses affixed around the three prisoners' necks. The court clerk read from a scrolled document. He could not hear the clerk's faint words except the final few, which echoed in his ears. "May God have mercy upon your souls!" The clerk then stepped away and the executioner placed burlap sacks over the three men's heads before retreating two steps to an awaiting lever. With an expressionless face, the executioner stoutly pulled the lever and the men dropped.

The ruffling sound of tightening rope resonated across the square. Dust erupted from the ropes as gravity stretched and twisted their strands. A dull thud resounded across the courtyard as the necks of two victims cracked. One body quivered as it slowly strangled, deprived of life's breath by the ever-tightening cord. The other two hung limp, their necks snapped upon the drop. For a full minute, silence hovered among the onlookers with only the rope's faint squeak as the bodies swayed, pushed by a gentle breeze. The life seeped slowly from the struggling man's grasp until he, too, rested limp, gone to another world.

Jeduthan hung his head downward in shame. How devious of humanity to inflict such cruel justice upon his fellow man. As silence retained its grasp upon the crowd, his eyes shifted toward his friend's sketch, the scratching lead resounding in his ears, mixing with the pounding of his own heart. Within two minutes, the crowd bustled with life again. Thousands of mundane conversations poured forth from the businessmen, merchants, laborers, and on-lookers, who were intent with getting on with their lives.

Editor Turner, as he prepared to leave, requested Bartlett to post his sketch as soon as possible to *The Lockport Observatory*. Upon receipt, he promised payment deposited in an account that the artist could retrieve at his convenience. Bartlett thanked the newspaperman while he continued sketching, and the editor departed upon his errands.

"A travesty! A huge crowd traveling from miles away to view the last moments of men's lives and then the haunting silence that overcame this crowd as God's hand reached down upon the condemned. Do you suppose, Will, it is the hope of viewing God's glorious retrieval of the dying men's souls that entices people to witness such horrific executions?"

"Don't know, old friend. Sounds as reasonable as any other excuse. Matter of fact, could you please write your impressions of the execution so that I can include it as a narrative with my sketch for *The Observatory*? Your impressions are quite moving."

"If this execution may have positive meaning, I would gladly pen my words." Jeduthan took out his volume of *Chaucer* and, with lead in hand, wrote upon a blank page.

A travesty!
A huge crowd, traveling many miles from their homes,
View the last moments of the Thayer Brothers.
The haunting silence overpowers the on-looking horde as God's hand
Reaches down upon the condemned, retrieving their everlasting souls.

"Here you are, Will. I hope this will suffice."

The artist read the passage. "Very nice! I believe your words will handsomely complement my sketch." Bartlett tore the page from the book and placed it in his sketchbook, along with his finished drawing. "We should post this as soon as possible, my friend."

The two again weaved among the mass of humanity toward the locks where Bartlett located the canal postmaster and conducted his business. Afterward, the artist announced that he tired of Buffalo and hoped to throw off its constraints, indulging his fantasies in nature's world once again. "Let us leave and explore, my dear Higby!" announced the artist. "Wanderlust calls me!"

Jeduthan readily agreed, as the city's confines had also pressed upon his soul far too long. He longed to seek the solace which only nature can provide. The pair retrieved Nimrod from the livery and set off northward, along the great Niagara River.

During the summer months, Jeduthan and his artist friend shared many adventures. At first, they cautiously remained alert for any wandering stranger who might be a disguised bounty hunter seeking his quarry identified only as *Jed Higbed, Scoundrel.* However, as summer waxed toward approaching autumn, Bartlett taught his elderly friend to enjoy each moment as if it were his last.

Although he could never quite achieve the same cavalier attitude and lifestyle that his artistic friend naturally exhibited, Jeduthan soon reveled in the natural and human wonders crossing their path. Among them was Niagara Falls with a goat-inhabited island amidst the falls' tumbling rapids. Others included the great whirlpool and the monumental gorge that delighted their eyes and ears, beckoning their investigating footsteps to trot amidst the intriguing settings. Jeduthan dreamed that these magnificent wonders would, some day, draw swarms of eager on-lookers when the full length of the canal opened for like-minded adventurers.

At Fort Niagara, where the mouth of a mighty river deposited the clear, cool waters from Lake Erie into the mighty Ontario Lake, a small militia garrison drilled under the sun's warm rays. These soldiers provided Bartlett's imagination a scene that sharply contrasted with nature's marvels. The men, sweating in order to maintain prime physical and mental conditioning in securing the nation's borders and thwart attack from unfriendly intruders, caused Jeduthan to wonder how much men would endure for an idealistic cause like liberty.

The scenery across the Canadian border struck him altogether different from American soil. The imperialism of that society proved itself upon Lake Ontario. There, the tall British Navy proudly flew their Union Jack, while the ragged, impressed sailors below slaved for their lordly monarchical masters.

Yet, for Bartlett, the ships added more material for his various sketches. His mixture of wild frontier shorelines where only savages dared to wander out of sight of the mighty ships' cannons and the great imperial fleet reeked of man's domination over God's wilderness.

As Jeduthan quoted from his beloved volume of Chaucer and his artist companion sketched all, from the magnificent to the lowly, the two men delighted in all they observed. They often boarded in small, quaint village taverns for weeks at a time, trekking into the wilds each day and tracking different courses as fate might lead them. One week they bedded down in an abandoned farmhouse while searching the neighboring forests for nature's wonders. Although the pair traveled very few miles by foot or on the back of faithful Nimrod, their imaginations trekked the wilderness thousands of miles during that long, wondrous summer. One day, however, the first snowflakes in the air signaled that their wanderings soon must cease.

The Erie Canal

The warm summer weather lingered through September and October that year. Yet, by late October, cold autumn winds began sweeping across the countryside. Nightly, the great chill breezes blew across Lake Ontario from off the vast Canadian steppes. Bartlett expressed his distaste for the northern latitudes and its accompanying blustery weather, but Jeduthan knew them well. Snow blanketed the hills overlooking his former hometown in northern New York from October through April each year. Old-timers said the snows were God's cleansing elixir upon the land itself.

The stiff, cold gusts chilled both men's bones as they tramped through the forest. That day, they searched for a rumored glen that contained a gushing water spring. It was said that its flow carved the rocks and narrow valley into a maze of twists and turns in which a man might lose his bearings and become trapped. Yet the geological wonder beckoned the pair nonetheless. However, they did not find their glen that day, nor the next, before two inches of snow blanketed the area and forced them to retreat.

As they approached their lodging after their arduous trek, Bartlett announced, "Higby! I believe it is time we return to the civilized world, allowing nature time to rejuvenate during this wintry season. I fear that if we do not move quickly we will find our trusted canal frozen and be stranded in the wilderness all winter."

"Leave the wilderness? My friend, we are not in a wilderness! Frontier, possibly, but we are not but a few days travel from civilization, I guarantee you. Come now, Will, we can hole up in a quaint village for several months and continue our adventures with the spring thaw."

Bartlett fumed. "We cannot hide indefinitely!" Calming, he continued, "I must inform you, my friend, that my agreement with the editors at the *New York Review and Athenaeum* requires me to physically report to their office in New York City, bringing my sketches and expense ledgers each calendar year. Accordingly, we must proceed to Buffalo and board a packet eastward."

Realizing the futility of arguing with William H. Bartlett, Jeduthan relented. The following morning the pair began a three days' journey following the river, trekking through ever-growing snowdrifts, until they broke upon the canal's route a few miles east of Buffalo. Jeduthan secured lodging at a canal side tavern while Bartlett inquired as to transportation eastward.

"Big news, my good man," stated the tavern keeper. "Tomorrow, the entire length of the great Erie Canal will link our western terminus with the waters of the Hudson and beyond. Only yesterday, our beloved governor, Henry Clinton, passed by this very tavern on his journey westward to officiate the opening ceremony."

"That is grand news, indeed, but..." cut off by Bartlett's call, Jeduthan concluded his business with the tavern keeper.

"Higby! I have heard that the governor has requisitioned our packet boat of choice, the *Seneca Chief,* and we will need to secure passage aboard another. Need not worry though, old man, the great ceremony has brought many packet boats to this terminus of the canal. Thus we will find bargaining for suitable passage easier," quipped the artist.

The two men stepped out of the tavern and viewed the length of canal. Here, so close to the western terminus, many carts, wagons, pack mules, and multitudes of people crowded the towpath, making progress of mule teams difficult. The pair sat upon a rock near the towpath, observing the increasing traffic passing hither and fro. After about half an hour, a strange sight appeared in the canal. A barge was slowly making its way eastward with eight sturdy rowers moving the boat at an incredibly slow pace. Bartlett stood and approached the canal's edge.

"Ahoy thar. Why is ye paddln'? Whars your mule team?"

Aboard the boat came the reply, "Cain't ye see the over abundance of traffic on de towpath? We'd be paddlin' cus thars no place for de mules t' haul us. We'd be carryin' cannon for de cerimoney on de morrow. We'd has on board twelve of de cannons, one for every mile we'd travel t'day." Bartlett looked puzzled, yet the boat's master only responded with, "You'll see, t'morrow, at de noon hour!"

Bartlett returned and sat beside his companion. "What do your suspect those canalers was trying to convey with the mentioning of a ceremony, cannons, and tomorrow at noon?"

"I don't know, Will. I am curious, though, about how and why you change into dialect at certain times with such little difficulty."

"Why, my dear Higby!" exclaimed the artist with a lingering southern drawl. "I feel that people are more comfortable when conversing in their own tongue. Though you might not be able to identify your own accent, it is very pronounced, I assure you. Additionally, a man such as me, who has traveled the world over, must effectively exhibit an ability to communicate with all sorts of people to obtain my necessities. So, be it Irish, German, French, Dutch, Swedish, African, Polish, Arabic, New Englander, Georgian, or even your New York twang, I proudly don the appropriate voice in order to converse capably. You, my friend, are a man of extensive vocabulary, and I adjust for that when I speak with you. While many we have encountered on our journey have limited vocabulary, if I were to speak to them with the wide-ranging word selection in which you are familiar, they would become perplexed and confused. Take, for instance, Pierceson, of so many months ago on the canal. What a vagabond! He only understood the words of a brute, thus I obliged him. I hope you understand what I mean."

"I think so. You adjust your voice and demeanor to best suit the moment!"

"Why yes, you are absolutely correct, old man. However, don't misjudge me. I don't mislead people. I only hope to communicate with them better."

The two men perched upon their rock seat and watched the sun recline in the evening sky before retiring to their tavern room at dusk.

Wednesday, October 26th brought forth a bright, crisp, clear morning. A heavy frost patched the grass lining the Erie Canal's towpath. Jeduthan, with Bartlett riding double, quickened Nimrod's gait, making their way toward Buffalo and the canal basin. There they were sure of finding passage in an eastbound packet. As travelers brought a fair monetary addition to many cargo-laden barges, some boat masters haphazardly installed primitive passenger quarters for a select few paying customers. Jeduthan and Bartlett searched when they entered town that morning for just such a barge.

The travelers arrived at the canal basin and spied fifteen separate barges tied upon the bank. Bartlett dismounted Nimrod and covering his eyes, peered into the shining water examining each boat as if judging their sea worthiness by their cleanliness. Luck would smile upon the pair when they happened upon the *Captain Swan.*

"Ahoy, young feller, you lookin' for passage?" hollered a grimy old man from atop the barge. Bartlett pretended not to notice him. "Mister, are you searching for a capable boat to take you along dis' here canal? Iffin' you are, de' *Captain Swan* is takin' passengers!" The barge master stretched out his arms and waved them in the air to attract Bartlett's attention.

Bartlett spied the barge, painted a dull gray with slime encasing its hull at the water line. "Yes, I am in search of passage, but is your barge clean?" grimaced the artist.

"As clean as da' bed you were conceived upon and softer yet to boot!" replied the captain. "I jes' today whitewashed the ol' *Captin Swan.*" Bartlett saw the sailor shift his eyes toward Nimrod. "I'd gladly take you and your horse flesh aboard."

Bartlett shifted his gaze to the horse stalls aboard the *Captain Swan* and noticed one of the four unoccupied. The captain continued examining Nimrod from afar indicating the boat master's true intention. The artist rubbed his chin and gazed upon the other boats as the captain stepped upon the ship's rail and continued his plea.

"Me boat is bound for Troy! Thar's where I'm to deliver me cargo of potatoes to market. I'd gladly feed you both as much potato soup as you like," urged the boat captain. "I even will take your horse aboard for no charge in exchange for his laboring alongside me mule, Gray Sallie. I'm sure they'll work well as a team."

"Cut our ticket rates also, old man! I will pay no more than two dollars for both Higby and I. Moreover, our horse flesh requires forage and iffin he works for you, he eats for free!" countered Bartlett.

The old sailor gasped as standard fare for passengers ranged from three to five dollars each. For a long moment, the boat captain rubbed his scrawny beard contemplating, before nodding in the affirmative. "I's Captain Petersen and I welcome you aboard. We leave immediately after Governor Clinton aboard the *Seneca Chief.* I have a party of passengers who hope to be the second boat to navigate the twin locks at Lockport. We will briefly tie at the pier below the locks to allow some passengers to exit before continuing along the canal. We do not stop except to change teams, and I will require your assistance getting your horse on and off the boat. Agreed?"

Bartlett extended his hand, sealing the deal with a substantial grip.

"Higby, let us stow on board Old Nimrod. We can then enjoy the celebration before returning to our luxurious accommodations and our journey eastward aboard the *Captain Swan.*" The two men led Nimrod to the canal's edge and, using a substantial hickory ramp, led the old horse onto the boat and into the stables near the forecastle. Depositing half the fare with Petersen, Jeduthan and his companion departed on one last adventure in Western New York.

Bartlett piped up, "Old man, today we view a truly historical event, the Erie Canal's grand dedication, man's greatest modern achievement. I am sure that a scene will present itself to my talented hands on this fine day."

Walking along the canal's towpath, the pair approached a large crowd gathered about the entry portal for the waterway from the great Niagara River, only a short distance from the expansive lake from which the canal received its name. Nudging their way toward the front, Jeduthan noticed on the far bank a substantial artillery piece pointing their direction, its muzzle elevated high.

Nearby, lay their former conveyance, the *Seneca Chief.* Upon its prow stood a collection of well-dressed gentlemen adorned, for the most part, with fashionable beaver hats. One gentleman addressed the multitude of humanity, waving his hands from the distant lake toward the first canal lock on the far side of the basin. Occasionally a burst of laughter swept the assemblage, but neither Jeduthan nor Bartlett heard the speeches that emanated from the group of well-dressed men. As the noon hour approached, the *Seneca Chief* was slowly poled by canal workers into the shallows, closer to where Jeduthan and his friend sat. Its destination was eastward to the Hudson, the first of many boats upon the Erie Canal.

Jeduthan's eyes followed the *Seneca Chief* as it entered the lock, the gate closing behind. Upon the stern stood a distinguished gentleman who held a fancifully painted keg in the air. Over the bustling crowd, Jeduthan could faintly hear the man pronounce, "I hereby dedicate this great waterway connecting the mighty Hudson with the waters of Lake Erie." The gentleman then poured the water from the cask into the mighty lock before he turned and walked toward the barge's bow and disappeared.

The water quickly began draining from the lock, and the *Seneca Chief* sank into the deep hole and out of sight. Soon though, the boat emerged from its cavernous den on its way eastward. Precisely as the celebrated barge emerged from the lock, the cannon that Jeduthan earlier spied upon the bank, roared forth with thunderous acclaim. The crowd cheered as the boat passed out of view down the canal. Moments later another roar, more distant, answered the first.

Looking about for Bartlett, Jeduthan found the artist firmly seated upon the lock's stonewall, lead in hand, intently sketching the scene. Approaching his artist friend, he leaned down and asked, "Could you hear what words the gentleman proclaimed?"

"Not a one, but I now understand why the cannons were upon the barge yesterday," responded the artist, without slowing his quick hand at sketching. "My parchment records only the visual, not the audible. That, my ripened old friend, I will leave up to you with your fanciful multitude of vocabularic abilities."

The throng of spectators soon began dispersing as Bartlett finished his picture and closed his portfolio. "Well, Higby, best we make straightway to the *Captain Swan* to occupy our cabin for the promised great Erie Canal voyage pledged by old Captain Petersen!"

The two hurriedly made their way along the canal's towpath, just in time to view their own vessel's departure into the depths of the second canal lock. "Higby, we must hurry! Petersen seems to have left us behind, the cad!" Running directly for the lock, both men drew near the vessel as it slowly descended into the chasm. With an easy step, the pair hopped from the stone lock's edge onto the barge. "Petersen, how dare you leave us!" cried Bartlett.

"I warned you that I would depart immediately following the *Seneca Chief*, did I not?" stated Petersen. "I am a man of my word. Are you? I have left and any who signed for passage upon my *Captain Swan* should be aboard." Wagging a menacing finger in the artist's face, Petersen concluded, "I don't stop for nobody!" Pulling away from the lock, Petersen signaled his team to begin its slow walk along the canal, the long rope attached to the barge's prow gently slapping the water every few seconds.

Soon, the two travelers reclined upon a pallet of potato sacks beginning a well-deserved nap when Jeduthan heard a cry near the stone lock. "Wait! Wait! Stop the barge! I have paid passage for my seat on the *Captain Swan*!" Bartlett shot up like a wild deer that had sensed danger. Jeduthan responded more slowly. The cry resounded from a portly gentleman carrying a substantial carpetbag. He quickly wobbled toward the vessel.

Prancing toward the boat's stern, Bartlett cried, "Come on man, you can make it! Petersen, will you stop for this passenger?" Petersen, at the tiller, ignored Bartlett's plea. The *Captain Swan* emerged from the cavernous lock and began its slow movement along the canal as the frustrated gentleman reached the last stone pillar of the lock. The man panted deeply, out of breath from his running. The boat, no more than five feet from the end stone inched forward. Bartlett again addressed the stranger. "Petersen will not wait, sir. I am afraid you will have to jump!"

The tardy passenger hesitated before he crouched his portly body as a cat might before it leaps upon its prey. However, the man's rotund stature was far from cat-like. When he finally hurdled for the boat, he fell short, crashing into the barge's slimy side and slid into the pale green canal water, seat first.

"Help me! I'm drowning! Throw a rope! Please help me!" the man cried.

Jeduthan snickered at the absurd scene of the fat man slapping the canal water frantically. Bartlett turned to his companion, shocked. "Why do you mock the poor fellow? Can you not observe the gentleman's inability to swim. He might drown!"

Jeduthan, with a fatherly calmness replied, "My experience at canal construction allows me an indulgent laugh at the gentleman's misfortune."

Bartlett remained confounded.

"Dear artist and companion friend, we need not worry. Let me demonstrate." Extending his body fully across the boat's rail and within a dozen feet from the stranded and flailing passenger, Jeduthan calmly said, "Sir, don't panic and listen to this simple advice." The man stopped splashing the water. "Calm your nerves and stop flailing. "Now, plant your feet into the canal bottom and stand upright." The overweight man did as told and, to his surprise, lifted his torso out of the water. "See, my good man, the water is only four feet deep. There is no need for drowning this day!" Jeduthan smiled at Bartlett.

The man stood, only waist deep in water, deeply embarrassed. Soon, he outstretched his hands as a child might when wanting to be picked up by its mother. However, the barge was well on its way, and Jeduthan rushed toward the stern to assist the soggy fellow. As Bartlett fished out the man's carpetbag from the drink, Jeduthan laid upon the boat's rail face first. When the stern passed the stationery fellow, Jeduthan grabbed one of his outstretched arms and, prying the man from the canal's muddy bottom, hauled him aboard. Nearly out of breath, both men lay side by side upon the barge deck, chests heaving skyward.

"Well, sir, I suppose you ought to inform me of your identity, for I hope not to refer to you as *mister soggy bottom* for the remainder of our journey. I guarantee that you are well deserving of such a title."

Smiling, the soaked stranger extended his arm in friendship. "I am William Morgan of Lockport. Your assistance is very noteworthy. Thank you."

After catching their breath, Morgan and Jeduthan moved forward where Bartlett continued his struggle lifting the soggy newcomer's baggage from the canal water. Finally, the artist heaved the dripping carpetbag upon the deck and exclaimed, "I retrieved your luggage, sir."

"Thank you, also. I hope we can share some time together before I depart. Lockport is about a five hour's ride from here, and I could use some comforting discourse along the way, our fine barge owner notwithstanding," explained Morgan.

In the distance, another thunderous cannon roared, shaking the canal waters with its booming tones. Jeduthan raised a questioning eyebrow.

Morgan lifted his hand as if to calm his new acquaintances. "No need to worry, gentlemen. We have nearly four hundred artillery pieces along the full length of this canal, signaling across our great state the moment of this wondrous engineering marvel's completion. Soon, my own tube in Lockport shall rattle the streets of the quaint village with its thunderous roar, and likewise all the way to Troy on the Hudson."

"How extraordinary! Such precision from a man late for his own packet boat," smiled Bartlett.

All three men broke into laughter.

"As soon as I can change from these muddied garments, let us sit and drink to our well being," announced Morgan.

"Agreed," smiled Bartlett as Morgan rose and disappeared into the aft cabin. He re-emerged after a few minutes a changed man. Dressed in a light blue frock coat with a lapel pin displayed prominently with gray woolen trousers, Morgan had all the qualities of a successful town elder. Bartlett pointed to the pin. "Mr. Morgan, may I inquire if you are a member of the Masonic Lodge at Lockport?"

"Yes sir, I am a founding member. Are you a member of the brotherhood?"

"Yes, for five years now I have enjoyed the company of fellow Masons. I fear though, our rituals are becoming unfashionable these past few years. I hope we can employ your fellowship in our time of need, just as we helped you during yours?"

"Of course," responded Morgan. "What may I call you?"

"I am William H. Bartlett and this is my companion, Higby."

"Higby? Our Sheriff Bruce has been in search of a man by the name Higby." Turning toward Jeduthan, Morgan asked, "Are you by chance that man?"

"Possibly," injected Bartlett not allowing his companion to respond to Morgan's inquiry. "I hope you may assist us when we arrive in Lockport."

"A brother in need, is a brother in deed. You may count on me, Brother William."

"When you and the others disembark, could you please move directly to *The Lockport Observatory* and using this note, obtain a package that Mr. Turner, editor of that fine newspaper, has retained for me? Afterwards, please proceed to the lower docks below Pendleton's

Cut and your city's fine canal locks and deliver my package to me in person. I would be greatly indebted to you, sir."

"No need for indebtedness, brother. We serve the same master," replied Morgan.

The three passengers conversed about various topics during the following hours, drinking leisurely from a bottle of port that Morgan secreted from his soggy carpetbag. Jeduthan remained relatively quiet as the two Masonic brothers spoke on friendly terms. Late in the afternoon, Jeduthan interrupted the pair and asked Morgan, "I have often wondered sir, about the basic tenets of Masonry?"

Bartlett spoke before Morgan could respond. "My friend, we are a close group of neighbors who come together to enjoy fellowship and to conduct mutual good deeds for the betterment of humanity. Often we meet in private at lodges such as the recently constructed building in Lockport to..."

Morgan cut his brother mason off curtly. "...to conduct secret rituals, devise covert handshakes, reveal clandestine codes, and share surreptitious information concerning our neighbors who we don't..."

"Shush Morgan. Higby, you must not listen to Mr. Morgan. He has obviously partaken an excess of rich drink and does not know when to keep quiet," interjected the artist.

Morgan hiccupped slightly and then produced an inebriated smile. "Mr. Bartlett is most likely correct. Pay little attention to my ramblings. I believe I should take a short nap before my departure at Lockport. Please awaken me as we approach," Morgan stated as he slowly nodded off in light slumber.

Bartlett remained silent for a long time afterwards. When Morgan's throat began a deep rumble indicating sleep, the artist spoke in hushed tones. "Higby, we will no longer speak of Masonry. Their belief system is noble. However, the rougher sort often practiced it improperly. Are we agreed, good friend?"

"Agreed."

The men lay on the barge's deck and viewed the bright stars and constellations as night overtook them. Jeduthan identified many of the star clusters in the northern clime before the sky clouded over and a thick mist disrupted their relaxed stargazing.

Soon, midnight approached and Petersen informed Bartlett of the approaching locks at Lockport. Bartlett awakened Morgan with a shrug. After refreshing his instructions for obtaining the package from Mr. Turner and the prescribed meeting place below the locks past Pendleton's Cut, the barge eased over to the canal's side and deposited Morgan upon the towpath. He quickly disappeared from sight in the enveloping darkness.

Petersen then off loaded his mule Gray Sallie, requiring Jeduthan to lead his faithful horse from the stable, onto a hickory ramp, and onto the soft dirt of the towpath. The barge waited a full half hour before workers guided the boat into the uppermost lock and began its descent down the five successive locks. The progress seemed unbearably slow. As each lock swallowed its barge, the sky darkened until the blackness revealed no semblance of civilization upon the shores. Only three lanterns shed light illuminating the slick cut stalls of the locks. An hour had passed before the *Captain Swan* entered the gorge and another three-quarters hour before reaching the planned rendezvous with Morgan. As promised, the portly Morgan waited upon the towpath, a small candle revealing his pudgy face.

"Brother Morgan, did you obtain the package?" whispered Bartlett.

"Yes, Brother Bartlett." Morgan tossed the package from the towpath into the moving barge. "I believe though, your friend Mr. Higby, has been compromised. Mr. Turner seemed rather perturbed at the late night intrusion. Nevertheless, after reading your note, he passed the package to me and I departed. However, before I had turned the street corner, I glanced back toward *Washington House* and noted that Mr. Turner had exited shortly after me. Pausing briefly at the intersection, he proceeded toward Sheriff Bruce's home at a quick pace. I hid among the alley shadows before proceeding to our rendezvous and do not believe I was followed."

"Mr. Morgan," interjected Jeduthan. "Please take time to go into the tent city and inquire after a young Irish lad by the name of Paddy O'Neil. Inform him that he should wait at the upper locks for his old friend, Higby." Extracting a silver coin from his trouser pocket, he tossed it to Morgan on shore. "Give the lad this coin and instruct him to remain at the canal basin inquiring after *Mr. Higby* that is bound for Tonawanda. I thank you very much. I am very much in your debt."

"You have your mission, my brother," stated Bartlett, holding his hand high above his head as if in some type of secret sign that Morgan repeated before disappearing into the darkness.

Jeduthan turned to his friend, "Will, I know very little concerning the Mason brotherhood, but its devotion to friendship is endearing."

The artist huffed, "Friendship is endearing! Masonry has become only a place to hide desperate men who cannot construct open friendship among all God's children. Come now Higby, let us rest for we have done all that is possible tonight." The two men lay upon their blankets, adjusting their spare clothing to provide as much cushioning as possible among the crates, barrels, and sacks aboard the *Captain Swan*. Soon the pair closed their eyes and allowed sleep to overtake them.[6]

Jeduthan awoke with a start. A cannon's roar echoed across the canal and a great impact pained his side, causing blood to trickle onto the boat's deck, staining the planks a bright red. From his stupor, Jeduthan gazed upward from his makeshift mattress into the eyes of Sheriff Bruce standing defiantly, pistol brazenly pointed at his torso. "How dare you attempt escape, Higby!" bellowed the sheriff. "I can assure you, there is no place to hide within my jurisdiction. Surrender, I say!"

Jeduthan shifted his eyes, finding his artist friend, hands bound and head bowed, acknowledging defeat. Nearby, Turner stood defiantly as might a conquering despot while Morgan lurked in the editor's shadow, devilishly rubbing his hands together, his beady eyes and sly smile revealing himself as the traitor. Jeduthan closed his eyes once more as he felt his heart sink.

"Higby. I say, Higby! Awaken, old man." Bartlett's voice rang in his ears as another blast reverberated through the chilled morning air. "Higby, I have some eggs and fried potatoes to share with you, my old

---

6 William Morgan was soon intertwined with events leading to a large-scale rejection of the Masonic Movement that reverberated throughout American society. For a detailed account see Rob Morris' L.L.D., William Morgan or Political Anti-Masonry, Its Rise, Growth and Decadence, Masonic Publisher, New York, 1883

traveling companion. Do awake and partake this meager breakfast with me."

Jeduthan opened his eyes to Bartlett's smiling face hovering overhead, plate overflowing with steamy, sliced potatoes. Regaining his composure, Jeduthan righted himself somewhat by propping his body upon his arm. "Will, what is that explosion?"

"An obtrusive man named Fleming has perched his body upon the barge's roof and is shooting wild game. He is very careless, and I expect some accident shall occur if he does not cease forthwith. Captain Petersen is fuming as it is. I expect his wrath will explode in a stream of oaths and obscenities much more poignant than Fleming's marksmanship. The old boat captain's son leads the mule team this morning and from where I have observed game emerging from the thickets nearby, it is likely the firearm wielding noise maker will pepper the youngster more sooner than later. Here, have some breakfast."

He accepted the plate and greedily swallowed the food as Bartlett grimaced at the actions of Fleming. The offender stood upon the aft cabin as Bartlett stated, a store-bought shirt gapping over his round, swollen belly. Jeduthan immediately recognized the man as a dandy and show off, for each time his gun roared he peered about with a large, toothy grin, looking for approval. A small group of children, no doubt his own, graciously endowed upon the amateur hunter a round of applause after each successful kill, of which there seemed precious few.

Fleming continued his gunfire for another thirty minutes, successfully driving into hiding any small animals that might venture toward the water, until the canal's course was barren of all wild life. Lacking sufficient live targets, the portly old man began shooting at inanimate objects including the canal water, nearby trees, and the occasional rock, scarring the beautiful nature with his vandalizing.

Soon, Petersen left the tiller and approached Jeduthan and Bartlett. In a hushed voice, the captain asked, "Gents, would you please assist me with overpowering Mr. Fleming and ridding us of his foolish gun fire?"

Bartlett responded, "I would gladly disarm the old cad."

Slowly, the three men made a course to the rear cabin, where each took a position around Fleming, surrounding him so he could no longer discharge his weapon.

"Mr. Fleming sir," announced the boat owner. "I desire that you cease firing that gun, as it is disturbing me mule teams."

"Your mules do not concern me! I will entertain myself as I please," Fleming announced defiantly, the gathered children receding to the safety of amid ship.

"Sir, may I remind you," Bartlett calmly remarked, "That Mr. Petersen is the captain of this floating barge and has absolute power over its crew, contents, and all passengers the same as if this were one of our mighty frigates sailing across the open seas. Please, cease your target practice as he has requested."

Fleming held the weapon boldly, his eyes narrowing. "I will not!"

Jeduthan, standing at Fleming's rear quarter, moved swiftly. He grabbed the gun's barrel, restricting its forward aim. Fleming pulled the trigger but only a spark resulted from the weapon's flint and steel. In spite of Fleming's protesting outbursts and string of verbal oaths, Bartlett easily disarmed the man, handing the weapon to Petersen for safekeeping. Fleming then retreated toward the boat's center and his awaiting family, who were cowering in a huddled group upon the deck.

"Foolish old man! His own children might have been the next victims from his carelessly discharging that weapon," quipped Bartlett. Throwing his hands up, the artist added, "And now he has driven off all nature's wondrous creatures from our viewing pleasure!"

"Don't you be worrying yourself, young man. The waters will beckon the little creatures again soon," stated Petersen. "Just you wait until night comes again and the frogs start a singing and the moon comes brightly shining. Then there be animals galore!"

Bartlett and Jeduthan returned to their places near the forecastle and peered down the long expanse of finished canal. Hours seemed to pass as the team continued their slow, lazy pace forward, dragging their quarry along at a steady speed.

"I remember months ago how I labored along this same route, removing stumps, rocks, and fallen trees from the towpath that Nimrod now treads. I worked here while running from my horrid past, that is, until you appeared at my tent flap, my artist friend. Oh, how my life has changed since those turbulent days." Pointing to a substantial bare barked tree, Jeduthan nudged his companion. "Look, my friend, there is where your eagle's nest once towered above the earth."

"Yes, you are correct," replied the artist, shifting his gaze rearward. "And back yonder was my stone seat you devilishly removed during my absence, filling your precious crater in the process." Eyes squinting, as if viewing a far distant object, he continued, "And, I believe, I can still see the earthen stain where your shoveling filled in the spot. True, what grand adventures we experienced these many months since that day!"

Pointing skyward, Jeduthan exclaimed, "The eagle still soars, free and undisturbed." A faint screech resonated as the men reminisced.

Bartlett reached for one of his traveling trunks and, digging through its contents, pulled from its recesses a parchment. Laying it flat upon the boat's railing, the artist pointed at the rock seat, the eagle's nest, and then slowly allowed his finger to follow the sketched line along the canal's path into the background.

"Higby, I now understand why our precious Lord has fated we remain companions for so long. You, my dear sir, are destined to captionize my sketching."

Jeduthan looked puzzled. "What, may I ask, are you talking about?"

"Do you remember when I first began sketching in your presence and you commented on the contrast between the eagle's perch upon yonder tree and man's impact upon the natural world?" Bartlett asked eagerly, as if an epiphany had overcome him. "You remember, do you not? Well, your words, so hastily conveyed at the time, would add a great deal to my visual, just like the short soliloquy you wrote following the Thayer Brothers' execution. Your words must accompany my drawings!" The artist beamed with excitement. "We have spent these last months traveling and exploring nature's wilds, recording the visual and now we must try to reconstruct your emotions and convey them to my patrons with short descriptive phrases."

Jeduthan remained puzzled.

"I draw. You write!"

"But Will..."

The artist extended his lower lip in sad disappointment.

"...Alright Mr. Bartlett, I will assist you..." Bartlett did not alter his sad face until Jeduthan added, "...in any way I can."

"Great!" exclaimed the artist. "Let us first examine my eagle's nest along the canal's towpath." Inspecting the sketch and frequently lifting their heads in order to sight the original bare barked tree, stone seat, and isolated nest, the artist gently inquired, "Well, what do you have for me, Higby?"

"Humanity tames the landscape but the eagle soars free!" quipped Jeduthan.

"No! No, that is no good. Try again!"

Jeduthan closed his eyes, remembering that moment when he first viewed the abandoned sketch. After a lengthy pause, his lips parted with, *"Eagles fly free, bound to no one. Humanity is duty bound by God to tend, tame and garden Earth's green pastures as grandfather toad is bound to nature's pond, ridding its murky waters of the ever-present mosquitoes. Only the eagle is truly free."*

Bartlett's eyes watered as if touched by a long forgotten memory. "Excellent, my dear friend. Moving, but thoughtful, reaching a deeper meaning that might slip past the engraver's steady hands upon copper plate. Here, try another." The artist dug through his trunk again and pulled out a larger sketch. It contained a lone canal boat gliding leisurely across an aqueduct spanning a large river. Upon the background, a fuzzy outline of a distant town, shrouded in haze, lay in the direction the packet boat traveled. In the foreground, evidence of wilderness abound with wild animals peeking from behind shrubbery, a looming cliff adorned with cedar trees clinging to its precipice, and a lone canal tavern dotting the far end of the aqueduct.

Jeduthan once again closed his eyes as he stated this caption. *"The passage of the canal, under the lofty bluff that springs at this place from the edge of the Mohawk, is one of the most beautiful of the many stunning features disclosed to the voyager on this great outlet to the West. No traveler sees a greater variety of fine objects within the same distance than the follower of the Erie Canal from Buffalo to Schenectady. The packet-boats are long drawing rooms, where the tourist dines, sleeps, reads, lolls, or looks out of a window; and if in want of exercise, he may take a quick walk on the towpath, and all this without perceptible motion, or jar... Of all the modes of traveling in North America, the most popular and the most delightful, to our thinking, is traveling by canal."*

"Superb, my dear fellow. A hint of practicality while explaining the benefits which humanity has endowed upon the Earth with the building of this canal."

The two continued writing captions, one print upon the next, until Jeduthan felt quite proud that he had productively aided his young companion.

"Now, we will place your name…"

"No, Will! I will not allow it, for that might compromise my identity. Please, dear friend, you take credit for the words," begged Jeduthan.

"I cannot, old friend, but if you wish to remain unidentified, you can adopt a *nom du plume!*"

"What, pray tell, is a *nom du plume?*" asked Jeduthan.

"It is a fake name, from the French, *pen name.* Many writers use them, especially political writers who fear revealing their identities. Benjamin Franklin, late founding father, repeatedly assumed imaginary characters when he wrote. For example, *Silas Dogood* was Franklin's *nom du plume* in his comments regarding the rights of man in the famed Declaration of Independence. So, *nom du plumes* are socially acceptable and fit your needs quite well." Bartlett paused, grinning in triumph, awaiting Jeduthan's response.

"If it must be, sign each caption, *N.P. Willis,*" Jeduthan capitulated.

"*N.P. Willis* it shall be," retorted the artist. "Why, may I inquire, did you choose that identity?"

"In honor of you, my young Will. *N.P.* for *nom du plume* and *Willis* for *Will is.* So, *Will is nom du plume!*"

Bartlett gazed at his elderly friend, puzzled but content. "Your choice, my dear Higby! Doesn't make a bit of difference to me, though I am honored, I suppose."

The two men gazed upon the setting sun gently descending the heavens aft. When darkness engulfed them, they made their way to the soft piles where they laid the night before.

During the night, the pair sought shelter from a chill wind, which swept down upon the small barge. The tiny covered-way amidship, masquerading as passenger quarters, was crowded with a morass of people and crates. A single sheet of canvas draped down the middle, separating the male and female passengers. Though cramped, the closeness of the bodies provided a sense of warmth and both men slept soundly.

The next morning opened bright and clear. Jeduthan poked his head from under the canvas, squinting in the crisp morning air. Autumn leaves, deposited by the brisk wind, littered the canal water and towpath. The lumbering mules plodded their ever-monotonous steps, sometimes crunching upon the scattered leaves.

Jeduthan sought out Bartlett, finding him in his accustomed sleeping position, covered in heaps of blankets, clothes, and spare canvas sacks, only his nose and feet protruding into the cool morning air. Deciding not to awaken his companion, he clambered his way onto the open deck and leaned over the boat's railing, stretching his stiff muscles.

Slowly, the barge eased toward the canal's side and gently bumped to a halt. A rattle of chains and a rustling of hooves upon the wooden planks signaled a changing of the mule team. He climbed upon the railing and leaped to the towpath. There, he observed young John Petersen, the barge master's son, exchanging the team for a fresh pair. Young John was perhaps eleven years of age, only slightly older than Jeduthan's own son, James. It had been nearly eight months since Jeduthan had last seen his boy. He wondered if his James matched this young man in strength and fortitude or had he fallen under the domineering spirit of his mother. Jeduthan shook his head trying to expel those images.

John Petersen's lanky frame took long strides, driving the mule team. Though the animals seemed to plod lazily along their path, the pace was more brisk than Jeduthan expected. He walked smartly alongside in order to fall in step with the boy and team. After a hundred yards, the older man struck up a casual conversation with the boy.

"John, when do you attend school?"

The boy peeked from the corner of his eye at the older man. Somewhat bothered, he replied, "Father allows us schoolin' durin' winter when we is stuck in da ice. Won't be long now 'til we be returning ta our books," the boy stated as he gazed upward into the cloud bank moving in from the north. "I's 'spect we'll get flurries t'night."

"If, at anytime you are released from duty, I would gladly assist you with a few lessons, if you so desire," stated Jeduthan.

"I'd be pretty worn after walkin' ten mile, Mr. Higby, an' usually we only eat and sleep durin' canalin'. Appreciate da offer, though."

Disappointed, Jeduthan remained silent for nearly five minutes. He found that he was soon breathing deeply from his efforts at keeping pace with the lad. "John, how long can teams pull this boat before they need rest?"

"Theys pull a good eight hours b'for we reload them. But leadin' a team is not easy, Mr. Higby. You has ta have a sharp eye ta avoid rough spots in de towpath. These las' few miles has been well groomed, but sometime thars' rocks, stumps, and de' like ta avoid. Jes' las' week, wees come 'cross an entire tree jes lyin' cross de' path. Father spent near half hour unhitchin' de' team and polin' de' hundred paces beyond da site before continuin'. Dis' a hard life, an' I hopes not ta be on dis canal till I die."

"I suspect, John, you could make more of your life, 'iffin you could read," responded Jeduthan, following the boy's accent much like Bartlett's tendency. The speaking style caused him an uncomfortable feeling and he determined not to fall into a similar habit.

"Do ya' s'pose, Mr. Higby? Like what?"

"Well John, many taverns operate along this canal, and I suspect you know where each is located. A well-trained eye, which you seem to possess, might easily lead a watery tour of nature-seeking city dwellers. Your skills with eloquent speech could well explain the marvelous wonders that our fine state and its untouched nature affords to eager travelers. That might be a fine occupation!"

"I s'pose you is right, Mr. Higby, iffin I could talk as smooth as you."

"The ability to communicate comes with patient, diligent practice and study, not much different from how you learned to lead this team along the towpath. Now, if you are interested, you visit me and Mr. Bartlett's area in the front of the barge this afternoon and I will teach you a little refinement."

"Thank ya, Mr. Higby! I be droppin' by when I's free," replied John.

The two continued walking in silence until they approached a large log jam. Six men were gingerly balancing upon the tangle of tree trunks floating in the canal, seemingly none parallel to one another. Young Petersen and Jeduthan stood in silence as the *Captain Swan's* captain clamored from the aft cabin.

"What's holding us up?" screeched the old man.

"There is a log jam ahead," hollered the young boy to his father's inquiry. "Looks to be a big one!"

The elder Petersen disembarked and passed by Jeduthan on his way toward the forward obstacle, muttering a myriad of curses under his breath. Young John sat down upon the ground behind the team. "We'll be here hours and Pa be fumin' most of da' time. Say, Mr. Higby, how ya' like to ride into da nearby town and fetch us some mighty fine drinkin' water? It's a natural spring and it's the best around these parts."

"How far is this village?" replied Jeduthan.

"No mo' than four mile and then we'd meet up on de' udder side at de' canal! I s'pose we'd be all aftanoon here befo' dis log jam be cleared. Take ya horse and follow dat path." John Petersen pointed toward a narrow farm road to the southward. "There, find de' spring and fill our canteens. Stay straight through town for a few mile till ya come to de' canal agin. There, we meet up with ya."

"John, what is the village named?"

"De' village is Clifton Springs. Ya can visit de' tavern if ya wish. De canal passes on its far side, but 'cause de' canal needs ta remain flat, we mus' foller a long outta-de-way route. It makes a great curve four times de' distance iffin' you follow dat path. I s'pose we'll not reach de' lock on de' far side for a'nudder four hours, maybe longer with dis log jam. 'Tis only a two hour walk directly, less iffin ya take Nimrod."

"Thank you, friend John. I expect I will take the path less traveled and see what adventures lurk in yonder village."

"You speak mighty fine, Mr. Higby! Meet us at de' lock. Be careful, 'cause ya know Father's rule 'bout leavin' folks who is late."

"Farewell, young John, until we meet once more beyond the village," was Jeduthan's parting words, as he unhitched Nimrod, mounted his steed, and headed down the farm road toward Clifton Springs.

The village lay only a few miles distant, just as young John Petersen had said. Jeduthan entered the main thoroughfare and proceeded to a nearby tavern to quench his hearty thirst from his mid-morning jaunt along the towpath. Even before entering the building, the unmistakable spicy aroma of pumpkin bread drifted into his nostrils. He had not enjoyed this tasty treat since  leaving Turin, nearly nine months ago. He breathed deeply and noticed his mouth beginning to water. As he sat at a vacant table, a short plump bar maiden appeared.

"Whatcha like, mister?"

"I noticed the smell of freshly made pumpkin bread. Am I correct?"

"Yessuh, you is."

"I s'pose I'd take a servin' of dat," he stated, slipping into the bar maiden's dialect.

"Yessuh. Right-o-way!" she responded. Disappearing through a doorway, she soon returned with a large plate covered with pumpkin bread. "Woodcha' like some ale ta wash down dat bread?"

"Naw," replied Jeduthan, now slightly enjoying conversing in native vernacular. He finished his hefty serving and left a coin upon the table before departing. Quite a change from the barge's daily serving of potatoes, he thought as he proceeded along the town's central street in search of the famed spring.

All felt right in his soul as he pranced past the town hall. It was a recently constructed building with a fountain decorating its well-kept lawn. A fine stream of water spurted upward several inches from its stone fixture. He decided to meander to the fountain and, carefully leaning down, extracted two long slurps from its cool liquid. A sulfuric smell penetrated his nostrils. Was this the fine drinking water that John

Petersen referred to? Jeduthan filled two large canteens and tied them to Nimrod's saddle.

Continuing on his way, he passed various shops housed in clapboard shanties. He spied a gathering of invalids upon one of these building's porch. One of these unfortunates had withered legs and leaned upon a crooked crutch. The infirmed man gazed upon Jeduthan's approach, sending a chill up his spine.

Changing his path, Jeduthan directed his horse eastward and exited the village without glancing back. He felt very uncomfortable by the invalid's piercing eyes. He nudged Nimrod into a trot and soon left Clifton Springs far behind; however, the accusative gaze he received in the town renowned for its medicinal waters worried him.[7]

Soon, he approached the anticipated canal lock. He dismounted and glanced westward down the length of the canal in anticipation of sighting the *Captain Swan*, but the barge was nowhere in site. Tying Nimrod's reigns to a post, he observed a notice board attached to the gatekeeper's shack. Displayed prominently were several notices. As Jeduthan began perusing the leaflets, his eyes widened with fear. To his horror, a flyer hung near the upper right corner with a sketched picture of him! In prominent letters the print read:

Wanted
Jeduthan Higby
Reward Offered In Turin, Lewis County
Crimes Against the Presbyterian Church

As if a common burglar, he reached for the notice and tore down his likeness. As a criminal might, he glanced about to see if anyone had noticed his actions. A young boy played with a small dog in a fenced lawn on the far side of the gatekeeper's house. A man lay leisurely on the stone lock, gazing into the bright sky, sunning himself in its warm glow, waiting for the next barge. A woman emerged from an outhouse

---

[7] Clifton Springs, New York is a quaint village with a natural sulfuric spring that many believe provides healing waters. In 1825, the first bathhouse was built at the small village and by the 1850s, Henry Foster established a small hospital at the sight claiming it to be a Water Cure Facility. More about Clifton Springs may be found at http://www.fostercottage.org/Menu/Main_menu.htm .

beyond. Nevertheless, nobody gave any indication that something was amiss.

Stuffing the notice into his shirt, its dry stiff paper scratching his chest, Jeduthan sauntered nervously toward the lock. He peered left, up the canal's route hoping the *Captain Swan* would soon appear, but there still was no sign of the boat. He sat upon the lock gates, his head lowered like a cowering dog. A few people, unmindful of the criminal in their midst, passed by him toward their various destinations. However, he made no eye contact. He contemplated hiking up the canal to meet the anticipated barge, but thought better of it. He decided to sit and wait, hoping to blend into the surroundings like a dark fish in a deep cold mountain pond.

Minutes dragged by, seeming like hours, before the trusted mule team led by young John Petersen appeared in the distance. He remained seated until John passed, a broad smile upon the boy's face. Mr. Petersen waved as his boy retrieved Nimrod, but Jeduthan only stoically rose and with the boat entering the lock, gently hopped aboard. He immediately found his artist friend, napping near their provisions.

"Will, I have been found out!" whispered Jeduthan.

"What do you mean, Higby?"

"Shush! Do not use my name here. I found this!" Jeduthan pulled the notice from under his shirt and allowed Bartlett to examine the parchment. "They have included a sketch, Will. Oh, what am I to do?"

Bartlett scrutinized the sketch and casually remarked, "Not a very good likeness, may I say. The authorities should have employed a better artist, one with more..."

"This is not a joking matter, Will! I am desperate!"

"First, my dilapidated old friend, do nothing. Sit, relax, and make no commotion. In ten minutes we will pass this lock and along our journey eastward," reassured the artist. Batlett opened his haversack and secured the notice deep within its confines. "Now, let us recline, peacefully and quietly for a while."

The two lay upon their backs as if asleep, covering their faces with spare clothes upon which they had rested the night before. Though the afternoon's weather was cool, nervous sweat poured from Jeduthan's face. True to Bartlett's word, the *Captain Swan* passed through the lock and soon lumbered along its way, leaving the gate keeper's notice board far behind.

After some miles Bartlett spoke. "Now, tell me all that occurred."

Uneasily Jeduthan began, "I walked with young John for an hour or so this morning while you still slumbered. However, when the barge encountered a logjam blocking canal traffic, he mentioned a nearby town. Seeing that the obstruction was significant and that the canal detoured around some hills, the young boy told me that I could venture on horseback to Clifton Springs. There, I could fetch some sweet spring water for our canteens. He reassured me that I need not hurry and to meet the *Captain Swan* beyond the village later in the afternoon. Therefore, I leisurely set off on my junket. Nimrod and I traveled only about three quarters of an hour before I sighted my destination. As I entered the village, I briefly visited a tavern along the main boulevard."

Bartlett perked up slightly with the mention of a tavern as he slyly let fly, "Higby, you dog!"

"Be serious now, Will! I consumed some sweet bread and then strolled leisurely along the town's street, admiring a quaint fountain in the village square. There, I stopped and completed my task with the canteens. A pungent odor imbedded in its taste, the water was far from sweet. Nonetheless, I took my share and while exiting the village discovered that infirmed cripples inhabited numerous shacks on its outskirts. I paid little heed to them excepting one that seemed to recognize my profile. Tapping Nimrod, I hurriedly exited town. As I continued my journey, the gazing eyes of that one cripple niggled at my mind. Had he recognized me? I tried to put the thought out of my mind, yet I still fretted. As I ended my journey at the gatehouse, my fears were confirmed. There, I found the offending poster, tacked upon its notice board. I removed it, shoved it within my shirt, and sat motionless until the boat caught up with me at the lock. Oh, Will, what will I do?"

"Do not panic, my elderly friend! No one on board has seen the notice and all will be well. We continue as planned, but we make sure that your given name remains *Solomon* until we quit our canal journey," Bartlett reassured him.

"Fine," Jeduthan nervously uttered.

"With that settled, let us resume our midday nap." Bartlett closed his eyes in serenity, but Jeduthan remained tense for a long time. Nevertheless, the boat's gentle rocking finally forced him into an uneasy sleep as they slowly descended toward the Mohawk River valley on their eastward journey.

A bell sounded and awoke Jeduthan with a start. Mr. Petersen's wife often sounded the bell when she was ready to serve her fair of potatoes and bean soup. However, when Jeduthan sat up, he spied young John Petersen sitting upon a potato sack, gazing earnestly into his face.

"E'scuse me, Mr. Higby," the youth barked. "You mentioned b'foe dat ya' could hep me b'come a bettr' speaker iffin I'd be willin' fo' ya' ta teach me some. I'd be ready now. It's brodder George's turn at de team."

Rubbing his eyes with his palms, Jeduthan responded, "Yes, what you say is true, young Mr. Petersen. Fetch me yonder a plate of soup and we will begin forthwith!"

The young boy scurried off and returned within moments with a hefty portion of his mother's soup, along with a treat, saved only for the Petersen children, a small square biscuit.

"Me ma says yous' enjoy de biscit fo' ya' helpin' me ta' bettr' speak," interjected the boy.

"Your mother should be praised for her interest in your betterment." The boy creased his brow, confused. Recognizing John's perplexed expression, Jeduthan simply stated, "Please thank her for me. Now, to speak more refined you must first slow your speech when talking with others. Most of your pronounced dialect comes from speaking too quickly. We will focus our first lesson on your greeting. As you approached me just a few minutes ago, you said, 'Scuse me, Mr. Higby'. The proper pronunciation is, *Ex-scuse me*. Notice how it sounds like three words?"

"Yessuh. Ex-scuse me," repeated John.

"That is correct. Now, let us analyze the rest of your statement." Jeduthan searched his artist friend's haversack and retrieved a sheet of scratch paper on which he wrote the following words. *You mentioned before that you could help me become a better speaker if I would be willing for you to teach me.* He next underlined the following words. *Before, that, you, help, become, better, speaker, if, I, would, willing, you.* "Now, the underlined words are your difficulties. Repeat after me. *Before, that, you...*"

John Petersen repeated the set of words, slowly and carefully, just as Jeduthan instructed. "Repeat them again, young John." The youngster did so, this time a little quicker with a few errors, especially *iffin'* and *willin'*. Jeduthan stopped the child and instructed his new student to slow down and try again. This lesson continued for nearly an hour before the youngster expressed confidence. Giving the boy the notes on the paper, he sent young John on his merry way, the boy jumping from one group of passengers to another, properly enunciating his practiced words.

"Ex-scuse me, better, before, willing, if, I,..."

"Looks like you have managed to unleash a little devil upon poor Mr. Petersen," announced Bartlett, as he reclined next to Jeduthan on their improvised bed. "He will not be able to relax his pronunciation in front of that boy for months without rebuke. You sure know how to relate to people, my friend!" Both men smiled.

As the sun set on the horizon and the sky's purple hues were swallowed by darkness, only the vessel's slow creaking through the calm waters, the shuffling of the mule team's hooves, and subtle glow of the barge headlamps penetrated the night.

Jeduthan awoke with a sharp pain in his side. Investigating, he found that his young traveling companion's left foot dug deep within his blankets seeking warmth from the cool morning air much like a puppy snuggling with its mother. Pushing his friend's offending extremity away, he became acutely aware that the barge leaned to one side with a distinct slant. Moreover, the trees, which normally traveled above the craft at the mule team's steady pace, now loomed motionless overhead. Inquisitively, he wiggled his way from the entangling blankets and peeked over the barge railing. He discovered the boat solidly beached, stuck in the muddy embankment. He nudged his friend. "Will, something has happened!"

Bartlett's steady snoring skipped a beat as he turned over inside his blanket cocoon. Jeduthan poked him again, without effect. In a final effort to arouse his young traveling companion, he yanked off the conglomeration of woolen blankets, cotton quilts, and assemblage of assorted clothing from on top of his friend. The cold air hit the artist with such fervor that he immediately righted himself, a scowl upon his brow. "Will, something has happened!" repeated the older man.

"Do you know, old man, that such drastic change in climate might bring a death chill upon a feeble body. Thank the God of nature that I am a tolerant soul, for any other person might have endured my wrath by such treatment!" announced the young gentleman.

"I am sorry Will, but our boat has stalled!"

"What do you mean, *stalled*?" Bartlett peeked from under the canvas and discovered the boat's condition. "Come my old friend, let us alight and investigate."

The pair put on their boots and made their way toward the rudder of the great barge. There, the two men spied Petersen sitting, relaxed, with the large pole he used to assist steering his vessel in his hand and a chaw of tobacco juice oozing from his mouth. "What be the delay, Mr. Petersen?" hollered Bartlett in his nautical slang.

"Water be drained from this here ditch. We is fast upon the mud. See thar," exclaimed Petersen, pointing in the direction that his canal boat faced. "Someone has done gone and run into the canal side and busted a huge chunk from the wall. We might be here for days, till de canal company sends a repair crew." He continued gnawing on a tobacco plug as he leisurely viewed the countryside.

"Mr. Petersen? Higby here used to work repairing towpaths last spring. I am sure he can patch that gap right up in no time and we can be on our way," announced Bartlett.

"'Tis' true?" inquired the boat master. "I twas goin' ta wait here, but iffin' you promise not ta learn my boy inny mo' ya fancy speakin', den I'd gladly hep you fill in dat gap and mebbe by midnight, we'd be on our way agin."

"I cannot agree to that, Mr. Petersen," responded Jeduthan. "Your boy has the right, if he desires, to improve himself, and if he comes to me, I will assist him."

The old man grimaced, squinting his eyes in defiance. However, Jeduthan remained steadfast. A full minute passed before Petersen caved in and assented. "Alright, Mr. Higby, iffin' dat boy be so determined, so be it. Now, let's try and seal dat crack and see iffin' the canal refills."

Jeduthan, Petersen, and five others, including young John alighted from the craft attempting to repair the blown canal wall. Picks and shovels were distributed and work commenced. Few of the young men talked as they hauled fresh fill for the canal's walls. The one exception was John Petersen who repeated his words, diligently all afternoon, much to the delight of Jeduthan. Noticeably absent from the drudge labor was Bartlett, who walked twenty-five paces beyond the break, sat upon a loose stone, and began sketching. Hours and hours passed, the men scraping dirt from the nearby woods and hauling the fill on large canvas sheets to the damaged canal sector. The gap slowly filled, the towpath gradually rising to its original height. The tiresome work might have been completed faster if other passengers assisted, but only the five men pitched in. Yet, before nightfall, the deed was complete.

Petersen placed his hands on his hips and satirically announced, "Now wees wait and sees if da water rises!"

"I expect you are correct, Father!" announced the younger Petersen in perfect pronunciation.

"Don't ye git uppity, boy!" exclaimed the father. Jeduthan could only smile at the younger boy's self-improvement.

An hour later, long after the moon lit the heavens, the barge creaked and moaned. By midnight, the craft floated and young John Petersen hitched the mule team by rope cable to the floating *Captain Swan* and got underway on their eastward journey.

The next day, the weather turned frightfully cold. Wind blew through the wooded hills and thin ice sheets formed along the canal's edge. Much of the time, Jeduthan plied his teaching skills on young John Petersen while Bartlett remained bundled in blankets, shivering in the cold. Sometimes the artist would pencil sketch the scenery, especially ice drapes hanging from rock cliffs near the towpath. However, he exhibited repeated dissatisfaction at the canal boat's pace, it never remaining long enough in one place for him to become inspired thus frustrating his attempts at canal scenery. As the temperate sun warmed the day, Bartlett turned his talented eye and sketchpad upon the *Captain Swan's* passengers and crew.

His first target was Susan Petersen, the youngest of the Petersen brood. At six years, she playfully jostled among the men travelers, even after continued admonishment from her diligent father. She danced and pranced for Bartlett too, teasing the artist with sneaking peeks and kissing sounds. The artist responded with playful banter as the little blond child would scamper through the barge, giggling and laughing. He soon cornered the child at the bow of the vessel and teased her as a "Little Princess with golden curls! Goldie Locks should beware of the terrible bears deep within the forest!" He reared upward as a fearsome wild animal and howled a screeching roar. The little girl scurried to her portly mother tending the stewpot, hiding among her apron folds.

Soon, though, the girl was at her teasing again. When she donned a red smock, Bartlett exclaimed, "Oh! There goes bright Little Red Riding Hood! Best avoid the forest and the awaiting wolves!" The artist then jumped upon his hands and knees and howled a shrill bark until rebuked by old man Petersen. However, the young lass laughed and leaped upon the artist's back and demanded a ride, to which Bartlett assented. Soon the pair were devoted playmates.

By midmorning, the artist convinced the young girl to remain still long enough for a pencil sketch. He worked diligently for five minutes until the young girl became restless. She soon pranced away, seeking other children to play with, leaving Bartlett sketching industriously. An hour passed as the artist skillfully added detail to the rough sketch. Details from the barge, the passing woods, and the mule team all enhanced the ambiance of the little girl in the foreground.

The sketch completed, Bartlett presented the drawing to Petersen. Much to the artist's surprise, the old man smiled approvingly, a significant change from the stoic, gruff old man's demeanor that the boat captain carefully nurtured. Petersen asked to trade an extra portion of rations for the sketch. Bartlett kindly accepted the proposal if the captain would allow him to offer his drawing skills to the other passengers. Petersen relented and the other passengers soon were lining up for portraits.

For three days, Bartlett sketched. He spent an hour drawing one attractive young lady named Gloria, pausing often to show his nearly completed well-proportioned sketch to the interested woman and her lady friends. Gloria giggled and flirted openly with the artist, wooing him as her *personal sketch artist.* She praised him for his natural talent of not only accurately portraying her physical beauty, but also capturing her charming personality.

Her lady friends' delightful air quickly turned to jealousy. The representative troupe therefore conspired with Bartlett in order to punish their arrogant friend to which the young artist readily consented. Finishing the portrait, he beckoned the ladies to comment on the masterpiece. Each took turns viewing the portrait and agreed, in mass, that his sketch truly depicted young Gloria's character. She reveled at the attention until Bartlett displayed the print for her own perusal. She reacted with horror and anger for perched upon the image's nose was a large green flying insect. She let loose a curdling roar.

Much to her chagrin, Gloria drew rancorous laughter from the entire boat. She stood up and with great force, slapped the artist's cheek and stormed away. Bartlett only laughed at the assault and continued sketching other portraits. The other young ladies learned from their arrogant friend to hold their tongues and remain humble, only praising the young man on his remarkable artistic talents. They feared flaunting comparable vanity might result in a similar fate. For his own part, Bartlett enjoyed the ladies' attentions and repeatedly teased each in turn with threats of warts, scars, or other embarrassing objects strategically placed upon their portraits. However much some of the ladies' pride might have been hurt, few remained unfriendly toward the attractive young gentleman from England for very long.

Later, during a bright sunny afternoon, Bartlett plied his artistic skills on Petersen, standing upon the aft roof, diligently steering his monster barge. The artist portrayed the old man as a great Herculean master, a great thunderstorm rumbling in distant skies. The old man remained steadfast, though, stalwartly going forth into the untamed wilderness. Examining the finished drawing, Jeduthan commented, *"Neptune steering man's destiny as he conquers the turbulent wilderness."*

"Fine caption, Higby! Petersen does not quite exhibit the formidable qualities your caption proclaims though." At that precise moment, the old man spit a brown stream of tobacco juice into the sluggish canal, a significant share streaming down his scraggly beard onto his tunic. The two companions smiled at each other before breaking out in boisterous laughter.

During the following days, the weather closed in and turned cold. Both Jeduthan and Bartlett abandoned their exposed positions upon the boat's open deck and moved their belongings into the central cabin as alternating snow, rain, and mist pelted the packet. Jeduthan became distressed as young John Petersen led the mule team slogging along the muddy towpath amidst the wintry weather. "Poor young boy, forced by his father to endure such hardships!"

The passengers inside the cramped cabin fared little better, most huddling in small, groups or using woolen blankets in hopes of retaining some body warmth. Even Bartlett seemed despondent, as he attempted to sketch in the poorly lit cabin. When water seeped onto a sketch, he utterly gave up, crumpling his frail body into a ball, and hiding amid sacks of potatoes. Hours passed, slowly driving wrinkles of anxiety upon the artist's brow. Jeduthan tried to examine his volume of *Chaucer* without success. Therefore, he too huddled amongst the sacks, observing the boredom that scarred his traveling companion. Soon, a visible crease developed upon Bartlett's brow, signaling an exploding rage eating away at his artist friend, much like the agony that a tick inflicts as it burrows into the skin of an infected host.

Abruptly, Bartlett bolted upward into a standing position. In a loud voice he demanded, "Why are we all cowering in this weather? We are not wet, and though the temperature is decreasing, it is not unbearable. Let us rejoice!" The passengers in the crowded cabin somberly looked up at the crazed young artist before drooping their eyes back inward, toward themselves. Frustrated, the artist demanded, "Higby, do something!"

"What would you have me do, Will?" Jeduthan calmly replied.

Bartlett contemplated a moment before blurting out as a traveling performer might for an expected recital, "Ladies and Gentlemen of the fair vessel *Captain Swan*! May I introduce to you, for your musical enjoyment, my talented consort endowed with extraordinary musical ability! We have traveled together nigh unto six months, while his joyful songs and blissful melodies have entertained me at my every whim. We have visited monumental wonders throughout the wilderness and he has captured, with a plethora of imaginative words, the miraculous scenes that I have reproduced upon many canvases. I give you, Higby, and his musical wondermental Schei..., She..., ah... What is it called again, friend?"

"A Scheitholt."

"Yes, musical instrument! Pull yonder instrument from its hiding place, Higby, and warm our hearts with its fair tunes." Jeduthan nodded in agreement and fuddled among his belongings, seeking and soon finding the instrument. "His repertoire is extensive, and I guarantee you, especially you elegant lady folk, fine dancing music, sounds to touch your longing hearts, all in addition to rip-roaring, down-home folk tunes."

Before long, most of the children on board emerged from their parents' protective, sheltering arms and, smiling with anticipation, awaited Jeduthan's first strum upon his instrument.

"I believe," announced Jeduthan to the gathering crowd, "My friend, Mr. Bartlett, will let loose with the words for this lovely tune, sure to melt the hardest of hearts..."

From atop the aft cabin, Petersen hollered down, "Don't ya' count your chickins, young feller!"

"Yes, even Mr. Petersen will pout as Higby plays..."

"*The Gypsy Lady*," concluded Jeduthan.

"Yes, fine choice, dear sir! Excellent choice! Join in all, if you know the words."

Jeduthan raised his scheitholt to his lap and lightly began stringing the tune and softly singing,

"An English lord came home one night, inquiring for his lady,
The servants said on every hand, she's gone with the Gypsy, laddie.
Go saddle up my milk-white steed, go saddle me up my brownie,
And I will ride both night and day, till I overtake my bonnie.
Oh he rode East and he rode West, and at last he found her,
She was lying on the green, green grass, and the gypsy's arms all around her.
Oh, how can you leave your house and land? How can you leave our money,
How can you leave your rich young lord, to be a gypsy's bonnie.
Oh come go home with me, my dear, come home and be my lover,
I'll furnish you with a room so neat, with a silken bed and covers.
It's I can leave my house and land, and I can leave my baby,
I'm a-goin' to roam this world around, and be a gypsy's lady.
Oh, soon this lady changed her mind, her clothes grew old and faded,
Her hose and shoes came off her feet, and left them bare and naked.
Just what befell this lady now, I think it worth relating,
*Her gypsy found another lass, and left her heart a-breaking."**

Clapping reverberated throughout the boat as Jeduthan ended.

"Next," interjected the artist, delighting in the passengers' enthusiasm, "We will provoke your feet into rapid movement and dance with an old Irish jig. Am I right, my dear Higby?"

"I suppose you're always right, Will." A rattle of laughter jumped through the crowd, led by four young ladies with whom the artist had teased the past few days.

"Get your dancing shoes ready as we rattle this deck with *The Irish Jig*." The children all gathered hand in hand and swung across the floor in a double ring, increasing in speed as Jeduthan plucked a rapid tune upon the strings, ending with all the children landing on their rears, arms outstretched as if a collection of synchronized dancers. Smiles and laughter rumbled across the New York countryside.

---

* Lyrics found online at http://www.contemplator.com/child/gypsylad.html , March 10, 2008.

Jeduthan introduced the next song by embarrassing Bartlett a bit. "Our next rendition will be in honor of someone whom my artist friend here used to consort with until her husband found out. *Crazy Jane!*" Bartlett half-heartedly protested by waving off Jeduthan's accusing finger. Mrs. Petersen snorted loudly like an excited swine chased by a rabid dog. The entire boat roared with cantankerous laughter as the musician strummed the tune.

However, Bartlett soon sought his revenge by prefacing the next song with, "I hope wonderful Mrs. Petersen might pay attention to our next rendition. *Mama's Little Baby Love Shortnin' Bread.*" This song incited nearly all passengers to join in singing, as Jeduthan replayed it over a dozen times while Bartlett danced with two young girls, back and forth within the cabin. On one occasion, the artist slipped and fell flat on his back, leaving the crowd roaring in good-natured amusement. Jeduthan ended the musical excitement with a rendition of *Home, Sweet Home*, which visibly brought tears to many.

Nightfall engulfed the boat and all quieted down in restful slumber, women separated from the men folk by a large sampling of linen stretched across the cabin's middle. Jeduthan spied Bartlett secretly sneaking a peek beneath the curtain and a brief *kiss and don't tell* rendezvous between his sly friend and an unidentified female passenger just outside his sight.

As the morning dawned and the eastern sky surged a crimson hue, the *Captain Swan* floated in the canal's still water as had been her custom for the past two weeks, gliding along at a steady rate of four miles per hour. All the passengers were lethargic, resting from the previous night's celebration. The lone exception was young John Petersen who pranced from bow to stern, practicing his precious words from the folded paper in his hand. Jeduthan studied the boy as the youngster approached each passenger in turn, exclaiming in heroic tones, *Ex-cuse me!* and then rattling off his remaining words, *Before, that, you, help, become, better, speaker, if, I, would, willing, you!* The boy would then bow slightly from the hip as if presenting a poem for a European royal entourage and then hop in gleeful ecstasy to his next target. More than a few times, he stopped near his father as if gloating in newly found sophistication.

However, he always remained out of the patriarch's reach, avoiding a quick slap from a stern father for his flagrant arrogance.

During the fourth round of young John's escapades, he drew near old man Fleming, still fuming from the embarrassment of wielding his firearm the previous week. He had remained aloof and snobbish even when his children joined in the singing the previous evening. Repeatedly, the old man admonished his children with loud rebuffs for displaying smiles and giggles when Bartlett teased young Susan Petersen and the egotistical Miss Gloria. Jeduthan remembered the same loud harsh voice emanating from his own father when he was a youngster, a father too busy for nonsense.

Today, Fleming was intently studying a newspaper. Jeduthan had noticed the paper many days before and once thought of asking if he, too, could peruse its columns in order to break the voyage's tedium. Yet, the old man's sole interest seemed to revolve around the scanning and re-scanning of this same periodical. Therefore, Jeduthan chose to not bother the old gentleman.

However, on this occasion, as young John approached the gruff old man with his typical greeting, Fleming raised his devilish eyes and confronted the poor lad. The boy seemed horrified, his voice fading into a subdued whimper as he stated the words written upon his sacred sheet.

"Listen, boy! You are obnoxiously bothering all on board, and I am frankly tired of your shenanigans. If you get within my reach, I will hog tie you and jettison your constricted body into the depths of this sewer of a canal where the snakes will feast upon your entrails!" The boy stood petrified, arm outstretched, still clutching his parchment. Fleming continued, "I said, you should retreat and cower, you ragamuffin!" However, the boy remained frozen. "I will show you what happens when I am defied!" uttered the cruel and callous old man.

Reaching for the boy's throat, Fleming narrowly missed severely injuring his quarry as the boy beat a hasty retreat, dropping his precious word selection at the old man's feet. Angered at the lad's escape, Fleming extended his hand upon the deck and retrieved the poor boy's list. Flagrantly and defiantly displaying the paper for the poor boy's hurtful eyes, the heartless man crumpled the parchment as if crushing the life from an annoying insect between his fingers. He bellowed a victorious cry as the boy further retreated toward his mother's skirts.

"Was that absolutely necessary, Mr. Fleming?" condemned Bartlett. "The young lad was only improving his diction. Do you have no sense of decency? We all should encourage our young people bent on self-improvement. Shame on you!"

Fleming only smiled an evil grin at the boy's anguish.

"I say, old man, your behavior wreaks the putrid stench of imbecility," interjected Jeduthan to his own surprise. "May God's vengeance convict you in the ever after!"

Fleming shoved the crumpled paper into his pocket and, grunting as a hog might before feeding time, lifted his sacred newspaper to his face to continue his reading.

"Higby dear fellow, don't waste your amazing vocabulary upon such a worthless creature. Let us seek out young Petersen and refresh his list," replied the artist, defiantly strutting past the old man. "Friend, hand me my beloved haversack."

Jeduthan gripped the haversack and handed it to Bartlett. The artist rummaged deep within the bag's confines and after several seconds announced, "Higby, I seem to have no more paper in my bag. I will need to access my trunk for another parchment."

Jeduthan's face shuddered. Another parchment? Where was the paper that held the wanted poster that he had torn from the notice board a few days previously? He glanced at Fleming, then toward the old man's pocket where poor John Petersen's word list still partially protruded. He was horrified, for on an exposed portion of the paper sticking out from the old man's tunic pocket, he spied the letters, *WANT...* Had he mistakenly used the last paper from his artist friend's haversack to scribble the boy's pronunciation list? If so, evil Mr. Fleming now held the key to his freedom within his vile clutches.

"Will! The wanted poster!" whispered Jeduthan. "I accidentally placed young John's words upon its reverse side and now the wily Mr. Fleming has it in his pocket; and it has my picture on it!"

Bartlett stopped fumbling through his trunk and turned, looking toward Fleming and the protruding poster. "Dear friend, we must retrieve said notice without Mr. Fleming's eyes falling upon your image." The artist's eyes wandered about the floating barge, focusing on Jeduthan, then Fleming, next Petersen, and finally upon his own trunk. "Higby, you will owe me immensely for the sacrifice which I am soon to endure for your well being." Bartlett retrieved an ornately silver inlaid mahogany box from within his trunk. Without opening it, the artist rose and approached Fleming. In a calming tone he stated, "Excuse me, friend."

Fleming peered overtop his beloved news periodical.

Bartlett continued. "I believe we were too hasty with our words a few moments ago, and Mr. Higby yonder wishes to express his sincere apologies for the utterances on behalf of the annoying young Petersen boy. He has implored me to offer, as consolation for any offense taken, this small gift from within his possession in return for the boy's list."

Bartlett extracted a small key from his vest pocket, opened the treasured chest, and revealed its contents. Within its confines lay two elegant bottles of fine bourbon. Fleming's eyes widened and then inflamed.

"Sir, you can inform the drunkard that I am a temperate man who frowns upon all who succumb to the evil temptations of drink. Be gone with Satan's elixir!"

"Well, perhaps we can come to another arrangement. What about…"

Precisely at that moment, Fleming reached into his pocket and extracted the paper for which the artist negotiations were intended, and viewed the list of words. Bartlett stopped. Slowly and with precision, Fleming flattened the parchment and turned the notice over. As if in slow motion, the old man realized its importance. His eyes gradually rose, ignoring the pleading artist and turned their impaling glare onto Jeduthan. Eternity seemed to persist as Jeduthan peered back into Fleming's stone cold, gray eyes; eyes that had haunted every moment of his life; eyes with which his father penetrated his soul when he could not meet expectations; eyes of his wife's unfulfilled desires; eyes of Turin's Presbyterian congregation as they hurled constant demands upon their over-worked and never compensated minister; eyes that penetrated his heart for years and for which he had fled so many months ago; eyes that he wanted to hide from forever.

Slowly, from the old man's cavernous mouth spilled the words Jeduthan had hidden from all these months. "We have a criminal aboard!" He stood and pointed toward Jeduthan while shouting to the ship's captain, "Mr. Petersen, I have found a desperado among us innocents!" His outstretched arm resolutely pointing an accusing finger. "There he sits…"

"Oh, shut ya trap, ol' man. I needin' be hearin' ya useless utterances. Ya had insulted me son. Ya has been terrifyin' de'whole boat with ya gun play. I will not be havin' ya spoil me friends who helped me fix de' canal whistle' ya lay upon ya fat rear. Now, don't ya not speak no more!"

Fleming opened his mouth as if to continue his diatribe, but Petersen waved him off. "Not one more word suh, ord' I'd be puttin' ya off me barge here and now!"

Fleming raised his finger in protest but Petersen defiantly bellowed, "Don't try me patience! Sit ya self down, and shut up!" Fleming sat with a huff, eyes glaring at Jeduthan. Bartlett retreated across the barge and sat beside his traveling companion.

"Higby," Bartlett whispered, "The old coot foiled my plan. Given enough time, he will undoubtedly report you. Thus, we must prepare for that eventuality."

Fleming's ire for young John Petersen subsided when his wrath turned upon Jeduthan. The old man's face turned beat red as he glared and fumed at the criminal which moments ago had been only an annoyance, playing his noisy scheitholt and inciting wicked passions among the people on the crowded barge. With Fleming's initial petition silenced by the barge's captain, Jeduthan returned the old man's glare trying to match his antagonist's intensity. However, try as he might, he failed. Fleming's uncompromising eyes revealed his continued craving to expose Jeduthan's identity. Time seemed to favor Fleming for as the canal boat drudgingly made its way eastward, a faint bell tolled its tone from a city on the eastern horizon.

Bartlett interrupted Jeduthan's thoughts. "Well my fine, fleeing villain, our plan is thwarted. Who would have taken that grumpy, old geezer as a temperate fellow? These past days indicated his disposition as a man recovering from a drunken affair, sobering only under the watchful eyes of a diligent wife. Nevertheless, our popularity aboard the old barge *Captain Swan* will not protect us long. When opportunity presents itself, I am sure our adversary across the boat yonder will attempt to contact a local constable and apprehend you as a scoundrel."

The artist smiled as he whispered these words into his friend's ear. "Now for a more successful strategy, we should wait until nightfall and bind the old teetotaler, hand and foot. Then, while I flirtatiously engage his wife, you can discreetly lower him over the side and deposit the old fool into the canal's muddy bottom. Before the glorious sunrise, his submerged torso will have been run over by a multitude of similarly laden canal boats to the extent that his corpse will never have the opportunity to rise to the surface, securing forever hereafter not only his silence on your past heinous crimes, but also shoring up the framework of this great man-made wonder. We could even return, someday in the future, and commemorate the spot with a substantial monument in his honor as an upright citizen in pursuit of a fiend!" Bartlett paused, waiting for some response from his companion that was not forthcoming.

"Low bridge!" hollered the boat captain.

Bartlett stood, hunched over, glancing forward. "Why look, Higby, we may be too late for my elaborate plan's execution! We are entering a town of substantial size."

Jeduthan's eyes left Fleming's for a split second, finding his friend leaning out the side rail of the *Captain Swan* as the barge maneuvered into a canal lock. A steeple, plainly outlined in silhouette upon the towering sky, alerted him of their arrival at the nearby town. Jeduthan returned to his quarry and found to his horror that Fleming was seated no longer but rather had waddled forward. Standing upright in the bow of the barge, the old man attempted to contact the worker at the lock gate. Jeduthan folded his hands together in front of his face, surrendering to defeat. He was sure that his end had arrived and he would be condemned. The lock gates soon closed with a loud clang, much like his cell door would tightly slam shut in the local penitentiary a few minutes after his arrest. Slowly the boat began to rise.

"I tell you, I have to report a fugitive! Who is your sheriff? Inform him now that I have the criminal aboard this very boat!" Jeduthan heard Fleming shouting to an inattentive canal worker. "You there, I insist…"

The rushing water soon equalized the lock with the forward water and the bow lock gate opened. Jeduthan heard the faint sound of one of the Petersen children's cry, "Move on, Nimrod, Gray Sallie." The boat slid forward, Fleming still pleading for someone to hear his complaint. Nevertheless, no worker took notice of the enraged old man.

"Low bridge!" roared Petersen once more. Jeduthan sought his artist friend, who had moved forward nearer Fleming and engaged speaking to the madman. Captain Petersen's announcement must not have reached Fleming's ears, for within an instant the low bridge made contact with the old man's head, flinging his tall, stiff hat off his head while at the same time, engaging his skull in an unequal match. The impact sounded like a pumpkin dropped from some grocer's grip, cracking upon the ground. The old man toppled, face first onto the deck, as his hat skidded along the top canvas-covered main cabin of the *Captain Swan*. Slowly, as the boat proceeded forward, the hat remained relatively still behind the low bridge as if a giant knife might move a vegetable along a smooth cutting surface until the main cabin roof abruptly ended and the fine beaver hat toppled upon the deck.

Petersen, viewing the entire episode, refused to abandon his position at the boat's rudder. Jeduthan believed a slight smirk emerged from the boatman's lips. Fleming remained where he had fallen, no one rushing to his aid. His wife and children lingered in the far aft portion of the cabin, not having witnessed the incident.

All remained motionless during a long, deafening moment. Seconds seemed like eternity before Jeduthan rose from his seat and approached the morbid sight sprawled face first upon the deck. He surveyed the body. He imagined Fleming's head had severed or split open from the horrid sound of the impact. However, the only evidence of injury was a faint trickle of blood oozing from the old man's ear. This hatless figure, sprawled lifeless upon the deck, reminded him of stories told by his younger brother of the great *Battle of the Thames* during the late war, tales of how many dead bodies littered the field, some with few physical wounds while others mangled beyond recognition.

He wondered if Fleming's blood was upon his hands. He worried that the nightmares might return. Clutched in Fleming's lifeless hand was the wanted notice. Jeduthan slowly bent down, wrenched the parchment from the broken man's tight grip, and shoved it into his own pocket. Beside Bartlett, only two other young boys witnessed the event, both children of Captain Petersen. Jeduthan raised a finger to his lips and signed secrecy to the boys, who sat petrified as the assumed dead man moaned a deep, penetrating grumble.

Bartlett bent down and with the help of Jeduthan, rolled the old man's body face up. Immediately, they realized the man's condition was not immediately fatal. A large bruise formed under his left eye and a little blood slowly issued from the same ear, but the old man still breathed, although nearly imperceptibly. He remained unconscious as Jeduthan called for Petersen's assistance. The boatman declared that he had no time to commit to passengers, but soon Mrs. Fleming streamed to her husband's side.

"Dear Lord!" she cried. "What hath thou suffereth, my husband?"

Bartlett answered her query. "Fine lady, your husband and I were innocently conversing about possible business opportunities along this fair canal when he, unfortunately, failed to observe the recent low bridge spanning our route. I narrowly escaped the same fate myself. If his impact had not instinctively caused my bending just as the bridge passed above us, I too would not be standing here reciting the tale. I am also grateful he was not standing where I recently occupied because I have no doubt we both would have been decapitated, our heads traveling along yonder cabin rooftop as did your husband's fine hat. Providence be praised for sparing both our bodies from more serious injury! I only hope the Lord will spare our everlasting souls when we meet in heaven."

Mrs. Fleming's eyes reddened and a tear appeared upon her cheek. With a quivering voice she asked, "Would you assist me, dear gentlemen, with moving my husband's injured body aft toward our cushions and help with his comfort?"

Jeduthan responded affirmatively, "I would gladly assist you, ma'm." As he lifted Fleming's torso and Bartlett grabbed his feet, the pair, working in tandem, hauled the man to his quarters. The three Fleming children cowered away from their father's seemingly lifeless body, for he had not groaned since being moved. Jeduthan etched an affectionate smile upon his face for the unlucky children; however, they did not respond in kind.

Laying the old man upon blankets spread by Mrs. Fleming and propping his head upon a small brown package found nearby, Jeduthan addressed the gentlewoman. "I feel my actions have caused your husband's unfortunate condition."

"Nonsense, sir! The Lord our God has a well-defined plan for each of our souls. Our gracious savior has rewarded poor Mr. Fleming for his many years, and if he is called to return to heaven today, it must be God's will. No one may cause God to strike down a man, be it you, me, your companion, Mr. Petersen, or even one of my precious little children. He is all powerful and only His will be done." She adjusted her dress to better sit near her husband's injured body, applying comfort as best she could. Bartlett and Jeduthan withdrew with no more words, leaving the God-fearing woman to tend her God-tempting husband.

Regaining their seats next to the artist's trunk, the two men spoke softly.

"Higby, we must escape while Fleming remains unconscious."

"I don't see why we need to leave now. I have the wanted announcement in my pocket."

"When the old man awakens, he will again try to alert the authorities. Though he may not retain the identifying portrait upon his person, he will no doubt spark an interest among any person he communicates with that there is a possibility a fugitive is aboard the *Captain Swan*. Accordingly, we have only one option available to us, we must leave. The closely arranged locks in Schenectady will slow the barge so significantly that by the time the old man can make contact with the local sheriff, we will be long gone, safe amongst the crowded cities further east."

Jeduthan thought about his friend's proposal before raising the question of obtaining Nimrod from the crowded stables aboard the boat.

Bartlett retorted, "We will wait for a moment when the steed is on duty at the tow rope. When we reach a lock, we will alight from the barge, proceed with our luggage toward old Nimrod, and instead of re-embarking the horse, we shall free him. Loading our belongings upon his back, we will proceed upon our journey. Few will even notice our escape." The artist smiled as a child might who has successfully conquered some unforeseen obstacle.

"I will do as you request, as I am too disconcerted to propose any other means at fleeing," agreed Jeduthan, and both men lay backward to warm themselves in the afternoon sun.

Fleming remained comatose the rest of the day. However, as night approached, he began groaning loudly, annoying many passengers aboard the *Captain Swan*. One set of petite sisters spied in on him while he slept, giggling at some of the more exotic groans emitting from the old man. Another man began making odds as to his survival, gathering a pool of money with a set date for his expiration until poor Mrs. Fleming chastised him for his devilish, gambling ways. As for Jeduthan, each moan meant the continued existence of an enemy who could reveal his wayward past.

As the sun began its slow descent into the late afternoon sky the second day following Fleming's wounding, his wife appeared before Bartlett and Jeduthan. "Please come, Mr. Higby! My poor husband has been calling your name in his semiconscious state and I fear his last words are meant for you!"

Jeduthan looked for his friend's support and the artist agreed to join him. Mrs. Fleming led the way to a private area that the woman set aside for her ailing husband. As the two men entered, Fleming seemed to wrestle from his sleep somewhat, opening his eyes briefly but not recognizing either man. "Darling, Mr. Higby and his friend, Mr. Bartlett, have come to visit you. They are terribly concerned about your condition. I have re-assured them that providence will provide."

Fleming attempted to speak but could only muster a single recognizable word, "Intemperance!" He then shifted his head and fell into a stupor once again.

"Dear Mrs. Fleming," stated Bartlett. "I am sure your husband will recover, but he might take a considerable time doing so. He may have delusions even after fully awakening, possibly lasting many days. My medical training at Oxford, though not complete before my creative indulgences resulted in changing my professional career to that of an artist, lead me to speculate that his skull's impact upon the low bridge might necessitate extensive recovery in an asylum of sorts. We have traveled a great distance on this wondrous canal amidst many of our state's interior cities but I can only recommend returning on the next available packet to Buffalo in order to find a suitable institution for your husband's impending recovery."

"But Mr. Bartlett, we have come so far! Shouldn't we proceed, possibly to New York City?" inquired Mrs. Fleming.

"No, indeed not, fine lady. I have been afloat upon the mighty Hudson, and I assure you that the swift current, combined with the hefty rapids you must navigate, will so shake your feeble husband that death will surely await him before he reaches the supposed safety of that fine metropolis. No, a smooth, non-jarring ride to familiar settings is in his best interest. Besides, you ought to remain home if the Lord decides to take your poor husband to a better place."

"I suppose you are right, Mr. Bartlett. Our excursion along this watery canal was really only intended as a relaxing holiday, but the weather and unpalatable food has robbed us of any pleasure. Moreover, my husband's unfortunate accident has added a damper upon any excitement we had sought. Only your sketching and Mr. Higby's delightful musical expose' a few days past have brought cheer to my wonderful children. Oh, thank you gentlemen, for your kind heart during this, my most troubling moment. May God bless your travels!"

Both men bowed slightly as they slowly retreated to their accommodations. "Higby, we need to escape tonight. Nimrod will soon be removed from the stables for his turn at leading the team. You gather our belongings while I speak to Captain Petersen." The artist disappeared as Jeduthan arranged the assorted blankets and two substantial trunks in order to quickly retrieve them at the next lock. Then he sat down, glancing along the lengthening shadows cast across the towpath.

Twilight engulfed the night sky as Bartlett returned. "All arrangements are made. We will alight at Schenectady's first lock, and Petersen will be on hand to release Nimrod." The boat continued on its steady rate for two more hours before reaching the lock.

Lights along the canal illuminated parts of the town as it weaved its route next to many streets and alleys; however, the two traveling companions were already far from the canal's watery path, seeking new lodgings at this late hour.

Troy

The two compatriots trekked northward into the pitch black of night. The wind picked up its momentum and a chill crept into their bones. Rain began to fall, pelting their overcoats with sleet.

Jeduthan knew that misery would rule the night if they did not find shelter soon. In addition, doubt rested heavy on his mind. Doubt of their destination, doubt in his companion, and doubt in himself. Might their hasty retreat from the canal boat's dry shelter and comforting travel have been a mistake? Should he protest their change of course and propose a separation between his own and Bartlett's paths? No! Try as he might, he could not call forth protest against his companion's intrigues for catastrophe seemed to lurk in all his own plans for the future. None of his well-laid plans ever came to a successful finale. His tendency to faithful obedience continued to permeate his personality. Therefore, he surrendered to Bartlett's will and plodded onward, leading old Nimrod by the reigns, following the artist through the cold darkness to an unknown destination.

After several miles, Bartlett paused under a large woodshed. Inside the accompanying habitation, the men could hear boisterous laughter and song. "Higby, we must stop soon as this rain will surely creep into our joints, leaving us as infirmed as old Fleming. I propose this tavern be our night's lodging."

Jeduthan summed up all his will and dissented. "I can not consent to another Irish Tavern such as we experienced in Lockport many months ago. Please, let us inquire instead at that modest homestead across the path for boarding where we might secure dry, comfortable bedding, along with a decent meal in the morning." The artist's forlorn frown displayed his displeasure. Yet the older man stood his ground. "Will, this is not a game! We must regain our strength by bedding ourselves in a warm, hospitable environ."

Surprised by his friend's steadfastness, Bartlett grudgingly agreed. The two men crossed the muddy road and soon Bartlett vigorously banged upon the framed door with his clenched fist. A considerable period elapsed before an older women cracked open the door and viewed the soaked men by her candle's light.

"Dear madam, could we impose upon your kind heart to allow two wet and suffering travelers a night's lodging? We have journeyed far this evening after alighting from a barge on that majestic canal which traverses your quaint valley and have been caught in this deluge, which might become the death of both our poor souls," Bartlett begged, swallowing his pride and producing a toothy smile. Seemingly not moved by his polite words nor obtaining any semblance of pity from the old woman, the artist extracted a shiny coin from his pocket, flashing its silvery surface so that the candle's light reflected back into the old hag's eyes. Her countenance changed remarkably.

"Well sir, please enter my modest household. We will gladly find you a warm meal and a soft resting place," she responded as Bartlett passed through the entrance, discreetly handing her the coin. "We had planned to open our home to visitors on a regular basis as we hoped many packets would pass through our fair city. However, the canal's distant proximity from my homestead has proven such a plan a failure. We are far too remote from the canal to attract any but the most adventurous travelers."

"Adventurous traveler that we are," remarked Bartlett pushing through the door and onto the rough wooden floorboards.

Jeduthan followed his friend into the home. He observed that the structure contained one large open room spanning from the forward portion of the building all the way to the back section with a substantial hearth on the right. A small ladder, mounted on the back wall, ascended to a second floor. He found the construction rather odd and mentioned so to the woman.

"Yes sir, you are quite correct. Me, I am Susan George, and my husband, God rest his soul, had only recently redesigned our ground floor to act as a tavern of sorts." Bartlett grinned slyly. "But he passed on two months ago. It was of a poor heart most likely, no doubt resulting from his vain efforts at changing our modest household into a tavern inn. It now be only me, my dear daughter Emilee, and young

Paddy. Emilee reposes up yonder fast asleep and Paddy is due back soon from the woodshed to stoke our fire. Do, gentlemen, have a seat at my table and allow me to serve you some warm soup left in the pot from this evening's meal."

Mrs. George gestured toward the table and three chairs opposite the hearth while she fetched wooden bowls, dipping two large ladles of steaming soup into them. As Jeduthan sat, he sensed his mouth watering caused by the sweet soup's aroma that had long evaded his nostrils during his extensive canal voyage. As their hostess placed the bowls in front of them and after each traveler had taken a long sip, a young man heavily laden with firewood entered the home. The freezing rain drenching the neighborhood made his hat droop low in front of his eyes, obscuring his face. Dropping his pile, the boy lifted his eyes and gazed upon the two men as if he had seen a ghost.

"Mr. Higby! Is that ye?"

Mrs. George snapped, "Now Paddy, mind yourself and keep your mouth shut for the peace and quiet of our guests."

"Course yous' is dead, but even yous' spirit remember young Paddy, Paddy O'Neil don't ye? Cause iffin ye don' den I's have taken a beaten' for nuttin."

"Of course I remember you. Madam, we met young Patrick some time ago, working together near the western terminus of the canal at Lockport town. He came to my aid in a manner not unlike yourself tonight. When I needed directions, this young lad volunteered as guide," explained Jeduthan.

"Dat's right, Missees George. I'd bin mighty helpful to old Mr. Higby," bragged O'Neil.

"I hope the young ragamuffin has profited you and yours to a similar degree, Mrs. George," retorted Jeduthan as the woman adjusted the soup pot lid.

"He has only arrived a week ago, much like you two fine gentlemen. Nevertheless, in that brief time, he has been a lifesaver to Emilee and me. He does all what we need done about the house and even holds down a paying job fetching firewood for near the whole neighbor-hood." Turning to O'Neil, Mrs. George signaled, "Now Paddy, you fix a bedding down spot for these two gentlemen. They will be staying the night. I will leave Paddy to see to your needs. It is late and I must retire."

Both men stood as Mrs. George left the room, climbing the ladder to the upper floor. O'Neil approached Bartlett. "I dunno ye, mister. But iffin' yous' be wid Mr. Higby, I'd trust ye." The artist smiled, and for once, said nothing. "Mr. Higby, I thought you'd been muddered. Two week ago, dis' man comes and says, 'O'Neil' says he, 'I's suppose to fine ye and tell ye to go to de upper locks an inquire for Mr. Higby,' and den he gave me a coin, jus' like you's done dat aftanoon back den. I'd do what he done asked and not more den twenny minut's later, de sheriff shows up, an ruffs me up, tryin' to make me talk. But I don' talk. He switches me, but I don' talk. He takes his belt and whips me, but I still don' talk. By dat time, I'd be about to talk, but I's don't know whats' to say, so I's just says innythin' dat pops into me head. I's says you is at da *Eagle Hotel*, and then da *Washington House*, then da *Mansion* before I'd break, whichin' I's sorry to do and tellem' yous' R-U-N-N-O-F-T, to Buffalo. Well, dey leave me alone din, as dey figure I's don't know nuttin'. But, I's not wait for dem agin', so I's lit out of Lockport for good. Innyways, deys no more work there an I's was becomin' lonesome for me people. So's I's figured I's make me way back to da big cittie and fine someone who I's could hook up with. Das when I's fine ol' missees George and her girl, Emilee. Dey's take me in and I's been here ever since. I's figure iffin' she feed me well, I's do's her chores an I's think I's might even have eyes for Miss Emilee. She's mighty handsome!"

"Well, O'Neil, I am sorry for what happened to you back at Lockport," stated Jeduthan.

"Don't be Mr. Higby. I's feel like a real man now and don't need no hidin' and it was you who set me free. I's been on adventures ever since."

"We too have been adventurers of a sort, young man. We invite you to join us iffin' ye be willin'," retorted the artist, dropping into an Irish dialect.

"T'ank ye' buttin' I's be stayin' round here for a while yet, iffin' ye don' mind. But iffin' ye fine yous need inny hep, ye jus' call for young Paddy O'Neil. Promise?"

"Yes that is a promise, O'Neil," reassured Jeduthan. "As for tonight, we need to get a dry place to rest and recuperate from this chilling rain."

"I's got ye all settled in, gents," replied O'Neil pointing toward the hearth. "I's stoke up a nice bed of coals and lay some soft blankets on de floor and in no time, ye be sleepin' like little babies. Yous get comfortable while I see to ye horse."

Jeduthan thanked the boy and reclined upon the blankets. Bartlett warmed his hands by the fire as the older man slowly closed his eyes and fell into a deep sleep.

Light shown through the window the next morning as Jeduthan awoke. He felt rested and relaxed, a feeling that had eluded him since Fleming's wounding. He sat up and searched for his artist friend, finding him quietly relaxed in a rocking chair, feet propped upon a short stool, toes wiggling in the radiant heat from the hearth's fire. "Good morn, old man. I think's I's found heaben'. Warm fire, plenty vittles, smilin' ladyfolk, and a young Irish lad at me callin'."

Jeduthan laughed at the image of William H. Bartlett, adventurer and traveler, fancying the life in a plainly furnished home. However, the Bartlett he had come to know was a master of deception. Nevertheless, though slightly mischievous, the artist was never conniving, devious, or hateful.

"I have sent young O'Neil fetching the morning post and after breakfasting with Mrs. George and fair young Emilee," a twinkle lit in Bartlett's eye, "We will be off in search of our final destination, ending our great Erie Canal adventure."

"Where do you have in mind, Will? I do not believe that your adventuring will ever come to an end."

"That is probably so, dear friend. Nevertheless, I must soon travel to New York City to deposit my sketches with my employer and settle my accounts. However, before I go, I will introduce you to my favorite cousin here in America. She is no doubt, my only cousin, but she still is my favorite! Moreover, she resides only a few miles from this spot, across the great Hudson in the bustling city of Troy. I, though, must carefully contemplate my plan of action, as her fastidious husband does not favor my company to the same degree. Now be off with you, as I contemplate." The artist shooed Jeduthan with a waggle of his hand.

The older man obeyed, withdrawing to the backyard where, displayed before his eyes, were the results of the magnificent ice storm of the previous night. The bright sunlight glistened off thousands of ice-covered tree limbs, bending low from the immense weight of frozen water. As the temperature warmed the air, water droplets gracefully fell from the overhanging trees, reminding him of a cold mountain stream sprinkling from a precipice. He spied Mrs. George at the well, retrieving a bucket of water while, running along the street, came O'Neil, newspaper in hand.

"Mr. Higby! Can ye please deliver this to Mr. Will?" The boy handed the newspaper to Jeduthan and without stopping his jaunt, directly reported to Mrs. George. Jeduthan glanced at the paper. It was the *Troy Sentinel*. The front sported the usual advertisements that dot the pages of most periodicals; apparel available at a shirt manufacturer; wagon wheel repair services at a local wheelwright; a special report concerning progress of the *Champlain Canal*; a large engraving of the *Erie Canal's* towpath.

Towpath! Jeduthan studied the engraving's details finding his stump, Bartlett's rock seat, eagle's nest, and far in the sky, a lone bird circling! This was Bartlett's sketch, published in the *Troy Sentinel*! He looked for a caption and below, in very fine print, he read, "*Scene Along The Erie Canal; Humanity is duty bound by God to tend, tame and garden Earth's pastures but only eagles are truly free.*" That was not his caption! They left out the important reference to nature's pond, grandfather toad, mosquitoes, and the natural world. Angered, he folded the paper under his arm and exploded into the inn's room where his friend rested in the rocking chair warming his feet by the embers.

"Will, the paper has printed our engraving!"

"*Our* engraving?"

"Well, your engraving, but my caption! Moreover, they have changed my words. I am..."

"Outraged? Angry? Irate? Annoyed? Don't be, my friend," retorted the artist.

"The paper totally mistook my meaning, Will!"

"They only had so much space dedicated for the engraving. It happens all the time. Many of my best sketches have lost their meaning to the engraver's knife. You must forget this incident, be pleased that your words are paraphrased, and continue on with your life. Don't fret over topics out of your control." The artist paused, letting those prophetic words sink into Jeduthan's mind. "Now, old man, please hand me my paper." Bartlett's outstretched hand dangled in midair a few seconds, waiting for his friend to lay the paper within his grasp. Jeduthan relented with a sigh. "Now, Higby, we will be leaving in a few moments and I require you to bind my trunks to old Nimrod and prepare for our journey. I expect a long hike today but do not worry, as we will have comfortable lodgings by evening. I will join you soon after I peruse the *Sentinel*."

Jeduthan obediently bowed his head, defeated by Bartlett's rationale. A wag by his friend's hand dismissing him signaled his retreat outside. There, he forlornly accepted his task and prepared for the pair's journey.

Taking their leave of Mrs. George and O'Neil, the companions left town following a farm road northeasterly. About mid-afternoon, they reached a towering bluff overlooking a grand river. "The Hudson, my boy!" exclaimed Bartlett as if he were announcing a wondrous natural monument.

"I know, Will," stated Jeduthan mechanically. "I traveled through this country many years ago as I brought my wife to the wilderness from Middletown, Connecticut. It does not impress me."

The artist's pouty lip extended, as if his feelings were hurt. "We must make for yonder bridge before nightfall in order to arrive at our intended destination at my planned time."

"What is your intended destination?" inquired Jeduthan, still expressing his discontent since the engraving episode of the morning.

"Cheer up, dear Higby! We will dine with influential society tonight, a very willing audience, I am sure, for your enlightening captionizations that the beastly *Sentinel* newspaper has so unfairly manipulated. Let us travel!" Bartlett extended his arm as if on some great safari surrounded by the wilderness' fierce creatures.

The sun descended into the western sky nearly as rapidly as the two travelers dropped into a canyon-like valley. Soon, the awaiting bridge graced their eyes. Stretching across the flowing waters a full 800 feet, it presented a grand sight, illuminated by the orange hues of the setting sun. A short, stumpy man appeared at the bridge's gate and Bartlett passed a single coin to him as payment. The man opened the gate and the two men, guiding Nimrod laden with all their belongings, crossed the mighty Hudson. They entered immediately a quaint village on the opposite shore. The town had placed a shingle at the bridge's end inscribed with *Lansingburgh*.

"Not far now, Higby! Here, we turn south." The two men walked forward in silence as the small, pleasant village thinned to only a few homes scattered along the road. Turning a bend, the approaching twilight illuminated a church steeple, standing erect and defiant, with one last ray of light reflecting from its brass cross adorning its imposing spire.

Jeduthan broke the silence. "Is this our destination?"

"Yes my dear Higby, it is! We must only find my cousin's residence in this fair city. Your eyes behold, or will on the morrow, the great metropolis of Troy. Just as in mythological times, we Greeks come bearing gifts, and I hope my beloved cousin Betsy Howard Hart will readily accept us with her customary reception."

Troy was a grand city indeed, very prosperous and thriving. Along the western portion of the path, larger and larger buildings seemed to sprout from the darkness. The smell of sulfuric coal smoke and the telltale signs of iron smelting permeated the air. This was truly the first large city that Jeduthan had seen, a far cry from the frontier villages along the canal.

"How are you related to your cousin Betsy?" inquired Jeduthan.

"Her father's, mother's, grandfather and my mother's father's uncle were uncle and nephew back in jolly old England, or that is how the rumor goes. I do not quite know how distant cousins we are, but my family and hers have been corresponding for years. When I chose to travel to this fair land, I sought her out. I visited them and we experienced many exciting times before I abandoned them for my grand adventure along the canal. We even traveled by carriage along the towpath with her father on a sort of field trip last spring. It was then I decided upon wandering the backwoods. The majestic sunset so captivated my senses that I felt a calling for the wilderness. I had only been gone from their

loving embrace a few hours when I stumbled upon your sorrowful personage."

"That I was, dear friend," replied Jeduthan.

"Now, old fellow, we will have the attentive eye of the most hospitable American I have encountered in this fair country, awaiting our arrival. Dear Betsy is the centerpiece and grandest hostess of this fine city. Her father, William Howard, a successful banker and merchant, has only recently endowed her with a fine, newly constructed home upon Second Street. As I visited her this spring past, it was only under construction and unoccupied. I met the architect, a young man by the name of Colegrove. He very much impressed me with his skill. I promised him a sketch of the building when I returned. Now that I have survived the perils of the western wilderness, I no doubt will uphold my promise." The artist paused to examine a street corner sign and exclaimed, "We have arrived, Higby! There, in the enveloping hand of darkness, stands our retreat." The two men stood in front of an imposing townhouse and, though the darkness hid its grandeur, the multitude of lit candles adorning the windowsills impressed them.[8]

---

[8] The best description of the Hart Residence is the excellent architectural investigation found in *The Marble House in Second Street, Biography of a Town House and Its Occupants, 1825-2000*, Rensselaer County Historical Society, Troy, NY, 2000. This work with the accompanying narratives by Douglas Bucher, Stacy Draper, and Walter Wheeler brought this Shimmering House of Troy to life. No visit to Troy ought to miss a visit and tour of this magnificent building. Many thanks to Stacy Draper for an in-depth look at the building and a delightful discussion of the Hart family, the original owners. (Summer 2008)

Bartlett approached, raised a large brass eagle knocker, and announced with its heavy clang his appearance. Swiftly, the door opened and revealed a short Negro woman, elderly, but with a refined face, gazing upon the stranger in wonderment. "Well, I's be! Hello, Massa Will! 'Tis good to see ya agin."

"Nice to hear your comforting voice once again, too, Aunt Sallie," replied the artist.

"Yous better get inside youngin', before de chill eat righ' down to ya bones," said the Negro as she beckoned Bartlett into the central hall. "It's bin too long dat yous been away. Misses Betsy, she will jes' be so pleased to see ya agin, too."

"Where is my cousin?"

"She be in de palor jes now, entertainin' I s'pose. I'll fetch her right away."

The old servant disappeared, leaving the two men in the warm hallway. After a few moments, the woman reappeared with a three-candle stand. "She be wid ya in a minit, Massa Will."

"Aunt Sallie, could you show my friend Higby where to stable our horse? We have been on the road for a long day's walk and with night coming along, our old steed needs rest. Higby, you can join Cousin Betsy and me after Nimrod is settled."

Jeduthan exited the home with Aunt Sallie. The old woman continued talking to herself about *Massa Will's* visit as they stepped into the street and untethered Nimrod. Leading, the old Negro woman walked along a short stone facade and through a tall gate. Loose stone underfoot crunched under Nimrod's weight as they passed through an unfinished garden. A few stark barren saplings stood guard in the dark parcel and loose marble lay scattered about, glistening in the moon's faint light. Stepping through the dark toward the rear shed, a pale glow reflected from the building's whitewashed brick. Its great height and sturdy construction impressed Jeduthan. When the old woman opened one of its heavy gates, Jeduthan was startled for in one of the building's five bays was a luxurious coach reflecting the candles' light with its polished brass fixtures. "Such incredible wealth," thought Jeduthan. However, the old Negro seemed unmoved as she continued jabbering on about how nice a visit with *Massa Will* would please her mistress.

Soon, Bartlett hailed Jeduthan from the residence's back stoop. "Higby, come in here! This way!"

Jeduthan quickly stepped to the rear entrance of the grand home and into the small hallway where his friend stood. "Let us enter the parlor where my cousin has already greeted me. We will stay here tonight, as I have told you we would, and look for suitable temporary lodgings on the morrow. Tonight though, do not mention any of our needs; only enjoy the company we meet."

The two men entered a large room decorated with three plush, low backed chairs along with one dark, wooden seat in front of a large desk containing spaces for ledger sheets and a substantial glass-encased bookshelf. There were paintings on all four walls of important personages, along with one portrait of their hostess. Jeduthan spied a faint signature on the portrait as *W. H. Bartlett.*

"Good evening Professor Higby." An attractive young woman adorned in a fine lavender silk dress sat on the wooden seat. Her eyes were a deep, impassioned brown that matched her long, auburn curls flowing over her shoulders. She outstretched an arm, offering her hand. Jeduthan clasped her milky, white hand and gently kissed its soft flesh. He smelled a flowery fragrance upon her being.

She continued, "I am glad you could join us. Cousin Will has explained your relationship and I am honored that my beloved cousin has inadvertently stumbled upon your acquaintance. I hope you will share, before leaving us, some of your vividly descriptive phraseology that accompany so many of Will's sketches." Turning to Bartlett she continued, "However tonight, let us first hear from you dear Will, of your wilderness adventures of recent."

Bartlett announced, "Professor, may I introduce my cousin, Mrs. Betsy Howard Hart." A loud cough resounded from behind the opened door. "Oh yes, less we forget, her husband, Mr. Richard P. Hart, banker and investor in our marvelous Erie Canal, which we have become so intimate with these past months."

"Good evening sir," Jeduthan stated, slightly confused by his friend's introductions.

"I am glad you have visited our good city, professor," stated Mr. Hart, hand outstretched. "I would love to discuss your impressions of our completed canal. Good God, it sure has cost me plenty."

Betsy glared at her husband annoyingly. "No talk of business tonight, Mr. Hart. Our guests are weary and should only relate pleasant thoughts concerning their adventures." She turned to Bartlett before continuing. "Pray tell, cousin, what adventures have crossed your path since last April?" Mrs. Hart's disposition toward Bartlett was considerably different from her own husband. She was warm, smiling, and flirtatious toward the artist while cold and abrupt with her husband. Mr. Hart conceded to her will and remained silent most of the remaining evening.

"After leaving your gracious abode, I journeyed forth, westward," explained the adventurous artist. "Sometimes I walked, sometimes I rode the stage, but mostly I glided gently along inside a lazy packet boat on the still waters of the canal." He used his hands to simulate his journey. Two fingers identified his vigorous walking, then jerky hands for the stage ride, and finally long gliding sweeps of his arms for the smoothness of the packet.

Bartlett continued, "I ate well the first week, until the canal boat became stranded in the mud. It was then I alighted and spied a work camp where I took board, offering my own hands at laboring on the canal's towpath." Bartlett secretively winked at Jeduthan. "The work was terribly difficult, and often I returned to my soggy tent with blistered hands and mud-caked feet, dead to the world. I could only drop upon my blankets in a heap, unable even to find the nourishment for which my poor bruised body ached. By and by though, my limbs became used to the drudgery of labor for, you see, as I removed stumps, rocks, felled trees and debris from the towpath, my body becoming accustomed to the hard work that toughened muscles." He flexed his forearms attempting to harden his muscles. Betsy grasped one arm and pursed her lips in awe of male strength. "But as I saw no fulfillment in the repetitive tasks for which many sell their physical strength, I drew my meager wage and departed. Soon, I journeyed forth with my sketchpad, eagerly seeking picturesque scenes to record for my clients William Cullen Bryant and the *New York Review and Athenaeum*. Immediately, I found my first scene that your own newspaper here in Troy has recently found fit to print. A contrasting view, one of man aggressively shaping nature for his own benefit and another of the last gasps of a natural world untouched by humanity. The caption was written by Professor Higby."

Jeduthan raised a finger in protest, however the artist added, "But the editors altered the caption to fit their own needs. Professor Higby's was far better than the *Sentinel's*."

Betsy turned, smiled, and inserted, "Do, professor, enlighten us with your original caption."

Slightly startled by the request, Jeduthan demurred. Bartlett began again with his narrative, but Mrs. Hart insisted. "Please, professor! Let us hear your enlightening words!"

Picking up the engraving displayed in the newsprint and holding it so that Mrs. Hart could view it in the candlelight, Jeduthan spoke. *"Eagles fly free, bound to no one. Humanity is duty bound by God to tend, tame and garden Earth's pastures as grandfather toad is bound to the waters of nature's pond, ridding its murky waters of the ever-present mosquitoes. Only the eagle is truly free."*

"How poignant and heartfelt! It radiates the contrasting beauty brought forth from dear Cousin Will's talented pencil strokes," beamed Mrs. Hart.

"Yes, heartfelt," stated the artist, slightly annoyed that he had lost the affectionate attention of his young cousin. "...To continue, I found lodging at the frontier town of Lockport, where double locks are carved from nature's hearth. It is there that I met the professor. He was entertaining the Marquis de Lafayette at *Washington House* with his musical instrument, the Schei..., Sheitt...,"

"Scheitholt," interjected Jeduthan.

"Yes, yes, whatever you call it. We dined together and soon became fast companions. Deciding to become adventurers together, we journeyed to Buffalo and witnessed the gruesome execution of the Thayer Brothers. Well, it was at that time that we decided to abandon the canal for the wilderness. We viewed mighty waterfalls, great battlefields of old, tall British ships sailing the enormous Ontario Lake, a mighty fortress guarding the swift Niagara's mouth, and even ventured into upper Canada. As the weather began to chill though, we set our aim to the canal once again, homeward bound. For nearly three weeks now we have endured crowded boats, smelly teamsters, rancid provisions, and even a dastardly villain before we stumbled upon your humble steps." Bartlett's lip protruded in his ever increasingly sympathetic expression.

"How great your adventures have been, cousin!"

"On the morrow, I plan to purchase passage to New York City, dear Betsy."

"Oh, no! You must stay longer," she begged. "I miss your company so, and there is stupendous news, a new school has opened in our fair community. You must come and visit its campus. Ever since Mrs. Emma Willard has blessed our city with her *Troy Female Seminary* a few years ago, others have showed similar interest in academia. Mr. Stephen Van Rensselaer gathered interested parties together last year to discuss and found a new polytechnic institute. It specializes, the men say, in instructing persons in the application of sciences to the common purposes of life. He has hired Mr. Amos Eaton as headmaster and *The Rensselaer School* has held classes this past year in the Old Bank Place at the north end of town. You most likely passed the building tonight as you made your way here to our home. Mr. Eaton has hinted that he might even open some classes to the fairer sex." Mr. Hart looked up with a start as if this was unwelcome news. "But as the tuition is twenty-five dollars, the student body is still very limited."

"That news is indeed splendid, dear Betsy, but I still need to leave to fulfill my commission with the paper," replied the artist.

A sly smile inched its way across Mrs. Hart's lips. Evidently, much like her cousin, Betsy Howard Hart had a scheming mind. "Darling Will Bartlett," she pouted. "I know how you so enjoy art. Daddy was only recently bragging about your talent and proved it with exhibiting your exquisite sketch of last April." The woman pointed to her portrait hung along the wall. All eyes moved toward the work. "I expect he would love to present the talented artist of such a wonderful portrait to the general population of Troy personally. Would you have time enough to postpone your southward journey until he may set up an expose'?" Mrs. Hart fluttered her long eyelashes alluringly at Bartlett, while her husband's eyes narrowed.

Bartlett characteristically paused, raised a wandering hand to his chin, stroking its short whiskers as if in deep contemplation.

"Please, dear cousin!" she begged.

"If you insist, yes! Of course, I will," announced the artist in a great show of affection.

"How wonderful! Mr. Hart? Will you, early tomorrow morning, stroll down to dearest daddy's home along the river and consult with him about making all the arrangements to present Cousin Will to our grand city?" She did not wait for an affirmative answer before continuing. "Now Will, what will you wear? I believe we can find you suitable clothing amongst my husband's suits. Oh, Aunt Sallie! Sallie, where are you? You never seem to be able to find the old woman when you need her. Oh, Sallie! There you are. Now, I want you to locate, among Mr. Hart's dress suits, a fine example for Cousin Will and alter it to fit superbly. We have a party to attend!" Betsy had worked herself into an excited fervor as Jeduthan yawned obtrusively. "Oh, my dear! I am so sorry. You must be exhausted, both of you. We will find room for you. Mr. Hart, show Professor Higby to our guest quarters. Cousin Will will be along soon."

Jeduthan nodded in agreement. He followed Mr. Hart into the hall and up an impressive stairway two levels to a large room containing an elaborate bed, reclining sofa, and a trundle.

"I hope you will be comfortable here. Our children are staying at our previous residence a few doors down Second Street, so we are able only to offer you sparse accommodations. You may need to pull the trundle bed from under because I believe Mr. Bartlett will be sleeping here also. I will send one of our Irish servants to see to your lavatory but as we still have some construction underway in the other rooms, she may not be available until tomorrow."

"Thank you for your hospitality, Mr. Hart. I will be just fine," responded Jeduthan.

"Then sir, I'll take my leave." Mr. Hart retreated from the room, leaving Jeduthan alone.

It was true, he was extremely tired, but still somewhat confused, and his mind was full of questions. A professor? Why did Bartlett exaggerate his adventures? Who was Mrs. Emma Willard and how was her new school different from other academies? Why did Mr. Hart flagrantly allow his wife to flirt with her young cousin? Although his artist friend sometimes stretched the truth, his cousin Betsy was definitely a schemer also. Her actions tonight demonstrated her abilities to get what she wanted. However, was she sincere?

Jeduthan hoped for answers, but for now, he welcomed rest. He pulled off his boots and for the first time in weeks, completely undressed as he snuggled amongst the soft bedding of the trundle. He left the main bedstead for Bartlett, as no doubt he would demand it upon his arrival later.

The next morning, Jeduthan slept late, awakening with an energized feeling. The soft mattress upon which he slept, with its clean sheets and the warm dry room added to his ecstasy. He turned seeking his friend but frowned when he did not see Bartlett's customary protruding feet and nose. However, evidence revealed that his friend had slept in the room, for the great bed's sheets lay disheveled and the artist's two trunks were sprawled on the floor, opened with their contents spread about.

He dressed, replacing his dirty shirt with a spare he found from his companion's trunk. He sported a dandy tie that he thought was appropriate for a professor. He found himself playing Bartlett's game, becoming whom his friend expected. He worried that someday, this facade would lead to his doom. Nevertheless, rather than resist, he consented to Bartlett's scheme. His fate rested solidly with his young friend.

Jeduthan descended the staircase as Aunt Sallie stood at the front door waving her arm vigorously to someone in the street. "I'll do jes' dat' Miss Betsy!" She closed the door and turned to find Jeduthan standing only a few feet away. She let fly a short squeal, startled by his proximity. "Fessor Higby? Ya' done scar'd me nearly to def. Ya' ain't s'pose to 'neek up on a soul such. Innyways, Miss Betsy told me to look afta' ya' today an we's be startin' wid some harty breakfast. Come 'long now, we's get you's fed right dis mornin'."

The old woman led him down the hallway and a flight of stairs into the kitchen. "You's sit right thar' an' I see's to your meal. Hope's you's like your eggs scrambled. Miss Betsy always wants her's dattaway. She an Massa Will, dey wen to' see da new school at dat ol' bank shack. Deys should be back by noon."

The servant heaped a large generous portion of scrambled eggs, three long strips of bacon, and four large biscuits upon his plate. The meal was so warm that steam filled the air. He closed his eyes and remembered at home how his mother used to prepare huge meals for the working boys. He imagined the smell of bacon saturating the homestead and freshly baked biscuits, sweetened with butter and grape jam, filling his warm belly so long ago. Often there was so much food that the pigs would feast upon the table remnants.

"I's asks you a question!" a ringing voice bellowed. It was Aunt Sallie.

"I am sorry, Aunt Sallie. The wonderful aroma from your superbly prepared breakfast overcame me. What did you ask?"

The old woman widened her eyes slightly. "We's eat like dis' everyday. I's asks ya', is ya' married?"

A little shocked, Jeduthan hesitated before replying, "I once was, Aunt Sallie. But that was far away from here and a long, long time ago." He somberly lowered his head.

"I's sorry for dey subject 'Fessor, but I's warn ya dat Miss Betsy likes to set peoples up afta' deys loss a wif. Iffin' I's be you, de less said, de better!" Aunt Sallie whispered with a wink.

The servant's question filled Jeduthan with worry. His abandonment of Florinda nine months before ached at his soul for the weeks he labored on the canal, alone. Then the adventurous Willaim H. Bartlett entered his life and became his friend. Over the summer months, his anger, resentment, and bitterness subsided. He then slept peacefully, his haunting memories of his wife fading, leaving him with blissful slumber. Now, he worried that the cruel memories would return for he was comfortably situated in a home rather than on some wide-ranging adventure with a trusted friend. Would nightmares beckon him to return to a life he so long ago abandoned? Aunt Sallie's voice interrupted his thoughts once again.

"I's gots so much work to do roun' here t'day, 'Fessor. What'cha goin' to do? Iffin you'd don' mine, I's be leavin' fo' a while to go to da butchr'. You's make you'self at home while I's be gone!"

"Aunt Sallie, I would gladly do that errand for you. I would like to see the town in the daylight and this would be just my opportunity. Would you allow me to seek out the butcher?"

"I's dunno', 'Fessor. You's be da gues' an' I's be da servant." She paused, eyeing Jeduthan's frame. "I's s'pose, iffin you's promise to not tell Miss Betsy, I's lets ya. She can be a hard woman when she's wants to."

The old woman gave simple directions to the town's butcher shop and instructed Jeduthan to ask "…for Uncle Sam. He's know's 'zactly what I's want. R'member, dey butcher shop is on Ferry Street." The Negro woman bid him farewell as she pointed him down the street.

He left the front steps and reaching the street, appreciated the sight of the impressive neighborhood. An imposing, two story white marble house with cellar windows, the Hart home was by far the grandest dwelling on the entire avenue. It's exquisitely arched window with spider web pattern framed above the street entrance testified to the owner's wealth and standing in the community. The other houses on Second Street were also fine architectural examples of superb construction, but none reached the grandeur of the Hart residence.

Tracing the path according to Aunt Sallie's instructions, he reached Ferry Street where he could see the river a few hundred paces in the distance. At the river's edge, a large, flat wooden barge rested, no doubt the ferry. On both sides of the street stood a variety of shops; a tailor, a dry goods store, a blacksmith's forge, two livery stables, and his destination, Sam Wilson's Butcher Shop.

Meandering toward the meat market, his mental image of a quaint town upon the mighty Hudson was rudely interrupted. On the far street corner, next to one of the livery stables, stood two burnt shells, skeletons of tall wooden structures, starkly contrasting with the other buildings on the street. They cast a dark shadow upon the boulevard as if a huge conflagration had consumed the entire block. The gloom that these two structures shed foretold a tragic history that must have recently enveloped the town.

Jeduthan dismissed the gloom and entered the butcher shop. Standing behind a wooden carving table was a tall, elderly gentleman with graying hair. Their eyes met.

"How do, young fellow?" The man did not recognize Jeduthan's advanced age. "What can I do for you?"

"Aunt Sallie from the Hart residence sent me here to inquire about some meat. She instructed me to ask for Uncle Sam, and he would know exactly what she wanted. Are you Uncle Sam?"

"That would be me, sonny," replied the butcher. He retrieved a set of spectacles from his pocket and gingerly placed them upon his arched nose. "Forgive me sir, I cannot see past my own arms without the aid of these blasted spectacles." He paused to adjust the glasses before continuing. "Yes, I am Uncle Sam. Most people seem to call that. Given name is Samuel Wilson, originally from Massachusetts, but now I call Troy home. What is your name, stranger?"

"Jeduthan Higby from Connecticut, but now a voyager of sorts." He worried that he might have exposed his identity, but the meat cutter seemed unconcerned.

"I knows Aunt Sallie, and I will have it ready in a minute." The butcher pulled a side of beef from his case. "I just slaughtered this beef last night and Aunt Sallie always asks for the rump." He began carving with his sharp knives.

"Mr. Wilson, why did Aunt Sallie call you Uncle Sam? I was expecting a Negro, the same as her."

"People have called me Uncle Sam nearly a decade now, son. They started when the national government contracted me to provide salted beef for our militia on the Canadian Front. I labeled the barrels U.S. as I thought all government property should thus be labeled along with my name, Samuel Wilson. Some fool soldier thought US stood for Uncle Sam, and I've had the title ever since. I don't mind though, and the bit of fame has helped out business, too." The butcher took a sheet of brown paper and wrapped the beef tightly, handing the meat to Jeduthan. "There you go, young man. You tell Aunt Sallie that Mr. Hart came by here early this morning, all itchy about something. I could tell he was very excited."

"Thank you, Mr. Wilson…"

"No boy, call me Uncle Sam! Everyone else does, so you should not be the exception."

"Sorry, Uncle Sam." Jeduthan turned and exited the building, the door closing quickly behind, loudly clanking the frame. The wind had picked up while he conversed with Uncle Sam and clouds appeared in the western sky. He recognized the weather all too clearly for as on the frontier such clouds were bound to produce heavy snows. Therefore, instead of returning to Aunt Sallie and the Hart home, Jeduthan decided to wander the town for the morning, scouting the streets and becoming more acquainted with the town's layout before the poor weather enveloped the city.

Along the riverfront wharves abounded, evidence of Troy's mercantile trade. New construction filled the streets even while remains of burnt buildings told a story of a great fire, which no doubt recently ravaged the town. Iron mills and forges dominated the Postenkill, a small creek that carved a large ravine in the town's center. Some of the shop buildings donned iron storefronts, an elegant luxury never found in frontier villages. There were also at least four bookshops serving the city. He was determined to browse their collections during his stay. However, what seemed to interest him most was the *Troy Female Seminary* only a few blocks from the town's waterfront. This must be Mrs. Willard's school, of which Bartlett's cousin referred. He had not believed that women should be ordained ministers and to see such a Seminary appalled him.

As he made a final turn onto Second Street and toward the Hart residence, he noticed a newspaper office advertised as the *Troy Sentinel*. He worried that its pages might reveal his sordid past. Therefore, he concluded to keep a regular watch, within its leafs, for any advertisement that may betray his identity. However, for now, he would play along with Bartlett's game of hiding in the masses of this crowded city.

He entered the Hart home from its rear door. The sound of his boots on the highly polished floor announced his presence. He looked for Aunt Sallie, but instead he heard her call "Fessor Higby! Dat you? We's be in here."

Bartlett was sitting on a sofa opposite his cousin. Passing by Aunt Sallie, Jeduthan secretly placed the wrapped meat upon a table behind the servant who picked up the package and exited quietly.

"Ah, Professor! Cousin Betsy and I have been gallivanting about town these past hours and have paid you no attention. Aunt Sallie informs us that you have found that wandering the fair streets of Troy have peaked your interest."

"Yes Mr. Bartlett, Troy does hold some interesting prospects. Most impressive, and yet disturbing, is the *Troy Female Seminary*. I do not approve…"

"Oh, Professor Higby! Please do not condemn our local female seminary," interjected Mrs. Hart. "It is not a seminary for ordaining the clergy, but more of a local school for girls. Many in our region frown upon women's education, especially outside the domestic realm. Only grammar school is offered to the weaker sex. However, Mrs. Willard's school has finally given women a chance to expand their minds farther than only tasks of domesticity."

"Then why the name?" inquired Jeduthan.

"So our investors will contribute. They frown upon higher education for women unless it is only to better understand our religion."

"That is correct, dear cousin," added the artist. "Women need an avenue to better themselves instead of relying only upon men. That is a truly noble pursuit! Possibly, in the near future, our dear female companions may someday even gain the franchise. I am definitely for it. I truly believe women are not the weaker sex, but by far the stronger. It reminds me of many of our great leaders. I was once told, *behind every great man stands an even greater woman.*" He paused before adding, "*...and a surprised mother-in-law!*" Bartlett giggled as his cousin raised her hand to her mouth, a little piqued. "You see, great men all have women who have tamed them." His comment caused a smile to appear upon the entire company.

Jeduthan sat opposite of the hostess and politely listened as his companion continued with his diatribe. "Women, at present, lack the basic education to function in our world. Here and now, they lack a legal identity. They cannot own property in their own names. They cannot act as guardians of their own children. They cannot even act as agents for their own benefit. No document signed by a woman has any legality in our community today. Therefore, I believe the first step in endowing women with any sense of worth, legality, or equity, must begin with educational opportunity. Only with education can the complexities of a man's world give women hope."

Mrs. Hart clapped her hands gently. "Oh, I so agree with you, Cousin. Women must be given hope!"

"...And to accomplish that goal, we must support the efforts of Mrs. Willard and her..." the front door opened and Mr. Hart's appearance interrupted Bartlett's little speech.

"Good afternoon, all," said Mr. Hart. "I have some exciting news for you, Betsy. I have talked to your father and he has agreed that Mr. Bartlett should be honored by a reception."

The hostess grinned and again clapped her hands delicately as her husband continued, directing the request to the artist. "Mr. Howard, your uncle of sorts, has requested that you be received by our most recent entrepreneur, Mr. Amos Eaton. He requests that you be an honored guest speaker to his popular and applied practical educational institute that is holding its second semester of classes here in Troy. Can I reply to Mr. Howard's invitation in the affirmative?"

"How fantastic!" barked Mrs. Hart. "You could speak on a practical application of your artistic endeavors. Yes, yes, you must agree, Cousin!"

Bartlett eyed Mr. Hart suspiciously, doubtful to his sincerity. However, he shifted his glance to his eagerly awaiting, naive cousin. If Mr. Hart meant treachery in this seemingly magnanimous gesture, the artist was determined to turn it back on him somehow.

He allowed a long pause to hover over the company before nonchalantly stating, "For you, dear Cousin Betsy, I acquiesce. Please Mr. Hart, convey to the prodigious banker, your father-in-law and my dear Uncle William, my sincere desire to be the honored guest of whom he seeks."

Mr. Hart's sly smile dissolved as his wife erupted in joy. "How wonderful of father! I know you will be superb!" Turning to her husband, she inquired, "When is the occasion?"

"Mr. Howard has requested Mr. Eaton to arrange for the lecture tomorrow evening," replied Mr. Hart dismally and mechanically.

"Fine! Done! Higby, we will search for suitable accommodations tomorrow morning. In the afternoon, we shall dine with my fine relatives and then meet the town elders in the evening. There, I will give them a lesson on the practical application of art. Cousin, I beg forgiveness for I must retire for the evening. An adventurous day has burdened me and I must rest. No doubt, tomorrow must surpass today's excitement. Good evening. Professor Higby, you must assist me with my plans for the morrow?"

The party stood as the companions departed for their upstairs room. Entering, Jeduthan announced, "Will, I thought we were going to keep a low profile here in Troy. How can we do that if you are invited to give a lecture?"

"Patience, old man! We cannot just abandon life because of some phobia that haunts your mind from a past existence. Besides, after I conduct my business affairs in New York City, I plan to return here, enjoying my cousin's hospitality at least until spring again warms the earth and we can set off on further adventures in America's wilderness. Maybe then, we could explore the trans-Mississippi!" Reaching into his satchel, the artist extracted a sketch of the double locks at Lockport and handed it to his partner. "Will you please enhance my sketch with a captivating maxim? You can take your time. I am in no hurry. Thank you, dear professor."

"And why," retorted Jeduthan, "have you saddled me with such a title? I grant you that I was a lay preacher, a learned man, and I do enjoy reading and exquisite language, however I am not a university trained academic. I worry, Will, that the compounding of our fabrications will lead to a tragic end."

"You mean, our lies?"

Bowing his head in shame as a defeated man, Jeduthan replied, "Yes, our lies."

"Again, dear Higby, I have everything in order. After finding your quarters tomorrow, you may lay low while I contend with my business in the big city. Tonight, though, we must rest."

Bartlett undressed and slipped into the feather bed, quickly falling asleep. Jeduthan was less assured of their future. As he lay upon the trundle, he could not find the same restful composure as Bartlett. Dreadful scenarios replayed themselves in his mind. What if a guest at Bartlett's lecture was from Turin and the *Troy Sentinel* already had a wanted notice printed for his arrest? What if a recovered Mr. Fleming were to arrive in Troy ready to reveal his criminal past while Bartlett was away settling accounts in New York City? What if… However, sleep finally overpowered him. Rest, though, evaded his mind.

A sharp jab in his ribs awakened Jeduthan the next morning. His eyes opened, terrified. He tried to move his arms but shackles tightly held them fast to the bedposts. Towering above him stood a tall man adorned in an all black suit wielding a long wooden club. A cold rain pummeled the sill as the wind passed through the windowpane's cracks. He could hear a resounding laugh as loud as thunder from a lightning bolt. He struggled but could not gain his freedom as the terrifying apparition declared, "There is nowhere to hide from your crimes! I have pursued your trail through the woods, amidst the crowds, and among the wilderness. You cannot hide any longer! There must be an accounting! You must come with me! Wake, you hear me, Higby! Come with..."

The light shined brightly through the bedroom window. Standing above him was Bartlett, his outstretched finger lightly prodding Jeduthan's ribs. "Come now Higby, we must accept our destiny today. Our future awaits us!" His friend's voice chirped like a blue bird calling for its mate in the early morning air. "I have promised sweet Betsy that I would find you quarters before I leave tomorrow for New York City. Now, hip hop! Be dressed! I will meet you on the front portico in a few moments." Bartlett left the room, his steps echoing upon the wooden floor while descending the elegant Hart residence's staircase.

Jeduthan righted himself from the trundle bed. His forehead beaded a nervous sweat from the terrifying delusion that haunted his night's dream. He breathed deeply as his heart attempted to regain its steady rhythm rather than its nervous cadence from panic moments before. He worried that with his friend's departure, the restless nights might return.

"Higby! Are you coming?" bellowed his friend from downstairs.

"Yes, I am coming!" Jeduthan quickly dressed and raced down the stairs and onto the portico where he expected his friend. However, to his surprise, he could not find Bartlett. Jeduthan stood for nearly five minutes before he re-entered the house, finding the artist in the rear parlor quietly conversing with Mrs. Hart. The woman's eyes gleamed with admiration as the artist completed his story.

"...and that is how I escaped certain death. Ah professor, I was just relating one of our many adventures to dear Cousin Betsy, but now I am ready. Good day, cousin," Bartlett announced as he rose. "May the entire town be green with envy after tonight's performance!"

"Yes, I am sure they must!" She fluttered her eyelids as the two men departed the house and turned down the Second Street.

After crossing Congress Street and placing several hundred paces between the Hart home and themselves, Bartlett piped, "Betsy Howard, a truly inspiring woman!"

"Yes, she sure is accommodating," retorted Jeduthan. "How is it that you openly flirt with your cousin, Will?"

"Be not offended, old aged one. Betsy has turned eyes before. Before she engaged Mr. Hart, many considered her the lily of the city. Her father manages many businesses in Troy and New York City, most recently enjoying a leading role in Troy's banking houses. His daughter would make a fine match for an ambitious man. If she had not already been betrothed, I might have taken a shot at conquering her virtue myself! How she became entangled with Mr. Richard P. Hart is hard to fathom. Nevertheless, our smiles, teasing, and amorous banter are more of a game than any illicit affair. Moreover, it sure does get old man Hart riled. That is half the reason I enjoy Betsy's flirting, for the expressions her old man displays. I expect that the girl would expose her..." Bartlett's voice dropped off as he extended a pointing finger toward the office of the *Troy Sentinel*. "By George, I think we have found you some suitable quarters, my dear quiet companion."

In the office window, directly above the *Sentinel's* shingle, was a small cardboard notice. *Room to let. Inquire within.*

"Let us approach this quaint periodical and inquire about the room." The men entered finding, seated behind an oaken table, a short dark-haired middle-aged man. Pressed upon the far wall were a large printing apparatus and multiple stacks of white paper. In the corner was a tight staircase leading upward, no doubt to the vacant room. "I am sorry to intrude sir, but I noticed your *room to let* advertisement in yonder window and I wish to inquire to its availability for a friend," stated Bartlett.

"Yes, we have a spare room just vacated by my daughter and her husband. I am Norman Tuttle, publisher of the *Sentinel*. Come, let me show you the room."

The man led the pair up the small staircase, apologizing while explaining that this was the only entrance. He opened the room's door, exposing its interior to his visitors. "We ask only quiet for the occupier and a rental of two dollars a week. We do not provide board; therefore, we provide no meals. Also, take care to avoid interrupting the printing office during working hours."

Jeduthan observed that the only furniture adorning the room was a small bed nailed to the wall along with a single freestanding chair and one small table. There were six pegs upon the wooden exterior wall for hanging jackets, but that was all.

"It is sparse, but sufficient. My friend here, Professor Higby, will take it. And for your help tonight dear friend, the first two weeks' lease is on my account." Extracting four coins from his pocket, the artist placed them into the awaiting hand of the proprietor.

"It is nice to make your acquaintance, Professor Higby. My wife and I live only next door and if you need entry while the office is locked, please inquire at our home and we will unlock the door. Please shut the door tight and secure the lock if you are here alone. We have only one key for this door and cannot allow you one. You are welcome to come and go during the rest of today until the fifth hour. I will secure the door then."

"Is that the time you close the shop?" inquired Jeduthan.

"No, usually we remain open until the seventh hour but I have been invited by Mr. Howard, one of our leading citizens here in Troy, to a special reception for his beloved nephew, an artist from England. So today, I will close early in order to attend," replied the printer.

A broad grin expanded on Bartlett's face. "My dear publisher, I am glad to meet you, for I am the artist of whom you anticipate meeting at Mr. Howard's reception. May I introduce myself? William H. Bartlett, at your service. I am on an errand for my dear friend here, who has accompanied me these past months on my ramblings in the frontier, and it is a pleasure to make your acquaintance." The artist winked at the printer. "However, let us keep this meeting private until tonight when we can greet each other as old friends in front of my uncle. I am quite anxious to see his expression." Reaching into his satchel, Bartlett pulled out a small sketch. "Mr. Tuttle, let me give you a small sampling of a sketch which I completed during my hiatus only this morning of my wonderfully sweet cousin Betsy Hart. Could you possibly engrave this simple sketch for your paper along with an announcement of tonight's lecture and present a copy to Mr. Howard? I am quite sure he would be very appreciative."

"I will do just that," smiled the editor. "Thank you, Mr. Bartlett. Please excuse me, gentlemen, as I go downstairs into the studio and begin the engraving process."

Mr. Tuttle disappeared down the steps, leaving the two friends alone in the room.

"Thanks for the room lease, Will. Do you expect to return from New York City within two weeks?"

"I expect more like a month, dear friend. That is why I wish to give you this." Reaching again into his satchel, the artist extracted a sketch showing Jeduthan standing on the prow of the *Captain Swan*, playing his Scheitholt while three young girls danced and paraded upon the deck. "This sketch will be a reminder of our long lasting friendship."

"It is wonderful, Will. I will treasure it by placing it upon the wall as my first possession decorating my quaint quarters." Jeduthan tacked the sketch to the wall and smiled.

"Good, Higby. Now, I want you to be prompt."

Jeduthan threw a questioning look toward his friend.

"We must meet at the reception tonight. My dear cousin will accompany me. Arrive at Cousin Betsy's at five in the evening. There, I must have a caption for that sketch with a fine selection from your superb vocabularic abilities for my lecture, so be prompt."

"I did not know I was invited."

"Of course, you are! You are my companion! So long, old man." Bartlett left Jeduthan standing solitary in the room.

Jeduthan spent the rest of the afternoon retrieving his gear from the Hart residence and obtaining livery services for old Nimrod. As he visited the grand home, he expected to see Mrs. Hart, Bartlett, or even Mr. Hart, however only Aunt Sallie greeted him, and she was in a hullabaloo. Scurrying from room to room, the old servant was preparing for the expected evening reception and had little time for conversation. Therefore, he quietly gathered his belongings and without interruption, left by the rear door.

After settling into his newly acquired lodgings, Jeduthan fondly reminisced about his summer's adventures. His growing adoration for his eccentric artist friend, their ramblings through the natural world, and their joyous adventures along the canal, all revitalized his manhood. Therefore, he felt indebted to Bartlett and yearned to present his friend a souvenir of their companionship that the artist might find of both practical use and sentimental value. He pondered his friend's attributes and settled upon his silver pocket watch.

He searched his knapsack and retrieved the timepiece. Inspecting it, he found the mechanism still operating smoothly. The crystal, though, contained two significant scratches. The first occurred when Jeduthan was only a young child. Inspecting the watch by firelight, he accidentally dropped it onto the hearth. He feared retribution from his tyrannical father and cowered for weeks, however the old man never commented on the damage. The second injury happened when his wife threw the timepiece at him after he had complained about her tardiness. Becoming enraged, she hurled it through the air toward his head. It would have landed squarely upon his brow if he had not evaded the flying object at the last moment. Thereafter, he packed it away and relied instead upon his unique quality to determine time by the sun's position. After that incident, he rarely erred when asked the time of day, which angered his wife even more.

As it was, this pocket watch was the only sentimental ornament that he retained from his great grandfather Zaccheus Candee, a man of whom he did not know. Zaccheus died while Jeduthan was still an infant. However, his mother had spoken kind words about the elderly gentleman. Jeduthan had been the first young baby the old man had held since his own children were born nearly fifty years earlier and the little squirming boy delighted the old patriarch. His mother related a portrait of the old man's thin lips parting into a broad grin as young Jeduthan crawled upon the floor, grasping at his wiggling toes. As a lasting bequest, he left to baby Jeduthan this simple silver pocket watch. On the back was inscribed his simple pedigree.

For as much as his unique instinct at guessing time rarely caused him to use the old timepiece, Will Bartlett seemed to have an opposite quality, never knowing the time and always arriving tardy. Therefore, Jeduthan decided to pass this simple personal item to his best of friends. However, before presenting it to the artist, he decided to cement their friendship by having one last name engraved upon its reverse side, that of W. H. Bartlett.

Jeduthan sought out Mr. Tuttle in the printing office and asked where he might find a jeweler or silversmith. Directed three blocks down Second Street, Jeduthan sprinted to the craft smith. There, he

asked the jeweler to add *W. H. Bartlett* to the list of names upon its
back cover. The jeweler readily assented and completed the task in a few
minutes. Inspecting the watch, Jeduthan decided it was appropriate.
While walking to his rented room, he determined to present the gift
to his friend before he departed tomorrow for New York City. The gift
complete, he dressed for the night's reception in Bartlett's spare tunic
and left his small room above the *Sentinel's* office, casually walking
toward the Hart residence.

Unlike the night of his initial arrival at the luxurious Hart home on
Second Street, tonight's night sky shown brightly with starry wonders
and a brilliant full moon. Approaching the Hart residence, candles
in every window lit the majestic structure. Jeduthan compared the
magnificent, impressive building to that which he imagined for only
with European royalty. The marble facade shimmered in the moon
light. Three large carriages lined the street in front, horse teams carefully
tended by splendidly attired coachmen. The brass handles adorning one
carriage luminously reflected the candle light from the home.

Approaching the walkway, he paused, a high, shrill sound startling
him. A puppy slid from under the largest of the carriages, advancing
toward him, sniffing about his feet. He leaned down and gently petted
the canine.

"Higby, my fine fellow!" Upon the front step, in the dark shadows,
appeared his artist friend along with another gentleman. "I am glad to
see you have arrived on time. Leave that wretched dog and come up
here where I can better see you. Ah, you look splendid. May I introduce
Dr. John Willard."

Jeduthan extended his hand in greeting to the aging gentleman.

"He needed some relief from the accumulated tobacco smoke within
the residence and I accompanied him hither to await your arrival."

"Glad to meet you, sir."

"Likewise," gurgled the kind doctor as he let loose a violent coughing
from his lungs.

"Are you well?" inquired Jeduthan.

The doctor continued his coughing for nearly a full minute before
responding rather feebly, "What ails me, sir, no man may conquer. I
offer you one piece of advice, young man. The remedy for old age is

the only cure worse than the disease. Advanced age knocks at my door. The only cure, I fear, is death. But death haunts our every moment and no one knows our time…"

"You are quite right, dear doctor," interjected Bartlett. "So we must not waste a single moment. I believe the stuffiness must have subsided by now. Let us re-enter the reception for, as you know, I am the guest of honor and if poor Cousin Betsy suspects my absence even for a moment, I will forever be apologizing." Bartlett led the two men inside and disappeared into the immense crowd, leaving the doctor with Jeduthan.

"Are you a medical or theological doctor?"

"Medical," replied Dr. Willard. "I have since retired from practice and have indulged my wife's fancy these past years. After we arrived in Troy, she has applied her many talents and opened a school for females. You might know of it, *The Troy Female Seminary*?"

"Yes, I have heard quite a lot about its novel ideas for educating women. Mrs. Hart is a true fan of your wife's efforts. We only recently debated the necessity of women's education and I wholeheartedly support your work. I hope I may meet Mrs. Willard."

"Of course you may. She is over yonder next to Mrs. Hart." Dr. Willard beckoned toward the far corner of the foyer. Standing next to Mrs. Hart was a dark haired, fair complexioned lady in her mid-twenties, far too young a maid to have been the wife of this distinguished elderly man. "Dear Emma!" cried Dr. Willard. "Please come over here and meet my new friend." Mrs. Hart pointed toward Jeduthan while mouthing a short message to her lady-friend before the woman broke away and approached the fine doctor and Jeduthan. "Emma, dear, this is Mr. Bartlett's intimate friend, Professor Higby, whom he has proclaimed so much about these past hours."

"Nice to meet you, sir." She extended her hand politely, her palm down, expecting Jeduthan to kiss her hand. However, to her astonishment, he grasped it firmly with his own.

"Hello. I am pleased to make your acquaintance."

A little sad faced, Mrs. Willard raised her chin slightly before stating, "I am quite surprised that your hands are so rough, professor. I expected to find your touch to be more womanly."

"I have been in the wilderness these past months. Struggles of daily life have hardened me, madam," he responded.

"What sort of professor are you, sir?"

Jeduthan panicked. He worried about jeopardizing his identity. However, if Bartlett's ruse was to continue, he must answer the question forthrightly. He responded by remembering his assignment as the Presbyterian minister to Turin's congregation which might somehow endow him with qualifications. "Professor of applied theology, natural sciences, and history. I hope some day to teach in a highly esteemed institution like your newly founded school here in Troy."

"How interesting you should mention, we..." From across the parlor, Mrs. Hart gently tapped her glass, interrupting Mrs. Willard's discussion.

"Attention, ladies and gentlemen!" All turned toward Mrs. Hart. She stood slightly elevated on what looked like a step stool. "We are here tonight to welcome back to our fair community my cousin and world renowned artist, William H. Bartlett of London. He has graced our gathering tonight and as you are my truest and closest of friends, I want to introduce him personally. Please welcome him!" Applause rang throughout the house as she stepped down from the stool, motioning the artist to take her place for a brief speech.

"Thank you, Cousin Betsy. Friends, I thank you for the warm reception this fine evening. I have traveled the wilderness now nearly a year and have found no company more appealing than that of Cousin Betsy, Uncle William, and your growing community. Since I last strolled your boulevards, many buildings have been replaced that the great fire of a few years past left as twisted scars amidst the beauty that is Troy. Soon, little evidence will remain of that terrible conflagration and your fine city will completely recover. I am also pleased to see Mrs. Willard's school quickly expanding with new campus buildings and I hope it will forever improve the station of women in the near future. Again, thank you for this fine reception."

The invited guests applauded Bartlett's short speech as an elderly gentleman stepped upon the stool. "Thank you, nephew." The older man had difficulty balancing and braced himself upon Mr. Hart, who stood erect and frowning, as if defeated. Jeduthan assumed the older man was Mr. William Howard, Betsy Hart's father. "Tonight, we, Mr.

Eaton and I, have appealed to Mr. Bartlett to lecture at yet another newly opened institution of higher learning, *The Rensselaer School for the Applied Sciences.*" A roar of applause shook the home for a second time. "Although he claims to be only a humble artist, I am sure that he will have a fine presentation at the new school housed in the Old Bank Place on the north end of town. For as long as I have known young Will, given a time and place to speak, he never leaves an audience jaded. Please, I invite all of you to his presentation, along with a significant number of other professionals, students, and esteemed guests who regularly attend the school's functions. You folks enjoy your evening." Another round of applause resonated.

At that, Mr. Howard stepped off the stool and the guests broke into smaller parties, tasting the many *hor'dourves* and small sweet appetizers prepared for the evening.

"Well, Professor Higby, how long have you traveled with Mr. Bartlett?" resumed Mrs. Willard. "We only briefly met the artist last February when Mr. Howard led a fund raising campaign for the *Rensselaer School.* At that time, he appeared quite provincial. However, after his adventure in the wilderness, he seems to have blossomed into a charming young man, full of life and vigor. Do you suppose the wilds of nature and the fierce savage countryside changed him and his old world style?"

"I assure you, Mrs. Willard, William H. Bartlett, at least the one I have come to know, is no dandy. He readily accepts challenges with daring and fortitude."

"Why Professor Higby, your choice of vocabulary hints at sophistication. It is just such style for which all humanity ought to strive. So many of our countrymen and women allow obstacles to restrain them rather than reaching for academic success. At the same moment, our learned leaders so often restrain our greatest pool of potential genius with the heavy hand of tradition. For example, Professor, the potential of women is repeatedly discouraged and stifled by our established society on mere pretense of protecting our virtue. What are your views on the abilities of women?"

Unhesitatingly, he retorted, "I, madam, believe God has endowed all his creatures with talent. Any talents that are wasted, consumed, exhausted, or inhibited is a shameful mark on humanity. That is precisely what drew my attention to Mr. Bartlett. He saw within me a potential talent which I was squandering and lit a fire in my soul seeking adventure and enjoying the beauty which God provides." He felt slightly awkward at his preaching and worried that he may have offended the woman until a broad smile breached her thin lips.

"You are a charmer, Professor Higby! Your words mimic my own ideology toward women's potential. I hope we may converse more on this subject at a later date. Come, dear husband, we need to take our leave if we are to attend tonight's lecture by young Mr. Bartlett. Good evening, Professor."

"Good evening, madam."

Many people had left the Hart home by this time, some riding in their carriages and some strolling down the street toward the evening's lecture of which Bartlett was to be the principal speaker. Jeduthan approached his artist friend who had spent most of the evening shaking hands and greeting people of importance to Mrs. Hart.

"Good evening, Mr. Bartlett," greeted Jeduthan. "It has been revealed to me of your debut at tonight's lecture. Can I inquire as to your topic?"

"Not only may you inquire, dear fellow, you must also prepare. I will be requiring your assistance."

Puzzled, Jeduthan asked, "How am I going to assist you? Don't you remember our plan of me laying low and not attracting attention! Already you have insisted on my new grandiose title of professor, introduced me personally to the most important citizens of this fair community, and now you wish for me to give a public speech on a subject of which has not yet been revealed to me? I beg of you, young friend, do not entangle me with such a scheme from which I cannot extradite myself."

"Your words betray you, my friend. Your extraordinary vocabularic expressions and terminology have destined you to become part of my expose'. What I can collect upon the white linen canvas, you convey with eloquent diction. Do you remember my sketch I left for you this afternoon? Do you recall that I asked you to caption its meaning before I left? Well, at this engagement for the *Rensselaer School*, I will need your best poetry to demonstrate to a skeptical audience the practical application for our art, both visual and auditory! Now, you make your way to the auditorium at the Old Bank Place and have ready your poetic words when I call for them. I must accompany Cousin Betsy and her father. I will meet you at the lecture. Goodbye and adieu, my vocabulary wielding cohort."

The artist graciously exited the parlor, the sounds of his boots echoing through the now nearly empty house. "Cousin, I am hurrying for your sake! I needed to finalize my..." His words trailed off in the distance night air, leaving Jeduthan alone.

He puzzled over his situation. Here he was, in a crowded city, with an alias, traveling with a popular and admired, though a little absurd, sketch artist who has taken a challenge to entertain, inform, and demonstrate a practicality for art of which Jeduthan possessed serious doubt. Now the sketch artist has included himself in the devilish scheme for no other reward except to retain the flirtatious attentions of another man's wife. Moreover, all the while, he was trying to keep a low profile so as not to attract law enforcers who, no doubt, were searching for a scoundrel of devious character.

He closed his eyes and prayed. Time seemed to stop as his mind filled with the wonderment that nature endowed upon him since his flight from Turin. The hard, laborious canal work; the newfound friendship of William H. Bartlett; the surrounding and all encompassing natural world enjoyed during his summer's repast; the adventurous canal boat journey; and now, the exciting society of Troy City. He took a deep breath, exhuming his worries and placing his fate in God's hands. Slowly exiting the Hart residence on his way to the Rensselaer campus, he attempted to think of a caption for his friend's sketch.

The Rensselaer School

More than a dozen fancy carriages, each with its own entourage of coachmen, footmen, and quarter horses, surrounded the Old Bank Place when Jeduthan arrived. Weaving his path between the coaches, he had difficulty reaching the walk leading to the campus' front entrance. A large oak tree flanked the building, and there he spied a young man amongst its branches attempting an unobstructed view of the proceedings within.

Entering the main hall, he understood the young man's eagerness at climbing the tree. The room was full of people, the many chairs and benches already occupied with eager attendees leaving only standing room for late arrivals like himself. Squeezing forward, he attempted to locate Bartlett, Mrs. Hart, or anyone he could recognize. However, Jeduthan failed in his attempt as the crowd was just too thick. Therefore, he retreated toward an exterior wall and leisurely leaned upon its cold surface as many people attempted to find seating.

"Good evening, ladies and gentlemen," came the call from an elderly gentleman toward the front of the room. His unusual height was striking. "Good evening. Please be seated and we will begin the presentation."

No one seemed to pay the old man any mind. The crowd did not lessen and few gained their seats. The old man's temper began to mount and his arms began flailing in an attempt to settle the throng, all to no avail. Finally, he stepped down and was proven as short as any common person. There must have been a stool underfoot similar to the speech-making platform at the Hart residence.

The next gentleman who stepped upon the elevation proved to be Mr. Howard, Mrs. Hart's father. "May we have order!" bellowed the banker and the crowd soon hushed. "May we have order! Find your seats for tonight's presentation." The room quieted into a myriad of whispers as more and more people found their seat. Nevertheless,

Jeduthan knew that many would need to continue standing, so he patiently secured his position along the wall.

As Mr. Howard retreated, four men brought forth a large lectern and positioned it in front of the speaker's platform, transforming the simple stool into a makeshift pulpit. Again, the aged man stepped upon the pulpit and began, "Ladies and gentlemen, I would like to welcome you to the *Rensselaer School for the Applied Sciences*." There was a pause as more people found their seats.

"Hello, Professor."

Jeduthan turned his head to his right and found that standing beside him was Mr. Hart. "I am glad you could make it into the room tonight. It appears Will Bartlett has packed the house."

"I expect an advertisement in the *Sentinel* might have more to do with it than my companion, Mr. Hart."

"Possibly, but I am afraid that poor Mr. Bartlett has met his match tonight. I know for a fact that he may be able to charm individuals in private homes, but public speaking is not his forte'. During his last visit, he made himself a laughing stock at a smaller party thrown in his honor at my father-in-law's home. Now, in front of this crowd, I am sure he will stumble."

Jeduthan glared at the man with distaste. Why would a person have such wicked intentions? Knowing a man's weakness, a merciless and unkind Mr. Hart intentionally lured Bartlett into an awkward position. Jeduthan knew that he must not allow his friend to be embarrassed. Therefore, Jeduthan began moving from his post to warn his friend just as the old man in the pulpit began speaking again.

"Ladies and gentlemen, most of you know that one of our noblest city benefactors founded the *Rensselaer School*. Mr. Stephen Van Rensselaer hopes to educate persons who may choose to apply themselves in the field of science to the common purposes of life. He entrusted myself, Amos Eaton, as its headmaster and principal instructor, with such objectives to bring his vision to a successful reality. I am somewhat proud to say that this past semester has endowed us with just such success. We here in Troy pride ourselves in our progressive ideas. Just one notable success is a peaceful solution to the slavery question in New York. The result is the abolition of the wicked institution within the state's borders taking effect within two years without bloodshed, uproar, or any angry mob violence." A mixture of light applause and polite silence passed through the audience. "Another success includes finding enduring qualities in our fine women, along with many untapped resources among our weaker sex. Here, at our school, we realize their potential also. With the help of generous, forward thinking men, like Dr. John Willard and his enthusiastic, passionate, and dedicated wife, Mrs. Emma Hart Willard, our community has established the first female institute in America, the *Troy Female Seminary!*"

The crowd stood upon mention of the Willard's and applause rang through the halls and spilled onto the street outside that must have resounded for several miles. Jeduthan's ears throbbed from the thunderous clamor in the assembled chamber. Mr. and Mrs. Willard rose and gently waved the audience quiet before Mr. Eaton continued.

"Tonight we have an honored guest as speaker. Our own Mr. William Howard, Esq. with whom our special guest resided for a short time last spring, first brought him to my attention. After a jaunt through the wilderness these past several months, our guest has returned enlightened by our vast natural wonders, impressed with our expanding industrialism, and endowed by our American ruggedness. A native of our recent enemy, Great Britain, but now I am assured, in love with the American spirit, it is an honor to present tonight, our esteemed guest and presenter, Mr. William H. Bartlett."

Mr. Eaton gestured downward from the pulpit toward the artist, who sat rigidly in a chair next to Mrs. Hart. Applause swept the hall. Bartlett hesitated before being edged forward by his cousin, stood in recognition. Mr. Howard reached his hand forward and gently pulled the artist toward the pulpit. As Mr. Eaton descended and Bartlett took his place, the crowd settled into an eerie quiet.

The eyes of all those people must have burned the artist's nerve. Jeduthan remembered a similar moment, the day when he preached his first sermon at Turin's Presbyterian Church. The gazing eyes shot cold steel swords through his heart. His pulse had pounded loudly enough to drown the dripping raindrops that beat against the glass window-panes. Every miniature noise had echoed through the chamber, from the sniffling of the young Regan child to the wind rattling the door. His friend now faced the same dread and he felt pity for the young artist.

Slowly, Bartlett began. "Ladies, gentlemen, students..." He paused, looking through the assemblage, slowly turning his head from one side to the other. "...Cousin, Uncle..." He continued to scan the audience before his eyes fell upon Jeduthan. "...And companion!" A broad grin expanded across the artist's face. His eyes gleamed with the comfortable, relaxed, and contented aura that Jeduthan adored for many months as innocence set free. He realized what his friend had done. Examining the room, seeking a friendly, non-critical, and affable face, Bartlett had found it in his traveling companion.

"People, methodical and practical people in our fair land, have repeatedly acclaimed praise for my sketches these past months. They have smiled, venerated, and applauded my gripping imagery, but few have seen the practical use for my vocation. As your school, here in this growing metropolis, beckons for the practical application of the arts and sciences, I have chosen to speak to you tonight about the possibilities for practical use of sketched art, along with the captioned word. Yes, practical use! Times are changing, ladies and gentlemen, when portraits will no longer be for only the rich and affluent. All humanity will benefit from the artist's brush strokes and the poet's clever words. Newspapers all across this land have already begun to experiment with engravings advertising great achievements. Only today, I visited the *Sentinel's* office and in a brief time, Mr. Tuttle engraved, from my sketch, a portrait of my dear cousin, Mrs. Betsy Howard Hart, announcing this evening's lecture." The artist reached into his satchel and extracted the newspaper. Holding it high above his head, he asked, "How many, in this room tonight, were intrigued so by Mrs. Hart's engraving as to investigate more in-depth the nature of her picture in this fine periodical?"

Bartlett waited as dozens of hands raised in confirmation. "If the announcement had been only in print, I am sure that many of you fine Trojans might have missed the invitation and be at home contentedly oblivious to tonight's celebrations and activities. However, beautiful Mrs. Hart's face beckoned you to investigate further which has brought you here. Publicity is only one of the many practical applications for an artist's imagination."

A round of applause shook the windows as Mrs. Hart rose and blushed in affirmation of the artist's premise. When the audience settled, Bartlett continued.

"Advertising also summoned me to this fine continent. The investors of the recently completed Erie Canal sought me in order to sketch their miraculous venture cutting through America's heartland. They hoped that their investment, as seen through my art, benefited not only humanity, but God's holy Earth. Thus, I set forth portraying and recording man's magnificent manipulation of the wilderness with sketches set about the famous waterway. I am proud to announce that I have fulfilled my mission. The *Sentinel* has published my work as engravings on several occasions, and soon these sketches will adorn fine newspapers across the globe." Jeduthan felt an inner glow as his friend came to grip his audience's imagination.

"Tonight, I will demonstrate a few more practical techniques I employ with my art. Cousin, would you please assist me?" asked the artist, gesturing for Mrs. Hart to bring forth a large, cloth covered frame.

Mr. Eaton assisted the woman by placing the frame upright and securing it in position for all to see. All made safe, the artist reached down and pulled loose the cloth, revealing a large sketch extending nearly a yard square. It depicted a beautiful scene of life on the canal, its weaving path disappearing into the background. The foreground, though, startled Jeduthan, his jaw falling slightly ajar. Sweat beaded upon his forehead. The drawing contained a man, seated in the bow of a canal boat with a scheitholt upon his lap. He was obviously playing the instrument as three young girls danced a jig upon the barge's deck. It was the exact depiction that Bartlett bestowed upon him earlier that day, except now, his sketch was hidden within the larger drawing. Had his friend turned into a fiend?

Bartlett continued. "May I present to this esteemed audience, an original print, as yet unpublished, that we will tonight transform from a sensual work of artistic talent to a practical, effective advertisement of our precious commodity. This portrait, which will be reproduced in a global periodical by week's end, is yet incomplete. In its original form, we can view the scenery's imagery with vibrant shading, and clever metaphoric meanings. However, when the engraver begins his craft of transforming my work of art onto his printing plates, the details will fade. The precise curves and angles of my musical hero will blur and my true meaning will surely be lost. Therefore, we need two additions to all successfully engraved art. Firstly, a clever caption must be included that will re-emphasize my true meaning. An original sketch would never require such a caption for the detail and imagery would be retained from my penciling. However, an engraver will lose its true meaning. He works with wood, copper, and clumsy steel knives. A caption, though, allows the engraving's observer to imagine my thoughts through poetry, as if they were replacing the lost passion that necessitates from the mechanical press' cold copper plates. Let me demonstrate."

The artist used a pointing stick and struck the print. "I am sure the patrons seated in the far corners of this fine establishment might not be able to view the sketch as well as, may I say, my dear cousin standing here beside me. Very similarly, the dulling by an engraver's knife will lose the passion found in the original sketch. But, add a caption and all can imagine my true meaning." Some in the audience whispered doubts as Bartlett inquired, "Professor, have you formulated the caption for my sketch?"

Jeduthan was stunned. Unable to take in the entire sketch, he was speechless.

"Professor Higby was with me when I sketched this scene, and I have full confidence he remembers our conversation. The importance of the written word enhances the passion of the pencil stroke. I am the visual artist, he the caption writer. Professor Higby, what do you say, faithful companion?"

Jeduthan felt hundreds of eyes shift toward him, each a possible witness to his treachery. He heard whispers, discreet murmurs, like so many in Turin's pews whispering each Sunday morning while he used to preach God's word.

Jeduthan felt his lips part and slowly say, "The harmony of nature and music warms the hearts and exalts the soul of the family voyaging along the glorious Erie Canal."

"Thank you, dear companion. Cousin, would you please write those stirring words at the base of the sketch for me?"

Mrs. Hart knelt down and added the words in bold letters.

"You see, ladies and gentlemen, the professor's words exactly match the image I wish to convey in this sketch. As the portion of the sketch containing the musician and dancing children are only a small bit of the overall portrait, my true meaning might have been lost in its publication. However, the words of Professor Higby add a cementing facet to the engraving. The object is not the scenery about the canal, but the happy family engaged frolicking in their adventurous canal boat expedition. Thank you, dear professor."

Jeduthan nodded to his friend's gracefully raised hand. Applause resounded and he felt a warm blush overcome his features.

As the applause subsided, the artist continued. "The final practical application for this sketch is called fracturing. This is the artistic employment of a pleasing and meaningful border for the artwork. Nearly always present with successful engravings, it too may expand on the artist's true significance of the portrait." Bartlett exited the pulpit and, using his sketching pencil, began a series of alternating images around the picture's border. "In this case, I will fracture this sketch with musical notes, canal boats, and musical instruments, repeated around its entire perimeter. This fracturing process completes the artwork and it is ready for the engraver and printer to reproduce in their periodical." The artist effortlessly finished the fractured border and remounted the pulpit. "I hope you have understood the practical application of visual and auditory art in my presentation tonight. I bid you good night and a fair adieu."

A roar of applause and shouts of acclamation shook the building. People began to rise, clapping their hands wildly, many shouting approval. The artist glanced toward Jeduthan along the wall with a broad smile and an affirming nod.

Jeduthan, in turn, peered at Mr. Hart, who still stood beside him, a distraught scowl upon his face. "I guess your plans faltered, sir. Mr. Bartlett once again steals the show." He pushed past Mr. Hart toward his artist friend at the front of the room.

A throng of well-wishers surrounded the artist, each hoping for an introduction. Most were young students, but there were also some more prominent citizens in search of the same recognition. Included amongst the pack was Mrs. Willard. As Jeduthan passed by, she reached out her delicate hand, touching his shoulder.

"Professor Higby!" she shouted over the roaring mass of spectators. Pushing closer, she continued with her mouth only inches from his ear in order that he could hear her. "I would like to invite you to my seminary tomorrow. I am impressed with your inventive use of the English language and would like to discuss a potential opportunity."

"Thank you, Mrs. Willard. I will drop by sometime after lunch."

Mrs. Willard nodded in agreement while he continued nudging toward his friend.

"Higby, my old compatriot, I knew you would not let me down!" exclaimed Bartlett, vigorously grasping his hand. "Let us depart this mob and retreat to your modest and peaceful accommodations."

The two men exited the building's back door, making their way through the rear alleyway. When clear of the building, Bartlett broke into a fast trot, causing Jeduthan's lungs to heave.

As they approached the *Sentinel's* office door, the pair slackened their pace and Jeduthan asked, "Why did you exit so quickly my friend?"

"It is better to make your exit when you are most desired than to become a bore upon your guests' sympathies," responded the artist as he gently pushed the door open. "Besides, I need to catch some rest before tomorrow. I must leave in the morning and I hate sad goodbyes, especially from the teary eyes of my Cousin Betsy. Please, you convey the news to her. I cannot bear it."

"I will," he responded. "Tonight, please bunk here."

"That was my plan exactly, old friend."

Jeduthan laid his heavy blanket upon the rough floorboards, allowing his younger friend the luxury of the mattress bed. Both men stretched their frames and lay in silence for a long while before Jeduthan broke the quiet.

"I have been asked to Mrs. Willard's school tomorrow."

"Now that is good news," the artist replied. "I suspect she might hope to employ you. Cousin Betsy has remarked that Mr. Willard's poor health caused a rift in the school's faculty. Some are very concerned about how Mrs. Willard will operate the school without her husband's guidance. I am sure she fears that resistance to a woman's leadership might cause vacancies. You might, my friend, be a potential replacement for some of the more traditional instructors at the *Troy Female Seminary.*"

"If I am a candidate, I fear my credentials may be inadequate. My alias might be questioned, or worse, investigated."

"Do not worry yourself, aged one. Your credentials are as solid as mine. Besides, you have repeatedly stated your desire to teach. This just might be your opportunity."

Jeduthan grimaced. "I know what I have said, but now that I am in the position to realize my dreams, I hesitate."

"We each have a destiny. Tomorrow, I leave aboard my packet for the big city, where I might catch my death or revel in riches. I might live to be a hundred, sailing the vast Mediterranean in search of my next scene or I might not awaken from tonight's slumber. We just don't know! If a person continues to fret about life's trials and tribulations, he will never find fulfillment." Bartlett stopped talking and for a long minute stillness hovered in the darkness. "Allow what happens to happen my old friend! Good night."

Jeduthan was restless during much of the night. Repeatedly he awoke to find Bartlett's deep, heavy breathing rhythmically resounding through the room. On one occasion, sleet pattered against the window-pane, causing a chill to engulf the area. By morning, the sun's rays etched the window frame's shadow upon the western wall and the room began to warm. In addition, a loud noise emanated from *the Sentinel's* workroom below.

Sitting upright, Jeduthan was startled to find his companion absent from the bed. The room's doorway was ajar and Jeduthan surmised that Bartlett departed in the early morning to avoid farewells. Hurriedly, he stood, dressed, grabbed his satchel, and exited the room. Vaulting down the narrow staircase, he passed Mr. Tuttle steadily applying his trade at publishing his newspaper and rushed through the outside doorway. He paused briefly, scanning the street in both directions before stretching his head back into the office inquiring of Mr. Tuttle for the packet boat schedule. The printer replied that there were two scheduled for that morning, both leaving from the small docks of the Marshall Textile Mill near Potenskill Creek.

Jeduthan sprinted down toward the river, hastily passing by Butcher Wilson's meat shop, rapidly skirting the livery where old Nimrod was boarded, and approached the ferry landing at the bottom of the valley. Crossing over the Champlain Canal, Jeduthan could see two boats departing from a small dock astride the Marshall Textile Mill. Standing on the prow of one, was Bartlett.

"Will!" exclaimed Jeduthan as he sprinted along the waterway trying to keep pace with the departing barge. "I did so want to see you off."

"Higby, did I explain to you my penchant of avoiding farewells?"

"Yes you did, but I have a gift!" The artist's eyes lit with childlike anticipation. "A useful gift, to keep you on time." Reaching into his satchel, Jeduthan extracted his silver watch. "I had your name engraved upon its underside as a token of our friendship."

"I regret that I cannot debark, old friend. This barge is chocked full of iron ore and cannot alter its course or speed without great effort. Captain Halstead has mightily demanded I remain aboard. I am afraid he will not pause on my account."

Jeduthan hesitated before commanding his friend, "Will, perch yourself on top of that large tub of ore, stretch out your arms, and catch." Bartlett obediently did as requested and Jeduthan tossed the watch across the canal into his friend's awaiting palms. "Now, you have no excuse to be tardy, my artist friend."

"You are correct," smiled Bartlett. "I will soon return to grace you with another adventure. So long, dear Higby!"

Jeduthan halted his run. The schooner *Troy*, aptly named, carried his friend away, venturing out into the wide river. Within minutes, Jeduthan saw a mast hoisted, a very unusual site for canal barges. Soon, the canal-schooner crept across the wide river, its bow riding low in the water and perched upon it like a defiant figurehead, was the indefatigable William H. Bartlett.

Troy Female Seminary

While the streets began to stir with shop keeps, pedestrians, and carriages, Jeduthan slowly plodded back to his room, paying little attention to the awakening port city of Troy. He worried that he lacked courage to face life's problems without the confident security of his friend. Now, with Bartlett's departure, he must tackle choices for which he alone must decide. The first would come in only a few hours in the office of Mrs. Emma H. Willard at the *Troy Female Seminary*.

Questions preoccupied his mind during those morning hours. In an attempt to relax, he purchased a *Troy Sentinel* from Mr. Tuttle. Scanning its pages, he was drawn to a poem entitled *A Visit From Saint Nicholas*. Its anonymous authorship only mentioned its previous publication a few years ago in the December 23rd, 1823 edition. Its fanciful story of a jolly old elf and his Christmas escapades caused a smile to breach his lips. Its imagery reminded him of simpler days. One line in particular piqued his interest.

> *...The moon on the breast of new fallen snow,*
> *Gave the luster of mid-day to objects below...*

The words touched his heart. He envisioned a scene of a crisp winter evening far away on the frontier. Its virgin landscapes illuminated by milky white moonlight. He remembered the many nights he spent gazing out his shop window toward the tall hills a few miles west of Turin. Their slopes glistened with powdered snow. Those evening moments seemed the only respite from the daily drudgery that his father, then his wife, and finally the community demanded from him during his past life.

However, that was many months ago during a previous life, not to be dwelt upon in the present. Here, in Troy, he eagerly yearned to start afresh, a new man. He hoped that Bartlett's prediction proved correct for he so desired that Emma Willard might give him an opportunity to test his teaching skills at her school.

He reached into his satchel in search of his silver watch, hoping that the brief time spent reading had not made him late for his appointment with Headmistress Willard. He did not find his watch, though. Sitting upright, he searched his haversack, checked under the bed, and opened the door into the hallway, all in vain. It was only then he remembered his recent gift to his precious traveling artist friend.

With humility, he calmly poked his head into printing room of the *Sentinel* and spied Mr. Tuttle at the press. "Mr. Tuttle? Do you happen to know the time?"

The printer turned quickly, a frown upon his face, his hands and apron stained with greasy ink. Annoyingly he replied, "I am sorry, sir. I am quite occupied at this moment. I must print two hundred copies of this newspaper before nightfall and have no time for interruptions."

Jeduthan retreated to his room and gazed out the window. People filled the streets, each scurrying about on errands. He glanced skyward but the sun was hidden from view by his eastern facing window. He noticed the shadows on the walkways, however, and determined that noontime must have past. Therefore, he set upon his mission to Mrs. Willard's school for his anticipated appointment.

He dressed in the borrowed suit left him by his friend and briskly walked through the streets of Troy to his rendezvous. A prominent shingle hung from a second story window marking the school's campus. It read, *Troy Female Seminary, Emma H. Willard, Headmistress.* He paused at the door with a sense of dread at what outcome this interview might hold for him. Maybe he should retreat and remain hidden among the masses! However, as he had verbally committed to the interview, not to appear might lead to additional unsolicited suspicions. Therefore, he opened the building's door and entered a well-lit foyer.

He found a young lady sitting at a lone table on the left side hallway. Upon his entrance, she looked up, revealing a pale, supple complexion. Her creamy white skin suggested a refined and pampered lifestyle, protected from the harsh environment of the wilderness and the out-of-doors.

"Good afternoon, sir," greeted the young woman. She stood, closing the book she had been reading and placing it upon the table.

"Welcome to the *Troy Female Seminary*. I am Amanda Dongan." Her high-pitched voice resonated in the hall. "I hope I can assist you today. Do you have an appointment to see someone?"

"Yes," he stated nervously. "I was asked to come this afternoon to see Mrs. Willard."

"Wonderful, I can direct you there. Please sign our guest ledger and I will lead you to her office?" She offered him a long quill pen. Recording his presence, he noticed that only a few others had signed in on that or the previous day. Notably, though, W. H. Bartlett and Betsy Hart were among the guests listed for the day before. Why had Bartlett and Mrs. Hart visited the campus the previous day? Had they arranged for his own appointment to see Mrs. Willard? He glanced upward toward the young girl's smiling face as he placed the pen within the folds of the guest book.

"Thank you, Mr. Higby. I am pleased to meet you." The woman extended her hand in greeting, much as a man might. Most women of whom he was familiar were not so forward. He vacillated, uncomfortable of his next move, but the young lady's hand remained extended. Unexpectedly, he noticed her stone grey eyes were transfixed upon his face. Most refined ladies were shy, however Amanda Dongan thwarted that stereotype. She was as resolute, firm, unwavering, and determined to grip his hand as any man might demonstrate his own equity to another. After a long, uncomfortable pause, he extended his hand, carefully gripping the girl's. Her grip was strong and confident, not weak and delicate as expected. If her skin had not been so smooth, he believed that her grip might be equal to any man.

She continued. "If you will follow me, I will guide you directly to Mrs. Willard's office." The girl briskly set off down the left hallway. He quickened his pace to remain close behind her. They turned two corners before the girl abruptly stopped and turned, facing her charge. "Wait here," she firmly commanded and then disappeared through the entrance to the headmistress's office. A few moments later, she reappeared and gestured for him to enter.

"Ah, Professor Higby!" Mrs. Willard stood by the only window, her arms folded across her chest. "I am glad to see you once again. I hope you slept well last night. There was a chill penetrating our fair village."

"Yes, very well," he responded.

"Thank you, Amanda. You may resume your station," Mrs. Willard directed the young lady. Amanda left the doorway, closing the heavy wooden door behind her. "Mr. Bartlett's lecture last evening was very enlightening. I was extremely impressed."

"Mr. Bartlett seems to always have that effect on people. He is a truly amazing person.

"Yes, he is very charming. Please, come in and sit," the headmistress instructed, pointing toward a plush cushioned chair opposite a larger sofa where she sat, crossing her legs comfortably beneath the folds of her dress. Jeduthan followed her lead and they sat opposite one another. There was an uneasy pause as the woman's eyes scanned his appearance. He felt her intense brown eyes judging him, sizing him up.

Jeduthan broke the silence. "I could not help noticing the great amount of construction in your fair city."

"Yes, it is true. The great fire left its wake upon Troy. Now the populous rebuilds. Out yonder window is proof of our recovery. The leadership of the First Presbyterian Church breaks ground upon its new building this very week. However, Professor Higby, I have not asked for this interview to discuss the vigor of Troy's recovery. I am very much impressed with your usage of the English language. Have you ever considered the teaching profession?"

The mention of the church caused Jeduthan nervously to shift his eyes to the window. However, he recovered when the headmistresses mentioned teaching. "I have, Mrs. Willard. The ministry called upon much of my earlier life, but as of late, I have explored a variety of interests that led to my association with Mr. Bartlett. Our adventures over the past year re-invigorated my intellect and I am traveling my way south in hopes of acquiring a tutoring position."

"Why south, sir?"

"I feel a change in clime might hold brighter prospects."

"Would you consider employment within our city?"

Jeduthan wavered. "I expect Mr. Bartlett's return in a month, so I am not seeking a position at this time."

Mrs. Willard's tone changed, more businesslike than Jeduthan had ever known from a woman. "Professor Higby, may I be frank? I am in desperate need of a temporary instructor for my girls' school. Moreover,

I am impressed with your language skills. Both Mr. Bartlett and Mrs. Hart attest to your noble character. Would you accept a teaching position at this institution?"

"Mrs. Willard, I am flattered that you might consider me, but Mr. Bartlett's eminent return would unfairly burden your charges..."

"Please, Mr. Higby! My husband's aging body is failing and I, as you know, will soon be left alone to face a hostile faculty in this experimental institution. Although we do have some allies in the community, most secretly hope for our failure." Her voice began to quiver. "My husband is an unshakable rock upon which this seminary stands, but I fear when he goes to meet his Maker, all of our hopes will rupture. I need friends on this faculty who will stay steadfast in the hope of educating our society's women. I know your positions on women's rights, in the ministry and in society."

"But..."

"Please, I am desperate..." Mrs. Willard paused, extracting a handkerchief from her sleeve to regain her composure. "Professor Higby, do as you must, but please consider the children."

The children? Jeduthan felt mortally wounded by those words. He had left his own children! Their eyes, the night he left, innocently closed with little anticipation of becoming virtual orphans on the morrow. He imagined their cries the next morning. *Where is father? Will father return tonight? What did we do to cause father to leave?* He gazed out the lone window, a cloud floated high in the blue sky above the river. The sun warmed the room and he felt the words depart his lips.

"Yes, Mrs. Willard, I will help. I cannot promise success, but if your students can benefit from my talents, I will graciously lend them to you, until my friend returns."

"Agreed!" Mrs. Willard announced as she stood and proceeded toward the door. "You may begin immediately. Amanda! Amanda! I will direct that Mrs. Dongan lead you to the classroom. I believe the subject is ancient literature." The young woman reappeared at the doorway. "Amanda, please escort Professor Higby to Miss Baker's former class. He is to be one of our new instructors here."

"Yes, ma'm. Professor, this way if you please." Mrs. Dongan led Jeduthan down the hall. Before turning the corner, he peered back toward the headmistress's office. Through the dim light, he could see the woman still at her door, the sunlight from her office illuminating half her face, revealing a broad, warm smile.

Moments later, he stood motionless at the head of the classroom. A large compendium of Greek literature perched on the wooden lectern at his fingertips. Grimly staring at him were twenty-six pupils, all seated stoically at their desks. Fifty-two glaring eyes, transfixed upon him, awaiting his direction. He felt as if he stood in front of the congregation again, each parishioner passing judgment on his character with their intense glare.

"Students..." he faltered. "Students, open your texts to the selection entitled, *The Iliad*." He watched as each young girl reached into her desk and retrieved the reader. Only a few opened the textbook. Jeduthan placed his finger upon the first lines of text and read aloud, "*Sing, O Goddess, the anger of Achilles, son of Peleus, that brought countless ills upon the Achaeans.*" When he glanced up from the page, he found blank faces upon many of the students. Two students rolled their eyes in boredom. Three others placed their head upon their desks, comatose, and one in the far back of the classroom probed her nostril with an investigating finger. He continued, "*Many a brave soul did it send hurrying down to Hades...*"

"Like us," retorted an anonymous listener in the crowded classroom. Jilted, Jeduthan looked up from the reading again, finding the children still disinterested. The room, though heated by a small coal fired stove in the rear, was chilled by wind filtering through the imperfect windows. Nevertheless, nervous beads of sweat appeared upon his brow.

One more line confirmed that teaching was not like preaching. Visions of bored congregations, sitting in front of him, flashed through his head. He wondered if he had really been that dreary or if these girls were expressing typical adolescent behavior, rebelling against authority.

He soon decided to alter his presentation in an effort of making the important themes become meaningful for the students. Yet how? He searched his mind for some connection that the *Iliad* might have upon these young ladies of Troy. Troy! Yes, Troy!

"Ladies, I could read verbatim from your texts the lines of poetry that Homer penned about that horrible, yet epic adventure thousands of years past, but I wish not for you to end your educated lives in

Hades. Therefore, I propose that we live the lives of Homer's classic and investigate the character's motives from that long ago conflict. It is quite appropriate that here in Mrs. Willard's school we study this story, for the epic began with a woman. A woman destined for Troy!" The girls' ears piqued, the disinterested raised their heads, and even the nose picker paused her gouging to hear his words.

"A beautiful woman, married to a Greek king, stole herself from his embrace and escaped from her captivity with her foreign lover, beginning a ten year long terrible military siege of an imposing metropolis aptly named *Troy.* Her facial beauty so captivated the known world that it purportedly launched a thousand ships!" The students were riveted. "And you, dear young ladies of Troy, are to become that woman. You will assume the role of Helen, daughter of the Greek god of gods, Zeus, wife to King Menelaus of legendary Sparta, and lover of Paris, heir apparent to the Trojan throne and..."

A student hesitatingly raised her hand. Caught off guard by her interruption, Jeduthan paused his soliloquy and asked, "Yes? What do you want?"

Standing she said, "Excuse me, Professor. I am Susan Livingston. Pardon my interruption, but are we studying ancient literature? I don't understand how women could play any important role so long ago."

"Thank you, Susan. I am glad you stopped me. Beware ladies, do not be fooled. Women have always played preeminent roles in history, as they will in our future. One short phrase which I have placed faith in my many years is that behind every great man stands an even greater woman." Jeduthan paused in the silent room, all the students now fully engaged before concluding, "And a surprised mother-in-law!" The classroom broke into boisterous laughter as he crossed arms and smiled.

"Ladies, as you read Homer's poem over the next few days, I want you to imagine that you are *Helen of Troy.* Listen to the poem's language for clues to her character, the images that haunt her, and the dread she fears. As a culminating assignment for the *Iliad*, I want you to create, in any medium you desire, a sketch, image, descriptive poem, carving, placard, soliloquy, debate, essay, or any numerous other items that expresses Helen's desires, motives, and hopes. I will guide you in the story with all its gore, adventures, heroics, and gallantry. However, only you can imagine the feelings of Helen, the sole woman for whom all these men dedicated their sweat and blood on their impossible ten-year adventure. Finally, the true meaning of this work of art should lead you in search of how you can use her character to become better women here in your own modern city of Troy."

He spent the next hour describing the *Iliad's* story of intrigue, adventure, bravery, and honor to his eager listeners. Quoting from the elaborate poetic verse, he followed with a detailed explanation so that all could visualize the character's suffering, tears, and hopes. At one point, he asked volunteers to role-play the duel between Menelaus and Paris. Just as the Greek is about to subdue his opponent, the Goddess Aphrodite spirits the Trojan away and into the bedchamber of Helen.

Many students eagerly arose to accept the challenge. When dismissal came, the previous lackluster students left invigorated with a sense of purpose that few seemed capable of only a few short hours before. Jeduthan felt good.

Afterwards, he picked up his texts and reported to Mrs. Willard's office. There, he was disappointed to find her absent. However, Mrs. Dongan reported that the headmistress desired that he return tomorrow at the same hour to direct an art class. He felt slightly confused, however he consented to the request.

Leaving by the same door he entered only a few hours earlier, he stepped lively down the street toward the *Sentinel's* office and his awaiting shelter. Passing by Sam Wilson's meat shop, he decided to stop in and pick up some sausage. He entered the shop and found a young man at the chopping block.

"Excuse me, may I purchase some sausage?" inquired Jeduthan.

"You may," replied the young man as he reached into a container extracting several links.

"Where is Uncle Sam?"

"He is in the country securing some beef from the local farmers. I am his son, Benjamin." The young man extended his hand in a friendly gesture.

"Jeduthan Higby."

"Professor Higby? I heard you speak only last night at *The Rensselaer Institute*. I was very impressed. I plan to attend classes there when Mr. Eaton has open enrollment next fall. Father was also at the lecture and he will regret not seeing you today for he talked at great lengths about you when he remembered your previous visit to our shop. It was hard to get a word in edgewise as he bragged upon you. Welcome back, Professor, and if you ever need anything at all, please do not hesitate to call upon us."

Jeduthan felt warm inside. He paid for the sausage, departed with a wave of his hand, and continued toward his lodging. Along the street, he spied Mrs. Hart waving furiously and calling his name.

"Professor? Professor? Please cross the street," she hailed.

He stepped into the muddy street and nearly fell into the slippery slime that lined the avenue's edge. Mrs. Hart caught her breath as he righted himself, avoiding catastrophe.

"Professor Higby, I have heard the news! Cousin Will has departed, and like his character, without a word."

"Now Mrs. Hart, pray not condemn the man. He dreads goodbyes. He nearly left me before boarding *The Troy* bound for his business in New York. He asked me to relay his sorrow for his hasty departure personally and I would have come by tonight if you had not caught me on the street just now."

"Did you say the canal-schooner *Troy* carried him toward his destination?"

"Yes, I viewed its name prominently displayed on its stern as he sailed forth into the river."

"That is strange. That boat is bound for Lake Champlain, not southward along the Hudson. Are you sure?"

"I believe so, but it was early this morning and I might be confused."

"Well, never mind. I am sure Will Bartlett will show up on my doorstep again in the not too distant future. I hear you are a sensation at Mrs. Willard's school!"

He grimaced. "How did you hear about me and Mrs. Willard's school?"

"News travels quickly in this city, my dear Professor. Mrs. Willard stopped by just after lunch to report that you accepted a position at the school. Additionally, only ten minutes ago, young Susan Livingston passed by my door and announced a splendid new professor who brought to life Homer's *Iliad*. She was tickled pink and hurried home to begin her studies. I have known that girl since she was a tot, and she has never looked as excited as she was today. No one has ever made such an impression on that child like you."

He smiled before excusing himself to continue his way toward his lodging, promising to visit often at the Hart residence. He entered the *Sentinel*'s office and Mr. Tuttle was at his usual place before the printing press. Jeduthan tried to ease his way past the old man without disturbing him but failed in the attempt. Mr. Tuttle stopped the machinery and turned.

"Professor Higby! I am glad to see you this afternoon. I hear good things about you at Mrs. Willard's school."

"My, how news spreads," commented Jeduthan. "How, pray tell, have you heard about me at the *Troy Female Seminary*?"

"My daughter is Mrs. Dongan." He paused. "Amanda Dongan, Mrs. Willard's assistant. She met you at the school's entrance. In addition, one of your students is my niece. I will not reveal her name for she would be embarrassed if you knew her identity, with you renting my spare room and all. Nevertheless, she was very excited, Professor. She is good at sketching, like your companion Mr. Bartlett and she sped through here in a flash on her way to retrieve her sketch board. I am sure we will see little of her the remainder of the day. You really gave her a spark! I don't know how, but I am..."

Jeduthan cut him off. "Thank you, Mr. Tuttle. I am very fatigued as of now. Please excuse me." He ascended the staircase as Mr. Tuttle watched. Just before entering his room, he peered down into the printer's room and found the old man grinning a broad smile. Jeduthan waved slightly before entering the room and shutting the door.

He had not lied when he told Mr. Tuttle of his tiredness. He plopped onto the bed with such force that the lone leg supporting the corner gave way, bending greatly under his weight. He feared that it might break at any moment, however it held fast and he relaxed. His mind filled with positive, fulfilling accomplishments. After so many months incognito, he finally felt productive. His first classroom experience reaped great benefits, including fulfilling his longtime goal as a teacher. Moreover, he was not just a traditional lecturer, but an inspiring and challenging instructor.

An added benefit also became apparent. The community expressed desire for him. With a new sense of achievement, Jeduthan reached into his bag, retrieved his sausages, and began gnawing at their juicy meat, imagining the adventures he would make on his own tomorrow.

A cloudless sky dawned bright and gay as Jeduthan strolled the delightful streets on his trek to the *Troy Female Seminary* and his second day as instructor. Entering the main seminary building, he again greeted Amanda Dongan at her post in the foyer.

"Good morning, Professor Higby," announced the young woman. "God has blessed us with an unusually warm day. Mrs. Willard has instructed me to lead you to the art room today. I hope you are ready to ply your companion's artistic talents.

Jeduthan looked confused.

"I observed you and Mr. Bartlett at the lecture the other evening and was truly impressed."

"Thank you for your confidence, miss. I assure you that I am second rate compared to my associate."

"You are quite modest, professor. Next Tuesday, you are to continue with ancient literature at the same time schedule. However today, the girls study portraiture. Come, follow me."

Mrs. Dongan turned and led the way through the halls. They passed several empty rooms and one full of students. He paused at the entrance of this room and viewed its instructor rigidly poised at the class front, reading from a text. Some students propped their heads up with stoic arms, eyes gazing blankly into space, tremendously uninterested. The teacher's voice resounded in a tedious monotone, from one arithmetic factor to another.

"Professor, I almost forgot. Mrs. Willard has left you this notice," interrupted Mrs. Dongan. She handed him a sealed envelope as the pair stopped next to a large door significantly farther down the hallway from his previous classroom. "This room houses the art students. I will introduce you to them." The young woman opened the door, the hinges creaking as an old wagon might on its journey westward on a great trek.

His first view of the classroom was shocking. Windows extended lengthwise the entire distance along one wall, revealing a panoramic view of the town's waterfront. Dominating the view was the Troy Iron and Nail Company's forge and the Marshall Textile Mill, the latter hiding much of the steeply dropping Potsenskill Creek that drained the town's upper elevations. Canal boats departing onto the river or ascending the watery ditch toward Lake Champlain and the upper reaches of the Hudson added a pastoral view for the growing cityscape.

His eyes shifted from the scenes framed by the windows to the many students seated on the wooden classroom benches. He recognized many faces, including youthful Susan Livingston seated in the front center, seemingly the most eager of all the students, a smile penetrating her round, milky face.

Mrs. Dongan piped in, "Ladies, I wish to introduce your new art instructor. Welcome, Professor Higby to our campus."

The class responded with a vocal, "Good afternoon, Professor Higby."

"Good afternoon, ladies," he replied, placing Mrs. Willard's sealed note upon the instructor's podium.

"Sir, I leave you now with your charges. If you require assistance, have a girl fetch me from my post," announced Mrs. Dongan.

"Thank you very much, I will." The young woman left the room with Jeduthan facing his large audience. "I regret that I am to instruct you in art class today," he began. "My visual art experience is very limited and I hope you will excuse my amateurish approach. I have, though, been fortunate at having spent the last half year in companionship of an exceptional artist by the name of William H. Bartlett." A noticeable alluring sigh floated through the room from an undisclosed source. "Do any of you know of whom I speak?"

Nearly in unison, a multitude of enthusiastic hands rapidly raised, smiles and batting eyelashes throughout. A young blonde girl asked, "Professor, can you describe how Mr. Bartlett obtains his images for his sketches?"

Another girl in the rear of the class piped up with, "And how does he exhibit such passion with his art?"

Pandemonium ensued as a flood of questions resounded from throughout the room concerning his companion's style, personality, wit, likes, dislikes, and even one bold question concerning his tastes in women. Jeduthan raised his hands to indicate a sense of order in the classroom before he once again began.

"Ladies! Ladies, my friend's style to the visual arts are very unique indeed. They are best described by one encounter Mr. Bartlett and I experienced during the summer months in the wilds of the frontier." The all female class quieted, leaning forward upon the edge of their seats with anticipation.

"I left my companion sitting upon the bank of an isolated stream while I busily led our noble steed to a nearby natural pasture. Returning, I found Mr. Bartlett, sketchpad in hand, not more than fifteen paces apart from a gigantic black panther, each glaring into the other's eyes. Neither twitched a muscle for what must have exceeded two full minutes. Me, petrified for our safety, remained perfectly still also, fearing any move on my part might bring the fierce creature's fangs upon my poor companion's exposed neck, sapping his existence from our lovely Earth. I scanned the ground for some type of weapon in which to protect ourselves, but to no avail. How could we survive? Soon, I discovered that my companion exhibited no fear but was trying his best to stare down this wild beast. I, being somewhat experienced with wild animals during my years on the frontier, realized that no mere mortal could successfully stare into submission such a terrifying fiend. Therefore, I prayed for deliverance. And it came, with Nimrod."

A single student interrupted, "Who is Nimrod?"

"Why, my noble steed, dear child. He came galloping from the pasture with such a frightful racket that the panther rebounded upward onto the near bank and disappeared into the dark thicket. My heart raced with excitement and relief for we were delivered from ruin. I approached my friend, and found that he had moved scarcely a muscle, except for his sketching fingers. His eyes continued their distant stare, not taking any notice of me, my old horse Nimrod, or even the trickling water of the brook at his feet. He remained frozen upon that spot nearly fifteen minutes until his sketch was complete, not a word exchanging between us. He never once looked upon his sketchpad until finished. His mind was so engrossed, so focused, and so intent on his subject that he must have become demonized by that panther."

A gasp emitted from one unknown student. Jeduthan paused, the classroom engulfed in silence. "Now, ladies, I believe I have given you what you asked for: an intense personal glimpse into a truly remarkable man. Now, you can demonstrate your artistic talents for me. I have made known my limited abilities at the visual arts and I apologize for my deficiencies, however my skill revolves about the written word. My story today painted an intense portrait of a moment frozen in time, a tableau of sorts. Moreover, each of you here today has etched into your mind some visual representation of that moment.

Your assignment, then, is to depict the story of Mr. Bartlett and the panther, in a visible sketch from any point of view you desire. I will give you an hour to complete this task before we will analyze each in turn. I warn you, do not invent items which the story did not include and do not discuss your sketch until I call time. Remember the moment!"

Smiles breached many faces as each hurried to their sketchpads and began drawing. Jeduthan walked among the class in silence as each girl approached the scene from differing views. He noticed that the older, more mature girls seemed to emphasize his companion's masculinity while invariably, the younger students focused on the prominent wild beast or the rescuing steed.

With the hour concluded, he called the class to order. Similar aged girls analyzed each other's sketches. Most critiques were complimentary, but there was the occasional boorish remark. Jeduthan hushed the offensive comments, emphasizing how the auditory story might have etched differing images unto different people. "One must appreciate passion in art," he cautioned.

Instructing the class to study their sketches before the next gathering, he informed the students that they would continue refining their drawing at a later date. He then dismissed the girls. A fair number of the older students approached the podium, personally thanking him for the lesson. As he shook their hands, he realized that each one of these girls were self-confident young ladies with forceful, energetic grips.

As the last of the students departed, he smiled. A warm glow passed through his body. Though he had done no preparation and expected only failure, the two classes were resounding successes. Moreover, he stumbled into these teachable lessons! What might he develop if given time to plan?

Basking in victory, he drew the shades and crossed the darkened room toward the classroom door. Just as he grasped the knob, he remembered Mrs. Willard's message still poised upon the podium. He returned, seized the note, and read the contents.

Professor Higby. Please join Mr. Willard and me for a journey to Albany after church on Sunday. We will attend a lecture early the next morning and return Monday evening. Dress accordingly, for the weather in our region is quite changeable.
Sincerely, Mrs. Emma H. Willard, Headmistress, Troy Female Seminary.

"How complimentary of Mrs. Willard," he thought. His association with this dynamic woman extended but only a few days and yet she had already invited him to an informative lecture in the state capital. Perhaps a retreat to Albany would do him good. Moreover, Mrs. Willard and he could use the time discussing more thoroughly the financial arrangements of his teaching position. Monetary concerns did not distress him for he retained the coveted church funds hidden within his scheitholt. Yet, if an arrangement was not forthcoming, suspicions might be aroused, an event that he wished to avoid if at all possible. Therefore, he scurried from the room, passing Mrs. Dongan with only a slight wave goodbye, and beating a hurried path toward the awaiting solitude of his room above the *Sentinel*.

Though he had not experienced boredom since meeting his esteemed artist friend many months ago, he was now on his own without duties, expectations, and few friends. He expected the long weekend held only monotony and tedium. However, this was not to be.

While gliding past the familiar shops lining the street housing the *Sentinel*'s office, Jeduthan noticed a young lady with a broad hat. She stood silently in the shadow cast by one of the burnt structures that had once been a grand home before the great fire of 1820 consumed its timbers. Her golden curls draped from beneath the hat's felt. Unable to view the female's face, he was sure she was sobbing, shedding heart-felt tears.

He approached, hoping in someway to console her when a gentle breeze exposed her pale face. It was Susan Livingston, his student of only a few minutes past. He wanted to turn away, but a sympathetic sensitivity engulfed his soul. He reached toward the weeping young student and touched her gently upon the shoulder. Startled, she wiped her eyes with her palms.

"Miss Livingston," he consoled. "Are you injured?"

She faced Jeduthan, tears streaking down her checks. "Good evening, Professor Higby," she managed to exhale between sobs. "I am fine. I often stop here on my way home to remember."

"To remember what?" he inquired.

"Home." She turned again to face the burnt timbers and the telltale signs of a brick walkway that forked before ascending a short set of blackened stone steps exiting into a once joy-filled portch that now was only an empty abyss. "This was my home five years ago. While father and mother sat upon the portico in a chair swing, I skipped along those bricks with my younger sister, cheerful and happy." She pointed forlornly toward the absent porch. "But then the fire came."

"How dreadful, dear child! How might I help..."

"During the night," she continued, unperturbed by Jeduthan's plea, "We begged father to repeat the story he often narrated to us during the Christmas season. We called it *A Visit from Saint Nickolas*. It described a wonderful visit by a jolly old elf to our house each year on Christmas Eve. There was a magical sleigh, pulled by flying reindeer, leaping upon the roof with a clatter and all the while, joyful songs emitting from the jovial rosy cheeks of the little man. All was gay and bright. However, that night, when we rushed to the windows in search of the familiar Christmas apparitions and newly fallen snow glistening in the moonlight, our eyes burned from the bright glare of towering flames. Clattering upon the rooftop was not old Saint Nick and his magical reindeer, but rather the sounds of cedar roof shingles crackling and popping like kindling. A firestorm engulfed the city. Wind blew at fervor pitch, flames swallowing each obstacle that challenged its destructive path! We retreated to our room, hovering behind our drawers, father sheltering our bodies against the terrifying heat while smoke blackened the air. The floor soon collapsed and I was thrown outward upon the singed grass along with father. Mother and sister, though, fell inward, into the bowels of the inferno. Bucket brigades formed in the valley, but we upon this hill were much too far from the river ever to expect help. Mother and sister perished that night while father lost his mind. For two years, we stayed with uncles, aunts, and cousins, before father regained his senses. He now works for Mr. Hart's *Troy Savings Bank* as a cashier, but he rarely talks to me anymore. He says I remind him of other times and other people. He might have disappeared for all it mattered, for he is only an empty shell of a man." She sobbed.

Jeduthan stepped closer to young Susan Livingston hoping his presence might comfort her grieving memories. Such a nightmare no child should endure! He placed his arm about her shoulders but his mouth could not utter any comforting words. She turned her eyes toward him and deep within, he could see his own daughter. Poor young Laura, a small child beckoning for her father's attention. However, he only sat at the barren wooden table, hands over his ears attempting to block out the child's heartfelt pleas. How wrong he was for abandoning his family and his little daughter. Was he any better than Susan Livingston's parent? Would a broken heart and tearful eyes haunt his memories always? What could he say to this tormented young lass?

"Miss Livingston, I wish I could console you with words, but I cannot. Let us walk." The two shuffled toward his room above the *Sentinel.* Approaching the building, he asked Susan to wait outside for a few moments while he bounded up the stairs and retrieved his scheitholt from his room. However, when he returned, Susan Livingston had vanished. He looked down the long street and saw no one. He stood in the dark, his hopes for consoling the young lass dashed.

He meandered to the rain barrel at the stone building's corner and peered into its dark contents. The blackness was so intense that it reflected his silhouette back into his eyes. He heard the painful sobs of his children ringing in his ears.

"Where is father?" echoed Laura.

"Will Daddy sing to us when he comes home?" asked young Philander.

A water droplet shook the stillness, disturbing the black water's reflectivity. He gazed into the darkening sky. It was void of clouds and only a faint star twinkled in the twilight. His face chilled, and as he reached to rub his cheeks, he realized the droplet that had disturbed the reflective blackness came from his eyes. Were these tears for Susan Livingston or his abandoned children? He did not know. Rubbing his eyes, he returned to his sparse accommodations, letting sleep overcome his emotions.

Next morning, he arose and searched for an eating establishment that would quench his desire for an adequate, home cooked meal. Tempted to wander to the Hart residence and inquire of Aunt Sallie for a spare plate of warm flapjacks, he dismissed the idea, worrying he might impose on Mrs. Hart's kindhearted hospitality too often. Instead, he strolled along Troy's boulevards searching for a quaint tavern. He could not find a suitable eatery and returned to his abode where he found Susan Livingston just outside his living accommodations on the far side of the street. Her eyes were no longer red in sorrow but beamed with excitement.

"Professor!" she called, extending her hand above the large straw hat adorning her blond curls. "Professor, may I speak with you?"

He hesitated little before stepping into the muddy street. While crossing, one of his boots sank deep in a sticky mud puddle, sucking his foot covering off his foot entirely. He stood motionless, balancing on one leg, a long stocking dangling in midair, half exposing his naked foot. Susan's beckoning suddenly changed to dread, concern, and finally into a giggling laugh, as she perceived her professor's predicament.

After nearly a half minute of balancing precariously over the sticky mud, he carefully placed an exposed knee next to the offending puddle and reached nearly a full six inches into its depths extracting his mud-caked boot. A deep sucking sound emitted from the hole as he pried the boot from the muck, auburn ooze dripping from its heel. He peered at the young girl with a seriousness that might frighten a fearless soldier. However, she continued her girly chuckle.

Bravely, he replaced his brogan boot upon his dangling foot, stood upright, and took three lengthy steps toward the girl, never taking his eyes from her face. On the third step, he again sank to his mid-calf in a similarly muddy hole. He looked down. His foot again covered in thick reddish clay. Susan vocally cackled an absurd snort, nearly falling backward upon the building's stone step at the sight of her professor.

"Young lady! I partially fault you for my predicament."

Susan hushed her laughing as Jeduthan slowly extracted his second boot from the pasty muck much as he did the first. Accomplishing the task, he pondered his condition and began to laugh. Susan soon joined him. He paced the remaining steps successfully and without incident. Sitting upon the stone steps, man and girl mused at his condition.

As both caught their breath, Susan spoke. "Professor, please forgive my abrupt disappearance last night. I became spooked all by my lonesome on the deserted street and I flew home." She lowered her head in shame before she mused, "But I am more fortunate than you, for I evaded the devil's earthly grip in the darkness that you could not in the brightness of day!" She smiled.

"Miss Livingston, I reward you for your wit, but it is not I that sought you, but you me." Looking at his mud covered trousers, he continued. "Now that I have paid a dreadful price for your companionship, may I inquire as to what brings you to my door?"

"I come to apologize, professor, and also to invite you to a religious revival today." Her eyelashes batted and face blushed. "We meet after lunchtime at *The Old Burying Ground on the Hill* where guest lecturers inspire us to live better lives. Most times, they speak on temperance. Will you attend?"

He stared at his muddy boots as he replied, "Why, Miss Livingston, I would be most honored. I hope you will not imply to the honored speakers that my muddied condition was a result of intemperance!"

She blushed. "Of course not, if you will not reveal my forwardness of inviting my teacher to such a social gathering."

"Your virtue is safe with me, fine lady," he responded taking Susan's gloved hand, raising it to his lips, and with a gentlemanly bow pecked a slight kiss upon the back of her extended hand. "For now, I bid you an affectionate adieu. I am in pursuit of a warm breakfast this fine morning."

"I know of a handsome place, professor, where you can dine on abundant eggs, breads, and pastries."

"I don't wish to further impose on your hospitality..."

Susan's lips tightened into a determined grimace. "Professor Higby, do not insult me as such! There is no impropriety for a good citizen to assist a newcomer to our fair city in finding a decent meal. Now sir, please follow me!"

She stood upright, tugged at the older man's arm until he relented and followed. She briskly led Jeduthan on a half-mile journey northward, past the Old Bank Place, and into the pastures beyond. Numerous times, he stretched his long legs into a jog to keep pace with the young girl. Her skirt nearly flew along the streets and lanes. Twice he feared that she, too, would slip and spill into the sticky mud as he did earlier but young Susan Livingston effortlessly glided along the boulevards, undeterred by possible calamities in her path.

He glanced westward at one point, viewing the ever present canal boats ascending the locks on their journey northward. The hooves of the determined mules plodding along the towpath brought forth pleasant memories of a young artist leading him from place to place on wondrous adventures. Once again, he was the follower of a determined younger personality who was, like himself, haunted by past catastrophic events. He wondered if personal misfortune often shapes such dominant personalities and if his own children's abandonment will result in similar character traits. He awakened from his thoughts as they approached a cottage a few yards from the canal.

"Professor, this simple bungalow contains the most fabulous chef in all the Hudson Valley. Her hearty meals could revive to healthy statures even the deprived warriors of the besieged fortress of Troy beyond the far ocean seas. Let us enter and partake of her bounty as the mighty Greeks did when the great bastion's walls were breached so many centuries before."

He raised a surprised eyebrow as these words flowed from the lips of his youthful companion. "My dear Miss Livingston…"

"You may call me Susan," retorted the girl.

"Alright, mademoiselle Susan."

"…And I will call you Jeduthan, at least when we are not in the formal setting of Mrs. Willard's school. Now, Jeduthan, let us enter!" She firmly pushed the cottage door inward and it opened. Inside revealed a simple tavern, six tables with accompanying low cut chairs with only one man seated nearby the rear entrance. His dress indicated a canal worker, probably one of the many independent teamsters plying his trade along the nearby course. However, what caught Jeduthan's attention was the huge feast upon the table. It contained a banquet of fried eggs, a basket of steaming biscuits, and three bowls containing mush, fried apples, and one unidentifiable white soup. The man paid little attention to the newcomers as the pair sat across the room at a vacant table.

"Jeduthan, I assure you this food is well worth the walk from town. I often spend time here, watching the hard working men enter and gorge themselves at these tables. This morning's patrons seem rather sparse, but the better for us," she smiled. A fat old woman entered the room and waddled to the pair's table.

"What may I serve you today?" she inquired.

Susan was quick to respond, taking charge of ordering while at the same time, causing Jeduthan to feel slightly uncomfortable. "We will have the same as that man over there," she responded pointing to the canal worker's table. Jeduthan began to protest when Susan shushed him with a waving finger. "Now, Jeduthan! We are taught at Mrs. Willard's school to speak when we have something we wish to say, ask when we have something we need to know, and demand when we desire something we want. I see what I want and I am not too delicate, shy, or timid in obtaining it. Thank you ma'am, and please bring us two plates." The fat old woman grunted and disappeared out the rear entrance.

There were a few minutes of uncomfortable silence between the two before he commented, "Susan, I am surprised with your comparison of this meager establishment's capacity and the voracious appetites of the Greek warriors of long ago. How have you come to know such details of Homer's story and poetry?"

"Our class discussion of recent has sparked my appetite for ancient Greek history," the girl replied. "Your story telling is superb and extremely vivid, the characters becoming lifelike in my imagination. The skits we performed in class also revitalized the story. Mostly, I believe our assignment motivated me. I never experienced a teacher before that encouraged a class to personalize a story as you did. We always studied the classic stories in history by routinely reciting passages, performing readings, and copying text. However, your idea of assuming the character of Helen is so relevant to young women that I can visualize her dilemmas and quandaries as if they are my own. I even see, in Helen, my..." Susan stopped her speech, lowering her eyes in shame as a slow tear formed and traced down her face.

"Dear girl, do not allow any shame you fear to overwhelm you. What transcribed between us last evening will never part my lips. Let us talk on another subject."

"No, Jeduthan, I do not mind speaking. Yes, Helen's problems are similar to mine own and I see their correlation. I am rejected by the one that should love me and I seek solace in another's arms."

"How do you know this?"

"I am rejected by my father. He will not embrace me. I try to speak to him; however, he will not listen. I try to write him but he will not read. I find myself seeking friendships that lead to disaster. What am I to do?"

"First, my young student, pray to our heavenly Father. He overcomes all. Secondly, use the talents that God has granted you. If you could describe your best talent, what would it be?"

She hesitated before shyly admitting, "Poetry. That is why your first lesson so engaged me. I love poetry. The other night, after your lesson about Troy, I went home and read the entire lyric that Homer penned in the *Iliad*. I read his lines late into the night, using candles and through their dim light, I beheld the images that each verse seared into my mind. I felt all encompassed by the story unfolding before me. And the story seemed to parallel my own catastrophe."

"Then you must hone that skill and apply the pen, child. I suggest you write a poem for your father."

"I have written him, but he does not read my lyrics. He considers it rubbish, without substance or usefulness. He believes me frivolous and..."

At that moment, the old woman returned with their feast. Susan wiped her face of tears and began to heap her plate with the fried eggs. "Susan, let us first bless this meal and ask for The Lord's guidance."

The girl nodded in agreement and Jeduthan began, "Father God, bless this food to our bodies and guide us in Your will. Allow our friendship to further Your kingdom. Relieve our fears and thank You for giving us hope through your Holy son, Jesus Christ. It is in His name we pray, amen." He looked upon the young girl facing him at the table. His sympathy poured out upon the troubled youth. She could not communicate with her own father, similar to his own difficulty in the past. He determined to help her avoid similar mistakes that had plagued him back home in Turin.

The pair ate the food lavishly, all which tantalized Jeduthan's appetite. He only avoided the strange pasty milk-white dish. The girl, though, scooped a large mountain of the mushy substance onto her plate. Staring in utter dismay, he watched as she heaped large pats of butter on its summit. The warmth from this strange food steamed as a volcanic mount might simmer and boil, melting butter acting as savory lava flowing its course down the food's mountain-like side. Astonishing as it was, the girl added even more butter, poking and shoveling the pats deep within the precipitous pile. Next, she added vast amounts of salt to the concoction before she topped the entire conglomeration with a vigorous pouring of maple syrup. Wide-eyed, he asked, "Dear girl, what may I ask is that substance?"

Susan smiled, her melancholy demeanor evaporating. "Oh, they are called hominy-grits. I just adore them. The woman who cooks for this inn is from Georgia, though you would never know it because she rarely speaks to strangers. I find her company quite rewarding, though. She declares grits as nourishment for the heart," she sighed. "Moreover, I believe her. Yes, I come here often, probably once a week, though father does not know and probably cares even less. After the catastrophe, I found this a sanctuary of sorts." She took the large wooden spoon and scooped a generous portion. "Here, Jeduthan, try some." She held the spoon precariously over the table offering the grits to him, some of the white paste dripping off the spoon's side and landing in small spots upon the table.

Jeduthan hesitated. "No, I will take my own, Susan."

She protested. "Come now, Jeduthan. Hominy grits prepared by an amateur are wretched. Let me make a deal with you. First, try some grits that I have prepared and then you try them your way. You can then decide," she smiled devilishly.

"Alright, I take your deal!" Slowly he advanced toward the hovering spoon still held by his young consort. His mouth enveloped the awaiting substance. Warm, salty, and with a hint of sweetness, the grits glided through his mouth, a taste all its own. He returned Susan's smile and said, "Your concoction truly is delicious. I believe I need to sample a larger portion!" Jeduthan heaped a liberal helping upon his plate and began eating, but quickly halted. He frowned. "These grits taste nothing like your serving."

"Correct you are, Jeduthan. I must admit that plain grits hold no sway over my palate. It is all in what you put into them that adds the savory flavor," she admitted.

A brilliant idea flashed through Jeduthan's mind. "You are quite right, Susan." He paused, raising his hand philosophically pondering. "Brilliant! Please, at our next class, I want you to remind me about grits. You are a genius!"

"True!" remarked the girl. "Now, let us finish here and begin our walk to Mount Ida."

Jeduthan expressed puzzlement.

Susan reacted to his expression with, "...I mean the burying ground! I have come to call the *Burying Ground on the Hill,* Mount Ida for its stupendous vistas of Troy and the Hudson are more liken to some great mountain. From its crest, no one may escape detection in the valley below. There, we will find the temperance lecture and religious revival scheduled for this afternoon. I propose we leisurely stroll back to town as our great meal has undoubtedly filled every crevice within my belly." She rubbed her midsection with her palm.

"Yes, it will be my pleasure to escort you to your meeting. Who is to be the speaker?" he asked.

"Reverend Nathan S.S. Beman!" announced the youth. "He is our Presbyterian minister and he has invited another special guest to speak to us younger folk. I think his topic will be *Intemperance* and its effects on our community."

"Now that should be a lively topic," Jeduthan said with a smile. He reached into his satchel to pay for the breakfast when Susan stopped him.

"Jeduthan, I will pay my own way if you please. Otherwise, rumor might suspect impropriety. Besides, you are my guest!"

Impressed by this young lady's boldness, he suspected the influences of Mrs. Willard. He responded, "I concede to your request." Each paid their own portion of the meal fare and then exited the tavern.

"Come, let us stroll to town along the canal and enjoy the rocky hills that form the valley of the magnificent Hudson," Susan announced, waving her arms in a circular pattern toward the glorious surrounding backdrop. Agreeing, he and the young girl walked slowly down the towpath, stopping often and admiring the gorgeous scenery. With no leaves to obstruct their view, newly honed rocks glistened upon the hillsides while some protruded within their reach, a few yards from their path.

Along one portion, the water had melted and refroze during the night. Amongst some shadowy overhangs, the slowly dripping water produced elaborately draping curved ice sheets that reflected the sun's afternoon rays. Susan stood behind one such unique formation that distorted her image through its icy barrier. Playfully, Jeduthan acted as if he would shatter the frail draping ice, however Susan begged him not to. Pleading, she instead urged him to allow the icy wonder to die a natural death by the sun's warmth. He smiled broadly, as his hammer-like fist faded into a gentle palm, acceding to her wish as a father might to the pleas of an innocent child. He would not soon forget this two-hour stroll with young Susan Livingston. All seemed right with the world.

Sin

A cool wind descended upon teacher and student as they approached *The Old Burying Ground on the Hill.* A gloomy cloud blotted out the sun's warm rays that had blessed Jeduthan's relaxed leisurely afternoon jaunt in company with his new young feminine friend. Reacting to the chill, Jeduthan lifted his jacket's collar while Susan extracted a shawl from her coat pocket, covering her exposed head. They crossed the cemetery by weaving their way through the headstones and memorials that seemed to litter the ground in a haphazard fashion. The cold stone and aged wooden planks etched with eerie epitaphs left little esthetic beauty in this place of the dead.

A crowd gathered on the far edge of the burying ground. No doubt, this was the meeting that Susan Livingston hoped to attend. Jeduthan followed her dainty footsteps across gravesites where, he spied the solemn group listening to a young preacher.

"...and my beloved, behold these dead who lay in this cold ground. They lived their lives with false hope, believing their works could save them from eternal damnation. However, friends, you still possess time to realize that only faith in Him will prevent you from sharing their same fate. REPENT and accept God's gift!" The preacher's voice echoed among the barren trees that towered above the gathering as a small choir began the familiar tune *Amazing Grace.*

Susan gently leaned toward his ear, covering her mouth with one hand and said, "That is the Reverend Mr. Beman. He leads the First Presbyterian Church here in town. Some have condemned him as a heretic, but I don't. Every time I hear him, my soul aches for forgiveness. He usually preaches a salvation sermon but I have it on good account that today's discussion will be intemperance."

She stopped whispering when three women turned their heads toward the couple in displeasure. Susan led her teacher closer to the speaker during the choir's final stanza.

"Ladies and gentlemen," Reverend Beman announced. "I wish to introduce today, a fine gentleman from the more remote parts of our state. He has recently traveled through many miles of wilderness at my request to address the brethren that call this city home. We are growing with great multitudes of immigrants coming into our fair region, not all with similar beliefs, customs, and cultures that we possess. We must strengthen our faith in the face of these newcomers and demonstrate that our town is Godly. Please welcome Reverend Mr. Charles Finney."

Jeduthan's heart seemed to stop as a hushed applause resonated through the assemblage as the guest stood. He knew this man! He emulated this same preacher with immediate calls of salvation in his church in Turin some years ago. He also remembered Bartlett's revelations from Lockport between a *Preacher Finney* and Editor Turner seeking a *Higby scoundrel*.

"Dear brethren of Troy!" began Finney. "Harken to Brother Beman's call!"

Jeduthan peered around nervously, looking for an escape.

"Beware of the traitor amongst you. An evil plague corrupts your hearts. He stands beneath these very trees! He slithers into our purse. He pursues our children. He invades our very homes! Oh Lord, I see him in our midst!" exclaimed the preacher as he raised a pointed finger directly toward Jeduthan. "There he stands! Full of pride! Writhing in selfish greed with your tithes! Condemn him, oh Lord! Strike vengeance upon his soul for his crimes!"

The preacher's piercing eyes glared at Jeduthan. They seemed to burn his heart as a hot iron might brand livestock. A faint whiff of burnt flesh seeped into his nostrils as a burning sensation broached his chest. He tore open his jacket, exposing his chest, and revealing...

He felt Susan slipping her warm hand around his forearm, seeking shelter from the brisk wind. He looked down but was somewhat startled for the youth gazed only upon the speaker. His hands felt clammy.

"...Oh friends, avoid sin's grasp. Intemperance's victims affect more than only one's body, but also the culprit's family, friends, and community. I implore you! Grasp the challis of sobriety. Seek God's wisdom in all you do and hope to accomplish, for it is by His will we live. Amen."

Susan tightened her grip as an *Amen* emitted from her lips followed by a beaming smile. "What a marvelous speaker, don't you agree Jeduthan?"

A nervous grin breached his lips as Mr. Beman retook the speaker's position.

"Brethren, go now, and sin no more! Ask God's forgiveness and accept His grace through His Son, Jesus Christ."

"What does he know of grace?" a woman's voice sneered a few feet away. Jeduthan turned and spied a woman standing alone, adorned in a long, flowing black dress near the rear of the gathering, arms folded across her slender frame. Her eyes glared at the speaker, seemingly as sharp as a Trojan's sword slicing the flesh of Greek warriors. He felt uneasy as her lips mouthed, "Hypocrite!" The word was unmistakable. Sharp. Fearless. Penetrating. He returned to young Susan Livingston at his side, the image of innocence and joyful youth. Her clear, childlike eyes contrasted sharply with the devilishly dark scowl from the sinister woman a few steps away.

"Jeduthan, let us approach Preacher Beman and I will introduce you," exclaimed Susan, a broad friendly grin shining upon her pale, smooth face. "Just possibly, perhaps, he will grant us an interview with Mr. Finney!" Her eyes hugged his heart as a youngster's appetite reveals its desires for a homemade fruit pie. Yet Jeduthan's heart ached with fright that Finney might identify him and his disguise forfeited for an adolescent's whim. He was saved by a tap on his left shoulder.

"Excuse me, sir. I believe I recognize you."

Both Jeduthan and Susan whirled around to find the dark woman addressing them.

"You," the stranger slowly stated, "were one of the featured guest lecturers at Mr. Renneslaer's school last week, weren't you?" She spoke with a slow, precise foreign accent, unknown by him, her words impeccably chosen. "And you, Miss Susan Livingston! Why am I not surprised to see you here! I see you are perched, once again, upon the arm of a fine and handsome gentleman."

Susan's broad grin faded and her eyes narrowed. "Good evening, Mrs. Beman. My friend and I were listening to your fine husband speak about sin. You, no doubt, understand the subject quite thoroughly," retorted the young girl.

"Miss Livingston, I just left the presence of your father who seeks your company immediately. He beckoned me to find your person and have you report to him." Pointing, Mrs. Beman declared, "There he stands, at lookout, beyond yonder cemetery gates. Go to him, young lady!"

Susan apologetically peered at Jeduthan. Her eyes revealed a child-like begging that a puppy exhibits when rebuked.

"Go, Susan. We will talk more later," he said, grasping her hand with a gentle squeeze before the youngster darted through gaps in the crowd.

"Please forgive the impetuous young lass, dear sir. She knows not her proper place." Mrs. Beman paused, awaiting a comment from Jeduthan. It did not come. "Sir, you have the advantage. You know my name but I do not know yours." Again, another moment of silence before Mrs. Beman glanced about, then down toward the ground, and finally raising her piercing eyes directly toward Jeduthan. Extending her hand for an anticipated kiss much like royalty expects from a loyal knight, Mrs. Beman announced, "Caroline Bird Yancy Beman, of Georgia! And you are?"

Jeduthan hesitated. "Jeduthan Higby, Connecticut."

"Pleased to make your acquaintance," she retorted, keeping her hand posted high in the air. He grasped it with his own, lowering her hand and applying a gentle shake. Slightly annoyed, the woman released from his grasp and continued. "I heard your remarks about that artist's sketch last week. Rather inspiring. Interesting use of descriptive vocabulary."

"Thank you for your comments, madam. The artist is William Bartlett."

"Yes, what a sweet young man. I remember him fondly. He visited our home in the spring, before his sojourn. We became quite intimate." She sinfully smiled, slowly inserting a finger between her red lips and into her seductive mouth as she exposed her polished white teeth.

Jeduthan looked away. "We traveled the summer months together in the New York and Canadian wilderness and only recently arrived in your fair city. Soon after his presentation, Mr. Bartlett left for New York City to settle his accounts and this morning, young Miss Livingston invited me to this gathering. I must say, your husband's words stir the soul."

The seductive smile disappeared from the woman's lips and a scowl returned at the mention of her husband. "Yes, he sure can stir people up. However, not everyone is as they seem, Mr. Higby. What leaves a man's mouth is only worth what a man may practice."

She sneered toward the gathered people surrounding her husband much as a serpent might inspect its prey. "But enough about the Reverend Beman, let us speak of pleasantries. I would very much enjoy an escort back to my villa. Would you do me the service?" She batted her eyes in faint helplessness until he nodded affirmatively. He hoped that relative safety would improve the further he placed his body from any possible inquiries from Reverend Finney.

He followed Mrs. Beman past three rows of wooden grave makers all inscribed with identical dates. The pair briefly halted and he inquired about the odd coincident. Mrs. Beaman nonchalantly acknowledged that the final resting places in this portion of burying ground were for paupers who perished in the great fire a few years before. She continued along the path to the far edge of the cemetery and turned upon the street leading down the hillside toward the business district. Jeduthan quickened his pace to catch up.

"I moved here a few years ago and have many confidants in the most prestigious families of Troy," she stated. "My previous husband, the late Mr. Benjamin Cudworth Yancy of South Carolina, was an American hero aboard the famed *USS Constellation* and later successful barrister at the South Carolina bar. After his passing, I retired to my estate in Georgia. I am sure you would appreciate the beauty of *The Aviary*, surrounded by hundreds of acres of America's pristine wilderness. My favorite spot overlooked the Ogeechee Falls, its beauty far exceeding any I witness in this wretched valley. Do you, Mr. Higby, have a preferred personal area where you relax?"

Jeduthan began to respond but Mrs. Beman's coarse voice interrupted. "I have been in this town now nearly four years and I am not much impressed. The oily filth in the canals and wretched wage slaves working in the iron and textile mills corrupt one's soul. Wouldn't you agree?"

Again, Jeduthan tried to respond but was cut short.

"Oh, dear man, will you look at that!" She pointed toward a young child chasing a large sow and seven little piglets in an enclosed alleyway.

"What perfect beasts that inhabit this town! The worst offenders are the wretched Irish. They live in squalor and spend their meager wages as soon as earned. However, there is nothing we mere mortals can do to remedy the miserable plague which they wreak on this town. Quick, let us continue further Mr. Higby, by way of Second Street where the better sorts inhabit." She turned and sallied across the boulevard, entering the upscale block, which he well remembered was Mrs. Hart's small community.

"I have friends on this block," Jeduthan was able to interject between the self-indulging comments of the preacher's wife.

"You do? Well, so do I! The shack occupying the corner lot is my friend Mrs. Van Ness. She and I play a friendly game of cards each Wednesday. Directly across from her is Mrs. Pawlings, a righteous woman, compared to most. Her only flaw remains her flagrant gossiping. I just do not know what to believe when it emanates from her thin lips. Sometimes she is just shameful, and her husband, it is rumored, fathered a child with their fifteen-year-old domestic servant. Some people might condemn the man; however, if you knew the real story, you would be appalled! Then there is that dreadful Hart family. They just recently completed an enormous mansion, parading for the entire town to see their fortune while we respectable citizens live in meager homes. I believe the old man..."

"I know Mrs. Hart," interjected Jeduthan.

Mrs. Beman stopped abruptly following Jeduthan's pronouncement. "Oh, do you now? That is very interesting." She twisted her head slightly, peering toward the Hart residence from the corner of her eyes. Soon thereafter, she continued. "Let us not dawdle, my esteemed companion. Come along!"

At that moment, Mrs. Hart appeared at an open upstairs window and called, "Oh, Professor! I am so glad to see you! Please stop for a few minutes."

Jeduthan looked skyward and nodded his head.

"Dear Betsy, I am afraid we are in quite a rush and can't..." exclaimed Mrs. Beman.

"Caroline, is that you! It has been so long since we visited. I will rush to the door immediately."

Mrs. Beman reached for Jeduthan's arm, tugging it slightly attempting an escape. However, he remained stationery. Her eyebrows elevated in annoyance, but abruptly changed as Mrs. Hart threw open the wide door of her home and raised her arms in welcome.

"Betsy Hart, dear friend! How wonderful you look and your new home is so impressive!" cried Mrs. Beman.

"Come in a few moments, please. How wonderful to see you both! We must have tea. Aunt Sallie!" The servant appeared. "Aunt Sallie, could you please prepare our guests some tea?" Aunt Sallie grinned at Jeduthan but the toothy smile dissipated when Caroline Beman entered the foyer.

"Yes 'um, Miss Betsy. Right-o-way."

"Come, Professor and tell me what has kept you from my company for so long," inquired their charming hostess.

"You no doubt know that I am engaged at Mrs. Willard's school, temporarily until Mr. Bartlett returns."

"Yes, I know. How has your teaching experience been?" responded Mrs. Hart.

"Challenging, yet rewarding. Mrs. Willard has been very accepting of my methods so far, and I believe the students are eager to learn."

"That is wonderful! I see you have met Mrs. Beman, our preacher's wife. Caroline, what brings you to our neighborhood this chilly afternoon?"

"Mr. Higby was escorting me back to the parsonage from a religious meeting at the cemetery on the hill and we found our way here. I was only just mentioning you and your wonderful new home to Mr. Higby when you burst forth with your encouraging smile." She looked around the room. "I just love how grand you have decorated this room and the home's design is just perfectly in tune with the neighborhood!"

"I cannot take credit for the structure's design. Daddy generously employed Mr. Colegrove as architect. Under daddy's careful scrutiny, we have just moved in. Some of the rooms are still unfurnished, isn't that correct, Professor?"

Jeduthan nodded in agreement. "Our first night in this town, we bunked in an unpainted room." Mrs. Beman raised an inquisitive brow. "...I mean Mr. Bartlett and I bunked."

Aunt Sallie entered the parlor with the expected tea and for the next ten minutes, the three spoke only in pleasantries.

"Well, thank you for the tea, Betsy. We must depart now before the weather turns wet. Where is your nigger with my shawl?" asked Mrs. Beman.

"Caroline, you know we don't treat our servants with such language. Please refrain from such vulgarity. Aunt Sallie is nearly like a mother to me," retorted their hostess.

"Come now, my dear Betsy. You mustn't allow black negro slaves to become too closely attached to your family. They are only property and nothing more."

"Caroline, what would your husband say if he heard such blasphemies from you?"

"Don't believe all you hear from that husband of mine. He may call for abolition, but he, too, has whipped the master's lash. The abolitionist himself has dealt in human slavery. He squandered most of my inheritance as he sold at auction the slave property from my beloved *Aviary*. I have been held in virtual bondage ever since, nearly a slave myself."

"No matter, Caroline, we do not resort to such vulgar expressions."

"As you wish, Betsy. Come Mr. Higby, let us be on our way," commanded Mrs. Beman as she arose and sauntered into the foyer nearing the exterior doorway.

Jeduthan looked to Mrs. Hart for his rescue.

"Yes, I suppose you must go. However, you understand, Professor, don't be a stranger. I expect a visit at least twice weekly. I will have Aunt Sallie cook up a stack of steaming flapjacks next time you stop in."

Mrs. Hart gently leaned on Jeduthan's arm and pressed her lips upon his cheek in a sisterly peck while Mrs. Beman glared. "You are like family, Jeduthan; always welcome." A broad smile pierced her lips.

"Come now!" Mrs. Beman demanded, exiting the Hart residence with Jeduthan in tow, tugging his jacket as if he were a dog on a leash. The two walked briskly as the weather was definitely changing for the worse. Three city blocks flew past before arriving in front of the large First Presbyterian Church of Troy.

"The parsonage is located behind the sanctuary. Would you like to come in and partake of some fruit?" Mrs. Beman seductively asked, pressing her torso against him. He could feel her robust breasts surrounding his arm and shoulder. Soon, she backed away, enticing him. "We could talk more about slavery and how we practice bondage in the plantation south." His heart raced for he understood the signals that this forbidden fruit flaunted before him. His body ached for her flesh, the pressing of smooth silky womanhood against his raw skin.

"Where do you and your husband reside?" he nervously inquired, his voice audibly trembling.

"He resides here, my dear man. He always spends his time here, amongst the saints and martyrs of the church. He never ventures forth from these dark, gloomy walls experiencing the freshness of our human world. I, though, do! Come, let me show you."

She raised a finger, beckoning him to follow. Somehow, forces pushed his body forward, uncontrollably following his seductress. The pair passed through the open doors, entering the cathedral-like sanctuary. A mist seemed to engulf him as wicked thoughts haunted his mind as her taunting drew him forward to the altar. Her black dress peeled away from her body, draping across the floorboards, providing a carpet-like softness for each of his steps. She lay upon the altar table, as a virgin might at an offering in a ritual sacrifice many centuries ago amongst the heathen. Her now bare bosoms thrust upward, only a muted veil concealing the delicate feminine folds between her thighs.

"Thank you, dear sir." The woman's words awakened him from his vision.

He stared into the darkening sky, the towering steeple adorning the First Presbyterian Church building silhouetted by the ominous clouds. A droplet of rain touched his nose.

"Rodney?" she bellowed. "Rodney! Come open this gate!"

A Negro servant emerged from a small door protruding from the church's sidewall. He ran with a slight limp, eyes glancing skyward, anticipating rain.

"Now open this gate before I thrash you, nigger!" She turned to Jeduthan, her scowl disappearing, replaced by a polite two-faced smile. "These niggers just seem ungrateful for all we provide them. They constantly leave us standing in virtual downpours while lazing about the comforts indoors. I tell you, only the lash will keep them productive." Jilted by Rodney's pace toward her she barked out other harsh words for the servant before returning to a counterfeit soothing tone with Jeduthan.

"It was so nice to make your acquaintance today, Mr. Higby. Your company is so very delightful, and I hope you will drop by my meager residence soon for a more intimate visit. Possibly, we can talk more about common courtesy that seems so foreign to the populous of this town. Good evening, sir." She curtsied, slightly revealing her round cleavage to his eyes. He responded with a slight bow as his temptress disappeared into the church, the Negro in close pursuit.

Jeduthan sauntered back, retracing his steps through town toward his lodging. Clouds persisted throughout the remaining afternoon and soon they hovered gloomily in the sky. The wind had yet to blow, but small rain droplets continued peppering him as he trekked toward his small lodging above the *Troy Sentinel's* office to sort out the meaning of the day's occurrences.

Chills ran through his bones as the droplets increased into a steady rain before reaching his sheltering room. He sat motionless upon his bunk, darkness engulfing his being. Had he only imagined Mrs. Beman's seductiveness? Did he secretly desire the preacher's wife, luring him into wickedness and immorality? Moreover, what of young Susan Livingston? Had he breached impropriety with his student during their morning's romp? Laying his head upon clasped hands, tears freely flowed down his exposed cheeks.

"Dear God, how much longer will my haunting memories and wicked desires wreak havoc on my mind? Please, almighty Lord, replace the wickedness with joyfulness and cheerfulness. I ask these things in Jesus' name. Amen." His voice quivered these final words despondently as he lay upon the straw mattress, falling into a turbulent asleep.

Repentance

Wind shook the window frame with frightful force. A whistling sound reverberated from the bare walls, the wind's fury heralding a turbulent day. Jeduthan arose, crossed to his lone porthole to the outside world, recognizing the all too familiar face of a wintry November day.

Last year, he stood, facing the incoming parishioners at Turin's Presbyterian Church, greeting each with an empty handclasp and in turn, each citizen strutting by him and entering the church's arched wooden doorway, a weekly ritual, devoid of significance. Yet, he played his part for all those many years, as was expected. Now though, far from that oppressive environment, he stands alone in a dank, dark room, answerable to no one. He was alone. He cast his eyes toward his empty bunk. At its foot lay his few possessions; a haversack, a broad brimmed hat, a pair of leather boots, two borrowed books, his copy of the *Troy Sentinel*, and lastly, his scheitholt, his former parishioners' money secreted within its bowels. Could possibly his continuing nightmares be a result of his fiendish retention of church tithes? Maybe his torment continued because Bartlett's departure left a void that was not readily filled. He did not know, but his heart burned. On this day, God's Sabbath day, while loneliness wrenched his aching stomach, he wished that someone would call for him, giving him hope.

He glanced into the street below, the drizzle icing random areas of the street as a lone female pedestrian turned the corner. A large scarf wrapped repeatedly about her face obscured her identity. Attempting a delicate balancing stride, she lost her grip upon the ground and fell upon her rump, revealing petticoats to his watching eyes. He smiled at the girl's misfortune, but as she righted herself, his grin faded.

Quickly slipping his boots over his bare feet, he bounded down the staircase and out the door. Bolting into the street, he reached the forsaken girl even before she had time to stand erect from her calamity.

"Miss Livingston, are you injured?" he cried while helping his young student to her feet.

"I suppose this is some comic coincident, Professor. Today, I stand before you embarrassed by a slippery street when only yesterday you stood before me, muddied by nature's weather. Please, dear sir, lead me into your shelter so that I may remedy my disheveled appearance," pleaded the young lady with an evident twinkle in her eye.

Jeduthan led the girl into the *Troy Sentinel's* office where she straightened her skirts and adjusted her scarf. "Thank you for coming to my rescue, Professor. I am glad to have caught you before you made your way toward church this frigid Sunday morning. I hope you don't think me too forward, but I hoped that you, being new in our community, would benefit me with your company at my church's worship." She lowered her eyes as a young child might when confessing to some misdeed. "I usually attend alone, Professor. Father still avoids the place. He says Reverend Mr. Beman's harsh words about Hell and damnation insults mother's memory. I don't believe father, though. I attend every Sunday." She paused, awaiting a reply. Jeduthan hesitatingly glanced toward the stairs leading up, toward his room. "I can wait, Professor, while you finish getting dressed. Services begin in about thirty minutes and the Reverend Mr. Beman's church is only a few blocks away."

Jeduthan nodded. "Yes, Miss Liv..." The girl waved a defiant finger at him. "Yes, Susan, I will attend services with you," he said self-consciously.

"Great!" the young girl enthusiastically blurted out. "I will wait for you here." She self-assuredly sat down and folded her hands upon her lap.

Jeduthan vaulted up the staircase. In his room, he quickly dressed in Bartlett's fine tunic. Before returning to his waiting escort, he stared at his scheitholt. Here was the best opportunity to rid himself of the torture that haunted his every night. Never greater was his prospects for returning God's tithes to the church than today, at Troy's Presbyterian congregation. He grasped the instrument, carefully separated the strings, prying from its innards the funds that he had secreted inside so many months ago. Yes, today he would be rid of this evil deed and repent his sinful ways. Hastily, he shoved the money into his trousers' deep pockets and bounded down the flight of stairs to his awaiting young student. His face beamed a broad grin as if freed from some great sin.

As he reappeared, Susan excitedly exclaimed, "My dear Professor, you are radiating enthusiasm like some zealot of old. What pleasant thoughts passed through your usually melancholy mind while you finished dressing?" She smiled slyly, not unlike the much older and worldlier Mrs. Caroline Beman the previous evening. He became uneasy.

Trying to conceal his newfound freedom from an awful sin, he responded to the girl's inquiry with, "Only that I am glad for your friendship, young lady. Now, let us depart. You lead the way." Soon, his sin of embezzlement, which had trapped him for so long, would be gone.

The pair briskly paced the few blocks to the imposing church building, speaking little as the cold wind bit into their faces, stinging their noses. Viewing the church building, he stood amazed. The previous evening, he had not noticed its substantial Romanesque architecture dominating the city block. It towered over the residential district as mightily as Olympus must over ancient Athens. Its sanctuary was similarly impressive. The vaulted ceiling soared above the pews, dwarfing the pulpit at its far end. How very different from his frontier chapel in Turin! Tithes collected here must dwarf his former neighbors' meager offerings.[9]

Susan led him forward past several older men to the second row of pews. Unlatching the high-whitewashed wooden pew door, she stepped gingerly into the spacious seating. He noted a small brass plate tacked onto the swinging door. It read, *Henry and Jane P. Livingston*. Stepping inside, he became acutely aware of the slightly elevated position that the pew took. Feeling slightly awkward, he leaned toward his companion's ear and whispered, "Susan, why does this pew sit so high?"

---

[9] Our story describes Troy's current First Presbyterian Church building. However, not completed until 1836, it is an impressive marble edifice. The church that stood on the site in 1825 was a conventional New England church with a sloped roof and tall steeple. Comparison prints of these buildings are in the Rensselaer County Historical Society's publication, *The Marble House on Second Street*, page 29.

She responded, "Shush, you will see in a moment. Right now, we must remain quiet for Reverend Mr. Beman will shortly address the congregation." Raising a discreet finger to her lips to quiet him, instructor and pupil sat gently back against the stark white walls surrounding their church seats.

An awkward quiet engulfed the sanctuary for many minutes before a pair of doors opened and four colored men entered with two large metal wheelbarrows. The men slowly descended the sanctuary, stopping at each pew to deposit metal boxes. Jeduthan carefully studied their progress. When the men reached Susan's pew, one man gently knocked upon the door before opening it.

The man's eyes glanced toward Jeduthan and then Susan before the young girl nodded ever so slightly. The Negro lowered his eyes, avoiding a stare, and with gloved hands raised one large metal box, and placed it below the seats where Susan and her professor sat. Immediately, Jeduthan felt warmth emit from below. The Negro slowly removed one glove while Susan retracted a small coin from her knit purse and dropped it into his outstretched palm.

At that very moment, Jeduthan became transfixed upon the Negro's hand, extended at knee level, attempting to hide the small financial transaction. Its skin was light brown and pitted with random burns, no doubt from his chore with the hot metal boxes. Veins protruded from its top portion and the jagged fingernails showed evidence of difficult work. They reminded Jeduthan of the hand of an old woman, worn by relentless labor in fields filled with briars and thorns. Nevertheless, the Negro's face exhibited youthfulness, possibly even younger than Susan. He wondered what sort of life this poor Negro endures that results in such disfigured appendages.

He was jolted by Susan's whisper.

"Professor?"

"Yes, Susan?"

"It is our custom here to have guests acknowledged by name. I expect that Reverend Mr. Beman will call on you to introduce yourself. Would you like for me to intercede on your behalf?"

"No, I will be fine," he whispered, secretly hiding a deep-seated dread.

A hissing sound escaped from a large set of pipes along the far wall, evidently part of an elaborate organ. He stretched his neck in order to locate the instrument when a group of people entered the room from a concealed entrance behind the pulpit. He lowered his head again, trying his best to remain concealed within the pew. The hissing sounds grew more intense until he felt his ears ache. Then suddenly the sound dissipated and ringing musical notes filled the sanctuary.

The musical prelude echoed off the tall white walls surrounding the congregation. The choir added their voices to the thundering organ's harmony and for the next ten minutes the Lord's music brought back memories of many hours in the pulpit amongst Turin's faithful. He closed his eyes, remembering the wondrous tunes which so inspired him in his youth, leading him into the ministry as his vocation so many years ago. As the selection ended, he opened his eyes again, ready to renounce his sins and refresh his soul.

A tall man entered the preacher's pulpit, the same person from the previous afternoon's lecture in the cemetery. There, Jeduthan, preoccupied with Susan Livingston and Caroline Beman, neglected to examine the esteemed Reverend. Average build, beardless, he wore a great black woolen coat contrasted only by a white neckerchief hanging from under his chin. The Reverend Beman, of which Susan was so fond, stood poised, erect, and dominant over his flock, judging each parishioner with piercing eyes. Silence hovered through the sanctuary, only the organ's low hiss disturbing the stillness.

After a long moment, the preacher, in a surprisingly soft voice, uttered a prayer. "Dear Lord, we thank thee for your patience and understanding, for we are hard-hearted. We turn our backs upon you every day, exchanging your gifts and the sacrifice of your son for the devil's sinful pleasures. Please forgive us our trespass and lead us to further your kingdom instead of the wickedness that Satan dangles within our sight. We are unworthy and too many of us refuse to acknowledge our sin's grasp upon our minds. Send into our callous hearts a straight and righteous arrow, piercing the iron curtain that separates us from you, dear Lord. When that drapery shall part, grant us that we shall see Him, who has forfeited His life for our salvation. We ask this and all our prayers in His name, amen."

Jeduthan raised his head from prayer and laid eyes upon a fearsome preacher, his eyes lit with fire and passion, with a stern glare casting its severe gaze upon the solemn congregation. "Good morning, beloved. It is so nice to be at Troy's Presbyterian Church this wonderful morning. I have a special message to bring forth this Sabbath..."

Jeduthan listened to the announcements, his eyes glued upon the pulpit, fearing the moment he would be called upon as a guest. He worried, "What shall I say? What shall I reveal? Will I be identified as a scoundrel before my first words echo from the walls?"

"...but before I deliver today's message, let us welcome guests amongst us. Please visitors, arise and introduce yourselves," echoed Reverend Beman's voice.

A small man rose, his head barely visible above the pew walls. "I am Patrick Scott, traveling through Troy on my way to New York City," announced the small man. "My new friends from the boarding house on River Street have invited me to your worship service, and I am glad to be here." Mr. Scott looked about and smiled an awkward grin even though his height must have limited his view of the other parishioners hidden deep within the confines of their pews.

Susan reached over and tapped Jeduthan upon the shoulder. She lifted her hand signifying that he should stand. Slowly, he stood, head and upper torso extending well above the pale white walls of the Livingston cell. He now had a clear view into many of the parishioner's seats and was surprised that two compartments to his right and one row forward sat the demur Mrs. Willard. A polite smile and nod from her comforted him. "Professor Higby of the *Troy Female Seminary*, invited by Miss Susan Livingston whom I regard with high esteem as a studious scholar and joyful Christian," he announced glancing downward toward the slightly blushing youth. An uneasy silence hung in the air as if his words reverberated through an empty hall.

As he descended again into the pew, he caught a glance of the forward most seats. Seated within its borders was Caroline Beman, the seductress whom had invaded his mind during his wicked fantasy the previous evening. Her eyes glowed, a broad devilish smile cracking her face, while one hand seductively lay upon her exposed soft cleavage. She allowed a restless finger to pierce her bright red lips as her pink tongue darted about its flesh as if to beckon him. He disappeared into the pew once more, feeling Susan's soft hand gently touch his forearm reassuringly while mouthing a silent, "Well done, Professor." Nevertheless, he felt as if he had betrayed his young, innocent hostess with his evil thoughts.

Two other men followed Jeduthan's example, rising and stating their names, residences, and who within the congregation had invited them to this morning's service. He paid them little heed as he stared blankly toward the preacher high upon the pulpit's pedestal.

"Oh, what a wicked world we behold," began the sermon. "Mankind, on this wretched Earth, continues an evil course. He denies the holy words that God composes in His good book. I walk upon our wharves and see, clear as day, the evidence of evil that haunts our nation, state, and community. Not two city blocks from this place where we now sit exists a den of iniquity, an institution that blots our community with a horrible stain; stains which will take many generations to wipe clean." Raising an accusing finger, Reverend Beman shouted, "Do not claim innocence, for each of you know of what I speak; an unimaginable crime against our fellow man. A theft from God's temple!"

Jeduthan felt uneasy, reaching into his pocket, feeling the coin and banknotes secreted there. His heart raced, taking short breaths trying to maintain a calm deportment as Reverend Beman continued. "A nightmare, in which I, too, am entangled. It is, of course, human slavery!" Jeduthan released a long, slow breath, relieved that the reverend's accusations and damnations were not directed upon him and his crime.

The preacher persisted for an hour upon the evils of human chattel and its horrendous effects on both Negroes and white people alike. The vivid descriptions of human torture, degrading existence, sexual misconduct, and enduring mental and psychological effects rang clear in his ears. Living so long among the wild frontier isolated Jeduthan and his former congregation from this evil. However, his experiences in the last few days, among Troy's respectable inhabitants, revealed the true nature which slavery cast upon a population.

"My travels through the southern states exposed how the wicked tradition leaves scars upon those poor souls who live within the confines of a society that accepts slavery as a natural state. Some even acknowledge it as a social good, rationalizing alternatives as worse than the disease. Here me now, dear brethren! We must lash out at those who call for compromise! We must dispose of all who claim a moral benefit at this peculiar institution! I call upon each of you to give the cry for freedom! Give now, before it is too late, for God's wrath is upon us!"

Jeduthan felt a warm glow in his chest as this man's appeals rang throughout the chamber. His face flushed with excitement for only once before had such an immediate appeal elevated his emotions to such fervent heights. That time was in Western, the small village where he heard Charles Finney bring to life God's scriptures. Now as then, the preacher's call excited the passions, pleading for immediate action. Jeduthan felt for the banknotes as a tall man rose to his left.

"Preacher! I pledge ten dollars for the cause," proclaimed the stranger.

"I pledge twenty dollars!" cried another from the rear of the sanctuary.

Jeduthan felt sweat form on his brow.

"Thank you, dear sir. God will reward you," the preacher announced. "He will reward all of us who grasp the realization of our own crimes. Repent, I say! Repent now, for God's vengeance will befall us! He calls on you, now!"

Jeduthan felt himself rise, extracting from his pocket his fist full of stolen banknotes. Raising them above his head, his lips exclaimed, "Reverend Beman! I commit all my worldly possessions to the cause of freeing our land from the grips of Satan. Please accept $300 dollars for the cause!"

A joyous clamor shook the hall. From all across the sanctuary, distinguished gentlemen rose, purses in hand, hailing the Reverend. Notes and coin dropped into the aisles, music rang from the choir, and the hissing organ came to life again in joyous melody. A true revival spread as women stood, wildly raising their hands praising God. Ushers traveled up and down the isles, collecting the spilled cash that rang off the stone floor much as a minstrel might at the finale of a successful performance. Jeduthan grinned broadly, the Holy Spirit filling his joyous heart as the sound of coin continued dropping into the collection plates.

Susan nudged him with the plate's edge. All was silent. The choir did not sing, the organ remained quiet, the congregation subdued.

Reverend Beman stood stoically, with grim, determined eyes scanning the worshippers. Jeduthan grasped the brass plate. It contained one banknote, three coppers, and two silver coins. He glanced toward Susan who cast her eyes toward the cold gray stones lining the pew's floor. An usher held an awaiting hand at their whitewashed door. Jeduthan felt himself mechanically pass the plate to the usher, adding nothing to its contents. He lowered his eyes in shame. He could not bring himself to part with the embezzled tithes. The banknotes remained tightly rolled beneath the recesses of his tunic.

As the usher's hand disappeared from the pew and the door gently latched behind, Jeduthan contemplated desperate action. He must stand before this congregation, admit to his crimes, and deposit the stolen tithes into God's hands. However, he could not bring himself to complete his humiliation. A tear ran down his cheek, and a cold chill blew across the floor as if Satan had scored a victory.

Survival

Susan stood to exit the pew as the last notes rang from the choir's final song. Jeduthan managed a fragile smile as he, too, rose, and opened the stoic cell door that had caged the pair during the religious services. The young girl edged past, leaving a faint sweet scent in the air, very pleasing to his nostrils. "The sweet fragrance of innocence," he thought. "How putrid my odor must be!"

Following close upon his hostess' heels toward the sanctuary's exit, Jeduthan was unable to reach the street because the gathering crowd stalled as a multitude of parishioners wished to greet their awaiting preacher before exiting and heading to their respective homes. He hoped to secure a quick escape, but to no avail. The crowded situation delayed their progress for over ten minutes before the pair stepped past the hand-shaking preacher into the church foyer. There, retrieving a shawl, awaited Mrs. Willard.

"Good day, my dear professor. I am pleased to see you partaking of services with us today," she stated pleasantly. "It is good to see you back also, Miss Livingston. We have regretted your absence these past weeks. How is your father these days? Regrettably, we see so very little of him."

Susan raised her voice cheerfully. "Father is fair. I, though, am reinvigorated. Your choice of Professor Higby as leader of our class has re-sparked my excitement for learning. He is a wonderful teacher and I have invited him to share my pew. I hope Reverend Beman is not offended."

"Nonsense, child! More of our neighbors should open their hearts to those looking for a spiritual home. Our gracious pastor continually cries for revival, and you, young lady, are living the word. Remember, the Bible teaches, *Love thy neighbor as thyself.* Fear no impropriety Miss Livingston," announced the *Troy Female Seminary's* headmistress as a broad, warm smile graced her face. Turning to Jeduthan, she continued. "Professor Higby, do you remember our engagement for today?"

Jeduthan responded, puzzled. He had completely forgotten the written invitation he received the previous Friday.

"I requested your accompaniment on an excursion to Albany," stated Mrs. Willard.

"Yes, old boy," piped in Mr. Willard, emerging from the cloakroom with two large overcoats and a gray woolen blanket. "We are visiting a preacher friend of the *Old School* in Albany this evening. As we travel together in my sleigh, we shall become better acquainted. By some accounts, your new teaching methods have rattled more than a few of the more conservative and traditional instructors at our fine institution. I hope we can converse more concerning these methods during our junket."

Jeduthan bowed slightly and turned toward Susan. "Please accept my apologies, Miss Livingston. I must beg your forgiveness. My employer calls."

Susan extended her lip as if hurt, reminding Jeduthan of his recently departed artist friend. However, she soon recovered her bubbly spirit. "I am fine, Professor. The Reverend's words revived me and I shall speed homeward to complete my assignment for tomorrow. Until then..."

She raised her hand expecting a tight, courteous clasp only to find Jeduthan delicately gripping her soft hand and gently pecking a polite kiss. He found his voice mimicking Bartlett's, "I bid you a fair, adieu." The Willards respectfully averted their eyes as Susan beamed an honored smile and darted through the church's heavy wooden doors.

"Well, Professor! I believe that young Susan Livingston has taken a fancy toward you," announced Mrs. Willard.

"I believe you are mistaken, dear madam," Mr. Willard stated authoritatively as he helped his wife with her overcoat. "I expect that young artist is more to her liking. Don't you agree, Professor?"

Jeduthan nodded, though his heart feared the old man was mistaken.

The packed foyer slowly emptied while the Willards adjusted their outer garments. Jeduthan patiently waited for the couple to lead him outside, but for some unknown reason, the pair continued stalling, greeting a great number of parishioners. Finally, a full five minutes after

Susan departed, only the Willards remained with him in the foyer. An awkward silence ensued before Reverend Beman joined the group.

"Professor Higby, may I introduce our preacher, Dr. Nathan S.S. Beman," announced Mr. Willard. "We all plan to ride to Albany together."

Jeduthan extended his hand nervously. "I am glad to make your acquaintance."

The preacher grasped his hand and forcefully asked, "Where do you call home, professor?"

Jeduthan responded, "From our western counties, sir. I have lived much of my adult life on the frontier, though originally I call Connecticut home."

"You, no doubt then, have heard of Reverend Charles Finney."

"Yes, I have," responded Jeduthan nervously.

"It is a shame that he could not attend our carriage ride today for he would have enjoyed the company of a neighbor. He only left this morning to return to his home county in order to continue spreading the gospel message to the faithful."

Turning to Mr. Willard, the preacher continued. "Well, John, we now only wait for Mrs. Beman to arrange herself before departing." Glancing into the empty sanctuary, the preacher bellowed, "Wife! Do not delay! Mr. and Mrs. Willard are waiting!"

Mrs. Beman sauntered slowly through the double doors into the foyer, in no obvious hurry. Her uncovered neck revealed cleavage between her soft plump breasts that recently tempted Jeduthan with sinful thoughts. "Be patient, husband! The cold wind has blown for the last two hours. I do not feel the urgent desire for another afternoon chill on my body. Oh, well now!" Recognizing Jeduthan, the temptress curtsied low.

Reverend Beman began, "This is professor..."

"Ah, we meet again Professor Higby!" interjected Mrs. Beman. "Dear sir, how fortunate. I do so hope I will share this dreadful journey with you, Professor. Possibly we can now have some tantalizing conversation..."

Jeduthan stared blankly as Reverend Beman tried to interrupt. "How do you know this man?"

Without losing her wicked smile, Mrs. Beman continued. "Oh hush, old man. I met the professor late last night following your little pity party in the cemetery. He escorted me home, after a short stop at a mutual friend's residence. I very much enjoyed our little escapade, Professor." She grasped Jeduthan's forearm and promenaded about his tense body flirtatiously.

With her polite voice, Mrs. Willard cut off the reverend from a bombastic outburst toward his wife. "Now that Caroline is present, let us please adjourn to our carriage. I expect the journey to take several hours and we may converse along the way."

Reverend Beman pushed forward, past his wife and exited the church, followed by the Willards and Jeduthan. The four reached the awaiting carriage and mounted before Mrs. Beman even emerged from the building. She slowly descended the stone steps, taking deliberate care to delay the expected junket. She took little care in hiding her disinterest in the journey and seemed to enjoy retaining control of the party's progress.

After finally arriving at the carriage, she climbed aboard and sat uncomfortably close to Jeduthan. He could feel the warmth of her body under the mass of blankets. She smiled at him, her pink tongue darting between her red, alluring lips as the carriage jerked forward along the street. Guided by two servants riding upon the buckboards, the carriage proceeded through the boulevards of Troy, the wind knifing into their exposed faces.

None of the occupants spoke until the carriage exited Troy city and bumped along the country lane southward toward Albany. Mrs. Beman's voice interrupted the party's silence.

"Dreadful little town! Few, if any people of real integrity reside there." She paused waiting some calculated reaction, before adding, "Present company excepting, of course."

"I believe your interjection of a so sorrowful opinion is uncalled for and unwelcome! I expect you to refrain from further outbursts," exclaimed the preacher in a commanding tone.

"Outbursts!" retorted the preacher's wife. "I will express my feelings anywhere and anytime I desire, Mr. Beman. That city is just filled with busy bodies that spend exceedingly large amounts of time gossiping. I just cannot believe how you are so oblivious to the nosey intrigues that plague your own church!"

"Woman! Refrain from your accusations. The Lord's house is holy. It provides sanctuary..."

"...For the spying eyes of wickedness," continued Mrs. Beman. "I tell you that more roaming eyes and twitching heads are found within those holy walls than is seen at a nigger's minstrel show. Every Sunday I hear neck bones crackling throughout the chamber likened only to bacon frying in a hot skillet, as your parishioners critique their neighbors."

Reverend Beman rose from his seat, a stern finger pointing threateningly toward his wife. "I demand that you control your phraseology, woman!" The carriage shifted upon its springs, unsettling the assemblage. Mrs. Beman retreated deeper under the blanket, closer to Jeduthan.

"Dear Reverend Beman, please calm yourself! Sit, for I fear you shall upset the carriage," interjected Mrs. Willard. "Professor, I am glad to see that young Susan Livingston has taken to you so fondly. Her reclusiveness since her father's catastrophe worries me. How is she performing in your classes?"

Rebuked by Mrs. Willard's unyielding words of warning, Reverend Beman slowly descended into his seat as Jeduthan responded. "I cannot deceive you, madam. At first, my entire class exhibited a lackluster interest in their studies. Soon, however, they warmed to me as I recounted my adventures with my companion, Mr. Bartlett. The mention of his name lit a flame in all the young ladies and Miss Livingston's attentions toward me derive from an infatuation with my close friend."

"Yes, Mr. Bartlett seems to have that effect on a great number of females at the academy. He is quite charming. Last spring, he visited our home along with his cousin, Mrs. Hart. We, too, enjoyed his stories and anecdotes," replied Mrs. Willard with a broad smile.

Mrs. Beman's eyes darted between her husband's and Mrs. Willard's before she straightened her posture and interjected, "I agree, Mrs. Willard. Will Bartlett is quite charming. We spoke at length before his departure and found we agreed on numerous points of mutual interest, including the natural rights of women. Natural Rights such as public prayer, child custody, property rights, and inheritance." She flashed a devilish scowl toward her husband.

Reverend Beman remained silent.

"Isn't that correct, husband? The good citizens of our community ought to protect a woman's rights to her own property. Our laws should reflect Godly principles of private property. All property!"

"Not if that property is human chattel! No human may suppress another's freedom through bondage," answered the reverend.

"True, human slavery is not God-like and we should have no business in perpetuating its existence. But how can we discard such a yoke that we, as a nation, bear?" retorted the preacher's wife.

Reverend Beman again stood within the carriage, raising an outstretched arm, and exclaimed, "Immediate emancipation!"

"Please, Reverend Beman, remain seated!" exclaimed Mr. Willard.

"Immediate and unconditional emancipation, I declare!" continued the preacher. "There can be no other answer to the slavery issue."

"Then why, answer me," demanded Mrs. Beman to her husband, "Did you, oh lordly master and protector, confiscate my inheritance and sell on the auction block my slave property before we left my home deep within the blessed land of my forefathers? How can you, a preacher who calls for immediate and unconditional emancipation, a distinguished man of God who claims the word calls for protection of women's rights, practice the hypocritical act of slave trading of another's property? You will be condemned, old man, when you face God's judgment day!"

Her words cut deep into Reverend Beman, rage overtaking him. Rising for a third time, he lifted his massive arm, and delivered a sweeping blow toward his wife. Narrowly missing her exposed face, she retreated within the blankets once more. However, the preacher, determined to discipline his accusing and insolent wife, attempted to strike a second time. This time, though, Jeduthan's outstretched arm intercepted the preacher's violent blow. An eerie silence pervaded the scene, Jeduthan's iron grip tightly restraining the preacher's thrust. He peered deep within Reverend Beman's eyes, raging with fiery flame. Twice more, the preacher lunged at his wife, Jeduthan blocking each blow and the carriage, all the while, rocking back and forth.

A bright beam of light flashed into Jeduthan's eyes, blinding him. A freezing wind passed across his exposed neck much as when overwhelmed with intense fear. He felt himself tumble repeatedly, and coldness pervade his hands and feet as if submerged into an icy river. As brightness continued blinding him, he felt a soft hand caressing his own. Its smooth, silky touch conveyed compassion and comfort. An uncomfortable contrast flooded his mind. The cold wind, bright light, and soothing touch confused him.

Eternity seemed to elapse before a soothing voice penetrated the light with the sweetness that only a child expects from a loving mother. The intensity of the light slowly dimmed and Susan Livingston's young face appeared, hovering above him, her lips moving ever so slightly, as a supple melody penetrated his ears.

"Oh, Professor, you are awake! I have been so worried these past four days."

"Miss Livingston? Susan? Where am I?" he inquired from his stupor.

"You are at Mrs. Hart's home," responded the young girl. "We brought you here to recover."

"Recover?"

"Yes, professor, recover! You have been in a terrible accident. Mrs. Hart graciously provided this room for your convalescence. You have been here four days now. I asked to tend you during the afternoon hours so that I could still attend classes. Father was hesitant at first, but relented when Mrs. Willard beseeched him."

"I remember a carriage ride..."

"You are correct, professor. The Bemans, the Willards, and you were on an excursion to Albany last Sunday when the carriage turned over. You sustained a serious injury and have remained unconscious these past four days. I am so glad you have finally awakened."

His eyes glanced about, recognizing the familiar room where Bartlett and he slept during their first night in Troy. He smelled wood burning and glanced toward a brick lined hearth where a small fire radiated heat throughout the room. The windows permitted a bright sunbeam to enter, showering the room with its brightness. He felt stiffness as he attempted to move his arms and twist his legs.

"Do I have broken bones?" he asked.

"No, you are physically fine. The doctor worried that the extended state of unconsciousness though would worsen your condition. However,

I knew differently." She smiled. "I prayed for your recovery, Professor. And God hears my prayers! You are now awake and healthy once more. Soon, we will be strolling along the canal again, enjoying ourselves just as if this unfortunate event never happened."

He raised his torso, propping his upper body against the bed's headboard. His muscles burned as he moved and his face must have shown the exertion by Susan's grimace.

"Please do not strain yourself. You must slowly regain your strength. Mrs. Hart left strict instructions for your awakening moment." She raised a small tray holding a cracker and small soup bowl of ornate porcelain. Carefully removing its top, vapors escaped into the air and an aroma of sweet broth emanated from within its depths. "Now, sir, I am to feed you this. Aunt Sallie swears it will revive you in record time."

She dipped a small pewter spoon into the liquid and raised it toward his lips, as might a mother when feeding a young baby its first solid meal. The clear liquid parted his lips and swished about his tongue, reviving his extremities as coffee might revive a chilled man on a winter's morning. He closed his eyes and felt his strength return as the young girl repeated the feeding ritual. Each spoonful was administered with a gleaming smile, reminding Jeduthan of his dear mother of so many years before.

"Susan?" he inquired. "Was I the only injury from the carriage accident?"

Susan's eyes left his own, glancing downward gloomily. "I regret not, Professor."

"Who else was injured? Reverend Beman!"

"No, he is fine. Reverend Beman arose from the snow unscathed. He turned rescuer, mounting an uninjured horse and returning to Troy seeking help."

"Mrs. Beman?"

"No, she too recovered, though slightly bruised and ruffled, but not seriously hurt." She cast her head toward the fire and Jeduthan glimpsed a tear form on her cheek.

"Not Mrs. Willard!"

The girl raised her free hand to her mouth, slightly gasping for air. "I fear, Professor, it is Mrs. Willard who shall pay the price of this tragedy. Her husband fell ill after returning to Troy and by nightfall had succumbed to his wounds. I am not sure of the causes of his demise but Mrs. Willard has shut herself in her home with only the old gentleman's body as company. She has not re-appeared since. She so loved that old man, more like a father than a husband. And he adored her. It was his money that supported the *seminary.* Mrs. Willard asked him to provide the necessary funds and without question, the old gentleman supported his wife's request. Now that he is gone, I fear the school might close."

"Do not fret, child. The Lord provideth. Mr. Willard is in a better place now where there is no pain and no fear. Let us take a moment in silent prayer for Mrs. Willard during her time of grief." He reached for Susan's hand and both closed their eyes reverently. He pictured the old man but had difficulty imagining the sorrow that Mrs. Willard must endure. A lone widow, cast adrift in a man's world.

"There is more upsetting news, Professor," Susan stated after a long silence.

"What is it, Susan?"

"Your companion, Mr. Bartlett. It is presumed that he succumbed to a watery grave the same day that you experienced your carriage accident."

Alarmed, Jeduthan exclaimed, "What do you mean, succumbed to a watery grave? I, myself, watched his boat depart for New York City."

"It is true, Professor, he left aboard the canal schooner *Troy*, but not bound southward toward the city but northward toward Lake Champlain. After an uneventful journey on the Champlain Canal, the vessel was last seen on the huge lake, floundering in rough winds. A nearby boat approached but was not able to secure a line before the waves swamped the schooner." She paused before outstretching her hand to cup his cheek. "No one aboard escaped!"

Jeduthan's head dropped in grief. Tears leaked upon his breast. He felt his chest heave as he sobbed. His mind raced. He remembered Will Bartlett's forever-optimistic smile, quirky anecdotes, and delightful company. Only to be smitten by an angry God. An angry, avenging God! He wondered if these dreadful circumstances resulted from his unrepented sins. Given repeated opportunities for redemption, he faltered and stumbled. Once more, Susan Livingston's gentle touch revived him.

"Professor? Reverend Beman will be conducting Mr. Willard's funeral tomorrow. Shall I inquire, on your behalf, that he add a memorial service for Mr. Bartlett during that somber time? Mr. Bartlett was very popular and many in the city will mourn for both men."

"No, Susan, I will request the favor."

"Nonsense! You are not in any shape to seek out the good Reverend. I shall and we will both attend services tomorrow," stated the young lady, a gleam sparkling in her eye which so often reminded him of his artist friend when he took charge of delicate situations.

He acquiesced to her demand with a nod of his head and the two sat in silence, Susan carefully administering Aunt Sallie's broth. He soon tired and after munching a few morsels from the dry cracker, slipped into a deep slumber. When he awoke, Susan had disappeared and Mrs. Hart sat next to his bedstead, carefully reading a small book. He remained still as he watched her eyes dart along the lines of text. As she turned a page, he caught sight of the book's title, *Works by Geoffrey Chaucer*. Her grey, intelligent eyes conveyed a seriousness that eluded his previous encounters with her and it puzzled him. She stopped as he audibly sighed.

"Well, Professor, I see you are awake. I do hope your strength has returned. I hope you do not mind me reading your volume. I find it rather enlightening," announced Mrs. Hart coldly.

"What is mine is yours, sweet madam. Please accept it as a gift. I no longer can enjoy its thoughtful verse without remembering my dear companion."

"Nonsense sir! Now do not be so melancholy. We have a powerfully busy schedule today, as you no doubt remember from your discussion with Miss Livingston yesterday. We have hot tea and biscuits available downstairs. Do you think you can dress yourself?" He nodded and Mrs. Hart rose. "Splendid! I have your garments arrayed upon the settee and, if you require any assistance, please just ring this bell and Aunt Sallie will come running. You do look so much better today. The color is back in your cheeks." She patted his face before she stood and quickly paced out of the room.

He sat upon the bed's edge, his muscles feeling weak. However, he gathered strength and dressed himself. Navigating out of the room and delicately balancing his weakened frame, he descended the staircase to the assemblage in the parlor. A vacant wooden chair awaited him upon his arrival along with Betsy Hart, her husband, Susan Livingston, and an unknown man with a long frockcoat.

"...and here arrives our recovering professor. Come and sit, dear sir," beckoned Mrs. Hart.

Jeduthan did as told, perching upon a hard wooden seat while the rest of the company remained standing. Nearby, a small table held a basket of biscuits and four small cups of warm tea. Slowly he retrieved one biscuit and began consuming it. A thick layer of salt covering the bread startled his lips. He rubbed the biscuit before again attempting a morsel only to find it cold, hard, and brittle. He bit hard upon its surface until it cracked into hundreds of fragments, scattering about the floor. He peered at the company surrounding him, desperately seeking a friendly gesture, but all frowned annoyance. Even young Susan glared.

"Come now Professor, no need making a mess, eating biscuits in my parlor," stipulated Mrs. Hart. "You are my guest; the companion to my dear departed Cousin Will."

"Yes Professor, moreover I trusted you with my heart," responded Susan. "I invited you to my church and your sins deceived you. How dare you make a mess in our community?"

"I agree," stated the unknown man. His coat parted, and pinned upon his breast was a silver sheriff's badge. He clasped a cold iron shackle upon Jeduthan's wrist. "We accepted you, invited you into our homes, fed and protected you, gave you comfort and all the while you were a fugitive, a criminal, a sinner!"

Jeduthan awoke with a start. Young Susan Livingston applied a cool cloth to his wrists as sweat beaded upon his forehead.

"Susan, how long have you been here?"

"I have not left your side since you first awoke yesterday except to change into this dress which Mrs. Hart loaned me for the funeral today. How are you feeling? Do you think you will have strength to attend the funeral and memorial service?"

He nodded. "Yes, I will not miss remembering our dear friends."

Susan smiled.

Discovered

Jeduthan stood before the menacing entrance of the Troy Presbyterian Church. His eyes were heavy and a deep sorrow showed upon his face. The bright sunlight warmed his woolen coat covering his shoulders. Seemingly, only moments ago, he stood upon this same flight of granite steps for a pleasant, brisk winter's ride to the state capital. Then, he was an accepted and admired member of the community, gainfully engaged teaching at a prestigious school where he felt that his presence and talents were making a positive impression on the young students. However, those hopeful moments met a tragic end in an instance of misjudgment. Now he stood, bruised, listless, and plagued by his sins. He felt the bank roll deep within his trousers, untouched but menacing like a coiled snake ready to strike. The dreadful nightmares had returned, intensifying and tearing his heart asunder with each moment's attempted rest.

Susan gently slipped her arm between his and the overcoat and nudged him forward. He turned his head as if only vaguely aware of her presence as he ascended, one stone slab at a time, deliberately, upward. An eternity seemed to pass with each stoic step reminding him of Jacob's ladder to heaven. Stumbling slightly on the final step, he entered the sanctuary. Only the quick steady arm from his female companion avoided a catastrophic fall onto the cold stone floor. The great doors opened inward revealing the church's gloomy interior, subdued with black draped cloth ornamenting the otherwise white walls of each pew.

Slowly, Susan led him along the aisle, toward an open casket near the alter railing. Peering over the flowers heaped upon the coffin's edge, he saw Mr. Willard's lifeless body, pale, cold, ridged; its gray skin drained of its warmth. Jeduthan approached with his hand tightly gripping Susan's, as if her strength might drain into his own body, hopefully rejuvenating his sagging frame. He heard a low, quiet prayer emit from the young girl's lips but he could only stand in self-pity, realizing how his own ego caused this man's demise. Another sin piled upon his mounting hill of wrongdoings.

Standing and adorned in black was the widowed Mrs. Willard, her skin only somewhat more flushed than her deceased husband. She remained quiet, head bowed in somber thought as her personal secretary, Mrs. Dongan, reached a delicate hand toward the visitors. Speaking in a muted voice, she announced the pair's attendance to her mistress, who raised a dark handkerchief to her eyes catching a single small tear as it escaped from its duct and slowly descended her cheek.

Without a word, the widow grasped Jeduthan's hand. Her grip was feminine, weak, cold, as if the self-confident female had met defeat, very contrary to that which he had become so accustomed to from this woman and others associated with the *Troy Female Seminary*. He wondered if this tragedy had permanently altered Mrs. Willard's dynamic and warm personality.

Susan prompted him onward and the pair circled the sanctuary, ending their journey at the familiar Livingston family pew. Upon opening the white wooden door, Jeduthan was startled by the sight of a man sitting motionless on the hard wooden seat. The occupant did not turn to recognize or greet the newcomers but rather sat erect, eyes set stoically forward toward the open coffin. Without pause, Susan stepped into the pew and sat next to the man without a spoken word. Jeduthan followed suit.

The prolonged silence engulfed the church as it filled with mourners, each making their way to the casket, stopping briefly to acknowledge the widow, and then circling the sanctuary attaining their proper seats. Mrs. Willard remained emotionless save for the one short-lived tear shed when Susan and Jeduthan took her delicate hand. One by one, family acquaintances filed past the widow, some with handkerchiefs raised toward their tearful eyes, others averting their eyes from the bereaved. Only Mrs. Dongan's soft lipped voice whispered words of greeting.

Minutes passed and the grieving line shortened until only Mrs. Willard and her faithful assistant remained standing. Outside, a low toned bell peeled its death toll. The younger woman motioned her widowed employer toward the front most pew and disappeared from view as the bell continued its rumble. Jeduthan spied a man sitting in a nearby seat extracting his watch, gazing into its clear crystal, adjusting its arms indicating noontime.

With the twelfth tone echoing through the grief-filled chamber, Reverend Beman appeared and slowly ascended his pulpit as a harpooner might position himself upon a whaleboat's prow. He held a long staff with his left hand and gripped a gargantuan volume under his right arm. His fiery eyes penetrated all the recesses of the church and Jeduthan felt intense emotion building within the preacher's frowning, convicted face. His lips parted and forceful words resonated off the walls.

"The payment for sin is death!" he roared. "We must all pay its price. He that is old, he that is young, even he that is vibrant and full of life; all must pay! Today we pay homage to a man who endowed our town with his presence these past years. A man who brought to our doorsteps hope for our young ladies with his vaulted *Female Seminary*. A man whose guiding hand calls forth the enduring spirit of..."

Jeduthan heard the preacher continue, but paid little attention to his ramblings. Of more immediate concern was the appearance in the seats of the choir of Reverend Charles Finney in company of a tall, erect man whose bearded face concealed a mysterious secret. However, Jeduthan knew the secret. The stranger's cold, steel gray eyes searched the church, scanning each pew systematically from his elevated position. His black coat parted ever so slightly and Jeduthan detected a silver badge concealed amongst its folds.

At that moment, he heard a whimpering sound within his pew. The stranger, who sat next to Susan, began sobbing. The young girl moved closer to the man, lifting her arm and gently caressing his shoulder as a mother might comfort a child injured by a mean spirited remark. Jeduthan thought, "Oh Susan, what innocence possesses ye!" The stranger was no doubt her father, who only a few short years ago had buried his beloved wife and child here at this very church, and today, so soon after his personal tragedy, was reliving those terrible, frightful moments yet again. Jeduthan inwardly wept for father and daughter, re-united in grief. They caressed each other's shoulders as two long separated siblings might express remorse following a long, unspoken disagreement finally settled by a mutual friend's untimely demise. Poor Susan, doomed to mother an ailing father, tortured by lost hopes and dreams.

"...we must continue His work in our country, ridding it of all semblances of treachery, which Dr. John Willard devoted so much of his life's work overcoming. Mrs. Willard, please accept our deepest regret for your loss." The preacher exited the pulpit. Immediately, another man mounted the platform. It was Reverend Finney.

"Brothers and sisters in Christ, please remain briefly. The Reverend Beman requests that I speak a few moments concerning an additional loss to our community. His name was William H. Bartlett."

Jeduthan perked up at the mention of his companion's name. Happy times flashed through his mind as he remembered the many adventurous moments the two shared. How quickly events overtake us. One moment people are filled with life, adventure, hope and then must endure misery, despair, and fright.

"I only briefly met this man and knew of his talents only through others. He, though, left an endearing mark upon many of us. His dear cousin, Mrs. Betsy Hart, fondly speaks of his lighthearted fancies and delicate, almost feminine manners. She remembers, as most that encountered this vibrant young man, his endearing wit. The demise of the canal-schooner *Troy* upon the treacherous waters of Lake Champlain has stolen from us a noble citizen who brought smiles upon the faces of many. Let us not forget, though, that the Lord our God may smite each of us, at any time, and we must accept His will, for no other power will prevail over those who believe. Let us pray..."

Preacher Finney began a prayer which Jeduthan himself often repeated during his many years in Turin's pulpit. Its familiar words were so unlike the vibrant life that his artist friend lived. With a closing amen, Jeduthan raised his head and viewed two men securing the coffin top. Within moments, six men slowly walked down the aisle, the wooden coffin suspended between their arms, followed by the veiled widow. The procession seemed to slow as it passed by the Livingston pew. Time seemed suspended as the sound of the pallbearer's heels upon the cold stone floor slowly slid past.

Jeduthan diverted his eyes. However, his ears caught the sound of a light tap against the pew walls. He raised his eyes toward the aisle and noticed that Mrs. Willard steadied her frame upon the pew's whitewashed wooden barrier. A small scrap of paper escaped her grasp and fell within the pew's confines as she continued along her dreadful path, passing his seat and departing through the sanctuary doors.

Jeduthan reached toward the scrap to pick it up, but before he could stand erect and return the paper, the widow had exited the building. He carefully hid the paper within the fold of his hand as the crowded church began to empty. Neither Susan nor her father stood during the processional and he felt slightly awkward. Mourners filed by and soon he regained his seat, awaiting his hostess' attention; however, he knew that the rendezvous with her father would delay any speedy departure.

Taking this opportunity, he delicately unfolded the scrap that Mrs. Willard dropped. His face cringed in horror. The words conveyed his most dreaded fear. Scribbled in shaky print was, *"My dear Mr. Higby, I have known of your identity since the night of the Rensselaer lecture. Mr. Bartlett informed me of your sordid past and trusted in my good offices for protection. Events of the last several days, though, along with the constant quibbling between the Beman couple, have reluctantly exposed your identity. I must warn you of approaching danger. The man with Reverend Finney is a sheriff and he seeks you! You must flee. God speed!"*

His eyes widened. He glanced toward the choir seats so recently occupied by Reverend Finney and his confederate, the sheriff. Neither man remained. Jeduthan skimmed the crowd but still could not locate those he most dreaded. Panic gripped him and he pushed his way out of the pew, leaving Susan still embracing her father. His haste seemed only to slow his progress more. He found himself surrounded by a packed multitude, all hoping to exit the church quickly, yet none seeming to achieve their purpose.

Sam Wilson appeared. "Hello, Professor!" he announced, a wide appreciative smile breaching his lips. "I am glad to see you are better. Drop by tomorrow, I have some new sausage which might touch your fancy."

Jeduthan grimaced a forced smile and a quick nod before the butcher faded into the mass. Next, he came across Mr. Tuttle, pencil and notepad in his old wrinkled hands as if he were gathering news.

"Professor, I am sorry to hear of your friend's death. I hope you are still comfortable in your room. We know that you have been absent recently and we have left the room vacant until your return. I will gladly obtain your belongings and send them to the Hart residence if you so desire," stated the short old man.

"No need," Jeduthan responded nervously. "I am on my way to the room even as we speak."

The old man nodded and then was surrounded by the throng. Jeduthan finally burst free at the church's granite steps and paced rapidly down the street. His hands shook from fright and a chill seemed to permeate his very core. He glanced back toward the church every few paces, but saw no one in pursuit. Even so, he quickened his step. He hoped to reach his room, obtain his belongings including his beloved scheitholt, and exit town before being lassoed and impressed by Mr. Finney's sheriff companion.

He approached *The Sentinel's* office, finding the door latched. He looked about the deserted street briefly before forcing his shoulder against the barred door. Its solid frame resisted his initial thrusts, which heightened his anxiety to a fervor pitch. Sweat began beading upon his forehead. He leaned against the small window that lit the interior of the printing room and could plainly view the rear door, slightly ajar, leading upward toward his room. He felt nervous as a carriage passed the street corner only a few dozen yards away. He glanced toward the ground, and then stooped, pretending to tie an unraveled shoelace. He hoped to avoid attracting undue attention. Luckily, the carriage did not pause but continued its lumbering path away. Again, he tried the door and with a firm shove, it moved slightly inward. Another substantial push should force the door and he would be safely inside.

As the door released its grasp and slid open, he did not hesitate ascending the stairs to his awaiting room. The exertion from scampering across town from the funeral, wrestling with the door, and now climbing the steep stairs began to wear at his strength. He noticed his collar bathed with perspiration. However, he dared not slow. Fear of the sheriff's shackles beckoned him to continue his escape no matter his physical condition.

Entering his room, he found all as he left it that wonderful morning when he energetically sprinted inside the room in preparation of attending church with the beautiful young Susan Livingston. He viewed his wonderful sketch left him by his devoted friend still hanging from its pin upon the plastered wall. The wonderful days from their magical adventure were only a dream now. Tragic events had long since marred those memories and now he did not have time to dwell on them any more. He ripped the sketch from its mounting and shoved it into his haversack before gathering his few belongings and departing out the office door and into the street.

A trickle of pedestrians filed along the walks and he felt many accusing eyes glued upon his being. However, no one stopped or acknowledged him as he entered the street, passing a muddy puddle. A thin luster of ice floated amongst its thick, red, brownish mud and he recalled last week when his activities with Susan filled his heart with laughter and gaiety. Oh, how he desired to return to that wonderfully fulfilling moment, when all seemed right with the world. Nevertheless, he must not delay.

His first impulse directed him toward Second Street and the Hart residence to obtain his faithful horse, stowed in the livery belonging to Mr. Hart. He quickly dismissed this errand, readily sacrificing his horseflesh in fear of a vigilant sheriff who would no doubt intercept him. Instead, he allowed his long legs to trace a direct path toward the river. He imagined that a few hours' walk along the canal southward would place him far from the reaches of his pursuers.

His plans were confounded, though. Approaching the water's edge, he viewed Susan Livingston calmly standing with Nimrod's bridle in hand. He approached his young student, her eyes tearing, ample evidence of a broken heart. His head hung low, ashamed for she must have deduced his plan and would rebuke him.

"Professor?" queried the young woman. "I suspected that I might find you here. You dropped this." She held out the small paper scrap that Mrs. Willard secreted to him in the church.

Jeduthan reached his hand forward expecting a reprimanding slap but instead received a loving embrace. He felt her bosoms press against the coat's lapel, an affectionate hug that stirred his inner warmth. How caring this child must be to hold in her arms such a cad as he. Her heart must flow with forgiveness far exceeding any he had known before. He began, "Please forgive..." but he could speak no more.

She whispered into his ear, "No sir, I need not forgive. It is He who forgives a sinner and we all have sinned and come short of the glory of God. Go! Take Nimrod and run. When you find that which haunts you, rest assured that it is He that shall overcome its powerful hold upon your soul. When you finally find that freedom assured to us by His power, return from your hiding place, and seek me. I shall wait."

Stepping away, sorrowful tears shedding, his hand lingered in hers. "Goodbye, Susan. You have a unique gift much like your beloved hominy grits."

Susan expressed puzzlement upon her pale, supple face.

"Life is all about what you put into it. Sweeten yours with butter and syrup and then treasure the memories! I know you have sweetened mine," he explained as he mounted Nimrod. "Remember me with this." Jeduthan extracted Bartlett's sketch of the children dancing to the tunes of a faceless musician at the bow of a canal boat. He gazed upon its delicate pencil strokes one last time before he passed it to his lovely young student. "Goodbye, sweet girl!"

He trotted southward along the waterfront, glancing only once over his shoulder viewing the beautiful young lass he was leaving behind. She remained standing, arm extended as if bidding farewell.

After a few miles along the river's bank, the weather closed in and a faint drizzle began to fall. A chill breeze blew as the drizzle faded and a fog bank obscured his view, steadily thickening into a soupy mist. Nimrod nearly slipped into the cold water twice before his master halted at a wharf. A steam-powered packet had just stopped to load some crates. He spied a few horses stowed in its hold. Inquiring of the captain if he would accept an additional passenger and steed, the old boat master replied in the affirmative and Jeduthan led Nimrod on board before the packet backed into the murky river.

Securing his horse, he slowly walked forward in search of a soft place to lie and rest. The emotional ride since awakening from his coma had taken its toll upon his mind and body. He needed rest. However, the packet was full of sleeping passengers and he found no available seat. He proceeded toward the forecastle where he spied, through the intensifying mist, a young man perched on the boat's prow. Jeduthan could not see the man's face but his right hand screened his eyes as if searching the indomitable fog. The figure moved not a muscle and remained as rigid as a warship's figurehead. Hanging from a short length of string dangled a small silver watch and upon the boat rail lay a sketchbook. As Jeduthan stepped closer, the boat's deck creaked under his weight. The mysterious figure softy stated, "My dear old man, is there nowhere you can hide?"

Historical Note

There are few fictional characters in **Nowhere to Hide**; however, we have elaborated on their respective interplay. For example, it is true that Jeduthan Higby left his family in Lewis County, New York in the mid 1820s; however, we do not know of his adventures. Truth be revealed, he might have left unnoticed one day and within a week arrived in Virginia to begin anew a fresh family, tossing aside all he possessed of his former life. However, we have no evidence one way or the other. Therefore, we felt it appropriate to fabricate his life on the Erie Canal, relationship with William H. Bartlett, and attachment to Emma Willard's *Troy Female Seminary* in order to bring to life some obscure events in American history.

Jeduthan's traveling companion, William H. Bartlett, is a true-life character. A painter and sketch artist, he traveled the North American wilderness (primarily British Canada and New York's Hudson Valley) in 1836 capturing natural portraits using a Romantic motif. Bartlett's most effective work included illustrating *American Scenery*[10] in cooperation with novelist and travel essayist Nathanial Park Willis in the 1840s. We enhanced Bartlett's biography a bit, for he would be in his early adolescence during the setting of our story. His demise upon the canal schooner *Troy*[11] sets in motion Jeduthan's re-occurring fear of detection and resulting flight described in our next volume.

---

[10] For a sampling of his sketches, see A Hudson River Portfolio at the New York Public Library web site, http://www.nypl.org/research/hudson/search/bartlett1. html , July 2008.

[11] This particular vessel sank in Lake Champlain in November 1825. A fascinating article by Bob Carroll Westport Marina Inc., PO Box 410, Westport, NY 12993, August 2000, describes the sailing-canal boat's discovery deep in the muddy bottom of the lake. http://www.westportmarina.com/troy/index.html. A detailed investigation concerning the boat's demise may be found at the Lake Champlain Maritime Museum website, http://www.lcmm.org/shipwrecks_history/shipwrecks/ troy_ss.htm, July 2008.

Events along the Erie Canal are factual including General Lafayette's visit to Lockport, the Thayer Brothers' execution in Buffalo, and the opening ceremonies of the canal. We have embellished the intrigues of Sherriff Eli Bruce, William Morgan, Erasmus Turner, and the Masonic Brotherhood; however, these men were indeed involved with mysterious circumstances and the ultimate decline of Masonry in upstate New York in the 1820s[12].

Life along the barge trip on the Erie Canal is representative of packet canal life. Dangers of fractured canal levees, imperfectly construction techniques, and low bridge obstacles constantly kept many canalers attentive at the tiller. We researched canal construction techniques, especially at Lockport and found references of the town's bombardment by explosions from the nearby Pendleton's Cut. Irish immigrants provided much of the physical labor completing the Erie Canal, however not all. Orange Dribble's new excavation crane provided critical service near Lockport, ushering in the beginnings of modern American large-scale construction that would pervade much of society within a generation. We hope that our story better demonstrates the difficult life of canal boat operations in the early years of the republic.

Adventures in and about Troy, New York brings to life the unique personages of a thriving city, recently rebuilt after a great fire in 1820. Nearly all the characters in these chapters are true to life including Samuel Wilson[13], Amos Eaton, Besty H. Hart, and even Susan Livingston. Her reference to the poem, *A Visit From Saint Nicholas*, is associated with her family history[14]. The founding of Emma Willard's school and the recent opening of the *Rensselaer Polytechnic Institute*[15] highlight the city's

---

[12] More on the murder of William Morgan may be obtained at http://www.freemasonrywatch.org/party.html , July 2008.

[13] Arlington, Massachusetts has erected a wonderful memorial to Samuel Wilson in honor of his in birthplace. However, he resided and operated his business in Troy when he gained notoriety. His gravestone in Troy is simple and plain by comparison.

[14] See Mary Van Deusen's genealogical site for much about the poem and Henry Livingston's descendants, including Susan Livingston, http://www.iment.com/maida/familytree/henry/index.htm, July 2008.

[15] An interesting history of the Rensselaer Polytechnic Institute and an excellent photo of its first campus may be found at http://www.rensselaer.edu/dept/library/yesterday/html/archives/buildings/old_bank_place.html July 2008.

importance as a center for innovated study. We were hard pressed to associate Jeduthan with these schools, so we searched our genealogical data and found that his descendants often called the old man, *Professor*. His association with the female academy is, sadly, only fabricated.

Of particular interest is the relationship of the Beman couple. An interesting work entitled *A Divine Discontent, The Life of Nathan S. S. Beman* (Mercer University Press, GA 1986) describes the quarrelsome life between the preacher and his troublesome wife. Caroline Bird Yancy grew up in a life of southern ease at *The Aviary* (aptly named for the *Bird* family). Married to Benjamin C. Yancy, a promising young South Carolinian lawyer, her life was rudely interrupted by her husband's demise in 1817. She returned to her childhood home and soon became acquainted with Rev. Beman. Both sought comforts of a spouse; however, their dual dominant personalities quickly clashed. Removed to upstate New York by his appointment as minister to the First Presbyterian Church of Troy, the pair often quarreled. Preacher Beman complained of Caroline's immature deportment while she insinuated that he was hypocritical by preaching abolitionism after he sold, at auction, her inherited slave property in Georgia. Their combative escapades often turned violent and eventually led to separation and divorce after fewer than four years.[16] As the couple's conflict climaxes Jeduthan's Troy escapade, we felt their characterization needed justification.

We hope that Jeduthan's story enlightens readers to an important period of American history when the foundations of the American character formed.

---

[16] Caroline Bird Yancy Beman resurfaces in Florida by 1840 where she marries Dr. John Gorrie, inventor of modern air conditioning. A biography of this gentleman may be obtained in Florida's Past; People & Events that Shaped the State, Volume 1, by Gene Burnett, Pineapple Press, 1988, page 31.